SHADOW LANDS

SAVAGE LANDS BOOK SIX

STACEY MARIE BROWN

Note from Author

As the people of Ukraine are experiencing unimaginable pain and suffering in this heartless war, I wanted to take a moment to state that though I use this country in a fictious conflict, one I established in my story long before the real war took place, I still had to express my support for this beautiful country. The strength of these amazing people. The courageousness of their fight for their country. The loss and terror they go through every day. I hope I conveyed even an ounce of their courage and bravery in my own characters.

Ukraine is the true hero and story here.

If you wish to help Ukraine, here are some ways to donate:
https://www.care.org
https://www.sunflowerofpeace.com/
https://www.icrc.org/en/where-we-work/europe-central-asia/ukraine
https://secure.projecthope.org/site/SPageNavigator/2022_02_Ukraine_Response_Web_UNR.html&s_subsrc=bt1

To Jason/Warwick

Just because this series is over doesn't mean we're breaking up. I will keep you tied up in my room until further notice.

ALSO BY STACEY MARIE BROWN

Contemporary Romance

Buried Alive

Blinded Love Series
Shattered Love (#1)
Pezzi di me (Shattered Love)—Italian
Broken Love (#2)
Twisted Love (#3)

The Unlucky Ones
(Má Sorte—Portuguese)

Royal Watch Series
Royal Watch (#1)
Royal Command (#2)

Smug Bastard

Paranormal Romance

Darkness Series
Darkness of Light (#1)
(L'oscurita Della Luce—Italian)
Fire in the Darkness (#2)
Beast in the Darkness (An Elighan Dragen Novelette)

Table of Contents

Brexley

The dying branches wailed from being snapped under my boots, each one a spine I cracked, a bone I broke, a life I took. They became a symphony in my head, a sonnet of sorrow and pain. Mixing with the bass of my heartbeat and the thunk of the box I carried drummed at my ribs, they sang with the guilt I bore with every step

I didn't feel Warwick through our link, but I somehow sensed him out there, vibrating the earth with his anger, howling his hurt in the dark. His emotions lashed out at me like invisible whips, telling me to stop. If I did, I know he'd convince me to stay, to turn right back around into his arms.

I couldn't.

The only safety for everyone was for me and the nectar to disappear. We were powerful separately but devastating together. Too many people wanted to use us, willing to hurt those I love—and worse, innocent bystanders—to get to me.

Trust became a precarious line when power and control were at stake.

And the person I feared the most was… *me*.

How many more would I hurt? Kill? Blood coated me, seeping through my skin to my soul.

Tad was dead. I murdered the most powerful Druid in history because he was trying to save a child.

From me.

It was like thinking you were the princess in the fairy tale only to wake up and find you were the evil queen the whole time.

The Villain.

It was why I continued to run. My legs grew weak, stumbling over streams and uphill, through dark sleeping towns, and across motorways, keeping to the shadows of night. I didn't stop.

I ran until the sun kissed the earth, returning for a new day, my body crumbling to the ground, no longer able to take another step.

Get up! Keep going. I struggled to push myself up, my arms and legs giving out next to a stream, my face thudding into the mud, my lids shutting with exhaustion.

And I let the darkness swallow me whole.

Chapter 1
Warwick

It was cold as fuck.

We had been out here so long my balls resembled ice cubes, clanking like bells every time the bitter wind snapped off the river. I hunkered down against the wall; my breath billowed in condensation, steaming up my binoculars.

"This is not good," Ash muttered next to me, peering through his own.

Frowning, I rubbed the blurry glass over the fabric of my coat and pressed them up to my eyes again. Lights glared off the Danube from across the river, and the entire fae palace was lit up. Hundreds and hundreds of figures moved around the citadel. Furniture was being carried indoors; servants and guards, terrified of their new patron, bustled in and out like there was a ticking time bomb under their feet.

Dragging my view over, I took in the quick construction on the far wing of the palace, already half rebuilt. The section that was blown up by the very same people moving in. Chance and quick thinking were the only reasons my sister and nephew lived. And they were most of the reason I stayed, why I hadn't fully gone over the edge.

"Fuck that bitch," I snarled.

"Think Killian will fight you to kill her first." Ash huffed out a thick cloud of breath, tucking his chin farther into his collar. It had to be past midnight, and the temperatures in the first week of December were already dipping below thirty degrees. "She's going old school with those uniforms."

Through the eyeglass, I could pick up the general details of the guards' uniforms. Black leather-like pants and shirts with long sleeves and an embroidered emblem on the front, which I couldn't make out from here, but I got the gist of who she was copying.

"Very similar to Queen Aneira's military." He shivered. Not sure from saying her name or from the bitter temperatures.

"Well, Sonya is a product of that time," I replied. "She idolized that psycho bitch." I scanned the area, taking in everything I saw. The armored cars, military trucks, servants, guards. Sonya was making herself at home in Killian's palace. Taking over the empty seat before he could come back. Majority of the people still thought he was dead anyway, so they welcomed their new leader without any fuss.

Budapest was in a strange limbo. Like a cartoon I saw once of a coyote hanging in the sky after running off a cliff until he realized he was standing on air, and then he fell. We were like him, hanging in the air. Waiting. Soon we'd realized we, too, were standing on nothing.

People in Savage Lands went along with their day, trying to simply survive, while rumors of General Markos's disappearance grew louder. Lieutenant Henrik Andor, his second in command, was trying to act like nothing was wrong and it was business as usual, but you could feel it in the air. The holding of breath before everything was about to crumble. When you merely survived day to day, escaping

4

gangs and death, starvation, and people willing to kill for a coin in your pocket, your senses became honed. You could feel a slight shift in the air. Something was off.

Wrong.

This city was all sorts of wrong.

Or maybe it was me.

Nothing had been right with me for weeks now as if I were on the precipice of falling.

"We better get back before I freeze my nutsack off out here." Ash got to his feet, grumbling at his stiff muscles.

"I'm sure you'll find someone to warm them up later." I shot at him, my eyes still on the palace.

"Who said it would be just one?" He smirked.

I wagged my head, dropping the binoculars and climbing to my feet. "Are you actually admitting there are two?"

"You mean my two hands?" Ash couldn't fight the grin hitching the side of his mouth as we strolled to our motorcycles. We both knew it wasn't his hands that were getting him off almost every night. You'd never know by how they acted during the day, but two people were slipping into his room at night, and shit got loud. It only grated my nerves and added to the anger and venom swimming in my blood, deteriorating the slight barrier I tried to keep up between me and the Wolf.

It had been just a little over two weeks since the night she left—since everything went to hell, and the Wolf was being held back by a thin thread. He wanted to hunt her down. Claim his vengeance. Exhibit his wrath. Devour his prey.

Violently. Brutally.

Make her *pay*.

Swinging our legs over the motorcycle, Ash and I tore off through the quiet streets. The only people out now were deadly and dangerous.

5

But most feared me.

The roar of our bikes recoiled off the buildings, the frigid air snapping even harder at my frozen skin. We zigzagged through the Savage Lands, making sure we weren't followed and stopping far enough away from where we had secured our new base, Vajdahunyad Castle, which wasn't a real castle in the technical sense. Copied from Corvin Castle in Romania, it was part of a Millennial Exhibition, built in an old park to show off the mix of romantic architecture of the time: Romanesque, Gothic Renaissance, and Baroque styles were highlighted in the Romanesque cloisters, mock drawbridges, moats, gates, carved portals, and spires. These were stunning back in the day, but the building had been left in ruins after the Fae War, ignored, neglected, and forgotten. Wildlife grew around it, concealing the gem in foliage, decaying over time.

Ash and I hid our bikes in the brush behind an old outbuilding on the east side of the park, slinking through the darkness across the large, overgrown common grounds, our senses at the quick for wild animals and enemies.

The moment we got within viewing distance of our new base, guns clicked as a handful of guards stepped out, ready to fire. Dozens of them, a mix of Povstat and Sarkis's people, were camouflaged in black and green. They looped all the way around the outskirts of the castle, guarding it against intruders twenty-four hours a day. My sister was even part of the patrol, most likely out here tonight with horse-face.

"Just us." Ash held up his arms.

"You're only giving me more reason to shoot." A man stepped out in front, pulling his balaclava up to his forehead. Tall and built, his blond hair hidden under a beanie, Lukas looked like that guy who should be out fighting crime and saving babies. The classic hero, where I'd be the villain.

A half smile curved up Lukas's mouth, his gaze coyly trailing over Ash, both pretending it wasn't their fault I was kept up half the night. Behind Lukas, I spotted the third member of the party that had me wishing for earplugs.

The demon's braided blue hair was the only color against her all-black outfit. Everyone had a job here. No one could float, so Kek picked guarding, thinking it would be the easiest job. With Lukas as the chief adviser of all the guards, I think she was finding it a lot more work than she figured. If they weren't on guard, he had them working out or practicing at the underground gun range.

"See anything?" Lukas cleared his throat, forcing his gaze off Ash.

"Mommy has officially moved in." Ash tucked into his jacket.

Lukas's head dipped; a streak of pain flashed quickly over his face before it was gone. I couldn't imagine having that heartless bitch for a mother. She cared more about power than her own flesh and blood.

"I'm actually surprised it took her this long." Lukas's eyes moved around, his head bobbing.

Sonya had soldiers on Killian's property before the dust even settled after the incident at Vĕrhăza. It only took her a few weeks to move all the old leader's shit out and hers in. She made sure everything represented her—not just a leader but as a *queen*. Unmistakably stating her autocratic rule over Budapest was a certainty.

With Markos quiet, off licking his wounds somewhere, it was still odd there was no retaliation from HDF. Sonya took that as a sign to take it all. With Leon dead, the human force in Prague crumbled within a week. But Sonya didn't want Prague; it already had a fae leader. An inept one, but she would not challenge him, not when she was handed an even bigger position in Budapest.

7

"Caden, Birdie, and Scorpion returned about ten minutes ago." Lukas flicked his head back to the castle. "Also…" His cheek twitched. "You might want to check on your friend. She refused to eat again."

Ash and I simultaneously jerked, knowing who he was talking about. Kitty. She had not bounced back from our time in Věrhăza. We'd been through worse things together, but something this time snapped her. Broke her so much she was giving up on living.

Ash nodded his head, his brow furrowing with worry. Whatever issue he had with her at one time evaporated when faced with life and death in the pit. In the end, we were family; the rest was just bullshit. Things were still tense, but his love for Kitty pushed that all to the side.

"Thanks." Ash moved around Lukas and Kek.

"See you later?" Lukas asked evenly, like it held no meaning.

Ash's gaze went from him to Kek, his head dipping again, before continuing toward the entrance.

"Do me a favor. Hang out in one of their rooms tonight. I'd like to get some fucking sleep." I grumbled, striding by them. My dick was having enough issues being at constant attention, panting and eager, like a dog waiting for his master to come home.

"You could always join." Kek taunted behind me with a laugh.

At one time, I could easily find a handful of women I could fuck into oblivion. Now I only wanted one. And that shit pissed me off. One of the many reasons I never let anyone in before. Not that I had a chance when it came to her. Brexley Kovacs had my balls wrapped up and locked down from the moment she walked into Halálház. Before I even had a clue what it was like to be inside her.

8

Where the hell are you, Kovacs?

Angry at her, at myself, I pounded up the steps to what used to be a museum but had long since been emptied. Passing another set of guards, Wesley and a girl named Sab I recognized from Povstat stood at the entry. Wesley nodded at us as we entered. The place had been ransacked and stripped, leaving nothing but a shell of high-arched decorative ceilings, turrets, and wooden beams. The entire place replicated the best architecture spanning from Austrian palaces to Dracula castle in Romania, making me feel like a harsh contradiction compared to the grandness and elegant beauty. I was dark. Cruel. I rolled in vengeance and fucked in the blood of my enemy.

My dirty boots clipped over the chipping tile floors entering the operations room, which held little heat. The place where the plundered stained-glass windows used to be was now boarded up, letting a draft in the room. Only on cloudy, rainy days did we light a fire, not wanting any smoke signal coming from this area.

Loud voices and angry magic stabbed at my frozen skin like nettles.

Fuck. Here we go again.

"This is *my* city." Killian leaned over the table, his finger stabbing at the wood of the makeshift table. "I decide what happens in regard to it."

"You sound exactly like all the rest of the authoritarian leaders," Mykel shouted back, his stance mirroring Killian's across the slab of wood. "And if you recall, my entire base, hundreds of my people, are dead because I was here trying to help you out. My city has fallen into ruin."

"And I am at fault for that?" Killian seethed.

"You can pretend you are innocent in all this, but you helped create this mess because of your *own* selfish appetite for power." Mykel hit the counter with his palm.

"And you're blameless?" Killian's voice lowered, tension vibrating off him.

"Your rise in Povstat wasn't because you are so pure of heart. You forget I was also part of the search for the nectar fifteen years ago. I know what you will do to get your hands on it. Don't talk of my greed and need for power."

Mykel stiffened, his chin flicking up, Killian's accusations knocking into him.

"This is all of our fucking problem." I busted through their dick-measuring contest, strolling up to them. "So just shut the hell up."

Scorpion snorted from the other side of the room, sitting back in a chair, Caden and Birdie flanking him.

I snarled at Scorpion, and he flipped me off. I wanted to hate the fucker, but I couldn't. Not even in the worst torture would I ever admit this, but I had faith in him. I trusted him with Kovacs. I knew he'd do anything to save her life, to protect her. Because of that I couldn't detest him, which made me want to hate him more.

Birdie nodded at me, but my attention slid from her to Caden. Instantly my guard went up, prickling like nails, stabbing back into my gut.

The anger I felt when entering wasn't from Killian

It was Caden.

His brown eyes flicked around, his jaw set, but I could feel it.

Vengeance, wrath, death.

A mirror of my own emotions.

His gaze shot to mine as if he could sense me too before he looked away. Neither of us had really spoken since that day in the lab. The day his father tried to rip my essence from me and give it to him.

Not a bit of me wanted to contemplate that day or

believe I shared anything with captain one-pump. Though no amount of denial could explain how I knew Caden would step out into the pit that final night in Věrhăza before he did, or how I seemed to sense him around, feel my own essence in him. The same hate and rage.

Killian cleared his throat, yanking my focus back to him. He had regained his health and strength, looking every bit the pompous ass he was before, though his dark cargo pants, long-sleeved shirt, and worn boots took him several levels down from douchebag.

"Report," he demanded.

Never mind. The douchebag was still flying his flag.

"Sonya's fully moved in. We saw hundreds of soldiers already wearing her insignia. Servants, tanks, armored cars. Looks like she took all Leon's military items and whatever you left and stamped her mark on it," Ash offered. "Thinking your crap is either at the bottom of the river or she's going to have one big estate sale this weekend."

Killian's shoulders tipped back as he sucked in air. I could tell it was hard for him to sit back and take this. The instinct to fight for your home and kick the squatter's ass to the curb had to be overwhelming.

Sonya was astute. Very shrewd. She hadn't played this game for so long to let it go easily. We had to play this smart.

"Repeat what you guys found." Killian motioned to the group across. They had been sent on a similar stakeout mission, but to HDF.

"From the outside, everything—according to him—is the same." Birdie motioned to Caden. It took Killian and Mykel a lot of convincing to let Caden go, but Birdie volunteered to babysit and make sure he wasn't signaling his old comrades. From the swelling rage I could feel coming off him, his hate for his father was severe. He

11

wasn't exactly on our side, but he wasn't on theirs either. Defected. Lost. Hurt.

Even though his mother was alive and resting in the next building, I could sense another one feeling the loss of Kovacs. She had been his anchor for so long, his best friend. Her presence would help him find his feet.

A nice person would want that for him. I, on the other hand, was happy to kick the baby bird out of the nest and see if he learned to fly on his own. This world was sink or swim. You figured it out fast, or it would eat you up.

"Half of the guards he didn't recognize," Birdie spoke for him again. Caden stared at the table, his hands clenching and unclenching.

"They're Ukrainian," Caden muttered under his breath.

"You know that for sure?" Mykel asked.

Caden nodded. "A few I recognized from my engagement party. They were with Ivanenko."

That had to twist a knife even deeper in his chest. Not only had Istvan forced Caden to get engaged to Olena, but behind Caden's back, he had ruthlessly been fucking her, seeding a child, to make sure he covered all his bases. Istvan could pass it off as Caden's or claim it depending on what happened. Caden's half-brother would now take his place as the true heir, Istvan disowning his previous family for this one. All for power.

"That means Ukraine leaders are still in a partnership with Markos." Mykel rubbed his beard. "I just don't know why he's been so quiet for the last few weeks. Why would he even give Sonya a chance to take the palace?"

"He lost the prison and a lot of his men that day." I folded my arms. The elephant in the room, which was always there, grew. We all knew who killed them. Even Mykel's men. "Also, his labs, the nectar, any relationship with

12

Romania were gone, and he destroyed his only alliance in Czech. He doesn't have a lot to stand on right now. Probably hiding under his desk with a bottle of pálinka."

"He'd be in Kyiv." A woman's voice spun us around. Thin, tall, and radiantly elegant, countering the cheap pants and sweater she had on, Rebeka held herself like an elite. She was bred for it; it was in her DNA, her bone structure. She still carried the bruises from her time in the labs and was painstakingly thin, but she looked far healthier than she had two weeks ago. Her shiny, long brown hair was down, softening her regal demeanor. The woman was beautiful, and human or not, you couldn't disagree she looked nowhere near her age.

"What?" Mykel swung sharply to her.

"*Anya…*" *Mother*. Caden went to her, taking her arm. This was the first time I had seen Rebeka out of bed. Being human, her body reacted and healed slowly to all the torment, starvation, and grief she had been through, almost putting her in a coma-like state. The healers had to force food into her through tubes. A few times, they thought they might lose her. "You should be resting."

"I'm fine. It's good for me to start walking around." She patted his arm. "I need to do something. I can't sit back."

Killian nodded at a chair, but she stayed standing.

"The lab you destroyed. It wasn't the only one."

The room went utterly still.

"What?" Killian's mouth parted.

"There's another one in Ukraine. He started building it about the same time he started his lab here."

Fuck.

The entire room hissed with the same sentiment.

"I guarantee Istvan is there." She swallowed, her hands reaching for the back of the chair to keep her steady. Caden

13

was right on her. "I know how he thinks. He would go there to reestablish himself and come back with an army."

"And you are just telling us now?" Killian exclaimed.

"I've had my mind on *other* things when I was lucid," she snipped back. The woman watched her best friend of years get gruesomely murdered right in front of her while feral monsters, who she knew as kids, tried to tear into us while her husband and his pregnant fiancé watched cheerfully from above.

"Do you know where exactly?" Killian pressed his palms on the map covering the table.

"No." She wagged her head.

"Are you sure you didn't hear anything? Any inkling where it would be in Kyiv?" Killian pushed.

"Killian." Mykel's tone was full of warning.

"You don't want to know where this other lab is? Where Markos is creating more of those monsters? You weren't there. You haven't seen what these pills can do… what these creatures become."

"Badgering her isn't going to help us learn anything more, either." Mykel volleyed, both yelling back at each other.

"Shut up!" Rebeka quieted them like schoolboys. "I don't know where it is. *However…*" She paused. "I know where he keeps all his plans. Every single important document he has. Where the documents for this other lab would be."

"Where?" Mykel stepped closer to her, his gaze moving over her.

Caden blew out, his head lowering. He knew exactly what Rebeka was talking about.

And I knew that… because he did.

I shouldn't. There was no way I should be aware of this information. But I could see the exact spot, every detail of the room, though I had never been in Marko's office.

14

"Fuck," I mumbled. "In the safe behind his desk at HDF."

Caden's head jerked up to me, his eyes widening. "How did you know that?"

My lids closed, hating the words coming from me because it was something I didn't want to be true.

"Because *you* know."

Chapter 2
Killian

My tight boots chafed my feet, the same shoes I was issued in prison. Věrhăza followed me, mocked me, continued to torture me, reminding me of all the things I'd like to forget. The scars would forever mark me. Figuratively and literally.

I paced up and down the length of the table, a headache throbbing between my brows. A constant weight pinned down on my shoulders as I tried to keep everything afloat. To fight every battle coming at us, to pretend I was all right in the face of it, to keep morale and hope going when everything seemed bleak.

"There has to be another way of finding this lab. Destroying it before Istvan can do any more damage." Mykel peered around the room. The dark circles under his eyes showed he was feeling the weight as well. I couldn't say I disliked him, but I could say I would like him a hell of a lot better if he were back in Prague. There were enough alphas and dominants in this room. And he kept forgetting—this was *my* country. *My* people.

The loss of his base, his people, the fight for survival for his own country, for peace, started here. I understood that. It didn't mean I had to like him being on my ass every day.

"We could send spies to Kyiv," Mykel added, rubbing at his dark beard, his light brown eyes staring off in thought. There were moments—a gesture, a look—when I could see the resemblance to Brexley, feeling like a stab in my gut. A stubbornness and determination in their expressions. I had never met Benet, Brexley's father, but heard Mykel looked very much like him.

We barely talked about her. Her presence was no less here, though. All the time. The massive elephant in the room we all tried to pretend wasn't. But we all felt her absence, the sting of her disappearance. The hurt and anger from what she did.

"No." I shook my head. "We don't have the extra people to send up there on a wild goose chase. Ukraine is heavily guarded and monitored." Ivanenko, the Ukrainian leader, had first been put in by Russia to be his puppet after the fall of the Otherworld. Istvan, seeing an opportunity to overtake a weak leader, had done just that. There was no doubt with Olena carrying Istvan's child, it was Markos ruling that country now.

"Then what do you suggest?" Mykel tossed out his arms. "We sneak into HDF and break into his safe?"

"Yes." I pressed my hands together, tapping them against my mouth. "That is exactly what we do."

"I know the place the best and the code to the safe. I can do it." Caden stepped closer to the table.

"Are you fucking kidding me?" Warwick growled, his head shaking. "You don't think you'd be recognized before you even got to the gate? You are one of the most well-known people out there. Your face was on magazines and banners."

"Now they say *most wanted* underneath," Scorpion huffed from the other side of the table.

"I agree with Warwick." That had to be a fucking first.

17

"You can't go anywhere near HDF. We need someone who can blend in with the soldiers. Play the part and go undetected. And isn't known at all to any HDF soldier. Especially as an enemy." I nodded around the room. "Which means almost all of you are out."

"I can do it." A woman's voice came from the doorway, her accent wrapping around my balls like a fist, squeezing. Instantly my shoulders slammed back, my head rising in defense as I swung around, ire already flaring my nose as I looked upon the human.

Red hair waving past her shoulders, bright blue eyes, and a curvy figure, though a lot of that had been lost due to the horrendous conditions in Věrhăza. Even under the cargo pants and sweater, you couldn't hide her sexual impact. There were small things that told you she was human, imperfections, if you looked hard enough, showing the burdens of life she had carried and gone through. Fatigue streaked her face. But there wasn't a person, fae or human, who could say she was not breathtakingly stunning. Rosie had this presence, like she had on stage when I saw her years ago as Nina Petrov, the young ingenue flouncing onstage. Seeing her perform had made something in my chest tighten, take notice, remember her years later. The play was horrendous; however, something about her had me returning to see it again.

That was before I got to know her. Humans were fragile, weaker, but she was a mix of softness and firecracker, which unsettled me. Her sharp tongue and stubbornness compelled me to scream or punch walls.

"No." My voice was sharp, my authority saturating the room with just a word.

"Excuse me?" She folded her arms under her breasts, her blue eyes narrowing in on mine.

"I said no."

"You said *no*?" She repeated my statement with a mocking tone. Her English accent had become part of her, even though she wasn't British. "I'm sorry, I didn't know you were my father and I was still twelve." Rosie stepped farther into the room. "You said you needed someone who could play the part, right?"

"Yes, but—"

"Anyone else here train in Stanislavski's method acting teachings? Can carry a whole play almost by themselves?"

"I saw it. It wasn't that great."

Rosie's chest puffed up, anger blushing her porcelain cheeks scarlet.

"I think she'd be perfect. She's human, which fits in there. Trained to fool people." Birdie motioned to her, a glint of mischievousness in her eyes directed at me. "Why not? Don't tell me you have a problem with her being a girl, since fae aren't sexist, right? Or is it because she's human? That makes you racist."

"I didn't say anything like that." For the first time in a long time, my words floundered, and I felt my face heating, Birdie's mouth twitching like she knew something I didn't. "That is not why."

"Then why?" Rosie tilted her head, and I whipped my head between the two women, feeling like I was walking into a sand trap. "I know you can't imagine me as more than a common whore."

My spine stiffened, her claim slashing across my chest. "I *never* said or thought that." My voice went low. Angry. Rosie's breath hitched, her gaze going to the side. "If something went wrong, you have not been trained to fight. That is what I am saying."

"I'll go with her." Scorpion leaned back in his chair, propping his feet up on the table.

19

"There is absolutely no way she is going in." I shook my head vehemently. "You either." I wiggled my hand at Scorpion. Besides Warwick, Scorpion probably stood out the most. Covered in tattoos, piercings along his brow, oozing "fuck the norm" attitude. He would stand out at HDF like a red in a sea of beige.

Rosie licked her lip, her gaze going down to the floor. I could sense her anger and frustration. "Whatever you say, *Lord* Killian." Though she meant it to be derogatory, my spine heated as the title fell from her lips, my dick hardening at her insolent tone, fury rolling my hands into fists.

I turned away, sucking in long breaths of air. What the hell was my problem? She was a *human*. Not at all worth my energy. Why did she irritate me so much?

"I came up here to tell you… we are out of painkillers and rubbing alcohol." Her voice still wrapped around me like a rope, forcing me to turn and look at her again. "And we are almost out of coffee."

"Whoaaa—whoa." Birdie held her hands up. "That should have been the first thing you told us."

Rosie and others had been put to work in the healing room we converted downstairs. Many were still battling the effects of the prison or nearly died fighting outside it. And daily, we had injuries from those going out on missions, unskilled fighters training for combat, or humans coming down with the flu.

It had only been two weeks, and we were still struggling to find our feet and get this place functioning like clockwork.

I nodded my head. "I will send someone to the market."

Rosie pinched her lips, dipped her head back, and marched out, leaving a whiff of her shampoo in her wake.

"Sending her is not a terrible idea." Mykel's voice

snapped me back, realizing I was still staring at the spot she left.

"No, it's a *horrendous* idea." I reacted instantly. "She totally stands out. Her hair is distracting." Her figure, her crystal blue eyes, her mouth.

"She can dye it. Or tuck it up in a hat." Mykel shrugged.

"She knows nothing of HDF. Where to go. How to get in." I heard myself. The defensiveness of my claims was way too much, but I couldn't seem to stop. "How to act like a soldier."

"She's an *actress*. They can pretend." Birdie continued to smirk, her hip leaning into Scorpion's chair. "You seem so adamant about her not going in. Why is that?"

I blinked at Birdie, my mouth opening in response, nothing coming out.

"If we are doing this. What we really need, for *whoever* goes in, are earpieces. Then Caden could walk them through each step." Mykel thankfully took me away from Birdie, returning to the topic.

Mykel lost everything in the bombing. He was carrying so much grief and guilt for not being there. All the children, people, his world, were taken in a moment, along with all his weapons and grade-A military devices smuggled from the Unified Nations. All of it was gone. I had lost everything as well.

"Now that's something I can do." Scorpion clunked his feet back on the ground, rising. "Got connections in low places. Give me a couple of days."

I dipped my chin in response as he strolled for the exit.

"Head to the market while you're out. Take backup," I yelled at his retreating frame, his hand waving in recognition. At one time, I would not take disrespect like that, but times had changed.

21

I had changed. Though I knew I wasn't the man they wanted here.

Andris's absence was like a ghost constantly hanging about, but no one spoke of him. I could feel his people's resentment in every decision I made as leader, their knee-jerk reaction to buck against me, to tell me to fuck off. Once I had been looked upon as more enemy than ally. Now we were forced to come together, and I was their temporary leader, along with Mykel.

Intuitionally, I understood if Brexley was here, they would follow her word as his. Or maybe they would just follow her. She had that quality—someone who was just born to lead. A common attribute we recognized in each other.

I fought. I bled. I killed. I sacrificed. I became Lord Killian by sheer will. I would not be a low-life ruffian ever again.

"Anya!" Caden yelped as Rebeka swayed, bumping into a chair. He grabbed her arm to keep her upright, Mykel leaping for her other arm.

"I'm fine." Rebeka tried to reassure them but failed miserably.

"You must rest." Mykel looked down at her with concern.

"Let's all take a break. Reconvene here tomorrow." I stated, suddenly exhausted and irritable myself. Everyone quickly responded in agreement, heading for the door.

"Farkas?" I called out, stopping Warwick. He curved slightly back, waiting for everyone to disperse.

"I just wanted to know… if you had sensed or gotten anything from—"

"No." His jaw clenched, fury flaming in his eyes, the single note vibrating the floor. Warwick's lip lifted as he turned, stomping out the exit.

"Always so loquacious," I huffed, leaning over the table on my hands, letting my head drop. I had to give it to Brexley. Her pull was so strong, not only did she have many of us willing to fight and die for her, but she had the most ruthless legend in the world bending at the knee. He was *only* here because she'd want him to be. To fight and protect this city.

Without her influence, did I think for a moment Warwick Farkas would be mulling around here, going out on missions, and finding us supplies? Fuck no.

"Brexley, where the hell are you?" I muttered, invoking power into her name, hoping she'd somehow hear me. Feel the pull back to us.

She had caused so much damage and death. Beyond anything anyone, including Tad, could have predicted. Her magic was raw and powerful. The stuff of legends. We called Warwick the legend, when I think it had been her the whole time.

As powerful as she was, the nectar was far more dangerous and unstable. With it, she had killed the oldest and most powerful Druid who ever lived. I felt the dark magic coming off his dead body, a hint that she and the nectar didn't just hold the power of a Seelie queen and her family, but they held the remains of black magic.

Brexley Kovacs had become the most wanted woman in the Eastern bloc. And the very item she had with her was equivalent, if not more, to the four treasures of the Tuatha Dé Danann. I couldn't deny I still coveted it. Desired that kind of power. Craved it.

And utterly terrified of myself if I obtained it.

The tension in my head pounded behind my eyes, my hands shaking. Fae healed quickly on the outside, but we didn't heal any faster than humans on the inside. I had not slept more than a few hours since our escape from the prison.

23

Nightmares plagued me, cutting deep into my chest, waking me up screaming, drenched in sweat. I had been through a lot in my time, seen and done things most couldn't fathom. But the horrors of Věrhăza, what nobody saw, the impact of wearing iron daily had taken a toll. I had to hide my shaking hands, my panic attacks, the dark voices in my head still calling for me to end it all.

As a leader, you could never show your weakness. Never show how scared and unsure you were. I could display nothing but strength and command.

While underneath, I was losing control.

Chapter 3
Scorpion

Early afternoon light peeked through the sections of window that weren't boarded up, echoes from the vast curved ceilings beating like hollow drums in my ears. Rushing down the marble steps, I moved to the basement level. Even if this place had never held royalty, the facade still parroted a decadence I could never understand. Living the last ten years mostly underground and in sparse buildings was comfortable to me. That had been a luxury compared to my youth. This superfluous excess made me uncomfortable in the fine, meticulously carved arches and banisters, painted with gold and dripping with details. Even gutted, this place made me feel like a dirt spot on white silk. It itched my skin and quickened my step.

Heading down the stairs to the clinic, I told myself it was to get a full list of items Rosie needed from the market before I headed out. There was *no* other reason I was heading straight to the healing room without even stopping to get coffee. I snarled at the half-truth clinging to the back of my mind.

I wasn't someone who backed away from the truth, who couldn't look at myself head-on if I did. But I pushed the rotting taste in my mouth away, clearing my thoughts and keeping my focus on finding the redhead. I stepped into the large room, which used to hold museum items, but now was chock-full of beds, patients, healing potions, and human medicines.

My eyes betrayed me the moment I entered, shooting to the spot in the far corner. I tried to ignore the tightening in my chest, the way my shoulders relaxed and locked up at the same time.

I spied long, wavy blonde hair and the curve of a slim figure curled up on her side, facing away from me. The girl who bit and clawed me, full of vigor and venom, boiling my blood with aggravation and overwhelming my brain with headaches, stared blankly at the wall like she was waiting for death. Even from here I could see her legs and arms twitching unconsciously, but everything else in her seemed to be empty.

My jaw clenched. Hanna was the last person I should give a fuck about, but the instinct was strong to stomp over to her and yank her out of bed, pushing her until the little viper struck back.

Her entire world had flipped on her. Everything she was taught, believed in, was ripped from under her. Her DNA had been changed without her consent. She had been brutalized, assaulted, and watched both her parents get viciously murdered.

Something I understood more than she knew.

"Scorpion, did you need something?" Rosie strolled up to me, though I couldn't snap my attention off Hanna.

Rosie glanced over her shoulder, following my gaze and then coming back to me. "She's been through a lot."

The softness in her voice jerked me to the redhead. I shifted on my feet, shaking my head like it didn't matter to me. "So have you."

"Yes, but I've already been through that moment when you find everything you believe in is a lie. Where you feel life is trying to take everything, including your soul, from you. Where the worst, most vile things happen. Stuff you can't even imagine. Some people don't come back from that. Hanna also has to deal with the murder of her parents and what Markos did to her. What he made her."

Air whipped sharply in and out of my nose. *Istvan Markos.* The rage I felt at hearing his name was overwhelming. I dreamed of torturing and killing him so slowly, he'd beg for me to end it. Everything he put us through, I wanted to do to him tenfold.

"She saw what the pills did to her fellow HDF comrades. What they were turned into. She's scared." Rosie folded her arms. "She's terrified the same thing will happen to her."

"The fuck it will," I growled, my words grounding out before I could even stop them. We all remember what those pills did to her ex-friends. They took on the fae essence in the pills, became the worst of human and animal. Feral monsters. Murderers. Mutants.

I would not let Hanna become that.

"Get me a list of what you need," I huffed at her, my feet already taking me across the room, my legs moving without any thought. Weaving through the beds, I spotted many people I recognized, one I knew as Ash's and Warwick's friend Kitty. She had been thin before, but now she was grotesquely so, nothing but skin and bones. She was hooked up to a feeding tube, looking like she was being forced to stay in this world.

Fae or human, Vĕrhǎza fucked us all up, even if we didn't show it on the outside.

Getting close to Hanna's cot, my mouth dried up, my tongue stuck behind my teeth, not knowing what to say. Sentiment or pleasantries weren't in my tool kit.

27

"Get up," I grunted, my fists knocking against my legs.

Hanna didn't move, her gaze not leaving the wall.

"I said *get up*," I demanded, my voice straining, trying to stay low.

Only a blink of her lids told me she was aware.

She was ignoring me, which was actually worse. Before I would get at least a glare, snarl, or a fuck you. This was nothing. I wasn't even there. I held no weight.

"Hanna…" I growled threateningly. Laying on this cot, longing for parents who would never return, for a time that would never come back, wasn't healthy. She had a lot to work through and had a long journey ahead, but it was time to start getting up. Living. Her parents would not want this for her. "I. Said. Get. Your. Ass. Up."

No response.

People feared me. I was not happy-go-lucky like Wesley. Maddox had charm even when he had been an asshole. I wasn't that person until you got to know me a bit. The most comfortable I had been with someone was Brexley. And that was because she was in every fiber of my being. I was only standing here now because of her. You had no choice with her. Every guy I knew, no matter how disgruntled, would be wrapped around her finger. She could approach the most feral, bloodthirsty dog and would have it snuggling on her lap in ten minutes, licking her face.

A.K.A… Warwick Farkas. But that bastard wasn't just licking her face.

Embarrassment and anger flared up my spine as Hanna left my demands and threats hanging in the air like tiny little butterflies.

Fuck that.

I shoved my hands underneath her, finally inspiring a yelp from her lips as I lifted her into my arms.

28

"What the hell are you doing?" she sputtered, squirming in my embrace.

This time I was the one to ignore her, acting like I didn't have a woman trying to wiggle free of me, my grip becoming tighter on her as I sauntered across the room.

"Let go of me!" Hanna snarled.

"List?" I paused in front of Rosie, a piece of paper in her hand. I flicked my chin at my pocket.

"Scorpion, let go!" Hanna wormed, her palms pressing into my chest. When she got nowhere, she turned to Rosie. "Help me."

Amusement twitched on Rosie's features, trying to hide her smile, stuffing the paper inside my jacket. Not doing a thing to stop me. I felt her pat my arm to continue on, as if she was all for getting Hanna up and out.

"Are you kidding me?" Hanna's face turned even redder, her legs kicking, letting me get a quick whiff of her. You could tell she hadn't showered or done anything in over a week.

"You stink, little viper." I curved toward the restrooms. Her cries grew more frustrated as she tried pointlessly to get out of my grip.

Hitching her up higher, I went into a private shower stall, turning on the water.

"Let me go!"

"As you wish." I plunked her down on her feet under the steady stream. The cool water caused her to belt out a string of curse words at me. Her thin cotton pants and shirt became like gauze as the water cascaded down her. My eyes darted to the side, trying not to notice how the material clung to her skin or how see-through it was.

"You fucking asshole!" Her hiss drew my attention back to see ire flaming from her eyes, her cheeks ruddy with fury.

29

"That I am."

"*Szarjál sünt!*" *May you shit a hedgehog!*

"Good to see you still have some fire in you." I smirked, tossing her a bar of soap. "Now wash up and get dressed. You're coming with me on a mission."

"A mission?" She licked at the water on her lips, my dick instantly hardening, which sent rage through me.

"Yeah, so be ready in fifteen minutes." I stepped out, slamming the door behind me. I squeezed my eyes shut and pinched the bridge of my nose, taking in deep breaths. I shook off the hum of adrenaline spiking through me and tightening my balls.

Fuck, I needed to get laid. Being tied to Brexley and Warwick kept me in a constant state of arousal. The energy they created just being near each other was intense enough for me, but when they fucked? Hell… people from all around could feel them.

It was torture. Not that I begrudged them fucking each other's brains out, but to be constantly pulled into other people's unrelenting passion was too much. Especially when you did not have anyone to take it out on.

My head shook, trying to dislodge the image of Hanna in the shower, the anger in her eyes, the hate on her lips, her nipples hard and showing through her shirt.

No! I yelled at myself. She might be feisty, but she was way too pure for me. I had a firm rule of not shitting where I eat. I kept sex and home separate. Never had I hooked up with anyone in Sarkis's army. I didn't believe in monogamy. So I kept sex uncomplicated—and paid for. And humans were never on my radar. What I liked… it wasn't for the faint of heart. And she was far too delicate and innocent. Plus, I think she *actually* hated my guts.

Twenty minutes later, I was a tad surprised when she

walked up to the main entrance where I waited. Dressed in the same kind of cargo pants, boots, black sweater, and jacket, her wet hair plaited in two braids. Her cheeks were rosy and her eyes sharp when they met mine.

Irritated.

I would take annoyed over devoid of life any day.

"Ready, little viper?"

"Don't call me that." She folded her arms, only making me smirk. "Where are we going, anyway?"

"Market."

"Market?" Her lip curled. "You got me up to go to the market?" She puffed out. "Only a man would think that is a mission."

A laugh came out of my throat, surprising even me. My head shook with a smile.

"I didn't say that was all." I turned around, heading out into the late morning.

The rich smells of things like főzelék and lángos wafted through the outdoor market, curling up my nose and grinding at my empty stomach. The heavy clouds held in the conflicting odors of horse manure, body odor, and the delicious foods being cooked to sell.

Tucking deeper into my hood to prevent my face from being seen, I glanced over at Hanna, also hidden under her hood. Her body was rail thin now. I knew she hadn't eaten a proper meal in a long time. Those of us who survived Věrhăza had lost so much weight and had been so starved that we still couldn't eat a normal meal. Our stomachs rejected it, but the whiffs of stew and fried bread dripping in cheese and sausage made me think I was up for the challenge.

31

"Want something to eat?" I nudged her.

"Aren't we here to shop?"

"We can do both." The pack on my back was full of items for the clinic.

I needed to wait for my connection to make contact. After the meeting last night, I had come straight down here, leaving a mark on a particular spot. A sign I needed to meet up. We called him *Dzsinn*, Genie, for all the things he could get you. I had found him in the early days of Sarkis's army. He had never let me down but was expensive as shit. He was deep in the black market, illegally bringing stuff in from the Unified Nations. No one knew his name or anything about him. The man had deep connections, getting top-of-the-line items. Most we could never afford, but I was hoping he'd make a deal this time.

"Come on. I know you're hungry. I could hear your stomach growling over the motorcycle engine all the way here."

She rolled her eyes but didn't fight me when I dragged her up to a Pörkölt and Paprikás booth, getting us a plate to share.

"Oh gods," she groaned, her teeth sinking into a bite of roasted pork and egg noodle dumpling, the sauce dripping from her chin. "This tastes so good."

I watched her dig in for another bite, her lashes fluttering in bliss from the warm food. It wasn't all that good, but compared to what she had eaten in the last few months, this was gourmet.

My stomach clawed to inhale all of it, twisting in hunger, but I stood there, holding the plate for her, watching her scoop up more, devouring and tearing into the meat like a feral cat. Her eyes flashed with a predatory look, darkening, a soft growling hum vibrating in her throat.

My breath caught. The sound and mannerisms sent blood to my dick and fear to my mind. My gaze rolled over her as she tore into another piece of pork. I slowly reached for a piece of meat.

A growl ebbed from her throat, her eyes peering up at me through her lashes, her lip lifting, showing her teeth. Guarding her food like a wild animal.

It only took her a moment to realize what she had done. Horror streaked over her features as she jerked back away from me with a gasp. "Oh gods," she whispered, panic swirling over her face, appearing as if she was ready to dart away.

"Hanna," I said, low and soothing, setting the plate on a table next to us.

She shook her head, tears filling her eyes, moving farther away from me. When I took a step toward her, her muscles twitched like a trapped animal.

"Hanna." I held up my arms, showing I was no threat. "It's okay."

"*Okay?*" she spat, wildness straining her vocals. "It's okay I'm turning into one of them? A monster?"

"You aren't going to become one of them."

"How do you know that?" Her voice cracked, her lids blinking rapidly. "I already am! I almost attacked you."

"I would take someone down for eating my food too." I shrugged with a smirk.

She shot me a look. "Scorp…" She started to turn away.

"Hey." I grabbed her arm, pulling her back to me. Widening my legs to become more even with her eyeline, I placed my hands on her biceps, forcing her to look at me. "Everything will be okay. I will make sure of it, little viper."

"How?" Her chest heaved out a gust of air, her eyes glossing with more unshed tears.

33

"I don't know, but I'll figure it out. You know I have no moral integrity." A smirk hitched up the side of my face. "I'll go far as I need to." My attention dropped to where sauce still streaked her chin. Unconsciously, I reached up, my thumb wiping it away, skating slowly over her skin and across her bottom lip before I licked it off.

Hanna sucked in, her gaze coming to mine. She stared at me unabashedly, peeling at my skin, at the barriers around me, suddenly making me feel off kilter. Exposed.

"Why?" Her blue eyes searched mine with complete honesty.

"Why what?" I cleared my throat, dropping my hands from her, my gaze going to the side.

"Why do you care?"

My attention snapped back, my mouth parting to speak, though nothing came out. The question rolled around my head, with no answer coming off my tongue in response.

Her gaze didn't relent. Bold and unyielding.

Shifting back, I folded my arms, peering down at my boots, her regard burning into my skin. The silence growing between us felt like claws and teeth.

"We better finish our list." I pushed my shoulders back, grabbing the plate and discarding it in the trash, leaping over the last few moments. Brushing my hands off, I started to head away when I lifted my head and spotted a man standing at the corner of a booth, his eyes on me.

Shrouded in a dark cloak, he tried to hide his identity, but I knew exactly who it was. Dzsinn's chin dipped, acknowledging me, then he stepped back, disappearing behind the stand, his average height and weight disappearing in a throng of dark clothing like a ghost.

"Come on." I motioned for Hanna to follow as I subtly shadowed Dzsinn.

"What's going on?" She picked up on the shift in my demeanor, her head snapping around, trying to find the reason.

"Remember, it wasn't just shopping we were coming for," I replied, weaving through the crowd of shoppers. Hanna was right behind me, following my lead without missing a beat.

I headed to our designated meet-up spot, a dark, seedy pub called The Lantern, where only the shadiest of smugglers and outlaws went. There was no sign, just a symbol of a lamppost stamped on the wall to tell you where you were.

"Stay close," I muttered to her as we started down the steps. Normally I would never take anybody with me to this place, let alone Hanna, but instinct told me she could handle herself and wouldn't do anything stupid. It said a lot when I didn't trust half the people I served within Sarkis's army.

The dimly lit underground pub smelled of stale, smoky air, unwashed bodies, and cheap musky alcohol. The crumbling brickwork added to the shabby feel. The bar was half filled with characters normal people would walk a mile out of their way to avoid. But neither Hanna nor I were normal. Most of these hardened, so-called tough criminals would crumble under the conditions we had endured.

In the darkest corner of the packed, windowless room, Dzsinn waited, his hood still up, his dark eyes darting from me to Hanna, a frown furrowing his brow. My expression stayed even as I nodded to her to take a seat. I slipped into the one across from him.

Dzsinn continued to watch her.

"She's good."

"Well, not to me. I don't fucking know her," he replied, a hint of an American accent in his gruff tone.

I leaned closer, enunciating every word. "I said she's good."

Dzsinn huffed, sitting back, but didn't argue. He knew if I said that, I was staking my life on it.

"Where's your other friend who usually comes with you?"

My muscles locked up, acid sizzling the back of my throat, my jaw slamming together. Peering to the side, I forced the words through my teeth.

"He's dead."

I still waited for Maddox to walk into a room like his absence was only because he was running an errand or on a mission. My nightmares recalled every gruesome detail of that bear ripping out his guts, lurching me awake in a panic because night after night I watched him die again, not able to stop it. Maddox's death was something I still hadn't faced, burying myself in all the other shit we were dealing with, hiding away from it.

Dzsinn dipped his head in respect.

"I need to get earpieces and undetectable body cameras." Keeping my voice low, I went straight into business, wanting to leap as far as I could from the memory of Maddox. "In the next day or two."

Dzsinn's eyebrows went up, sitting back in the chair.

"That's extremely exclusive stuff. Only the king's distributors traffic that kind of equipment."

King Lars was a shrewd man. When the wall fell between worlds, and all the human-made stuff failed under the weight of the magic infusing the air, he started producing items to take their place that could work in this new world. He had the top scientists and developers engineering it while having the scariest motherfuckers known to the Otherworld distributing his products throughout the Unified Nations. Dark Dwellers. Times had changed since their prime in the Otherworld, back almost two decades ago, but they were still known to be hired assassins. Silent, ruthless, and deadly.

If you saw one, you were already dead.

"Can you get it?" I pressed him.

Dzsinn pondered me for a moment. "Yeah. I can get it, but it will cost you."

"I figured." I snorted. "What's your price?"

His mouth stretched in an unsettling smile. "Besides my normal fee, plus rush costs?" A smug smile hinted on his mouth. "A future favor."

Fuck. I didn't move, trying not to show any emotion. In the fae world, favors were just as binding as a promise. Once you agreed, you couldn't back out no matter what they asked you to do.

My throat bobbed, and I shifted in my chair, feeling Hanna's gaze bounce between us, once again picking up on the change in the air.

"That's my price," he confirmed.

"No," Hanna spoke at the same time I said, "Fine."

My attention twisted to her. She shook her head, worry in her expression, understanding this was a heavy price.

A muscle in my cheek jerked as I turned back to Dzsinn. "I agree to the terms."

Dzsinn grinned smugly. "Midnight. Tomorrow night. At the boat dock."

I nodded, about to rise.

"Oh, and tell *Lord Killian* that King Lars is watching everything happening here *very* closely. There are also whisperings about some powerful nectar finally being found. Its magic equals the treasures of Tuatha Dé Danann."

Hanna and I froze.

"What?" I tried to control my voice, a trickle of sweat beading down my back.

By the glint in Dzsinn's eyes, he was aware of everything going on and that I was connected to it. Dzsinn had his ear to the ground, to the wall, and in the air. He made sure he was informed of everything going on. That's why he was so good at what he did. Though I wasn't expecting him to know about this.

"That *girl*..." He stood up, peering down at me. He was an average size, but his dominance made him seem ten feet tall. Information was power in the fae world. "She might need to be warned." Rapping his knuckles on the table. "She has been classified as a threat and has their majesties' personal bounty hunters coming for her." Dzsinn nodded at Hanna and me. "Tomorrow night." With that, he slipped out of the tavern in a blink, no one remembering they ever saw him here.

"Oh my gods... was he talking about Brexley?" Hanna whispered hoarsely to me, her eyes wide.

"He was." My throat struggled to swallow. It was automatic, the impulse to reach out for her, to sense the hum in our link. But there was nothing. An empty void of darkness.

Brexley was being hunted by so many groups, but I had heard about the reputation of the royal bounty hunters. They never failed.

We had to find Brexley before they did.

"Brex..." I muttered to myself. "Where the fuck are you?"

Chapter 4
Brexley

A slow, steady rocking roused me from a deep sleep, my lids lifting to the dim light of twilight. In the distance, I could see the sunset slipping quickly over the horizon, the darkness encroaching. Disoriented, fear spiked through me, not understanding where I was or what had happened. My mind was heavy, my muscles limp and sore, my head pounding.

My gaze darted around the covered wagon I was in. I laid on worn, musky pelts, crates of aging vegetables, cans of beans, and salted meats stacked around me. The sound of the creaking wood of an old wagon and the rhythmic steps of dozens of horse hooves tapped at my ears from outside.

Trepidation thickened my throat. Sitting up, I noticed I was still wearing my prison outfit. It was ripped and caked with mud and dried blood. My hair hung in filthy chunks around my face. My mind scrambled, trying to recall my last memories.

Recollections flooded my mind—running through forests and towns, over mountains, down ravines, like something out of my control was pulling me. I sprinted for hours, never slowing my pace, until my body gave out,

39

collapsing by a stream. The memory of why I was running—
what I did—slammed into me like a tsunami.

"Oh gods.," I croaked, tears brimming my eyes.

Tad.

I killed him.

My friend, someone I considered family, my lifeline in
Halálház. I was about to hurt Simon, and he pointed all my
magic at him instead to protect the boy. I killed so many of
them. I recalled their faces, frozen in fear, slaughtered by an
invisible army. All because I couldn't control my power…

The nectar.

Sucking in with panic, my hands frantically searched the
pelts I was on, knocking against an object hidden under a fur.
Relief blew from my lips as my fingers curled around the box,
pulling the familiar burnt container to me. When I peered
inside, the substance lay innocently, empty of its past crimes,
devoid of power. It was so small, so unassuming compared to
the magic it contained and what it could do.

The extreme conflict of wanting to toss it into the river
to never see it again was defeated by the utter sick terror of
letting it out of my grasp. To cut off part of me.

With a lurch, the wagon came to a shuddering stop, a
man's voice hollering out, "We camp here tonight."

Movement exploded outside, dozens of voices rising
from behind the canvas separating me from them. Sucking in,
I rammed myself against the board, my attention sweeping
the space. I grabbed a can of beans, tucking the box in my
waistband.

Boots crunched under dirt and foliage, a tall shadow
walked next to the wagon, coming around the back. Pushing
myself up more, tension bracing my muscles, primed to
defend and attack.

The flap was pulled open, and a large murky outline
filled the entrance.

"Our vagabond is finally awake." His raspy but oddly soothing voice struck my ears.

I stayed silent, ready to fight if he came for me. My body shook with exhaustion, weak, but survival pumped adrenaline into my blood. I would fight to the death if I had to.

There was a flick of a match, the man lighting a lantern in his hand. The soft glow of the flame kindled to life, revealing half his face.

I swallowed down the small intake of air. He was not what I was expecting.

He looked to be in his mid-twenties, far younger than my mind put with his voice. The man was alluring and rough at the same time. A contradiction like his voice. He was dressed in dull, worn pants, a long-sleeved Henley shirt, a thick long jacket lined with fur, and his waist belt was loaded with guns. He had dark hair, thick scruff, and dark, sultry eyes, which felt like they could undress you and slit your throat at the same time. He wasn't classically handsome, but something pulled you to him. Seducing. Enthralling. Mysterious. I had this feeling he could make you crawl over glass to be near him.

Definitely fae, but I had no idea what type.

"I'm sure you are quite hungry," he stated, looking at the can of beans in my hand. His gaze darted up to mine. His lips didn't move, but I still felt like he was smirking at my weapon of choice.

"Who are you?" My voice came out withered and broken. "Where am I? How did I get here?"

"I found you, half drowning in a creek bed." His voice slunk around me, goosepimpling my flesh. "As to where you are… about a day's ride from Košice."

"Košice, Slovakia?" I exclaimed in disbelief.

41

"We either left you there to die, or you came with us. You were not conscious enough to let us know your choice." His dark eyes tracked me like he was trying to pry more information out of my head.

"How long have I been out?"

"Over two days."

My mind tried to wrap around the prospect that I had been unconscious for two days, vulnerable, crossing a border into another country. Two days since I escaped Věrhăza. Two days since I killed Tad and hundreds of others. Two days since I left Warwick...

It was what I wanted, to get away from the people I loved, to protect them, but now I felt scared and homesick. The link to Warwick and Scorpion was severed. I was completely alone with people I didn't know or trust.

"Even unconscious, you wouldn't let go of that box." He nodded to the bulge tucked into my waistband.

No emotion or reaction reflected back at him, no sign of my terror that he'd figure out the truth of what it was.

"Who are you?" I asked.

"I could ask the same of you."

A bonfire flamed outside the caravan, crackling against the stars and icy air. The commotion of people chatting, laughing, and moving around pulled my attention outside.

"What is this?" I nodded at the wagon. Did I just land myself in some outlaw gang?

"Come see for yourself." He waved me on, stepping away from the entrance, leaving me in darkness.

I took in a heavy breath. There was no other choice. I was far from home, with no money, food, or transportation. I was stuck until I could come up with a solid plan.

Taking one of the pelts to keep me warm, I followed him out of the wagon, climbing down the steps into the freezing

42

night air. I trailed after him around the wagon before I came to a complete stop. My mouth dropped as I took everything in.

"Holy shit," I muttered. In the short time since stopping, this open area had been transformed into another world. Lanterns hung from the dozens of wagons circling the huge bonfire in the middle, keeping the wind out and heat in. Over twenty canvas-covered wagons holding supplies and brightly painted vardos circled around like a wall. The vardos, which were houses on wheels, were decorated with intricate and ornate details and designs, gilded in gold trim, and painted in bright colors, something you would picture a cliché fortune teller in. These were rundown, though that almost added to the magical eeriness in the air.

Dozens and dozens of people milled around, setting up tables and chairs. Pots were put on the fire to cook, drinks, plates, and utensils set down on community tables. My attention went to the various people. All ages, types, and sizes: a woman who had the skin like a lizard, a man who had a horse's tail and hooves, a little girl who walked on her hands because her legs were actual frog legs. They reminded me of Carnal Row, where the fae could partially turn into their other form to entice the customers. Why were they in half-forms here?

Most appeared normal on the outside, dressed in variations of the guy standing next to me, but something told me they were not. By the energy in the air alone, I knew most, if not all, were fae.

I stared in awe, watching the horse-man pull out two pure white horses from a trailer type of wagon, their coats and manes glinting like stardust. The roar of lions from another wagon shivered up my spine.

"What is this?"

43

"This is our home. Our family. Our livelihood." He turned to me, his voice once again making me shiver with anticipation. "It's where the freaks and shunned of the fae world, those who don't fit with their own, can find a place." His dark eyes moved over me as if he knew I was one of those people. "I am Jethro."

"Laura." I muttered the name I used in Halálház.

The side of his face tipped in a smirk, as if he also knew I was lying.

"Well, Laura. Welcome to Circus Mystique."

Chapter 5
Caden

Icy night wind whipped off the Danube, stabbing my frozen face with painful pricks. My muscles juddered like they were hopping under my skin.

Always restless. Always ready to attack.

My finger twitched around the trigger of my gun, my gaze darting around, taking in everything. My senses were overloaded all the time now. The magic in the air I had never really thought about sparked against my nerves. The lapping of water snapped in my eardrums. The smell of the dank, musty water, fish, pollution, and gasoline from the boats made me feel nauseous. Had it always been this bad and I just didn't notice?

My chest knotted, pushing back the truth that I was too afraid to acknowledge. Hiding it deeper under the layers of rage.

"You and Birdie stay here," Scorpion instructed me. I couldn't stop the rush of anger at the nerve of a *fae* ordering me around like I was some foot soldier. The fact I was even here, guarding his back, twisted more ire through me. Gritting my teeth, it took everything in my power not to strike out, fury constantly bubbling under my skin, which seemed to be the only thing I'd felt since *that day*...

Actually, that wasn't true. Fear was another one, but that only fueled my anger. And what burned my veins with fire and more rage was the unrelenting drive for sex. I had a normal, healthy appetite before all this shit. Typical for a human man in his early twenties. I had taken a few women to bed because sleeping next to Brexley without touching her gave me the worst case of blue balls imaginable. I always had my pick of girls willing to be with me at HDF, but I wasn't a playboy. Not really my thing. I chose to be with Brexley over them.

This was different. What was raging through me was a desire I almost couldn't control. A need so deep to not just have sex, but *fuck*. Relentlessly and brutally. The need itched my insides like I wanted to tear out of my own skin.

"He won't trade with anyone he doesn't know." Scorpion peered around the boat dock, his posture suggesting he was on the defense, prepared to fight at any moment. "Be on the lookout up here." He frowned as if he could feel the same thing as me. Something was off, coating the air like a bad taste in your mouth.

"Yes, I know how to do this," I snipped, feeling like some moody teenager going through puberty. "I am a trained officer."

"Yeah, inside the cushy walls of HDF." Scorpion scoffed. "But the moment you had to fight outside of them, you were captured." *By me*, he left off.

"Fuck you." My body lurched for Scorpion before my brain even had a chance to think. He reacted to my threat, his chest puffing out.

"Whoa! Whoa!" Birdie jumped between us, holding up her hands, pushing us away from each other. "Both of you

46

calm the hell down. We're supposed to be on the same side, remember?"

"Right." Hanna snorted, her head shaking, our eyes meeting across the two fae. I could see the same struggle in her. All our lives, we were conditioned and trained to hate fae, to kill them without mercy. Since our "capture" by Sarkis's army, her going into Věrhăza, and my being treated like a lab experiment by my own father, nothing was solid underneath us. Nothing made sense anymore.

I was fighting with them now, but it didn't mean I was totally on their side. I had no side. And the more I felt the truth tapping at the back of my neck, the awareness of what was happening to me, the more isolated and alone I felt.

Scorpion glared at me but took a deep breath, his gaze going to Hanna for a moment. She didn't flinch from his heavy stare. "You coming, little viper?"

Her lips pressed together, and she turned to head down the dock without a word.

A small sigh came from him. "Birdie?" He tipped a brow at her.

She nodded at his unspoken words, only a strand of her white-blonde hair peeking from her hood. You could see the bond, the closeness between them, the years they had known and worked together.

Had they ever fucked each other?

My lip curled at the image, and a wave of irrational anger flared up my spine. The instinct to step closer to her, to block her from Scorpion's view, almost rocked me back on my ass.

What the fuck was that? Turning away to get ahold of myself, I took a deep staggering breath.

"You okay?" For such a tiny petite thing, she had a deeper, scratchy voice that clawed down my back, making

47

my dick hard. Which only pissed me off more. My fingers rolled so tight, the skin over my knuckles started to split.

"Fine," I huffed, shaking my head and moving behind the embankment wall, getting a better position overlooking the docks below.

"Seriously, pretty boy, you are really tightly wound lately." She crouched right next to me, her gun ready, her tiny frame giving off so much heat and energy my teeth sawed together. I inched away from the way her energy had my body reacting.

Her brows furrowed, watching me scoot away like I was six and she had cooties. She rolled her eyes, setting her focus on Hanna and Scorpion slipping through the darkness to the pier where they were meeting his contact, Dzsinn.

Clouds slid over the full moon, fog rolling off the river and drenching everything in a murky eeriness. My shoulder twitched again, the sensation shifting me in our hiding spot, turning my head behind me. I couldn't explain it, but something felt off tonight. It was heavy in the air, like the atmosphere was playing a song trying to warn us, but the night only reflected the croaking of frogs, the soft lapping of water against the embankment. Nothing out of sorts, but I couldn't seem to settle.

Birdie looked around, her nose scrunching up.

"You feel that?" I watched her look around.

Her head snapped to me. "You do?" Her head tipped, scrutinizing me. I hadn't told anyone what had happened to me at the labs, nor had Warwick uttered a word. It was difficult to articulate the hurt and shame of your own father feeling so little for you that he tested his theory on you before he did it himself. I felt violated—uncomfortable with what happened to my body without my say.

I was overshadowed with shame to realize how blind I

was for so long. Gullible and stupid. I even turned on my best friend because I still wanted to believe my father over her accusations. Another struggle was the discomfort of no longer feeling in control. I was tied to someone I hated, and he was with the woman who should be mine.

I wanted to punch myself for not admitting it sooner. For being so cocky, taking her for granted, thinking she would love me forever and would never slip through my fingers. Now Brexley was gone. Her loss was more than just physical for me.

"Why shouldn't I?" I muttered, my jaw struggling to move between my gritted teeth and numb muscles.

Birdie shrugged. "Not usually something humans can sense anymore."

I locked up. "What does that mean?"

She shot me another *what the fuck* look. "Nothing, pretty boy. Just saying. The slight surge in the air from magic is something humans don't really notice."

"How do you know? You're not human. Maybe we do." I could hear the defensiveness, the attack spitting from my mouth. "You don't fucking know."

"Seriously, what is going on with you?" she snapped back at me. "You weren't this much a dick when you were chained up as our prisoner."

"Maybe that's why," I huffed. I knew I was being an ass, which was not normal for me. I had been brought up to do my duty, to be the well-mannered prince of HDF. Charming, strong, smart, and refined. Now, I couldn't seem to control this beast inside, the fury crawling out of me, and she seemed to bring it right to the surface.

Movement down at the pier turned our focus. A boat motored up, three silhouettes climbing out of the small craft. Everything about their dark outlines had me tensing up. I could tell the smaller one was in charge. He had that air about him.

All were fae.

"Dzsinn." I heard Scorpion address him, their voices easily carrying to me, though they should have been far out of earshot.

"Everything's in there." Dzsinn nodded to the container his men dropped at Scorpion's feet.

Scorpion leaned down, examining the product inside. He nodded as he stood, handing him a thick envelope. "Thank you."

Dzsinn peered in, checking it was all there. Satisfied, he glanced back at Scorp. "I will let you know when I need to call on that favor."

Scorpion dipped his head in understanding.

Icy air licked at my spine, prickling the hairs on my arms as if tiny ants were crawling over my skin, screaming in warning. My head twisted behind me, confirming my fear. Dozens of figures in dark clothes, branded with an insignia I had never seen before, darted out of the shadows. They were heading for us, loaded with weapons.

"Csapda!" Ambush! Birdie screamed to Scorpion below as a shot rang out, cutting the bitter air with a ricochet.

It only took a moment for everything to combust with gunfire, everyone scrambling to hide. Birdie and I ran behind an old ferry booth, shooting back at the assailants. Gunfire came from the dock, retaliating against the group coming toward us.

"Who the hell are they?" I poked my head out, firing at anything moving toward us. There were so many. "They aren't HDF." I knew their style, the way they moved and would attack.

These guys moved with precision, but not as a unit.

Almost as if they were barely trained. They lacked cohesiveness. They seemed to be of all ages, women and men. Our attackers were skinny and weak but determined to kill us.

"I don't know." She pulled another gun from her jacket. Double fisting them, she leaned around me, firing both at once, each shot dropping a body.

"Damn." I blinked back at her, causing a hint of a smile on her face. The sound of a boat engine spun us to the dock. Dzsinn and his men fled the area.

"Scorp!" She shouted down where he and Hanna were. Hanna covered Scorpion as he picked up the box. They bolted off the pier without cover and joined us behind the abandoned ferry booth.

"Who the hell is shooting at us?" Scorpion hissed. "It's not HDF, right?"

"No." Hanna's back was to the wall, but she stood there almost like she was in a trance, her chest moving up and down. "It's not HDF."

"Then who?" Birdie fired on our attackers. Emptying the chamber of one of her guns, she seamlessly tucked it back into her coat, yanking out another automatic from her thigh, and continued to shoot without pause.

Why did I find that so hot?

"They're no longer human." Hanna swallowed, her eyes glossing with emotion.

"What?" Scorpion's head darted to her for a second, his gaze running over her as she stood there, frozen.

"I can feel them," she muttered, her throat bobbing, her hands strangling the handle of her gun as if she was trying not to move. "They're like me."

"Like you?" Birdie's forehead furrowed.

Hanna turned her head to Birdie. "Monsters."

51

Scorpion growled under his breath, his head in shaking in disagreement, but we all understood what she was talking about.

They were on the pills. Human-fae hybrid freaks that were turning into the fae essence they were given. I had seen a couple of my old classmates firsthand turn into these monstrosities and attack us. They became almost impossible to kill.

"Then they have to be HDF." Birdie's gun blasted at the approaching enemy.

"No." Hanna shook her head. "I don't think so."

"It doesn't matter!" Scorpion yelled. "We need to escape!"

They continued to move in from all sides; we only had the water as an exit, and that was yards away.

"Szar!" My gun clicked empty.

"I hope you have a plan like the one in the market." Birdie yelled at Scorpion over the volley of bullets, pulling out yet another gun attached to her ankle and handing it to me.

I blinked at her.

"What?" She shrugged at me. "I like guns."

"I was hoping you had a plan." Scorpion took back her attention. "Like the one in Sarajevo."

"Oh yeah, that was a good one." She nodded. "You had that brilliant one in Vienna."

"Masterful." She and Scorpion went back and forth as our enemy descended, getting only yards away from us. They were the kind to joke until the end, while Hanna and I were the serious ones.

I could see the tension in Birdie's frame, her fear hidden behind her badass demeanor.

"Ahhh!" Birdie cried out as a bullet grazed her arm. It was like I watched it hit in slow motion, the blood spraying out, her body jolting as another one hit her thigh, the force taking her to the ground.

Terror. Rage. Vengeance.

They boiled under my skin, shutting off everything but the desire to kill whoever hurt her.

In that moment, I was no longer in my head. Something deep in me roared with retribution, a force I could not contain bellowing out in a cry.

Nothing could touch me.

Death was afraid of me.

I was to be feared. Revered.

The roar of motorcycles, gunfire, and screams of death snapped me back with the sting of a rubber band, dropping my body, my energy heaving out of me.

"Oh, hell yeah," Birdie cheered out. "Distraction!"

My gaze lifted to see Warwick, Ash, Lukas, and Kek barrel in. Warwick used his clawed scythe to slice through the attackers as Ash and Lukas gunned others down. Kek smiled with a sinister joy, snapping their necks without lifting a finger.

Warwick was everything the rumors suggested. Brutal, ruthless, detached, and quick. He gave no thought to the one he cut in half as he sunk into the next. Killing without mercy and with no effort.

A true warrior and legend.

I fucking *hated* him.

With a swing of his claw, the final head rolled off into the river; the now silent streets were soaked with blood and littered with body parts.

His gaze lifted to mine, stirring up more of my hatred, when I heard Birdie call out for him.

"Legend!" She limped over to him with a grin, ignoring her wounds. "Can I say you have impeccable timing."

He nodded at her, his eyes shooting to me again like it was my fault he was there.

Even worse, I knew deep down… I had called him here.

53

Chapter 6
Warwick

"Repeat that again." Killian stared at us from across the table. Tonight a fire crackled in the hearth, illuminating his clenched jaw. We all were back in the command room, except Birdie, who was getting patched up downstairs, and Caden, who took off the moment we arrived back here, getting as far from me as possible.

I was all for that.

"The men were my mother's." Lukas folded his arms, hiding all traces of emotion. "It was her insignia they wore." When their bodies were all scattered across the road in parts, it was easier to get close and see what was embedded in their tops. A woman with wings curved into a harp. It was a symbol used by British monarchies in the past, but for fae it meant something completely different. A secret emblem to all the fae living among humans before the wall fell. Over the centuries it had been twisted into a symbol of fae purity. Representing pure fairies as the true rulers and fae being above all humans.

"You said the people fighting were human?" Mykel paced in front of the fireplace, maps and plans spread over the table, the two leaders working late into the night when we returned.

Scorpion's gaze went to Hanna. She stared at the ground, shifting her weight between her feet.

"We've been watching them for two weeks. She only had a handful of guards at the palace." Killian looked to Ash as if he could make the pieces fit. There were over two hundred tonight, far more than what we saw night after night at the palace. "Where did they come from?"

"Maybe Leon's troop is still faithful to her," Mykel responded.

"They weren't trained soldiers." From the back, my voice ground through the room, turning every head to me. "Men and women, young to old. Most were extremely malnourished. They were people you'd find in the Savage Lands, not a skilled army."

"They were like me." Hanna's voice barely rose above a whisper but somehow screamed through the room.

"What?" Mykel whipped to her.

"They were on the pills." She swallowed, lifting her head like she was facing down an internal battle. "I could feel them."

"Feel them?" Killian tilted his head.

"I can't describe it, but I just know. They were all turned into monsters."

Killian pressed his hands into the table, his head bowing, exhaling in and out slowly. "This is how she will solidify her rule and stay on the throne. She will make her own army."

"My mother will use and kill her *own kind* to stay in power, and human lives mean even less. She can easily toss them away." Lukas confirmed Killian's claim.

"But how did she get the formula? I thought the lab was destroyed?" Mykel scratched at his beard with frustration.

His question had my mind jumping back to when Kovacs and I were first brought to the labs, Sonya's voice responding to Istvan as we were being taken to the dungeons below.

"Actually, I would like to see the labs. I need to understand what is going on and am quite interested in the process."

"She stole them straight from the source." I wrapped my hair back in a tie, the adrenaline from my kills still rolling in my veins, needing an outlet. "Istvan took her and Leon on a tour of the labs when Kovacs and I were brought there."

A scoff filtered from Killian, his head shaking. "I have to give it to her. She was even ten steps ahead of Istvan."

The woman had been sleeping with the enemy for years, building up her plan to take over. Sonya was old school. No instant gratification. She played the long game, setting up all her pieces to ensure victory. She was the next Aneira. Cruel, clever, shrewd—maybe even smarter because she had learned from the past queen's mistakes.

More than Istvan, Sonya had been the biggest threat, but no one saw it coming because of how subtly she wiggled in and took over. Her beauty, charm, and pretty words had the fae completely enamored with her as their leader.

She wouldn't stop there.

"They're all dead?" Killian straightened, his hand running over his forehead as if he had a headache.

"Yes." I nodded, glancing at Ash, Kek, and Lukas, the enemies' blood still covering us. "We made sure."

"Most fun I've had in a while." Kek tugged on her blue braid with a mischievous smile.

"What?" Ash's arms went out in a feigned hurt.

"Guess you'll have to step up your game tonight, fairy." A coy smile tipped up her mouth, her one shoulder lifting. "You too." She winked at Lukas.

Lukas's face went red, his gaze going to the floor, but I could see a small tug at his lips, his eyes shooting to Ash, then back to the ground. He was a shy one compared to Kek and Ash.

Killian's lids closed briefly. He seemed ready to snap in a million pieces. The moment he opened his eyes, he was back.

Noble.

In charge.

"We'll talk more about this tomorrow and start planning for our next mission." He nodded at the container Scorpion had put on the table. Two body cameras and a handful of high-tech earpieces. "Get some rest." He dismissed us.

He didn't have to tell me twice. My body ached with unshed energy.

Anger.

Violence.

I needed a shower. I needed a drink. I needed to punch the shit out of something. But most of all, I needed her.

My muscles clenched as frustration and ire made me want to obliterate everything around me. To kill. To feel death in my hands.

Or fuck the entire whore house until my body gave out.

But I didn't do either…

Fuck you, Kovacs. A snarl flicked at my lip. I was nothing more than a housebroken lap dog.

"Warwick?" Scorpion called after me. My boots thumped up the steps and headed for the front door. I needed to get the fuck out of here. "Hey, asshole!"

With a growl, I stopped, turning back to another person I wanted to kill, but because of Brexley, I couldn't, which fueled my fury. She was part of him, shared something with him like a fucking annoying twin brother.

"What?" I snarled.

Scorpion ignored my response, his eyes darting around, then motioned for me to follow him.

"If you don't talk soon, I will snap your neck." I huffed, begrudgingly following him to a small room off the side.

"Then shut the fuck up," Scorpion volleyed. "Believe me, you are the last person I want to spend extra time with, but this is about Brexley."

My entire body tensed, my shoulders rising, but he had my undivided attention.

"I didn't want to say anything to Killian until I told you." Scorpion kept his voice low. "When Hanna and I met my contact the other night…" He swallowed, hedging how to say the next part.

"Spit it out."

"He knew about Brexley."

"What?" I stepped back, a slight panic huffing into my lungs. "What do you mean he knew about her? How?"

"That's the least of our worries." For the first time since I'd known this guy, he looked nervous. This only tripled the adrenaline in my system. I could feel the air pumping heavier in and out of my lungs.

"The king and queen of the Unified Nations have somehow found out about her—*and* the nectar. Worse, they've classified Brexley as a threat."

Sucking in sharply, my entire body rose higher. Fear and panic slammed into me, almost blurring my vision.

"Their bounty hunters are coming for her."

In a breath, I had Scorpion against the wall, my fingers digging into his throat.

"You waited until *now* to tell me." Every syllable shot out like a dagger, my anger expanding my frame.

"Get the fuck off me." Scorpion struggled against my

grip. I locked my hand firmer around his throat. Fury bloomed behind his eyes, but he stopped fighting for a moment. "You weren't exactly around to tell, fucker."

Any time I wasn't on a mission here, I was out searching, going through any town she could have passed through. He was right; I took off for days at a time. I would hunt her down. Find her. Even if she clearly didn't want to be.

I released him with a snarl, stepping back.

"Still nothing for you either?" Scorpion muttered a few moments later.

A wave of emotion burned up my esophagus, and I turned my head to the side, slightly shaking it.

"Think it's on purpose, or her powers are still depleted?"

"I don't know," I muttered with a shrug, hating that this conversation was even happening.

"We have to find her soon, especially if the Unified Nations have sent their bounty hunters after her."

"You don't think I fucking know that?" I barked, my boots squeaking over the floor as I paced. If the rumors were to be believed, the pair who worked for the royals never failed to get their mark. *Ever.*

This time I would be standing in their way.

"Look, I know you want to find her, to tear apart this world, kill every person, including me. I get that. I want to find her too. You aren't the only one who feels…" Scorpion tapered off, a nerve flexing in his cheek. "But what the fuck are we supposed to do? She could be anywhere by now. Anything could have happened to her. She could be—"

The look I shot him slammed his mouth shut.

"No." I shook my head vehemently. "She's fine." Before, when the link went dead, there was still a sense the person was alive. A vibration within the bond. This time I couldn't feel anything, like she had died and taken everything with her. But I knew she was alive. A sixth sense in my gut connected me to her beyond the link.

Though we knew all too well, alive was far from all right. Knowing that made me want to lose my fucking mind. I had lived centuries; my time with Kovacs was a blink in the scheme of things, but I couldn't handle not being connected to her for a moment. To not know where she was. To not hear her voice, see her smile, feel her skin, taste her, capture her moans. Everything felt off.

Wrong.

I saw no color.

"Anyway, thought you should know." Scorpion huffed, strutting past me, leaving me spinning in more rage. I was a bomb ready to go off at any moment. And this country was a powder keg—on the precipice, about to take down the entire Eastern bloc with it.

I would let it, too, if Kovacs wasn't in the middle of it.

"Fuck!" I slammed my fist into the wall, bits of it crumbling to the floor. I felt destructive. Sadistic. Vicious.

Useless.

I should be able to find her. To feel her. To know exactly where she was.

If she wanted to run. I would have run with her. She couldn't protect me from her. It was too late for that. She had already leveled me.

Needing to get the hell out, the impulse to raze this motherfuckin' city to the ground thrummed in my pulse. I needed to kill, fuck, or pulverize someone until I felt nothing.

Walking out into the night, I headed for my bike, determined to act on at least one of those.

Water sprayed down my back, blood and sweat streaming down my skin, circling the drain. My knuckles were splintered, and bruises along my jaw, torso, and eye throbbed with pain. The alcohol in my system pounded in my head.

My forehead pressed into the cool tile, aiding my headache. I had fought the last three hours straight, knocking down fighter after fighter, the underground ring pinned against me, almost killing one before they dragged him away. Yet I still vibrated with fury.

It was another business Ash, Kitty, and I started back in the day. One I had taken part in a lot then.

I hoped tonight would take the edge off. It hadn't.

I knew what would—what would soothe the beast in me. But she fucking left me.

My dick was hard, aching. Desperate for her, to be inside her.

"Kovacs." I flipped around, pressing my spine into the wall, my hand wrapping around my girth. Closing my eyes, I tried to reach out for her, my mind flicking through memories of my dick fucking the shit out of her pussy.

A small groan puffed from my chest, my hand gripping harder, thinking about how she felt clamping around me, how the shadow of her tongue would glide up my chest, lick through my ass.

Gritting my teeth, I rubbed harder, needing it to hurt because I no longer felt anything anymore. I had a taste of her, of every color, and I wanted more. The need to release, to burn through my anger, had me grunting with the effort.

The communal lavatory entrance squeaked open, and the sound of several pairs of bare feet padding the floor daggered ire through me. This used to be a public restroom for the museum, but Killian had half the stalls turned into private showers. I thought at 4 a.m. I'd be safe from people. Safe to jack off without interruption.

61

A man murmured, too low for me to hear, followed by a woman's laugh.

I hissed under my breath, knowing why they were here. Maybe it was from the magic swimming in our veins, in our DNA, but fae were nymphos. Some more than others, but as a whole, we were constantly horny.

The shower at the far end turned on, the woman snickering before I heard the man speak again, but this time I realized not only did I recognize the voice, but it was a different man.

Fuck.

I knew that voice better than my own since it talked a hell of a lot more than me.

"On your knees, my beautiful blue demon." Ash's voice was low, full of sensual playfulness. "Wrap your lips around his cock."

The slap of skin hit the wet tile floor, a groan from who I figured was Lukas following soon after.

"That feel good?" Ash spoke so sensually, his tree fairy energy taking over the room. "Want me inside you?"

"Yessss…" Lukas moaned out. "Gods, Ash… I want you in me so bad." Lukas hissed.

My dick hardened in my hand. Normally, I would leave, not wanting to be part of this, but being mostly drunk and twisting with frustration and rage, my cock ached for more than just a halfhearted release.

The energy wrapped around my erection to the point of pain, which turned me primal, only caring about pleasure. Begging to feel *something*.

A deep, strangled cry came from Lukas, Ash's groan following. The slap of wet skin and flesh being pounded into burned through me, my mind picturing Brexley bending over in front of me as I hammered into her.

I stroked faster, pre-cum spurting from my tip.

Air caught in my throat as all their moans and sounds of sex echoed louder and louder through the bathroom.

"Finger yourself, Kek." Ash's tone wasn't a command, but the seduction in it practically made it one. "Let me watch."

There were a few moments of wet smacking before I heard Kek.

"Not enough, fairy. My pussy is used to you now. Craves you."

A growl came from Ash. Through the slits in the doors, I could see Ash moving away from Lukas, picking Kek off the ground. Her legs wrapped around his waist as he slammed her spine into the wall, plowing into her without hesitation.

Her scream shot shivers of magic through my nerves, pounding more blood through my cock.

"Kek..." Ash croaked. "Gods, how do you feel this fucking good? I want to be constantly inside you."

Kek only cried out in response, not holding anything back. She let it be known how she felt fucking him.

"Shit." Lukas rumbled, his hand reaching for Ash's hair, yanking and twisting his head back until his lips covered Ash's in a hungry kiss. Lukas gripped himself behind Ash, positioning before he thrust into him.

They all groaned in unison, hissing and swearing as they fucked each other. The magic in the air strangled to the point I started to sweat under the stream of lukewarm water.

The relentless sounds of sex became a backdrop to my own need. My lids shut again, my hips punching up against my hand. My arm ached, and my muscles burned as I strangled and twisted my dick harder. My mind reached for her, clawing at the emptiness between us, trying to find any way in. To peel every level until I found her.

My spine prickled, my release coming, but it wanted more.

It wanted her.

"Princess." I howled internally, her face flashing in my memory as cum scorched through my shaft.

High-pitched cries tore through the space along with the hard slaps of skin, ruthless energy pounding the fuck out of the room as the three of them orgasmed at once. It was an electric shock to my nerves.

Hot, thick cum erupted from me, a grunt carving into my throat, my mind ripping from reality as my release took me.

It was so fast, I was sure I imagined it, but I thought I saw her sleeping, curled up in a pile of pelts. Her eyes burst open with a gasp. Then it was gone.

Back in the shower stall, cold water cascaded down on me, my chest heaving for air as I slumped against the wall. I squeezed my lids against the pain of being back in reality, the moment of bliss gone.

Lost in my thoughts, I tried to recall what I thought I saw, but it drifted into the far reaches of my mind. My rage was pushed back, though, fatigue loosening my muscles enough that I required sleep.

Noise from the door opening pulled my focus as the three of them padded out.

"You're welcome, Warwick." The smirk in Ash's tone was not lost on me. I knew that asshole too well.

He knew I was here the whole time.

"Fucker," I muttered. I swear I heard him laugh down the hallway.

Naked and not giving a shit, I shuffled to the room I was using down the hall, falling face-first into my pillow.

It felt as if I only closed my eyes a moment before I was woken up, my nose itching with the need to sneeze.

"I swear to the gods…" I grumbled into the pillow, my eyes still shut, burning with lack of sleep. "If she has any fingers anywhere near my nose…"

"Oh, don't worry. She didn't have her fingers anywhere near your *nose,* massive one."

Chirp!

With a growl, I rolled my face deeper into my pillow. Kovacs running off was bad enough, but she left me with her fucking pets to babysit.

Grunting, I turned my head back, my heavy lids prying open. Opie was standing on my shoulder, wearing a skirt of leaves, his chest wrapped with deerskin. He'd designed a harness attached to his shoulders, carrying the tips of antlers behind him like wings. They had been left behind in the agriculture part of the museum next door. His beard tinted a bright green, his mohawk hair pink.

"*Lófasz,*" I grumbled, shutting my eyes again.

Chirp!

Exhaling, I twisted to see the imp sitting on my ass, wearing a leaf choker and animal skin shorts, her fingers up and flying around, flipping me off.

"Yeah, fuck you too," I replied. "And get your fingers away from my ass."

Chirp!

"I know they always say that when they're *awake*." Opie huffed.

Chirp!

"No, that was a misunderstanding."

Chirp! Chirp! Chirp!

"It was too!" Opie stomped his hairy feet into my arm.

Chirp!

"Shut. The. Fuck. Up. Both of you." I sighed again, rolling over, Bitsy flying to the side.

65

"Ahhhhh! Bitzy, hide! The armed missile is launching! Run!" Opie waved her up to the pillow as she bitched me out, her face scrunched up, her fingers circling the air like windmills.

"Fuck my life," I muttered. Before, I was a feared mythical legend. Still was to most, but these two little cockroaches did not get the memo. Since Brexley's disappearance, they had decided to attach themselves to me.

At first, I had hopes they would be able to find her like they did in Prague, but as if she was bubbled in some druid spell again, they couldn't pinpoint anything.

Pushing off the bed, I grunted, the bruises along my ribs still sore, my hand aching, and fuck, my dick was raw. Disappointingly obvious, it was not because I had been inside her.

The half-drunken memory of the night before, getting off to my friends fucking each other, had me sighing into my hands. I rubbed my face, trying to wake up.

"Seriously, even off duty that thing looks like it's going to clobber small villages."

I turned to see Opie and Bitzy sitting on my pillow, staring at me with wide eyes and rosy cheeks.

"Does it have an off switch?"

"Is there a reason you're here?" I grabbed briefs from a pile on the chair, yanking them on. "You know I've eaten imps for breakfast before."

Chiiiiirp!

"No. Not in that way." I paused. "Shit." I tipped my head back with the realization I understood her, my head shaking as I lowered it, grabbing a pair of pants off the pile. "Fuck you, Brex," I muttered under my breath, zipping them up. "Leave me with your pets."

"Pets?" Opie stood up. "How dare you!"

66

"What do you call annoying things that follow you around, nip at your ankles, and beg for treats?"

"I don't beg for treats." Opie folded his arms.

"Mushrooms?"

"Oh… yeah… those I'd beg for."

Chirp!

"Go annoy Ash then. I'm sure he'd love you to wake him up."

"We came from there. He was already *'up'*." Opie air quoted his fingers.

Chirp! Bitzy curled her fingers, matching Opie.

I scoffed, tugging on a shirt. I shoved my feet in my boots.

"Plus, we thought you'd want to know some information we found."

I looked up, waiting for him to continue. "Well?"

"I don't think you deserve it now." He huffed and turned away from me.

I stood up, breathing in, trying to control my rage. I headed for the door.

"Wait? Don't you want to know?" Opie whirled back to me.

"Tell me or don't. I'm not wasting my time waiting for you to get over some tantrum."

"You really need sex, big man. Your blocked-up pistol is making you grouchy." Opie sighed and let his arms drop. "Fine. Only because you asked so sweetly."

My hands rolled into fists, but I tried to stay calm.

"We were able to sneak back into the palace." Opie put his palm up. "Oh, my gods, what's she done with the decor? Can I say I really love it—is that bad to say? I mean, Killian's designs were nice, but Sonya has a flair—"

"I swear to the gods, brownie, if you don't spit it out, I will use you as a flare."

Opie glowered at me but continued. "So you know the labs Killian had underneath to test the pills?"

"Yes?" I swallowed.

"She's doing the same."

We had already come across them last night, but from what Killian said, his labs could only test a handful at a time.

"But it's worse… like sooooo much worse. Like—"

I growled.

"Okay, so you also know the passages underground I had to open for you?"

Chirp!

"*We* had to open for you?"

"Y-es." I gritted, my patience almost gone.

"And you know the old prison, the stinky one—though I kinda miss the shower days. Those loofas felt so good when you scrubbed just right…."

"Brownie," I barked.

"Right, well, that was also left abandoned?"

Acid started to fizz in my chest, sensing where this was headed.

"Get to it."

"Sonya has cleaned out the wreckage and built a bigger lab and testing area in there, using the cages as pens to hold them."

"Fuck." I felt blindsided, but at the same time, it made sense. She had no one to fight for her if she declared war on HDF. She needed soldiers.

Victims.

The place was massive, built to hold thousands of prisoners.

"How many cages are filled?" I stood frozen, dread already pumping through my veins.

"From the lower ones that weren't destroyed in the bombing?"

68

"Yes."
Opie swallowed, his hands twisting.
"All of them."

Chapter 7
Brexley

The dark night twinkled with thousands of firebulbs, as if the stars themselves descended to shine their magic on us. Colored lanterns, torches, and small fires in metal bins lit a path to the huge red and white striped tent. Many of the vardos were set up as booths along the path, selling food and drinks, some performing outside theirs, luring in the spectators.

Like a child, I stared in awe at the scene before me, drawn to the lights like a magnet. The sultry music coming from the speakers coiled in my ear, whispering the promise of escape, of dark desires, and freedom from the woes that bind you.

Carnival Mystique reminded me of Carnal Row, minus the outright sex, though I had no doubt it was still on offer in the dark corners. Adults and children alike flooded through the gates, eager to see the freakish shifters slinking around, performing for the audiences who had bought tickets, persuading them to dig deeper into their pockets for more coin. The aromas of roasted peanuts and chestnuts filled the air along with the sweetness of candy that looked like painted clouds.

"How do you like it?" A raspy, deep voice slipped out of nowhere, a tall form making me jump.

"Jethro." I slapped my hand to my chest, inhaling my surprise. "You startled me."

The more days I passed with this group, the more of an enigma the mysterious ring master became. Jethro was definitely fae, or at least half, but what exactly he was, no one knew or spoke of. Not even his troupe.

His dark eyes peered down at me, the light from the flames glinting off them, making him appear frightening... and sexy. Even more so tonight. Dressed in black pants, a dark maroon jacket, and a top hat, he was the epitome of a ring master—but not one who entertained children. Jethro oozed sexuality and wickedness, leading you willingly down the path of debauchery. If he had been at Carnal Row, he would have had everyone clawing to get into his establishment. To be the one he chose for the night.

"You must come and watch." He tipped his head, saying no more as he slipped away into the shadows, heading toward the big tent, leaving prickles dancing down my arms.

"Damn," I muttered to myself.

"There is something about that man." Another voice jerked me to the side, this one belonging to a dark-haired, beautiful woman I'd seen around camp this week. She and her grandmother were fortune tellers and stayed in the nicest vardo, doing card readings and séances for extra money as they traveled through towns and villages.

I had been introduced to everyone in the troupe, from animal handlers to the trapeze twins. Only a few had made any attempt to talk to me since.

"You are an outsider to us. We don't trust outsiders." She tipped her head, her eyes flicking to me.

I actually understood that.

71

"You should go watch him. Jethro is…" She let out a heavy sigh, wrapping her heavy wrap around her shoulders, filled with words she did not say. "Intoxicating. He's unbelievable to watch. A different person when he's *Maestru*." *Master* in Romanian.

The sexual way she said it made my eyebrows lift.

Her mouth twisted up, almost in a dare, like she knew dark secrets about him.

"I'm Zelda." She said her name like a performance.

"How… fitting."

"My name is about as real as yours, *Laura*." She smirked back at me. "We all play a role here. Humans love the cliché. They want danger and excitement, but only in the comfort of what they know. Just enough outside their comfort to intrigue, but not enough to scare. Did you know I have very little talent for fortune telling? My twin brother is the one who got the gift from *Bunica*." *Grandmother*. "But have you ever seen a male fortune teller? One seeking the future in a crystal ball or doing a tarot card reading?"

"No." I realized in all the books I read that the depictions were of women wearing exactly what Zelda was wearing tonight—her wrists draped in trinket jewelry, bright scarf in her hair, white blouse with a bodice, and a long, layered skirt. A costume.

"This is our life. The show is how we survive. We give them the show they want. We stay in our roles." Her tone went serious, and she tossed me a shirt she had been holding under her shawl. "Be sure you stay in yours, *seamstress*." She twirled around, heading back to her vardo.

Peering down at the torn item in my hand, I sighed. Jethro had stated the same thing to me earlier this week. If I was to stay, I had to pull my weight. I was trained to fight; I knew where to punch someone to knock them out instantly.

Now the thing getting me by was my unexpected skill in mending clothes.

And here I thought prison hadn't taught me anything useful.

With the prickles of eyes on me, I lifted my head. The soft light from inside a vardo outlined the figure in the doorway, watching me. Sucking through my teeth, I forced myself not to flinch back.

Esmeralda.

Or at least that was her stage name. The matriarch and the main fortune teller. She lived up to the part. Her hair was graying, but she was still beautiful in an outfit similar to Zelda's, but with less skin showing. She was swathed in mystery, her granddaughter and grandson paling in comparison to the intense power she gave off.

Her brown eyes dug into me, peeling back my skin as if she could see inside me, reaping my soul and taking all my secrets. No emotion, but it was like she was reading me, seeing my strange aura, though I knew she couldn't. Perceiving the blood staining my hands, aware of the things I was running from, and seeing nothing but trouble.

Tucking the shirt inside my cloak pocket, I turned away, her intensity crawling up the back of my neck as I jogged toward the big tent, keeping to the edges of the festival to stay away from the circus goers.

"Hey, sweetheart." A blond, nine-foot bearded man with an American southern drawl grinned down at me, smoking his cigarette as I approached the back entrance of the tent.

"Hey, Hank." I grinned back, my most honest grin in a while.

Hank looked like he was half giant or something. Scary when he didn't smile, he had muscles larger than my head and legs thicker than most trees, but he was the sweetest one

73

I had met here. The only one asking how I was, calling me sweetheart, and making sure I got enough to eat. He was a happy, jolly guy with a boisterous laugh, except when I saw him rehearsing his axe and gun tricks with his partner and wife, Lulu. There, he was focused and terrifying, throwing them faster than the eye could pick up as she spun on a giant wheel.

Where Hank was tall and broad, Lulu was short and tiny. I mean, she didn't even hit four feet tall. They were an awkward pair, but they had two kids, so somehow, they made it work.

"First time seeing the show, huh?" Hank talked slowly, his sentences drawing out. "Better get in there, don't want to miss when he takes the stage. He's somethin' else, sweetheart." He pulled away the canvas, waving me in.

The backstage area was filled with performers. White horses were decorated with jewels and feathers, their riders in almost matching outfits. Jugglers, hoopers, and trapeze performers roamed the space, and the back area was alive with loud noises, adrenaline, hairspray, and cheap perfume.

Music swelled from the stage as I snuck around the side, staying in the shadows. The lights went off, making the spectators in the packed seating gasp, before a single light went on Jethro. He absorbed the light, claiming everything, including every speck of attention, as his.

You couldn't keep your eyes off him. He radiated every fantasy you desired, every sin you wanted to commit.

"Ladies and gentlemen, boys and girls… Are you longing for the most dazzling, magical, death-defying show ever? Do you want that and more?

His deep, seductive voice rose through the tent. My skin prickled with energy, having no idea what to expect. I had seen nothing like this before.

The crowd screamed out, stomping their feet and clapping. Starry-eyed fans cried out, "Yes! More!"

Chanting. Pounding.

In one instant, everything flipped. My breath stuck in my throat, excitement twisting to utter terror. My heart thumped as flashes of death flickered through my head, the distinct taste of dirt and adrenaline coating my tongue, the smell of piss and sweat filling my nose. I could feel their blood covering my skin. The memory of the crowds' chants growing louder with each kill. The pounding of their feet.

The sound of the patrons in the tent chanting for the ring master curled up my spine, bending me over, blurring my vision and stealing my air. I was back in the pit. Fighting for life, murdering friends, and hearing them cheer for more.

"Let me hear you!"

The assembly amped up their excitement until it rung in my ears, sparking panic through me. Wind gusted through the tent flaps, and a flicker of lightning crackled in the air, making some in the crowd gasp with excitement, thinking it was part of the show.

I needed to go. To run. Yet my legs refused to move, my muscles frozen in trauma.

"This night, we will twist the facts, contort what is possible, and shed you of your boundaries. Don't fight the lure of your most wicked dreams, where truth and logic no longer apply. This is the place where you are truly free." The fanfare upped like it was drilling into my bones, my body shaking. The dim firebulbs around the sides crackled again.

"Welcome to Circus Mystique! Where your fantasies come true!" Jethro's voice rose to a crescendo, making the audience go wild.

A small cry came from my throat as I felt my terror manifest. Lightning snapped through the tent right as the lights were brought back up, dozens of them bursting, sparks flying up like firecrackers.

The spectators trilled with *oohs* and *ahhs*, thinking this was some great magic trick.

But I knew better.

Through the shadows and obscurity, Jethro's gaze found me.

A sharp inhale tucked in my throat, his attention zeroing on me as if he somehow knew I was the culprit. His jaw clenched before he turned his head back to the audience, becoming *the Master* again.

I didn't hesitate. I bolted out the front entrance, knocking into a few people running late for the performance. The frosty night air mushroomed in front of me, my skin hot and sticky, stinging against the sudden icy temperatures.

My feet took me down the path, heading back to our camp, which had no barrier between the circus and us, except the lights grew fewer, the darkness crawling over you like a blanket.

Coming to a stop, I took in huge gulping breaths, my muscles quivering. Trepidation shoved at the energy gurgling inside me, swallowing down the sharp edges of dread, guilt, and grief.

My lids shut, and images of Tad burned through my mind. His expression when my magic hit him, how his frail form flew through the air, his dead eyes staring up at the sky.

A deep sob churned in my chest, wrapping around my lungs and strangling out the oxygen. I had not faced what I had done. The fact I had killed my friend—and hundreds of others. And I couldn't now. It was too much. The weight would crush me until I would no longer get up.

It wasn't just the fear of losing control. It was the revelation that I liked it. Wanted more. The high of reaping souls—of giving and taking life. To use the magic at my will and avenge. End all my pain and suffering and take everyone down who caused it except my invisible army. They didn't see any difference… they harvested lives with no distinction to appease their master.

It wasn't just the nectar I feared; it was myself.

A tickle pricked up the back of my neck, and the sensation of being watched curved my head around, standing me up slowly.

Everyone was in the large tent or in the carnival section; this area was quiet. Still.

Fog curled over the ground, wrapping around the forest we butted up against. A shiver ran down my spine, an alarm triggering my heart to pound.

My eyes took in everything. Trepidation danced on my bones, and a brush of icy wind licked through my mind, whispering something I could not hear. The need to run back to the big tent wormed through my legs, stepping me back cautiously. Larger plumes of air rolled out of my mouth as I circled around, the sensation growing stronger.

Watched.

Hunted.

A twig snapped and I swung back around, almost letting out a scream.

Only two feet away was Esmeralda, her dark, creepy gaze on me.

"Holy shit!" I stumbled back. How the hell did she sneak up on me like that?

"I see you." She moved closer, her voice rough. "And I see *them* too. Death surrounds you, girl. And it will destroy everyone for you." With that, she turned away, gliding back to her vardo, leaving me shivering, but not from the cold.

"Princess…"

My eyes bolted open with a gasp at the deep rough voice and the sensation I wasn't alone. My core pulsed with the need, desire like water trickling over my skin. It was only a wisp of wind, a ghost with aqua eyes hovering over me, and the moment my eyes were fully open, he was gone.

My heart slammed against my ribs. My skin was hot though the air was freezing. Sitting up, my attention darted around the wagon, looking for someone who wasn't there. Did I dream it? Or was the link coming back?

Conflicting emotions of happiness and fear knocked into each other. If the bond was starting to return, there wasn't anywhere I could hide. Not from him.

Leaning against the sideboard, I breathed in and out, trying to calm myself. My heart ached for another moment, another second to feel him near me. Tears filled my eyes, my mind twisting me up so much, I could even smell him. If violence, lust, and rage had a scent, it would be Warwick.

Rubbing my face, I dropped my gaze to the corner of a box hidden under my pillow. I tugged it to me, the weight of the nectar inside heavier than you'd think. It carried the weight of that night twenty years ago. Like a time capsule, it waited for the day to be let out and rediscovered.

My shoulders dropped with both relief and sadness when I peeked inside. It still lay there with a dull emptiness. Maybe I had only dreamed about Farkas. Though it wouldn't be long before it came back, probably drawing more than Warwick and Scorpion to me.

The urge to chuck it into the river, hoping for it to be forever buried in the silt and mud, clashed brutally against the need to keep it close and protect it.

My fingers reached out, the desire to hold it and feel it come to life consuming me. I wanted the magic to take over, burning power through my bones. Reason and logic collided in me like a gale force wind, spinning my head and flushing blood quicker through my veins. Jerking my hand back with a heaving cry, I slammed the box shut, tossing it back on my pillow. My back shoved into the sideboard, my legs pushing me back as if I could escape the force field it was trying to pull me into.

Sucking in and out slowly, I tried to calm myself, my gaze still on the box.

"Death surrounds you, girl. And it will destroy everyone for you." Esmeralda's words clung to me like a bad dream, her sentiment clawing at the back of my brain and tightening my chest.

Growing up, fortune tellers, seers, and tarot cards were seen as entertainment. Fake. Rebeka once had a cool theme party with tables set up with fortune tellers, but none of us believed it was anything but show. Their predictions were so generalized they could apply to anyone.

Inside the walls of Leopold, life tried to stay in the lines, pretending it was the time before the wall fell. Before we found out fae and magic were real, living among us, and our world was now theirs.

Esmeralda was no fake. Her statement peeled away all my barriers, finding the truth I was hiding, which I was terrified of.

Death would destroy everyone *for me*. I had no control and no understanding of the true power that filled me and the nectar that night. It was magic no one had a name for, no one could define, because it didn't exist. It was royal fairy magic, black magic. It was death, grief, and pain from so much loss and sacrifice on the field.

79

The need to reach back for the nectar rocked through me like a drug I craved. My skin crawled with the need to move, the memory of Warwick's voice still pounding through me.

I had to get out.

Tugging on my boots, I wrapped a pelt around me and slid out of the supply wagon I had taken up as my lodging. Every wagon, even the carny one, was full, so Jethro carved out a space for me to sleep between extra wagon wheels, food, and medical supplies.

Frigid air hit my lungs with a punch, and ice covered the grass and roofs of the wagon. Thick fog clung heavily to the trees, winding itself over the frozen ground. Dawn hinted on the horizon, dulling the stars in the sky.

My legs took off, heading for the thick forest beside my wagon, the fresh, crisp air clearing my tumbling mind. The canopy of trees engulfed me in shadows, my flesh shivering.

The sound of a slow-moving creek hit my ears before I came upon it. Squatting down, I cupped my hands into the icy water, splashing it on my face, sending a hiss up my throat.

Overhead an owl squawked out a loud cry, breaking the silence, the sound shivering down my shoulders.

The goosebumps covering my skin didn't ebb as the chill from the water disappeared. Once again, I felt the spike of warning creep over me, pushing my shoulders back. My gaze scanned the forest for any movement. Person or wild animal. Though I was more afraid of a person.

There was no doubt I was being watched from the darkness.

Kalaraja always seemed to find me. While Warwick would come barreling for me, Kalaraja would enjoy slithering up to me, playing with me.

I had many out there looking for me... looking for what I carried.

That chilly sensation fluttered up the back of my neck and through my mind again, like a howl in the wind far away.

Deliberately, I rose to my feet, my gaze searching for any movement. My pulse thumped against my neck, anxiety thicker with each passing second.

I took a step back. Watching. Waiting.

Then I spun around to run but came to a dead stop, a cry barking from my chest.

Esmeralda stood only feet from me.

"Megbasz!" I jumped back in surprise. "How do you keep doing that?"

She stood there, her dark brown eyes on me, her hair in a messy bun, a heavy pelt draped over her shoulders covering her thin frame, highlighting her bright pink, fluffy slippers.

"Are those bunny slippers?" I did a double take, the assaulting color and cute floppy ears contrasting her eerie persona. They made me think of Opie. I missed him so much. I even missed waking up to Bitzy's fingers in my nose.

"Yes," she replied dryly, her lips pinching as the ears on her slippers flopped around. She didn't speak again, the air filling with awkward silence, my feet shifting under me.

"Well…" I nodded my head, starting to move around her. "Gonna head back to camp now."

Her fingers wrapped around my wrist, stopping me. Her eyes were hazy with a faraway look. "You will only know death if you don't learn control."

A gasp hiccupped in my throat. "Wha-what?"

"He's here. He stays close to you. So does death. They loiter at the edges."

"Who? Who's here?" A spike of trepidation filled my throat as her death grip tightened.

"He says he would do it again. Forgives you."

A flush of cold heat plunged through me.

81

"Forgives me?"

Her hazy eyes flickered. "He fears what you are… what you can do if you don't learn control."

"Who?"

Esmeralda blinked, her head shaking as if she was coming out of a trance. "Dammit. It's too early for this crap," she grumbled, her hand dropping from mine, snarling out at the woods as if there was someone there. "Before I even had my coffee."

"What is going on?"

"That old man is quite persistent."

"What old man?"

"The Druid," she huffed, folding her arm, her head flicking out to the space beside me. "He's right here."

Chapter 8
Killian

"Is that your move?" I tipped my head at the seven-year-old across from me, a bit of his tongue sticking out the side of his mouth as he contemplated his play.

Simon's sharp blue-green eyes peered up at me while he shifted his chess piece slowly to another square, gauging my reaction.

"Look at the whole board." I smiled as I watched him try to assess me, pick up on any clues I might give away, which was a huge part of not just learning chess, but life.

A soft knock sounded at the door, and I tried to ignore the sensation zinging through me. My gaze stayed locked on the boy, not going to the figure entering.

She stood for a moment, irritation radiating over her.

"You *called* for me?" Her accent immediately wrapped around my dick, making me almost jerk upright in the chair. Even if it was fake at one time, she'd played the part for so long that she could no longer distinguish herself from the character.

My head turned to the curvy redhead in the doorway, air hitching in my throat. Her beauty unnerved me. She was exactly what you would picture as an ingenue on stage. Full lips, crystal blue eyes, porcelain skin, and an incredible figure made her appear soft and sweet.

Nina might have been, but Rosie had a spine of steel and a will of iron.

My weakness.

My dick stirred as her smell wafted more into the room.

"Yes, come in." Clearing my throat, I shifted in my chair by the fire, the misty day giving us the cover to get some heat into the freezing rooms.

Rosie stepped in, realizing I wasn't alone when the closed door gave her a full view of the room.

"How about this, Uncle Killian?" Simon hovered his piece over a square. He had taken to calling me that when we were in the cabin, and I never corrected him. I would never admit it to anyone, but whenever he did, I felt a warmth, a sense of belonging I never had before.

Rosie's gaze landed on Simon in the chair across from me, her feet coming to a stop, her eyebrows scrunching together in confusion.

"You have to imagine several steps ahead and every outcome I might play against you. Take a moment and study the board. I'll be back." I rubbed his head, standing to my feet.

Rosie stood in bewilderment.

"What?" I strolled to her.

"Are you babysitting?" Her mouth parted, her lids blinking with disorientation.

"His mother and Zander are on duty, and his uncle is out, so I said I'd watch him." Simon didn't really need to be watched; the place was safe for him to run about, but I actually enjoyed spending time with him. He was the only one who wasn't giving me a headache right now, including the woman across from me.

"Why?" I added defensively.

"I don't know…" She shook her head. "I just never imagined you liking kids or being around them. I can't even picture you as one."

"Well, there's a lot you don't know about me." I snipped, irritated I was so one-layered in her view. Why I cared what a human thought, I don't know. "And yes, even if it was long ago, I once was his age too."

A memory of where I was at his age came to mind. I was existing—not really living—at an orphanage, where I was starved and beaten daily. I eventually stowed away on a ship, desperate to escape that hellhole. I could still smell the salt in the air and feel the crash of the waves as the boat rocked violently, the water dripping down my face, soaking my threadbare clothes. The terror as I was dragged out of my hiding spot and dropped at the feet of the most feared pirate in the world. I was a scrawny, unwanted street rat, but I held my chin up and stared back at him, pretending I wasn't petrified. Maybe like when I look at Simon, there was something about me that he took pity on. Respected. He saw I was scrappy, but he must have known I'd fight and kill to get where I needed to because he not only let me live, he made me part of the crew. Part of that world. Taught me how to survive. Gave me a family.

It was where I met her.

Where I got my name.

Where I became a man.

Where my heart was broken.

Where I decided nothing would stop me from being even better than the man who took me under his wing. The man I grew to hate. I would be worthy. I would be good enough. I would be rich and powerful. I would become a king.

Or the closest thing to it.

"Can't picture you ever playing or getting dirty." She folded her arms. "Did they even have dirt back when you were a kid?"

I moved into her in a blink, forcing a gasp from her throat, my hands fisting at my sides to keep from wrapping them around her beautiful neck and tugging hard on her red locks.

"You know *nothing* about me or what I was like," I growled, stepping into her more. Our bodies aligned, her heat pressing into mine, the soft scent of her shampoo filling my nose. She looked like she wanted to retreat, but she stood firmly, her jaw tight, her blue eyes flashing up to mine in defiance. "You have no idea how dirty I can get. What I've had to do in my life before your grandparents were even a thought. So do not challenge my character, *Nina*." She flinched at her real name. "You won't like the outcome."

"You think I'm afraid of you, *Killian*?" Her tongue hissing my name in ire did the opposite of what she was trying for. My blood rushed below my belt, my chest heaving. "Being alive so long, you'd think you'd be better at it by now." She motioned around the room. "Where is your castle now, *Majesty*?"

The rage and exhaustion circling me daily snapped my willpower like a twig. My hands gripped the back of her scalp roughly as I yanked slightly on her strands, pointing her face to me as I towered over her, pressing her into me. Her eyes blazed and her nose flared, her jaw clamping together. She was ready to fight.

It was at that moment I realized what I had done, the line I had crossed… with a person who had experienced so much trauma and assault from men. Her husband, the whorehouse, Věrhăza. She had been raped by those to whom her husband

86

owed money, then forced into prostitution to pay off that vile piece of shit's debt.

I was no different.

Jerking back like she had electrocuted me, I turned away from her, running my hand, which still echoed with her heat, through my own. My body radiated fury, my chest heaving with disgust.

"Simon, why don't you go down and visit your Aunt Kitty," Rosie spoke sweetly to the boy. "I think it would really help for her to hear your voice."

"Is she doing better?" Simon jumped up from the chair. "Is she awake?"

"She's the same, but I know your visit would help a lot." Rosie nodded in encouragement, watching the boy run from the room to go see her.

Kitty's condition seemed to only be declining. The prison destroyed her will to live. To be part of this world.

I couldn't help feeling the weight of it on my shoulders, more guilt weighing me down. Markos may have upped the ante on torture, but it was still my prison. Something I had built. The cruelty, beatings, and the Games—all existed in Halálház. I didn't oversee it once it was up and running, but that didn't lessen my accountability.

It wasn't until I was a victim of my own creation did I truly understand the depravity of what I let happen and felt the weight of my ego.

I heard the door shut behind Simon. The buffer between the tension was gone, letting it thread through the room like webs. Exhaling, I placed my palms on the table, my back to her. I stared blankly at the map of Leopold and HDF lying on top.

"Killian," Rosie spoke after a while, my name like a melody on her lips.

"I'm sorry." I croaked, the words struggling to get out of my chest.

"What?"

"I said I'm sorry." I stood upright, turning around, though I still wouldn't look at her. "I shouldn't have touched you like that. I apologize."

"Apologize?" She folded her arms with a smirk. "Wow, I don't think I've ever heard you use that term before."

I cleared my throat, peering back at the map, the *entire* reason I summoned her to me. Somewhere in the back of my head, I heard myself laugh at that. "Now to why I called you here."

"No." She shook her head, her arms dropping away.

"No?" I shot back.

"I know why you called me here." She walked up to me, her blue eyes tearing through my soul, kicking through every barrier. "Do you think you hurt me? That I'm afraid of you?"

My shoulders went back. "I shouldn't have grabbed you like that."

"Why?" She tilted her head.

"Because… well… because of…" I stumbled and tripped over my words.

"Because I've been raped, or because I'm a prostitute?"

"*Was*." The word popped out of my mouth before I thought. What Rosie had done to survive was shamed by many, especially humans. Though I respected her drive to live and didn't look upon it with disgust. The opposite, actually. I respected her. She was scrappy and tough, and she would do whatever it took to survive. Something I understood.

Though the idea of her being with other men caused rage to flood through my muscles.

"You're not a prostitute… I mean, that's not all you are.

88

And that isn't why." I clamped my mouth shut, wondering why I had just said that.

It was clear she didn't like me, nor I her. I had no idea why we were talking about this.

"Because I've been assaulted?" She replied with no emotion.

I dipped my head.

"How fragile do you think I am?"

"I'm sorry?"

"You think you're the only one who has gone through a lot in their life? I was ashamed for a long time, a shell… Some days, I wished to die. But that was long ago. I realized I had to pick myself up or I'd drown under it, giving them all the control. Those monsters in Vĕrhăza aren't worth my tears, nor is my ex-husband. I am proud of who I am and where I'm at now. So I appreciate your self-absorbed struggle with yourself over how *you* think I should be handled."

She marched up to me until I was pressed back into the table. The woman was like a lion.

"*I am* the one who gets to decide that. *Me*. And if I don't like something, you better believe you will know it." She tapped her finger on my chest. "And tugging my hair?" A derisive smile twisted her lips. "That's beginners' foreplay. You'd have to do a lot more than that to even set the minimum bar for me. And you are far too uptight for that, *Majesty*."

Blood roared in my ears, clamping around my cock. The compulsion to grab her and throw her on the table, ripping off her clothes and kissing that mouth until she moaned for more, consumed me. I'd bend her over, thrusting deep into her until she was hoarse from screaming my name as I fucked her over the maps on the table, showing her what the man beneath the title could do.

Desire whipped me like a lash, making me dizzy. Rage

89

and confusion roared through me, needing an outlet. But decades of training myself, restraining my old impulses to take what I wanted when I wanted, kicked in, locking me up.

A nerve in my jaw twitched, my lungs ignoring the need to take in more oxygen than normal, keeping them steady.

Controlled. Unaffected.

All a lie.

Rosie scoffed, stepping back from me as if I proved her right. I was too noble to ever show emotion or let go. To her, I was a run-of-the-mill, entitled asshole she had met countless times before, with a larger ego and grander words than what I delivered.

She had no idea that barely under the surface, I was illicit, wicked, and depraved. I had robbed, killed, betrayed, and lied to get to where I was now.

"Skipping all the bullshite so we don't have to be in each other's company longer than necessary." She licked her lips, crossing her arms, preparing for a fight. "I will be going undercover into HDF. It's already planned."

"No," I barked, my mood snapping quickly to anger.

"I talked it through with Mykel. Caden will walk me through every step."

"You think I give a shit what Mykel says?" My voice rose. "He is not in charge here. I am! And I say no."

"Well, I say no to your no."

"What?" I wagged my head. "That's not a thing."

"Yes, it is. See, I just did it. I'm ignoring your no. And still going."

"No, you are not. I am the leader here, and I say no."

"Well, you're not the leader of me, so I say yes."

"Oh my gods!" Frustration caused me to rake my fingers through my hair, a strangled cry vibrating from my throat. "You are the most irksome woman I've ever met."

"Thank you."

My boots pushed past her, pacing a small area.

"It is far too dangerous. I need someone who can react to anything at any time."

"You mean like an actress? My life has been one long improv."

"I've seen you act." I scoffed.

Her eyes lowered, her jaw locking down, my insult reddening her cheeks. Then something shifted in her, a coy smile hinting at her lips.

"You saw Nina act. Young, innocent, and unaware of the world… Nina." She shifted closer to me, her nearness forcing my lungs to hitch as her body pressed into mine. For some reason I didn't move away. "No life experience." She tilted her head up to me, her blue eyes unflinching as her fingers trailed down my chest. "So naive to men… to *sex*." She licked her lips, drawing my attention to them. That single word went straight to my dick, which rose with a heavy pulse like she had enchanted it. "She had no clue." Rosie's voice went low and husky, grazing my ear. My chest was no longer in control as it heaved in shallow pulls. Her hand slipped down, running over the erection in my pants, causing me to suck in. Damn, I was hard. My body vibrated with the need to fuck.

It had been a while, my country and my title coming first over everything else. Brexley had been the first in a long time I had been attracted to. That's not to say women hadn't been through my bed, but they weren't anything more than sex.

I was so tense that Rosie had me so taut with one touch, and I felt drops of pre-cum dampen my trousers.

Anyone could get this response from touching me, right? It wasn't her—not a *human*.

Her knuckles rubbed over my pants again, turning my

91

dick to steel. My hips curved into her hand, my need for her to touch me more shaking my muscles.

A smirk fluttered her mouth as she leaned in, her mouth close to mine. "How simple it is to fool and distract a man." She dropped her hands, stepping away, her brow tipping up. "How's that for acting, *my liege*?" she taunted.

A mix of anger, embarrassment, and even more arousal battled inside me as I realized what she had been doing. Heat scorched my face at how easily she had me in the palm of her hand. And how badly I still wanted her and hated myself more for that.

"You think that's all it would take? Batting your lashes at some soldier? This is a *serious* mission." I cleared my throat, moving away from her again, trying to gather myself and my ego off the ground. I hated being played with. Normally someone would lose a hand or head for that, but this woman seemed to only rile me up more. "You are not going. And that is final."

"*I am* going, and that is *my* final. I make my own choices. Not you." Indignation brightened her eyes. "I won't have another man telling me what I can and cannot do. I understand the risks. I will not sit back any longer. This is my war, my fight, too."

"What if you're caught? You can't fight." I threw my arms out.

"I know how to shoot a gun. Don't treat me like I'm some helpless girl."

"It's not because you're a girl. I wouldn't second guess sending in someone like Brexley or Hanna. They have been trained. They know what to do if things go wrong."

"Hanna has been helping me. Training me in moves and how to act like a soldier." Rosie put her hands on her hips. "And guess what? Brexley is gone and Hanna can't go in.

Neither can most of you. I'm human, and none of them there know my face. And Wesley is going with me. It's not like I'm going in alone."

"Wesley?" My frame jolted to a stop, unable to fight the instantaneous reaction exploding in my chest, my head already shaking back and forth. "Fuck, no."

"Why not? He's a good fighter. He would blend in with the other soldiers." Her shoulder lifted, a tiny smile on her lips. "As much as he can."

I noticed him flirting with her before, hanging around the healing room when she was working like a pathetic puppy. His intentions were obvious.

Did she like him back? Whatever came over me roared with resentment, tinting my vision green.

"No way in hell he is going in there with you." My tone crawled from the depths of my gut, my control breaking apart.

"Why?"

"Because I don't trust him to protect you." I had seen him fight. He was well trained, but it didn't fucking matter. I couldn't sit here knowing they were on this mission together, their bond intensifying from the situation they'd be in. What if something went wrong? I shuddered to think what could happen to her if he wasn't on the top of his game.

And I wouldn't be able to do anything.

"That's not up to you. I do trust him," she spat. "The mission is tonight. We can't change it now, no matter how much you stomp your feet like a child. I'm going, and so is Wesley."

"Wesley is not going."

"Then who is?"

"Me."

93

"I can't believe this," I muttered, my eyes shutting as I pressed against a stone wall. The foggy night wormed through my clothes, chilling my skin. I gave myself a moment to revel in my own gullible stupidity. I was played. And what made it worse, I might not have stopped it even if I had realized it.

Nina was innocent and beautiful to watch on stage, but Rosie was a master of her craft, twisting you up and spitting you out in whatever way she wanted… and you'd only ask for more.

How did I go from putting my foot down to her going to not only flipping on her going but confirming myself as her partner? Because the sweet ingenue conned me. She may call it acting, but it was pure unadulterated manipulation.

"You didn't have to come," Rosie murmured. "If I recall, *everyone* was against you coming, and Wesley would have been just fine protecting me."

"Damn right I would have been," Wesley responded in our ears, his suggestive tone rebounding through the earpieces Scorpion got us from his connection. "Guess I'll have to show you another way. How about a date with me?"

I heard Hanna snort.

"Playin' with fire there, Wes," Birdie muttered, clicking her tongue.

"Shut up, everyone." Ire gnawed at the back of my neck, cutting Rosie off from answering. Their flirtation grated on my nerves. "This is only for communication about the mission, not trying to get laid." The proper noble manner I had imposed on myself for so long was crumbling, reverting me back to my old pirate days. Vulgar and rude.

Rosie was right. *No one* wanted me on this mission. My face was too recognizable as the leader of the fae. However, being noble and very powerful also came with perks. My powers of glamour were far superior, and I was more than capable of fooling the human eye.

That was the excuse I used, anyway. Righteously and firmly. My decision was laid down as law, saying Wesley was better to stay on lookout, along with Hanna, Caden, and Birdie. Hanna and Caden had knowledge about the schedule and pattern the guards would have.

While across the river, Scorpion, Ash, Warwick, and Zander were checking out the old ruins of Halálház. Two of them knew firsthand what the setup had been like inside. It was a recon mission only, needing to get more information about what Sonya was up to over there.

Should I be back at base, overseeing both missions? Yes. There was no doubt that, as a leader, I should be there. Yet here I was, and I couldn't seem to regret my choice. The thought of not being with Rosie to protect her made me more unsettled than the idea of turning away from my rightful duty.

"Through the brush and ivy, you will see a hidden gate." Caden's voice came into the earpiece. "It's by the graveyard. Brexley and I used it all the time to get in and out unseen."

Rosie and I slipped across the street, staying in the shadows, heading for the spot he described.

"More to the left," Caden stated. I had a tiny camera on my chest, letting him see where we were going and what we were doing. While the others were dotted around HDF with sniper rifles, Caden was set up with a small monitor to guide us. The equipment was top-notch, but he still needed to be within a hundred-yard radius of us so things wouldn't break up. "Let's hope they didn't find it and lock it up."

"That would be bad," I grunted. This was our only way in; if it was locked, mission over.

Rosie pushed through some overgrown foliage, finding the entry, her teeth nipping at her lip as she tugged on the gate.

With her second attempt, the gate squeaked, opening stiffly, the hinges almost rusted shut, leaving very little room for me to get through.

Hiding my anxiety, I sucked in, slipping from the outside to the inside of HDF. I never imagined I would be sneaking inside the walls of Leopold as a spy and not walking through the gates as a king.

"Pass the graveyard and head south," Caden said, though the glowing lights of the old parliament building towered far above the quiet streets and timeworn flats, steering us toward it like a beacon. "The entrance to the barracks, where you will find extra uniforms, is on the northeast entrance."

Slowly, we wormed our way through the streets. It was late, but it felt eerily off. Not a single flat had even a light on. Anxiety crawled up the back of my neck, and far away, a singular male voice boomed through the quiet night.

Rosie turned to me, her brows furrowing. Her human ears could not pick up on what I could hear.

"Sztrájk!" Strike! "Megöl!" Kill!

Grunts and a war cry echoed through the air in unison, scraping an eerie sensation down my bones.

"What is that?" Caden asked.

"We're about to find out," I muttered, motioning for Rosie to stay behind me. Coming to the end of a street where it widened into the huge plaza of HDF, we stayed tucked in the shadows.

My chest twisted with dread as I took in the scene before me. A gasp came from Rosie, her mouth dropping.

"Are you seeing what we are seeing?" I whispered, hoping the earpiece could pick it up.

At least a thousand soldiers were lined up in hundreds of rows, performing drills screamed out by an instructor on a higher platform. Not one was out of sync or was messing up. Over and over, their rifles with spears stabbed at an invisible enemy, practicing killing with robotic precision.

What was strange was none of them wore HDF uniforms. They were all in black.

"Strike! Kill!" the man upon the platform ordered in accented Russian.

"Caden…" I swallowed. "I think we have a serious fuckin' problem."

Chapter 9
Scorpion

This place creeped me the fuck out.

The ruins of Halálház lay over the terrain like tombs, left abandoned in the exact position as the day it was attacked by Sarkis's army. Carnage on the surface, while worms and rats ate away at the intestines far below.

I was one of the people who snuck close enough to lay the bombs that night. Little did I know, underneath my feet was someone who would change my life. My entire world would recenter itself because she lived.

Even though I didn't miss the tie with the asshole next to me, on the receiving end of their endless sex drive, without it meant Brexley was absent. Not just physically, but from my soul, leaving a hole I never realized was there until she filled it. My friends had become my family, but I never truly let them in, keeping everyone at arm's length because it was easier. In my life, I knew nothing but bereavement, and in our world, there would only be more. Getting attached meant feeling continual loss.

With Brexley, there was no choice. She was rooted in my blood. Was part of me. Family. Because she wedged herself in, she must have left a crack open for others to sneak in. More specifically, one other slipped through, filling my thoughts and pounding my chest with worry.

It irritated the shit out of me. That wasn't me. I didn't think about women unless I was enjoying one. Keeping work and sex separate. I didn't spend every moment fretting over their well-being or fantasizing about being inside them or having endless dreams and thoughts about them.

Never.

I would never admit my skin itched, knowing a certain blonde was over at HDF on a mission, and I couldn't protect her if something happened. Not that she couldn't take care of herself. It felt oddly wrong when Killian separated us. That I felt off if I wasn't near her.

Stupid. It's not like I cared about her more than just a buddy. Like Birdie. Though I hadn't jerked off to Birdie like I did that fucking human hybrid.

Snarling, I peered through the binoculars, my gaze going over every inch of the old prison.

"Looks abandoned." I shrugged, handing the pair to Warwick next to me.

"It's not abandoned, lizard." The brownie on Warwick's shoulder folded his arms.

"Scorpion." I gritted through my teeth. "And why the fuck are you here again?"

"Because, *spider*, none of you can make it without me." *Chirp!*

"...aannddd Bitzy," he added quickly.

Chirp! Chirp! Fingers went up in the air.

"I didn't forget you. You just weren't listening. You'd think with those ears you would have heard me properly."

Chirpchirpchirpchirpchirp!

"Both of you shut up," Warwick growled at the two on

99

his shoulder. "Or I'll be chucking you both into the river below."

"They seem to forget, Bitz, they can't survive without us." Opie sighed, tugging at his black beanie, which looked like a sock with a knot at the top. Bitzy was on his back, both of them wearing skintight black leotards, with a black sock tied around their face, black bird feathers glued at the corner like eyelashes. "Silly peons…"

Chirp! Bitzy flung up her middle finger in agreement.

"They know this place better than anyone. And can open locks," Warwick grumbled. "Believe me, otherwise I'd be eating a brownie with imp sauce right now."

Chirp!

"Yes, technically, he would be licking you, but not in that way."

Chirp!

"I know he keeps threatening us with a good time. But all talk and no action."

Warwick growled under his breath.

"Where are they being held?" I asked Opie, making me reconsider all my life choices because I was now asking sub-fae for advice.

Damn you, Brexley.

"They are being kept in the back section of the prison. It was the least damaged." Opie pointed in the direction. "The sewer tunnels lead you right there."

"Fuck, no," I huffed.

"The only way in is a private door on the side," Zander spoke up, motioning at the southwest side. "It was the door you and Brexley escaped out of that night I helped you."

"Oh, the night I got to punch you in the face?" Warwick snorted. "Yeah… Good times, pony-boy. Like to do that again."

100

"Not sure your sister would approve." Zander shot back, a hint of a smile on his face as he looked through the binoculars.

Warwick growled under his breath, only making Zander smile more. I could tell Zander was enjoying the hell out of poking at Warwick. I didn't know them well, but it seemed Eliza and Zander were in that first stage of love where they couldn't stop touching each other. Drove Warwick insane, which made me happy. The man was already hanging by a thread being without Brexley. It would take very little to tip him over.

A rumble from the ground froze me in place, the sound of several heavy vehicles laboring up the incline to the ruins. Blinding light from headlights had us duck down farther behind chunks of cement blocks.

"Szent szar," Ash muttered as three enormous tanks and two armored trucks rolled up, stopping at the end of the road.

The four of us didn't breathe. The door Zander had just been pointing at opened, and a guard strode out, heading to the last armored car. All of us reacted when his face came into view, opening the car door to a beautiful blonde in the back seat.

A snarl rose into my throat at seeing him, my body locking down in response.

"Majesty." The man bowed to Sonya.

"Captain Boyd." She nodded at him. "Are they ready?"

"Kapd be a szőrös faszom!" Suck my hairy dick. Warwick sneered to himself, his head shaking, probably thinking the same thing I was.

I wished I had killed him when I had the chance.

"Yes. Everything is set, *my queen*."

I heard Ash inhale sharply through his nose. "That fucking bitch," he snarled protectively. Probably thinking

101

about Lukas. That guy really did have a shit family. Sonya wasn't only setting herself up to be leader of the fae; she was going to be queen. And I doubt that would stop at the Hungarian borders.

Of course Boyd was with Sonya. Probably had been the entire time. I always wondered why he had been working for Istvan. Now I realized he was a spy all along—for the future Seelie queen.

"Good." She crossed her legs, not leaving the car. "I want a big show. I want everyone to see us crossing the bridge and heading for HDF. There can be no doubt left this city is mine now. One ruler for all. We will together squash Killian's pathetic excuse of an uprising. The humans will know their place once again. Servants to us."

Boyd grinned. "Exactly, my lady. Can I say how happy I am that you are finally in charge? Putting fae back where they rightfully belong?"

"Yes." She preened. "Now don't let me down, Boyd. Andor is expecting us soon, so let us not dally."

General Andor? Wasn't that Istvan's second in command? What did she mean he was expecting them? Weren't they on opposite sides? What the fuck was going on?

"Yes, my queen." He bowed again, closing her car door and motioning back to another guard at the prison entrance who propped the door open, shouting a command.

The rhythmic boom of hundreds of boots hitting the metal stairs in sync tapped at the back of my neck, my heart beating with dread. Acid coiled in my stomach as I absorbed everything she said, fear spiking through my nerves.

This was supposed to be a simple scouting mission. Check out what the Brownie had told us about Halálház and the labs. Yet in one moment, everything took a sharp turn, tilting everything on its axis.

Soldiers started coming out of the door loaded with guns. Their movements were robotic, and they were dressed in black leather with her insignia like we saw the other night.

The outfits reminded me of the days of the Seelie Queen Aneira.

Sonya's army lined up and marched down the road as more and more flooded out, joining them. They kept coming, hundreds and hundreds of them.

Her car pulled away with the tanks, leading the marching troop right to where Killian and Rosie happened to be breaking into HDF at this moment.

"Eliza... Simon." Zander shuffled back. "We have to get back to base. Warn them and get everyone out."

Fear was wild in Ash's eyes, his head nodding in agreement. Warwick moved with them.

Fear twisted my body another way, overriding everything else.

Our team at HDF had no idea they were coming. They were focused on the enemy in front of them, not coming behind.

"Scorp! Where are you going?" Ash yelled at me when I moved the opposite way.

"HDF! I have to warn them!"

"They know. Caden does." Warwick replied, his jaw setting. The energy coming off Caden lately was the same as Warwick's. They never talked about it, the tension between them only getting worse, but we all knew something happened in Istvan's lab... that they carried the same magic.

Warwick's statement didn't stop me. I started running, only one thought coursing through my mind.

Hanna.

Chapter 10
Caden

"Caden… I think we have a serious fuckin' problem."

The camera was dark and grainy, making me doubt the images coming back from Killian. Heat clawed down my spine, locking down the influx of anger and terror underneath. I despised my father, what he had turned into, what he had done, especially to my mother and me, but this was like a knife to my gut, hacksawing at everything I knew and understood. My home, my very foundation, which was already crumbling under my feet, was now the headquarters for our enemy.

I trained my whole life and was programmed to be a proud HDF soldier, believing I was on the right side. A patriot who would one day lead as my father had. Now as I looked through the square, I found nothing recognizable.

"What? What's going on?" Birdie's voice came into my ear. My eyes automatically went to where I knew she was stationed along the wall. Only I was able to see what Killian and Rosie could; the rest were only connected through our earpieces—equipment so deep in the black market, my father couldn't even get it.

"Can you get closer?" My heart thumped stronger in my chest, still hoping the black uniforms with an embedded insignia were a trick of my eye, that the hazy night was affecting the camera.

The camera danced as Killian and Rosie snuck closer, hiding behind the Kossuth Memorial—an old monument dedicated to a long-ago Regent-President Lajos Kossuth. It was their last line of defense before it opened up on the enormous square filled with training soldiers. Their backs were to us, but I could see they were women and men, mainly young, but some appeared rail-thin and fragile as they held their rifles, stabbing them in the air. Their movements were rigid. I knew the signs. They were all on the pills.

"Strike! Kill!" the instructor on stage yelled out. The camera was close enough to see him this time, his voice coming in clearer, taking me back to ballrooms, champagne, and decadence. To the sick little fuck who I wanted to punch in the face every time he was near.

"Holy shit. It can't be…" Killian's tone made my stomach drop, catching the same thing I did.

No. My brain wanted to reject it, not letting me connect the two opposing sides. Two worlds that didn't belong.

The son of Prime Minister Lazar.

"Sergiu." I breathed out, my eyes locked on the weasel of a man onstage instructing the troops, colliding with the entitled, lazy son of a bitch I grew up knowing. The fucked-up asshole Brexley was supposed to marry.

"Sergiu?" Hanna exclaimed into our ears. She had also known him, not like Brexley and me, but Hanna knew him enough to understand his character. "What the hell is he doing here?"

My question exactly. Why was he dressed in the insignia of the fae? Leading them like he was a captain?

105

Images flickered in my mind—my father holding Sonya, Alexandru, and Sergiu at gunpoint, turning against his allies, taking them prisoner before Věrhăza was attacked by Povstat. In our world, that kind of insult would cause war against nations.

My throat tightened, and my skin flushed warm, clashing against the freezing air, my mind spinning with thoughts.

"What the fuck is that little twat Sergiu doing here? Wearing Sonya's mark?" Killian's smooth voice went low, edging on guttural, feeling the deeper threat on the hold of his kingdom.

Not one person here didn't remember him watching us fight for our lives in the pit, snickering, until he was the one my father turned against.

Alexandru Lazar was smart, shrewd, and knew how to play the game to survive. Romania's allies were few, and losing Hungary...

Sergei was too arrogant and conceited to see anything but his own ego.

"Daddy put him there." I gritted through my teeth. I never enjoyed the backstabbing and maneuvering the leaders did, but I knew their plays well. I understood more than anybody what Alexandru was doing—saving his own skin. Tossing away his country, his people, hoping he would be inside the protected elite circle as the human hold came tumbling down. With my father running off, leaving the field open, Lazar saw Sonya was gaining control, and he had no chance against her. He tossed all his morals away to survive as she took power.

Getting Sergiu in her fold, working for her, was probably one of the many ways Lazar was solidifying his place. His safety within her reign. I would have no doubt many of these people building her army were from the streets of Romania.

Sergiu screamed at them in repetition, thriving off his own anger, his ego reveling in the dominance and power he wielded. He was standing on a house of cards, but the idiot was far too self-absorbed to see it. The little prince was playing dress-up for a war he wasn't prepared to fight.

"Fuck," Wesley hissed. "Romania is with her? This is so much worse than we thought."

It was, and I still couldn't understand how this happened. Where was Andor? He was my father's right-hand man. Wasn't he in charge? How could my father just have abandoned HDF? Left it to this?

"Get out," Hanna spoke. "This is far too dangerous."

"No." Rosie's British accent flared in my ear. "We are too close. We're here. We're never going to get this chance again. There might be more inside that lockbox than just the whereabouts of the lab."

More rope snagged around my lungs, knowing my father was in Ukraine, building his own empire. Pushing Ivanenko out, taking over his throne, power, and well-trained military. It was why my father wanted me to marry Olena at one time. To be the one to take Ivanenko's position while father stayed in Hungary. Our power expanding wider and wider.

As an alternative, if I couldn't step up, he was fucking my fiancé behind my back, impregnating her to make sure no matter what, we were "in bed" with them.

The rage and hate I felt for my father roared through me, my lungs heaving and my vision blurring. To my father, I was never enough for him. Never the son he wanted. Never strong or disciplined enough. So, he tried to mold me into a legend, but that I couldn't even do right.

He left me to die, even hoped I would, so I would no longer be a concern. A threat to his new son and wife.

I wanted to destroy my father.

I wanted his death.

The sensation was so overpowering, my stomach rolled with nausea. It vibrated through my muscles, sang in my veins, embedding into my DNA.

Into my *fae* DNA…

I rankled with fury. I could feel that legendary asshole everywhere. His magic changing me. Tying us together.

What scared me the most? I liked the power. The magic curling around my spine, making me stronger than I could ever dream. And that pissed me off. I didn't know what was happening to me. My morals still fought against what felt natural. I was becoming one of them. The enemy. The soulless. Though, I seemed to feel everything more. My senses and emotions were heightened to the point I couldn't breathe.

"There are stairs to your right, which lead you down into the training rooms." I shook myself from my dark thoughts, zeroing in on the mission.

I agreed with Rosie—keep going. There was nothing I wanted more than to take my father down.

I heard Killian take a deep breath. As leader, he shouldn't even be on this assignment, but as stupid as it was, I kind of respected him for it. He wasn't sitting on the sidelines like my father did. I had always idolized Brexley's dad growing up. Benet was the first to ride into a battle. He stood with his men, and he died with his men. He wasn't behind a desk, ordering others to die in his name without also risking his life.

"I decide if we go forward or not," Killian bade, his camera turning to Rosie.

"We're too close," Rosie protested, shooting him a look.

"I would be ending this mission if my men were here and not me. I would not put them in harm's way for something they are not prepared for, getting them killed."

Through the camera I watched Rosie fold her arms, her jaw rolling, her gaze not leaving Killian's

"I swear to the gods, Red." Killian muttered, the camera shaking with his head. "We go on, you listen to *everything* I say, you got it?"

She nodded her head.

He sighed again.

"We go on three. Do not stop for anything," he instructed. Tension rose in my throat as Killian peered out. The troops were still doing their drills, the shadows of the foggy night providing some cover to the vast square. "Okay, one, two, three…" Killian shot out from behind the statue, moving so quietly, his feet like a cat's, darting like a bullet to the stairs. Rosie worked hard to keep up, her breathing laboring in my ears.

"Go down and turn immediately to the left once you're through the doors." The camera flickered as Killian and Rosie headed underground. I knew every inch. The smell of sweat and damp musk from the showers. The squeak of the lockers, the piles of training clothes heaped in the laundry baskets. The gym and training area was more of a home to me than the flat I lived in far above. It was where I felt the happiest. Not under my father's eyes, where I always had to prove myself more than anyone else. I still felt free in the world down here.

The camera flickered again when Rosie and Killian entered, the light blinding from the darkness outside. They turned left toward the locker room. The normal noise of booming voices, showers, and lockers slamming was gone.

The room was eerily silent. Not one person was there.

This was the easiest access point to get up to the higher levels without notice, as the doors above ground were always guarded. Or at least they were when my father was in charge.

"Guess you won't be needing those HDF uniforms to change into now," Wesley replied dryly into our earpiece.

"This—" The microphone connection went out. "Was bad even before—" Static. "Decided to change sides," Killian said.

The monitor wavered and crackled.

"Come on." I hit my hand against it, trepidation oozing into my stomach. The camera cleared up. "Okay… there are stairs down the hall. They lead you up to the ground floor. From there you will have to go up the back stairs to my father's office. There is a hidden key to his office behind the painting in a lockbox." I had told Killian and Rosie the numbers for both the key box and his safe box before we left, just in case.

They were almost to the stairs when a voice called out behind Killian. "Hey!"

My heart stopped in my chest, knowing that voice almost better than my own for how many times it yelled at me.

Bakos.

The man I thought of more as a father than my own. He was tough but fair, and I respected him so much.

"Where are you two going? All *trainees* should be in the quad." His tone dipped how it always did when he was disappointed.

"Caden?" Killian hissed at me.

"It's Bakos. My HDF instructor." I replied. "Turn around."

Slowly, Killian and Rosie twisted to him, showing the man now before them.

110

His hair graying slightly at his temples, Bakos still wore the HDF uniform.

"I asked where you were going?"

Killian didn't move or speak.

"Eltévedtünk." We are lost. Rosie's voice was thick with Hungarian. Not a breath of her English accent could be heard.

Bakos tilted his head, his gaze sliding to Killian. "You look familiar."

I could hear my pulse in my ears. Though Killian could glamour, some humans could see through it. Bakos was so void of bullshit, I could imagine him cutting through Killian's too.

"Identify yourself," Bakos ordered, stepping closer.

Killian still didn't respond, acting like a stooge on the pills, void of any personality or thought.

Every step Bakos took, my throat tightened.

The camera glitched for a second, forcing me to suck in.

"I gave you an order." Bakos was almost in his face.

"Trainee Cece and Kope, sir," Rosie said with no emotion.

Bakos's eyes drifted from her to Killian. I took in the subtleness of his gaze, the caution and knowledge something was wrong, the huff in the back of his throat like he could see through them.

"He knows," I hissed into their ears, panic curling around me as the screen went fuzzy for a longer time. "Did you hear me? He knows."

Bakos had drilled so many things into us besides the skill of fighting. Instinct. Intuition. He also pulled Brexley and me to the side because of our positions and who we were to my father. He gave us a code. If we were ever compromised and could not outright say it because lives were on the line, we uttered a phrase that meant we needed help.

"Tell him, *rám férne egy cigi.*" *I could use a cigarette.* I

111

wiped at the trickle of sweat sliding down my face. It was equivalent to I need help. Neither Brexley nor I smoked. It was a red herring. "Helikon."

Killian coughed as if he wanted to tell me I was fucking nuts. I probably was, but an instinct I couldn't even explain washed over me. "Say it."

"Fuck," Killian muttered under his breath, clearing his throat, speaking to Bakos. *"Rám férne egy cigi."*

Bakos jolted, his eyes widening. "What?"

"Helikon." Killian uttered the name of the particular brand that stopped being made after the fae war, our country going back into the Dark Ages.

Bakos stared at Killian, trying to keep his expression blank, his body rigid.

Please, Bakos, hear me... know it's from me.

"Hey?" Another deep voice boomed from behind all of them. "What the hell do you think you're doing?" A man stomped up, and instantly I felt my world teetered again. Andar's assistant, Tibor, who was a two-faced condescending asshole, marched up to them, now dressed in all black with the fae queen insignia.

"You two should be in the square preparing for tonight." He pointed at Killian and Rosie, then turned to Bakos. "And you were fucking fired. Andor no longer needs or wants your assistance here."

"I work for Markos, not Andor."

"Well, Markos is no longer in charge." A slimy grin slid over his mouth. He would have made an excellent politician. "And finally, I get to tell the great, perfect, heroic Bakos to get the fuck out of here."

Bakos's attention shot back to Killian, his gaze going right to the camera on his chest as if he could see it, my old teacher looking straight at me.

"The only way you get me out of here is if you force me." Bakos twisted around, walking backward, turning Tibor's back to Killian. "Come on, Tibor, you know you've dreamed of doing this."

Bakos was short, but he could put Tibor on the ground in less than five seconds. Of course, Tibor was too arrogant and stupid to acknowledge it.

"You're right." Tibor rubbed his hands together. "Been looking forward to this for a long, long time."

"There was a reason you failed my class." Bakos bounded back farther. "Your ego outweighs your lack of talent and utter stupidity."

"Te geci!" Motherfucker! Tibor headed straight for him. Bakos easily leaped out of his way, socking him in the face with a soft hit, his gaze shooting over Tibor's shoulder. It was minuscule, but I saw his chin flick, his eyes going to the stairs, then back to Killian with a nod.

Telling them to go.

He was creating a distraction.

He knew I was involved somehow. Knew that S.O.S code was from me. He just handed me all of his trust, and he had no clue what for, but he still did it. For me.

"Go!" I yelled into their ears. "Go!"

Killian and Rosie didn't hesitate, darting for the stairs up to the main level, Tibor too distracted by Bakos's fists to even notice them.

The earpieces crackled and hissed, the screen going fuzzy the higher they ascended.

"Shit, what's going on?" Birdie's voice cut in and out, the equipment going on the fritz, but that was no longer my concern.

A sensation crashed down on me, magic stabbing at the back of my head, filling me with images, prickling everything

113

in my body. The screen blinked out completely, as if the electricity from my body had fried the device.

Turning my head to the river behind me, the fog tangled up in the bridge joining the two sides. The sensations grew stronger, creeping over my shoulders and shivering through my muscles. I could feel the pounding of their feet, hear the hum of the tanks.

"Oh, gods," I uttered, my breath stumbling.

"What?" Hanna crackled and popped, her voice barely there.

"Everyone get here to me. Now!" I yelled, tugging out the useless earpiece.

I knew what was coming. What was heading straight for us.

Because Farkas just showed me.

Chapter 11
Killian

The plush carpet absorbed our footsteps. My hand was on Rosie's lower back, pushing her to move faster.

"What the hell just happened?" Rosie whispered when we cleared the bottom level, bringing us to a hallway of painted arched ceilings and stained-glass windows facing the Danube on the main floor. "Why'd he help us escape?"

"Wasn't about to stop and ask." I had no idea what had just happened, why an HDF captain helped us, or what that phrase meant, though it clearly meant something vital. Something important enough to trust it over two intruders.

"Okay, Caden, now where?" I muttered into the earpiece, my gaze sweeping every corner of the dimly lit passage, my body alert to any threat.

Nothing.

"Caden?" I repeated his name. The silence pulled my attention to Rosie. Her blue eyes widened with alarm. "Caden, are you there?" Silence. "Birdie?"

"Wes?" Rosie tried herself.

Dread weaved through my ribs when none responded.

"I don't know if you can still see where we are, but we can't hear you."

Not even a crackle of static. The equipment was dead.

"Fuck." I hissed under my breath.

"What now?" Rosie swallowed, her head dancing around, keeping watch.

"We find our own way." At this point, we were in too far to abandon the mission. Sonya's threat level went from a three to ten in a blink, but that didn't take away from Istvan's. I'd known his character far too long to think he gave up. He would return to take back what he thought was rightfully his.

"Come on." I motioned for Rosie to follow, finding another set of stairs down the hall, taking us up to the second floor. With my glamour and our dark clothes, it might fool someone from afar, thinking we were part of them, but random soldiers running around up here would be suspicious.

My pulse tapped rapidly against my throat, my arm out, protecting Rosie as we came into a hallway. Peeking out, I double-checked for movement. The corridors were too quiet for such a huge, bustling place. This was an army base, home, and government building all in one. There should be endless activity and people moving about.

HDF was like a graveyard.

Stepping out into the passage, I held the air in my lungs, trying to listen for any sounds. The back of my neck prickled. My senses were far superior to humans, and I could easily hear and feel them before they could me. But with Rosie behind me, I took extra precautions.

Right on my heels, Rosie trailed after me. Caden had given us a rundown of the HQ. Drawn up a sketch of the layout. We knew the lock combo and how to get in just in case something happened, but being in the space was far different.

Following my instincts, we snuck down another passage, my eyes landing on a painting Caden had described.

116

I snorted, my head shaking as I took in the painted image of Istvan, the first *king* of Hungary, also known as the "King Saint Istvan." General Istvan Makos clearly idolized him and also wanted the title of "King" and to be thought of as a saint. Saving everyone from themselves… twisting everything he did in his mind like it was a calling or destiny. He was the chosen one.

All bullshit.

"Narcissistic much, Markos?" I muttered under my breath, shifting the painting to find a keypad.

"Guess you two do have something in common, luv." Rosie's lilt caressed my ear, making my fingers almost slip up, her voice curling around my body. My shoulders tightened, and I pretended the way she said love didn't make me hard.

The keypad unlocked, relief flooding my lungs as I plucked the key from the hiding spot.

One step closer.

A loud boom of doors shutting in another part of the building echoed through the empty hallways, voices resonating in low murmurs, rushing blood through my veins, shoving the key into the lock.

Footsteps thumped like drums, moving closer to us.

"Hurry." Rosie's head whipped around, her feet prancing.

The door clicked open, and I pushed her in first, my hearing picking up two sets of legs treading toward us. My heart slammed in my chest, my hand fumbling as I shoved the key back into the hiding spot, barely able to straighten the painting before their footfalls hinted around the corner. Slipping inside, the door shut with a soft click, locking it behind me, figuring whomever it was would keep going.

The voices stopped in front of the door. Panic surged,

117

my gaze flying around the room, my heart thumping in my ears. Bookshelves, desk, chairs, but nowhere to hide. My attention went to the windows, trying to calculate if we could climb out before they entered.

The doorknob twisted, accompanied by the scrape of a key entering the lock.

Fuck!

Spinning, I grabbed Rosie, yanking her with me, instincts working faster than my thoughts as I dove us behind the long curtains on either side of the windows, her on one side, me on the other. I sucked in and flattened my body against the wall as the door swung open.

It was strange, but it was like I could smell Brexley here, as if her fear and heartache were imprinted against this very curtain. I didn't have the connection to her as Warwick and Scorpion did, but there was still something between us. Something that made me feel like she had stood right here, her own terror bleeding into this very fabric.

"All of this will be cleared out." A man's brittle voice resonated against the walls as he stepped into the room. "Except for his papers in the safe, we can make a bonfire from the rest for all I care. I wouldn't mind watching him burn with it. All those years, he made me and my family suffer under his thumb. The blackmail... screwing my wife behind my back. He will see who is in charge now."

Another person followed the man in but didn't respond.

"Have a seat."

"I will stand." Emotionless and low, the second man responded. Something in it struck a chord with me, the familiarity scraping up the back of my neck.

"Yes, fine." The first man moved. From my position, I could see a glimpse of graying blonde hair and barrel chest, his arm decorated in medals, moving behind Istvan's desk.

118

Lieutenant Henrik Andor. Markos's second in command. I knew my enemies and had seen him enough in the Leopold gossip papers to recognize him. Always behind Istvan, stiff and scowling. His frame was much huskier than Markos, though Istvan's arrogance and personality shoved this man far into the distance. Nothing but a bitter aftertaste left in your mouth, you'd soon forget.

"State your business. I have much to do this evening."

"Her Majesty is on her way?" The voice clashed against my eardrums, spurning the emotion of hate in my gut.

"Queen Sonya will arrive soon with her troops. Everyone in this city will know who is in command. And I will no longer be anyone's second."

My body jolted, my gaze meeting Rosie's across the way, her eyes meeting mine with the same terror.

Andor and Sonya? What the fuck was going on?

"Thank you for finding their whereabouts so quickly." Whose whereabouts? Trepidation poured through my blood, my intuition gnawing at my bones. "You will be compensated accordingly, Kalaraja."

Air evaporated from my lungs, acid burning up the back of my throat. It took everything in me not to leap out and cut his throat, tasting his blood on my lips. I knew all about this sick fuck. He had been working for Istvan for years, purely for money; the guy had no loyalty to anyone but the coin, hunting and killing for pleasure.

Kalaraja, Lord of Death, was the name given to him when he became this monster. Few knew much beyond that. Had known the boy, Hazem, as I had. We had a past.

The taste of revenge for his betrayal coated my tongue; the memory of him and the raw anger flushed through me.

I wasn't surprised he had backstabbed Markos for whoever would keep him flush in kills, though I never even

119

considered Andor to be anything but Istvan's lap dog. In this cutthroat world, I should know better by now.

No one was faithful.

My attention shot to Rosie, her stunning features and terrified eyes twisting me up. I turned my head away, cutting off any feeling stirring inside, reminding me of the weakness I let myself have once. What a woman could do.

I had learned long ago never to trust. Never to love again.

"I have discovered Ms. Kovacs is not with the rebel army."

Andor's head jerked back, showing me more of his face, surprise hinting on his lifted brow, probably the most emotion he showed. "Are you sure?"

"Yes. She and the nectar disappeared the night of the prison break," Kalaraja stated. "There are rumors growing louder of sightings of her. And that the King of the Unified Nations has sent his bounty hunters after her. He has spies all throughout the Eastern bloc… he and the queen are aware of what she is capable of. They want to destroy her and the nectar."

Bile lunged up my throat, fear I never thought possible wrapped around my lungs. King Lars and Queen Kennedy had the best of the best.

They would not fail.

"King Lars?" Andor popped up his other brow. Kalaraja must have nodded because I saw Andor's head dip, his hand rubbing at his forehead. "We must find her first, then. We need the nectar. I want it."

"There are reports she has been spotted with a gypsy caravan near Ternopil."

"Ternopil?" Andor stiffened, his chest huffing up higher. "She's in Ukraine?"

"Rumors."

"How well do you trust these sources?"

"They have not failed me yet."

"Then go find her!" Andor barked. "We will pay whatever you want, but get to her before Markos or Lars's men get to her. Get me the nectar now!" He hit his fist on the desk.

"My expenses and payment up front."

Andor's jaw gritted, but he turned to the bookshelf behind him. Tugging on a book, he pulled away a set of hollowed-out books, displaying the safe behind. My lungs caught air, locked on the very thing we had come here for. Andor typed in a code, and after a soft beep, the door unlatched. Opening it, I spotted dozens of files. All private information Istvan wanted to keep from the world.

Andor pulled out an envelope, plucking handfuls of 20,000 forints.

"This should be enough." He shoved the wad at Kalaraja. "Now go. I will not let Markos win this one. He will pay for what he did to my son. For the years, he belittled and threatened me. He will watch everything he's ever wanted slip through his fingers before I gut him. He thinks himself so smart. And all this time, I've been waiting to strike. But I need that nectar."

"Yes, Lieutenant."

"King," Andor gritted.

Oh, fuck. This was why he was with Sonya. He thought he would be by her side. I wanted to laugh. What a moron. The woman was like a black widow. If for one moment he, *a human*, thought himself special and that he would benefit from her, he was sorely mistaken.

"My apologies, *King*." Kalaraja's voice was flat, but I knew him enough to hear the tightness in it. To know he'd

121

love to slice through Andor's throat. And someday, when Andor no longer paid enough, he probably would.

A knock sounded on the door. "Come in," Andor replied, switching back to the killer in front of him. "Kalaraja, find her. Kill her. I don't care how, but bring me back the nectar."

My eyes met with Rosie again. *"Brexley,"* Rosie mouthed, her expression in utter panic, tears building behind her eyes. She didn't say anything more, but I could sense the next words like they were my own. *We need to find her now.* And in that one look, I felt the urge to tear this world apart to find Brexley *for her…* for me. Duty of my role be dammed. And more than anything, I wanted to kill the man who was just assigned to hunt her down and exterminate her.

"Yes, my liege," Kalaraja said, exiting the room as another man stepped in.

"Sir, Her Majesty and her troops are just arriving."

"Good." Andor tucked the envelope back in the safe, shutting it. "Is everything set up?"

"Yes. We are set to attack Vajdahunyad Castle at your command."

My blood went to ice, and I forgot everything else, air stopping in my lungs, my eyes locked on Rosie's.

Vajdahunyad Castle.

"No survivors. Slaughter them all. I want Killian's head on a spike by the end of the night."

"Yes, my liege." He bowed, heading back out the door, Andor on his tail. My bones ached to move. Time seemed to stop when Andor left the room, the door finally clicking shut behind him as I listened for his steps to recede.

Busting out from behind the curtain, my only thoughts were on getting to my people, my legs bolting for the door.

"Killian!" My name uttered through her mouth was like

its own magic, halting me in my tracks. And twisting me back to her.

She darted for the safe, the reason we even were here. She bit down on her bottom lip, her fingers tapping over the keypad.

"Hurry." Panic almost overtook me, my fists tapping against my leg. I needed to get out of here, needed to get back to the base. I shouldn't have left at all and been the leader they needed and not been selfish. I ignored the fact that if I hadn't come here, I wouldn't have known about the attack or about the hunt for Brexley.

Rosie moved quickly, the safe opening, her hands reaching for the piles of documents. I moved back to her, grabbing them from her hands, twisting her around, and shoving them in the slim pack on her back. Whatever was in these files would have to wait.

"Come on!" I zipped the bag up, already beelining for the door.

They had found our base.

My people had no indication of what was coming for them. They'd be caught unaware... and if I couldn't get to them in time...

Their blood would coat my hands forever.

Chapter 12
Brexley

Metal squeaked from the rusting Ferris wheel, the carriages rattling against the chilly breeze. The pounding of hammers, voices, and the roars of hungry tigers nipped at my ears, pulling my focus.

I heaved out in frustration, opening my eyes. A few dimly lit streetlamps cast more shadows on the old Ferris wheel rotting in the background of the overgrown National Revival Park in Ternopil. The Ferris wheel was more like a headstone marking the life which used to exist here, groaning and howling like a ghost of its former self.

It was our last night in Ternopil before we moved on. The carnies were tearing down the tents not far from us, making this place deserted again. For two nights, lights, music, laughter, and awed guests had filled this section of the park, escaping into the enchanted world where they could forget their suffering. Those years they had suffered under Ivanenko's tightfisted reign while he lived in luxury.

"You aren't even trying." Esmeralda's scratchy voice huffed with irritation, jerking my head to her. She was wrapped in a heavy robe and her bunny slippers, sitting back on a bench, chugging from the flask she was holding, a fae-marijuana joint burning in the other. "You are wasting my time. My energy. Plus, I'm freezing my tits off out here. Try again!"

Shifting on my knees, the cold cement bleeding into the fabric of my pants, I closed my lids, trying to push away the defensive wall that wanted to protect everyone from what I could do. A trickle of sweat glided down my back, challenging the ice-cold temperatures biting at my exposed skin. The sun had long ago fallen behind the trees, the carnival patrons back in their homes fast asleep. Fae were naturally nocturnal, but I learned quickly the carny life was even more so. This was when they came alive, thriving in the shadows and the seedy illusions that could trick the eye and mind.

"Concentrate, girl," Esmeralda snapped.

Exhaling, I tried to open myself up, blocking out everything, but all I heard was the hammering and commotion of the carnies in the distance. Grinding down on my teeth, I dug deeper, shoving all the commotion away, drilling my thoughts on my magic, unearthing that fire deep inside.

The noises in my head pounded harder. My skin prickled. I could feel death everywhere in this place. Pain, starvation, suffering over the generations. This land held a lot of history. A lot of suffering. Ghosts lingered on the edges, waiting for me, and if I opened up a little, they would devour me.

A strangled cry came from my throat, my head tipping back in frustration. "It's not working."

"No shit." Esmeralda puffed out a long billow of smoke, her head turning to the side. "Yes, yes, I know!" Esmeralda barked, batting her hand at the air. "Back off, old man. You

125

are grating on my nerves too." She took a swig of *Ţuică*, a plum brandy that was probably homemade. "My grand-children are annoying enough assholes, and on top of that, I have to deal with your lot." She shook her head, unhooking her ankles, making the ears on her pink bunny slippers spring around. "And they wonder why I drink and smoke." She sucked on her roll, puffing it out. "The Druid says you're the one blocking yourself." She stood, shuffling over to me. "The only thing you are fighting is *you*.

The Druid.

Tad.

At first when she said he was with her, I thought she was crazy. But it wasn't long before it became clear. Esmeralda was the real deal. Her mother was a seer who could see fae auras back before the wall fell and they were still in hiding. Her father was from a druid line, watered down enough that she didn't inherit most of the druid qualities, but enough that she could still sense them. Interact with that level of magic.

I still couldn't believe it, that night by the river, telling me Tad was there.

"What are you talking about?" I shot back defensively, thinking she was either full of shit or I had been discovered. My sins finding me, my truth of who I was made known.

"The Druid. He's here. Yammering in my ear until I couldn't take it anymore." She moved her fingers by her ear like a mouth. "Won't shut up about helping you... training you to control your magic... and keeps mentioning something about nectar?"

"What?" I stepped back, my insides turning to lava as my skin iced.

"Yeah, yeah, I'm getting to that. Back off!" Esmeralda waved her hand at the air in annoyance. "He says he sees things, that you are clearer to him. That he sees the

126

connections between you and the nectar. It's dangerous. Deadly. Very adamant about you learning to control your own magic. Never to use this nectar again."

"What? Why?" Hackles raised, I held the box to my chest, defending it if anyone tried to take it. "It's my magic too. It's part of me."

"No." She shook her head. "You might be connected through circumstances, but that magic was never yours. Not meant for anyone. That kind of power will only destroy. You must learn to be without it. To find your own power." Her head tilted at the nectar, her brows furrowing. "What the hell is that, anyway? Looks like something my cat barfed up—"

"Hey? Girl." Esmeralda snapped her fingers in my face, bringing me back to the present, peering up at her. "I'm perfectly fine going back to my wagon where it's warm, where I have a chocolate biscuit and weed, and leaving your ass to do this on your own."

"I'm trying."

"No, you're not. You're not letting yourself. Stop being so stubborn, girl" She tapped my head.

"How am I fighting myself?" I tossed out my arms. We had been working for hours, yielding nothing.

"Your fear," she replied. "You are scared of what you are… what you can do."

My stomach tightened, the arrow of her words hitting its target. It was instinct to protect yourself from danger, from hurt, and my mind slammed shut the moment I felt any barrier going down, any chance my power might slip out.

"I can't help it." I rolled my frozen fingers into my lap, exhaustion riding over my shoulders. I wasn't sleeping well. Besides the guilt, shame, and fear I held, there was an anxiety I couldn't place. Or I could, but I didn't want to say it out loud. The need for him ached so badly I almost couldn't bear it; the desire to call out for him pounded in my heart with every beat. The craving was worse than any drug.

At the time, I felt I was a coward for running away. I couldn't face my actions. Now I looked at it differently. I had to leave. It was something I felt in my soul, something I needed to figure out on my own. Warwick would never have let me go.

"What do I do?" I scrubbed my temple, my head thumping. I wanted nothing more than to wrap my hand around the nectar and use its strength to lift mine. The need didn't go away. It was something I had to work through. "Please… I don't know how to do this."

Esmeralda's eyes suddenly glossed over, her gaze far off though she looked right at me, her demeanor changing as she cleared her throat.

"In death, I see you much clearer, my dear. I can feel your fear holding you back." Esmeralda's tone and speech pattern went softer and slower. She was no longer there. "Sorrow and grief bind you—they're choking you. But if you don't learn to control it, there will only be more."

A sharp gasp of air burned down my throat, tears building behind my lids. Even though Esmeralda stood in front of me, my senses were picking up another, knowing who had taken over.

"Tad?" I croaked.

A soft smile curved her mouth, head dipping.

"Tad…" My eyes filled up with tears. "I-I can't do this."

"You can, and you must. You are strong, Brexley. You have been through more than anyone I have ever met at such a young age. That girl I saw in the Games… she never gave up. She fought."

"And killed." I hoarsely replied, trying to keep back my emotions. "I. *Killed.* You." A tear fell down my cheek, the heartache and grief so raw, I was afraid to let it out, knowing I might buckle under it. I couldn't think about the lives I took, the anger at Istvan for what he had done, for murdering my father and taking everything from me. The hate and guilt mixed and gurgled inside me like a volcano, and if I let go…

"No." He reached out, touching my face. I no longer saw or heard Esmeralda; it was Tad I felt, his voice I heard. "You didn't fight to kill. You fought to survive. For life." He patted my cheek. "And you freed me from the twisted confines of my body. A cage I had been locked in for too long."

"How can you forgive me? Look what I did. What I was about to do… to Simon. I killed hundreds of people, and I didn't even care. I just wanted to destroy Istvan."

"That's why you must learn your powers and control them," Tad replied. "There is no escaping yourself, child. You must face it. Head on, like I know you can. I'm not saying it will be easy, and I'm not saying I don't also fear what you are, but you have no choice. I see that now. You are strong enough to do this. You have to. The war is still coming, and it is much more than any of you thought. And the nectar is the most dangerous thing of all. It cannot be used. It is too much. Power like that, magic from the Otherworld… just like the treasures became, the nectar should not be used in this world that it is no longer meant for. You understand?"

I nodded, my lips trembling, wishing so badly I could bring him back, to take away what I did that night. Have the real man here with me.

"There is only forward," he said, his hand brushing my cheek. "And just because I'm not physically present doesn't mean I'm not here. I will always be with you as long as you need me."

"I need you," I whispered so low I barely felt the words come out of me.

"Then I am at your side." He touched my face again before his hand fell away. Esmeralda's body jerked, her eyes blinking rapidly, her lips twisting up in a snarl. "Dammit, old man! You do that again, and I'll conjure your ass into my crystal ball." Her chest puffed up, flaying an arm at the air. "Trap you inside like a snow globe and shake you like a maraca."

I snorted.

She blew out, her shoulders falling. "I wish that crystal ball was more than a prop for tourists. So cliché and contrived." She took another drink from her flask. "But I will smoke a roll of sage and sprinkle salt in my ass if it gets you off my back, druid." She grunted at him, then snapped her fingers at me. "Hurry up and figure this shit out so I can be left in peace. He can haunt you for eternity," she grumbled, stomping back to the bench, bunny ears wiggling wildly. She flopped down, wrapping her robe against her tighter, muttering under her breath.

I blew out, feeling heavy.

"Brex-ley." I swear I heard a voice graze the back of my neck, so light it was almost nonexistent, a voice neither male nor female, but it strangely calmed me.

Shutting my eyes, I exhaled, lowering my shoulders and emptying my mind. The squeals of metal from the Ferris wheel, the hollers from the carnies, and the roars of lions slowly faded into white noise. Concentrating on my breathing, I opened up against the terror, the tightness in my belly wanting to close back down, sensing the embers under the sequestered fire, ready to inflame and forge.

My skin prickled as ghosts buzzed my skin, their voices growing louder in my head, sparking fear in me.

Instantly everything died away again, popping me back to reality.

"We're gonna be here all night," Esmeralda grumbled, rolling up another smoke. "What? I am being supportive. I'm still here, aren't I?" She talked to the air beside her.

Settling back on my butt, I tried again. Slowly the sounds dissipated, and all I could sense was the thump of my heartbeat, the taste of the air still hinting with sugar and burnt caramel, the smell of straw from the horses.

Wind lashed through the dilapidated park; a fizz of lightning flickered above. The spirits swooped in closer, the hundreds of voices muddled together, their energy slipping past me, trying to take my energy. Sweat beaded my hairline, pushing deeper into walls I built up around the volcano burning inside me. The power could be dimmed and hidden, but it could never completely go out.

This was me. *My* power. Not the nectar's. The magic in my blood was raw and wild, but it was all mine.

It was mine to learn.

Mine to control.

I focused my energy, trying to strike lightning near the Ferris wheel.

Nothing happened.

"Dammit!" I grunted, leaning over my legs with exhaustion, feeling my link with my magic dwindle away.

"Was something supposed to happen?" Esmeralda took a hit, then stomped out her roll with the heel of her slipper.

"Yeah." I rubbed my temple. We had been here for over three hours, and I felt completely fried. "I think I need a brea—"

Pop! The crack of a gun going off jerked my head to the sound. Birds and bats took off from the trees between us and where the carnival was, screeching into the dark night.

Clipped voices rose, sounding anything but friendly.

My gaze leaped to Esmeralda, her eyes wide.

The nectar. I had left it in my wagon.

131

Jumping up, I darted into the trees, voices getting louder. I kept to the shadows, sneaking up on camp, terror rolling my stomach into knots.

"Wait up, girl," she whisper-shouted behind me, shuffling up to where I stopped behind a tree, peering out. A small bonfire in the middle of the broken-down camp flickered enough to light the area.

My chest squeezed as I took in the scene. Many of the carnies stayed near their wagons, but a few of the men, including Hank, stood next to the Master of Mystique. Jethro's frame was stiff, his chin up as a handful of soldiers dressed in gray uniforms descended from their horses, a tall built one approaching Jethro. The guards' backs were to me.

"La dracu." Fuck. "Corrupt guards. *Poliție murdarăr."* *Dirty police.* Esmeralda sneered in Romanian behind me. "They stop us for nothing and take anything they want for themselves. Food, money, jewelry… *nemernici."* *Bastards.* "Every country. Different uniforms, but all the same."

None of the guards moved. They stood stiffly by their horses like they were waiting for an order.

A tingle on the back of my neck slid down my spine.

The lead guard stopped in front of Jethro, his voice too low to hear from where I was. Jethro looked at something in the guard's hands. He lifted his head, shaking it.

"Are you sure?" The officer's voice barely made it to my ears. "We've heard reports otherwise."

"Your reports are wrong." Jethro's jaw gritted. "There is no one here by that name."

Another chip of dread tumbled down my vertebrae.

"Let's see if that answer changes when I ask your group of freaks here." The guard swung around, holding up a picture. "Has anyone seen this girl…"

A scream tore up my throat as I slammed my hand over

132

my mouth, my teeth cracking together to keep it from escaping. *What the hell was he doing here?* Terror drove through my veins, locking oxygen out of my lungs. It charged through every wall, peeling back all my defenses, flaring the magic that was just starting to wake back up, linking the bonds I tried to cut.

I felt *him* before I even looked.

My skin flamed with heat, my heart slamming in my chest like I finally came back to life. As if every dull color around me sharpened. His body heat licked at mine, daring me to look.

My head twisted to the side. Aqua eyes glowed in the darkness, boring into mine. Hazy and see-through, but I had no doubt he was there. The link surged through all barriers to find each other, my fear calling him near.

Warwick Farkas.

Dressed in all black, he had his hair pulled back. Dirt and cuts marked his face, but the sight of him rushed both joy and terror through me.

Fury rattled off him. A rumble came from his throat, his gaze shredding through me. *"Kovacs..."*

"Come forward now, or we will look through your camp ourselves. My men will turn over everything. And if things get broken or burned..." The guard's voice tugged Warwick's focus to the scene behind me. To the soldier who held a picture of me.

Tracker.

Dressed in a Ukrainian military outfit. Captain of his troop. I had no idea what had happened or why Tracker was wearing it, but I knew Istvan's connection to Ukraine, and the possibilities scared the shit out of me. Tracker wouldn't be anywhere without Istvan. That suggested Istvan was no longer in Budapest, but with Ivanenko and Olena in Ukraine.

Warwick's gaze locked on Tracker, his shoulders rising, nose flaring with wrath, his gaze dancing over Tracker and every single detail of this place. Taking in the carnival's name on the side of the wagon.

Fuck. I couldn't have him find me. Especially now.

Locking down, I sliced through the link, cutting him off. My heart ached the moment I did, his shadow disappearing, a small whimper sizzling through my chest, the vibration of his angry roar echoing in my soul.

It felt like I had cut out my own heart.

"Step forward now and give her over, and we will leave you in peace," Tracker boomed, peering around the campsite. "You are hiding a fugitive. A dangerous one at that. I promise you it will be worse for you later if you don't assist us now."

Esmeralda glanced at me, then at the picture in his hand. I remembered taking it. Rebeka had us pose for the magazine at a ball a few months before I went to Halálház. The girl in the picture with the glossy hair, expensive dress, and made-up face was pretty and elegant. Being trained to be a wife to some abusive nobleman or leader. She was also naive and arrogant, having no idea what lay in front of her, the sharp turn her life was about to take.

The woman Esmeralda saw was nothing like her. The young, innocent girl hadn't made it out of Halálház.

"*That* girl isn't here." Jethro folded his arms, his subtle gaze drifting around. Either to find me or to make sure his people understood.

Hank moved in closer, towering over all of them, his arms folding. "Nope. Never seen the likes of *that* girl before."

Tracker's mouth pinched, dropping his arm. "Fine." He nodded at his guards.

Now I realized why they stood there so stiffly; they were waiting for an order.

134

Their minds were no longer their own. The effects of the pills coursed through their veins. That meant destroying the lab hadn't stopped Istvan. I should have known better. I knew his mind well; he would have several plans in place. And I had a feeling Ukraine was a much larger part of this than I ever knew.

The guards stepped out, heading straight for Esmeralda's vardo, kicking over tables and chairs along the way. Zelda and her twin brother Leander stood in front of their home. Zelda fumed with anger, her arms crossed, not moving.

"Move," a guard ordered.

"Du-te in pizda ma-tii!" Go into your mother's twat. She spat at him in Romanian. Leander yanked her away before the guard could do anything. They went into the vardo.

My body moved before I even thought, heading for the men. A hand grabbed my arm, yanking me back.

"No," Esmeralda hissed, shaking her head.

"I can't let them destroy everything you own. Your home."

"You don't think they will anyway?" Her grip was strong for a little old lady. "That's not how they work. Plus, we protect our own. No matter what."

"But I'm not one of you. Why would you protect me?"

"Jethro just made you one of us."

"What?" I gaped, peering back at him with shock. His word was law here. He was head of the family, and what he said, they'd abide.

"I don't know who you are or what you've done... but the Master just made you part of the family."

135

Chapter 13
Warwick

The claw weapon on my back hit my spine with each strike of my boot pounding across the pavement, my chest heaving with icy air. Every minute counted, and it felt like the clock was moving faster than I was. My legs stretched, trying to gobble up the path as we ran for our base to warn them what was coming. Ash kept up with me, Zander a little ahead in his horse form, galloping toward the entrance.

The guards around the base leaped out, causing him to rear up as the three of us came barreling for them, their guns drawn until they saw it was us.

"What's going on?" Lukas lowered his rifle, his shoulders locking back, going into defense mode as if he could sense something was wrong.

Zander prodded the ground with his hoof.

"Go." I snapped at him. "Go find my sister."

He neighed, galloping off.

"Your mother." Ash turned back to Lukas, heaving for air. "She's coming."

"Coming?" Lukas's eyes widened. "What are you talking about?"

"We don't have time for explanations," I growled. "Just know she has teamed up with Lieutenant Andor at HDF, and they're all advanced this way. They found us."

"Andor?" Lukas's mouth parted. "I don't understand. He's human, right? Why is he with my mother?"

"Doesn't seem to matter anymore." I glanced over at Ash. He gave me a nod, neither of us having to talk. He would get them updated while I headed for Mykel.

The soles of my boots hit the tile, leaping up the stairs and heading for the command center where he would be waiting for us all to return. Bursting through the door, I found him pacing in front of the hearth, Rebeka sitting in a chair by the fire, sipping some tea. Both jerked to me when I entered.

"We were found."

"What?" Rebeka's cup hit the table, tipping over as she stood.

"Sonya. She and Andor are in some alliance. They're headed here. She has tripled her army. They're all on the pills."

"How long?" Mykel's voice was low.

"No more than an hour."

"Wait... no, this is wrong. Andor?" Rebeka's eyes widened in shock. "He has joined Sonya? That is not possible. He was my husband's second." Rebeka, out of anyone here besides Caden, would know him the best. "I mean, I knew he and Istvan didn't always see eye to eye, but to side with the fae?"

"She offered him more than your husband did," Mykel said matter-of-factly.

"What about Caden? Do you know if he's okay?" Rebeka bit down on her lip.

"I don't. Scorpion went to warn them, though."

Mykel nodded. "We can't do anything about that now. We have to get everyone here to safety." He leaped past shock

137

and went straight into action. "Rebeka, go down to the clinic, get everyone up. We need to evacuate those who can't fight now," he ordered her. To her credit, she nodded, instantly moving for the door.

"I assume the guards outside know?" Mykel's eyes lingered on her until she left, then turned back to me.

"Yes. Ash is catching them up on the latest, and Zander went to my sister's bunker, letting them know."

Mykel nodded. The only emotion I saw was his throat bobbing as he swallowed, and I could see his mind racing with plans and actions.

"We don't have the numbers. They will slaughter everyone here," I stated bluntly. "I don't know how many HDF has, but Sonya has hundreds, maybe close to a thousand. We are far outgunned. Plus, on the pills, they are stronger and harder to kill. Putting up a fight would be pointless."

Mykel's head dropped, his mouth pinching. "Okay. Then we run."

No one wanted to abandon this place, but we had no choice.

"Get the word out to everyone you pass. They take only what they can carry and meet in the square. I will be down there to give them more information as soon as I can." He reached over to the papers and maps on the table and, by the handful, started chucking them into the fire to burn. Getting rid of any information or documents. "Go."

I turned around, jogging out of the room. By the time I made it downstairs, chaos had erupted. Notice of the attack had already spread like wildfire. Hundreds of people moved around, heading for their loved ones, or getting back to their rooms to grab their belongings.

Rebeka ran up the stairs to the main floor with a child in her arms, more people from the clinic behind her.

"Rebeka." I grabbed her arm. "Where's Kitty?"

Rebeka's face creased into sorrow, her head shaking. "I tried… I tried to get her, but she wouldn't come."

Boooom!

A blast went off in the far distance, rattling the chandeliers above our heads, causing screams and panic from the children.

Rebeka's horror-filled gaze met mine, and she tucked the kid in closer to her chest, the orphan crying into her shoulder.

From the pitch in my ear, it sounded like the explosion was maybe a mile off. Sonya wasn't even trying to hide their approach, conveying to the city who was in charge.

They had gotten here a lot faster than I expected.

"Go!" I waved her to the door, my feet already hitting the steps, rushing to the clinic.

A few healers were still there helping the ones who needed more care and help to move, but my gaze locked onto the bony figure in a bed a couple of rows back. Striding forward, I bared down on the cot, my teeth crushing together, my chest aching at what I was seeing.

Head shaved, with sunken cheeks, her already slim figure was nothing more than bones. She stared blankly into the distance. If I hadn't seen her chest moving up and down, I would think she was dead.

"Kitty." My fear burned with anger. "Get up. We need to go."

She didn't respond. Not even a flicker in her gaze.

"Dammit, Kitty. We are about to be attacked. Now get up."

Nothing.

A strangled growl rose from my throat, my fist rolling into balls. "If I have to pick you up and throw you over my shoulder. I will."

139

Her dark eyes finally darted to me, a look I knew so well, lowering her lids. It was her 'if you do, I will kill you' look.

"If that's what I have to do."

Her lips parted. "No."

"You are not staying here."

Another look.

"I'm not going to let you die."

Her gaze went back to the wall, telling me that was exactly what she wanted. She had lost her will to live. Her desire to get up and fight another day had perished. Losing her business, home, and very identity had broken her, but Věrhǎza stole her soul, demolishing what was left of her.

Another bomb shook the ground, sprinkling bits of the ceiling down on us. They were getting closer.

"Get. Up!" My teeth ground together, my feet shifting. I wasn't good with emotions.

She didn't respond.

I went to scoop her up with a growl, but a figure darted in front of me, blocking me and stopping me in my tracks.

Ash went down on his knees at her bedside, leaning closer to her.

"Kitty…" His voice was soft. "Listen to me." He swallowed, reaching out and curling his hands around hers. "I've been such a fool. And I am sorry." His voice croaked. "Took me a long time to acknowledge it… to see my ego and broken heart lashed out at you for something you couldn't control any more than what I felt for you." He swallowed, his thumb sliding back and forth over her knuckles, like we had all the time in the world, while more bits of ceiling came raining down. "I'm sorry it took me this long to say something. But seeing you now… what happened to you in Věrhǎza. It put everything in perspective, and I realized I'd been holding onto a grudge—anger and hurt I no longer feel, but didn't have the guts to admit to or let go of." He reached up, stroking her cheek. "I'm sorry I turned my back on you. And I'm sorry I broke the promise to always be there for you. You are my family. First and always. I love you so much."

Kitty's eyes broke from the wall to Ash's, something I hadn't seen in her face for a long time hinted on her face.

Hope. Love.

Not romantic love, but the deep love we had that spanned centuries—lasted through the highs and lows, through death, starvation, torture, poverty. We had been there for each other through it all and always had each other's backs.

"Warwick and I can't exist without you." Ash jerked his head toward me. "You know I can't keep him in line alone. That takes an army."

I swear I saw a hint of a smile on Kitty's mouth.

My forehead scrunched together, and I grew antsier as time ticked on, but for some reason I knew to stay quiet. This had been decades in the making. Their pain and hurt kept me in the middle, tearing apart the only family I had, besides my sister and nephew, but honestly, these two had been with me longer through much more shit.

"Please. Don't give up on us. We need you." He squeezed her hand. "We need you to fight. Janos was tough, but Kitty is a badass. She doesn't take shit, and she doesn't fucking give up. Ever. I need my sister. I need you to want to live, to not let those assholes in prison win. They don't deserve to have you. To take you from us." Ash kept her hand in his, rising to his feet as another boom echoed not far away.

"Fuck," I muttered, about ready to grab them both and run.

"Now get the fuck up." Ash's voice was low and even, but powerful.

Her gaze drifted up to where he held her hand.

141

"I will help you every step of the way, but *you* have to get up. *You* have to want to."

There was a moment I thought she might turn her face back to the wall. Give up. My body inched forward, ready to take her whether or not she wanted to go.

Ash's arm went up, blocking me.

"Kitty." He whispered her name. Her gaze went back to him. I saw it in that moment. The determination lining her forehead. Her chin dipped, and she started to sit up.

Air I didn't even know I was holding whooshed from my lungs.

She struggled, fatigued with dehydration and hunger, but she sat fully up, blinking back emotion as she stared at Ash. My family was back. And I recognized that only Ash could have gotten her up. The one who broke through and put that flame back in her gut. He had always been our glue. Our foundation.

She wobbled as she rose, but she got up with just his hand as support.

The building shook as another bomb went off right over our heads. Commotion and cries came from above. Lights flickered, some going out, more debris trickling down on us.

"We don't have time." My arms went under Kitty, lifting her up. "Put a blanket around her," I ordered Ash. He quickly bundled her up, and we both took off for the door.

"Get out now!" Ash yelled at the last healer, still packing her bag with medicines. "Come on!"

I didn't wait, my legs taking us up the stairs. People ran every which way, and I zigzagged through the throng, getting out into the night.

Groups swarmed the area with what little they had, terrified and unsure as the sound of gunfire and thousands of feet stomped toward us.

Mykel, Rebeka, Lukas, and Kek were together, organizing groups. Ash and I made our way to them.

"Sonya's men are coming up the north side," Mykel said to me the moment we walked up. "HDF from the south."

We were being surrounded.

"We have to get everyone out of here." Ash peered around at the mounting people.

"Only way is to slip out into the park." I readjusted Kitty in my arms, though she weighed nothing. "In small groups."

"Lukas, I need all shifters who can carry people, anyone willing to help some of the sick and small children," Mykel instructed.

"Yes, sir." Lukas nodded, disappearing into the throng.

"Uncle Warwick!" Simon's voice rang out in the air, whirling me around to see my nephew running for me, his arms wrapping around my leg. Zander and Eliza were right behind him.

"Warwick." Relief filled my sister's voice, her attention going to Kitty. I could see shock turn to hope in my sister's eyes. She hadn't grown up with me like Ash and Kitty had, but they had been in her life since she was born. "So glad you are okay."

"Zander, would you be willing to shift? Carry some of these people out of here?" Mykel asked.

"Of course." He dipped his head.

A ball of fire flung through the air, crashing into the roof of the base, tossing us to the ground. I hit the dirt, covering Kitty's body with mine as debris exploded from the roof, cutting through my clothes and skin.

"You all right?" Mykel scrambled over to Rebeka and the several children she was protecting.

"Yeah. I think so." Rebeka looked over each one, nodding her head.

143

Everyone around was slowly getting up as more gunfire hit the castle's outer wall.

"We have no time. We need to go now!"

The moment I stood up, about to reach for Kitty again, I was no longer there. I could feel the pull, driving through me and yanking me to her as if she owned me. She fucking did.

My shadow stood in a woodsy area, my chest sucking in at the sight of her hiding behind a tree. Seeing her felt like she ripped open my chest and healed it at the same time. Her long dark hair lay down her back, and a dark cloak wrapped around her shoulders. Another person stood with her, but I took no heed of anything but Brexley.

Anger. Passion. Hurt. Love. I felt every emotion seeing her. This woman came into my life, flipped it, and took over. And I bowed to it. To her.

And she ran.

As if she felt me, her body stiffened. Her head swung to me, her almost black eyes glinting off the firelight yards away, her mouth parting.

"Kovacs," I rumbled. I wanted to strangle and kiss the fuck out of her at the same time. Before I could utter another word, a voice tugged my attention away from her.

"Come forward now, or we will look through your camp ourselves." I breathed in, my gaze snapping on the man who just spoke. My muscles locked up, fury rising as I looked upon the traitor. I wanted to rip him in half with my own bare hands.

Tracker.

He was holding a picture of the girl who was groomed to be a real princess. But not *my princess*.

I no longer heard the words he said. It didn't matter. He had found her.

Worse, Tracker was dressed in a Ukraine uniform with

men who appeared like robots. Their eyes were dead, their bodies robotic. They were on the pills.

This meant Markos had already assembled an army in Ukraine. He wasn't shamed or defeated. He was rebuilding stronger with more money and weapons, thanks to Ivanenko. He would come back for Hungary. For all of the Eastern bloc.

I needed to find her. I would fucking find her. I took in every detail, anything that could help me track her down.

I felt the link start to dissolve, pushing me away. "No," I snarled, but it was too late. "NO!" I roared, my tendons strangling as I screamed up at the sky. She slammed the wall down between us, ramming me back into my body.

"Warwick!" Eliza screamed my name, twisting me around to see troops coming up the path for the castle. "Come on!"

Peering over, I saw Zander had shifted back into his horse self, Eliza and Simon on his back. I scooped up Kitty, running her over to them. She was barely conscious. Standing up had taken most of her energy.

"Take her!" I shoved Kitty at them. Eliza wrapped her between her and Simon, keeping Kitty from slipping off. Zander was bigger and able to bear more weight than a normal horse.

Eliza looked at me, her chest falling. "Come on."

I shook my head, turning to Zander. "Listen, pony-boy. You have the most important things in the world to me. Get them out of here and protect them with your life, or I'm coming for yours."

Zander neighed, flicking his head. Probably a fuck you, but I took it as a yes.

I whipped to Mykel. "You need to find a way to destroy Halálház, Sonya's labs. We need to take out her ability to keep making more. Can you do that?"

"Yes… but what are you doing?" Mykel hustled Rebeka and some of the children toward the last escape we had.

I didn't answer him. "You have a place to go?"

"Yes." He nodded. "Killian told me of a location if anything happened to him."

"Go," I ordered. "Go now and don't look back. Get them all to safety. I will find you guys later."

"Where are you going?" Mykel insisted.

"To find your niece," I grunted, turning to Zander and slapping him on the hindquarters. He took off with a snort. "Now go! I'll distract them for a bit."

Mykel appeared concerned, but he nodded. "Get Brexley home to us," he said, then ushered everyone left to follow, not looking back.

Realizing I wasn't alone, I peered at Ash on one side and Kek and Lukas on the other.

"You guys should go."

"And miss out on the fun?" Ash scoffed.

"Not a chance, Wolf." Kek grinned, her eyes turning black, staring off at the soldiers heading for us. "This is when things get exciting. Plus, I'm great at *distracting*."

"Damn right she is," Ash muttered.

Lukas snorted, his head bobbing, cheeks slightly blushed.

"Yeah," I breathed out. "I know." Firsthand. "Things could get really dangerous," I rumbled, pulling the claw off my back, swinging it around to get a better grip. "And death is highly likely if you follow me."

Ash tugged two guns from his waist. "Only way we know, brother."

Chapter 14
Scorpion

Flames rose from already dilapidated and rundown buildings. The poverty and hopelessness of Savage Lands tasted bitter on my tongue. The encampments that overran the area were now mostly vacant. People off the main street were hiding in fear from the army that just marched through, terrorizing and threatening.

Sonya and Andor had made sure everyone understood there was a new order in Budapest, setting fires and destroying camps along the way to Vajdahunyad Castle. Nothing about the march was subtle or quiet. It was deliberate. Wanting to cause fear.

"Why?" Hanna muttered next to me, a nerve in her cheek twitching. "Why would they do this? They were already suffering out here."

"Because fear is the best way to control people. To have them surrender to what is happening and not fight back."

When I got to HDF, I found Hanna almost immediately—intuition that took me right to her. Birdie, Caden, and Wesley were also with Hanna, watching a bigger army than I ever imagined behind the wall of Leopold.

Killian and Rosie had not been heard from since they lost their connection to them.

"Sonya has a troop coming. They will be here soon." My lungs burned from running so fast, the troops nipping at my heels. "Then they are all heading to our base. They want to take us out and make sure Killian is no longer an issue."

"I know." Caden's Adam's apple bobbed, his jaw tensing.

My brows furrowed. "How do you know?"

Caden rubbed the back of his neck, a vein popping in his jaw.

"We can't wait for Killian." Birdie spoke instead, her tone full of distress. "We have to get back and warn everyone."

"Ash, Zander, and Warwick are warning the base. I came here to inform you guys what was happening. They'll be here soon." My gaze drifted to Hanna. She hadn't spoken a word. Her attention was on the fae-like troops, her hands flexing and unflexing as if she was fighting an eternal battle. Struggling with the urge to join them… or slaughter them all.

"I'm not leaving." Wesley shook his head. "They are still in there." The *'they'* meaning Rosie. I had seen him around her enough to know when my friend had a crush. Wesley was always infatuated with a girl, especially the ones that didn't fall under his charms right away.

He loved the chase.

"We don't leave anyone behind," Caden clipped. I didn't know him well, but he seemed like a completely different person from the guy we held hostage not long ago. If I didn't know he was human, I'd think he was fae. He had an energy coming off him that reminded me of another asshole. A legendary rage filled that dickwad too. "Plus, they're already here." Caden's eyes went past me.

The thumps of marching feet iced up my neck, jerking me to see Sonya's troops had already crossed the Széchenyi Chain Bridge, heading up the promenade, their weapons glinting in the moonlight.

"*Ó, hogy baszd meg egy talicska apró majom.*" *Oh, may a wheelbarrow of small monkeys fuck it.* Birdie grumbled, yanking out another gun from her thigh holster.

When Killian and Rosie finally emerged from HDF with the bag full of documents, the regiment was at least twenty minutes in front of us, giving us no time to talk. We raced through the city toward the base, seeing the aftermath the troops left in their wake. The devastation her army was already causing in our city.

Would our group get out in time? Would we be too late to help?

Anxiety drove me faster, and I came to a skittering stop across the lake from Vajdahunyad.

"Fuck," I whispered, horror seeping into my lungs.

Bullets and explosions howled through the night from the castle area, the man-made, algae-filled lake reflecting the fire igniting the roof.

Suddenly, my legs dipped underneath me, heat burning through my gut.

"Scorpion!" Hanna grabbed for me, keeping me upright. Something inside me tugged, feeling the pull, like part of me was trying to come back to life again, gasping for air and crawling its way through my soul.

I knew with every fiber what it was, who it was.

Brexley.

It was more a feeling. A wisp of her shadow brushing

my skin. A sense of being centered for one fucking second before it was hacked off like a dead limb. I bent over, gasping for air, my body reacting to the sudden high and the low.

"What's wrong?" Birdie was on my other side.

"Nothing." I gulped, straightening. "I'm fine." The flicker of connection was gone, but the emptiness didn't pull me under this time. I could barely feel it, and maybe it was my imagination, but I held onto the tiny buzz I could feel of her.

Gunfire and cries snapped me away from whatever it was, returning to the horror before us. Thousands of silhouettes moved closer to the base, raining hell down on the castle. I hoped Warwick had gotten to them soon enough and was able to get most out to safety.

The soldiers flooded both sides, and I knew we all felt helpless, especially Killian.

Caden hissed under his breath, fury dancing off him like sparks. "No *fucking* way."

"What?" Birdie swung to him.

"That asshole thinks he can distract them long enough," he growled. "Four of them against thousands." Caden shook his head, his eyes going back to the burning building across the lake as if he could see right through it. "Fucking idiot."

"What are you talking about?" Killian asked.

Something told me I already knew the answer to this.

"Warwick." Caden flicked his chin to the base. "Him, Ash, Lukas, and Kek."

"What? How do you know?" Rosie blurted out.

"I just do." Caden's response made my hair stand on end.

Rosie wagged her head in disbelief. "So they're trying to fight against this?" She waved her arm at the overwhelming numbers marching in on the base. "There is no way they can defeat that many. They'll be killed."

"They're not trying to defeat them." Killian's head lifted in understanding. "They are trying to give our people time to escape. But you're right. They will probably be killed."

"Then I say we go assist them." Birdie, already holding two guns, switched out her smaller one for a faster automatic, handing the other one to Rosie. "This girl is good with newbies."

"No." Killian shook his head, reaching to take the gun Birdie was handing Rosie. "There is no way you are going to be part of this."

"Funny." Rosie's fingers curled around the gun. "I don't remember asking for your permission."

Killian opened his mouth again.

"And before you shove that bullshit that you're a fae lord and I have to do as you say…" She cocked back the weapon. "Remember, I never voted for you."

"You don't vote for leaders," Killian exclaimed. "We inherit them through lineage or challenge."

"Then I challenge you to fuck off."

I snorted out a laugh. I was really beginning to like her. I could see why Wesley was keen on her, but I had a suspicion he wasn't alone.

"What's the plan?" Wesley asked me, stepping in next to Rosie, trying to take her attention from Killian. "There are too many to sneak up on. We'd be killed in minutes, not doing a bit of good." He motioned to the tanks and the mass of soldiers.

Inhaling deeply, I peered across the lagoon.

"We head straight." I nodded to the castle.

"What?" Rosie's head swung to me while Birdie and Wesley peered at me with mischievous smiles.

"Like that time in Kosovo?" Birdie's eyebrow popped up.

"Something like that." I grinned, flashes of memory coming back to me. One of my tattoos covered the deep scar running across my torso from that conflict.

"Fuck, yeah." Wesley's head bounced.

Killian let out a long sigh, understanding immediately. "Then let's go." He nodded toward the disgusting, freezing swamp. A foul musk prevalent even during the colder months could be picked up. The boats and tourist stuff were long gone, so we would be swimming across. Birdie, Wesley, and I had fought in some harsh environments, so I knew they would be okay. I was shocked how easily Rosie and Hanna went in. Hanna at least had training and was probably put through extreme circumstances, but Rosie was proving herself beyond measure.

"What?" Rosie glanced at Wesley, catching him looking at her with awe as well.

"You're a badass." Wesley grinned at her as the frigid water hit our stomachs with a punch.

"You think this is the grossest thing I've been covered in?" She lifted her eyebrow, stepping farther in with a smirk. "Luv, this is nothing." She went in, keeping the gun and backpack above her head as she progressed across the small lake.

Killian's nose flared, and I noticed the glare he shot Wesley before he realized it and forced his expression to go blank, trudging into the water behind her.

Flames flickered off the water, the cries of death and battle and gunfire ringing in the air. The seven of us traveled quickly across, but Caden was the first to reach the shore, rushing out without hesitation. His clothes clung to his solid frame. He was built from years of training, but the guy seemed bigger than I recall, his back heaving with rage as he moved through a passage between buildings.

"Caden?" Birdie hissed his name, but he didn't respond, his legs picking up his pace.

"Shit!" I scrambled after him, Birdie and I getting to the end of the passage at the same time.

We both stopped.

In the middle of hundreds of hundreds of faux soldiers was exactly who Caden had said. Kek, Ash, Lukas, and Warwick battled the tsunami of endless men coming at them, their chances dwindling by the second.

Warwick was battling at least ten, while I noticed a guard push in closer, his rifle pointed at the legend's head. My mouth opened to yell, to warn him.

A roar sliced through the night, Caden's shoulders expanding as he picked up a rifle from one of the dead. His back muscles flexed as he hurled it like an axe, the spear on the end slicing through the guard's neck like a guillotine. Blood gushed out, his head only hanging on by a tendon, his body dropping to the ground. Warwick whipped around to Caden. The Wolf's face was smeared with blood and vengeance.

They only glared at each other for a moment before they both jumped back into fighting, Warwick's claw hacking through two soldiers at once. It was only a moment, but watching Caden and Warwick fight near each other had chills running down my limbs. Their movements, the energy coming off them—it was the same.

Birdie's small gasp next to me told me she saw the same thing.

Footsteps pummeled the pavement behind us, the rest of our group catching up, jolting Birdie and me from our spot. Guns blazing, the rest of us leaped into the fold.

Ignoring the bitter cold seeping into my clothes, adrenaline spiked my body with heat while tearing through a layer of soldiers coming behind Ash and Lukas.

"About time you fuckers arrived," Ash smirked as he shot one and sliced into another with a sword.

"Sorry, we decided to take a little dip in the lake first. Get refreshed," I countered, jumping behind one and snapping his neck.

A bundle of guards went flying back, and I craned my head to see Kek, her eyes pitch black, an evil smirk on her face as she tore through another row.

"Someone is having fun." I swung around, stabbing a guard in the throat with a dagger. "But I think we need to get the hell out of here."

"I couldn't agree more," Ash replied, a bullet grazing his temple. "Like now."

It wouldn't be long before their number started to overrun us completely. Killian and Wesley shielded Rosie as she shot everything that moved. Her combat skills were not even on the playing field of what was needed here. It was only time before they got one of us.

"We need a diversion!" Birdie yelled at us. "Or we're toast."

Scanning the area, trying to come up with an idea, a memory tickled the back of my head, swinging me around to the tiny blonde. "B, remember how we escaped that prison in Istanbul?"

Her eyes grew wide as she took down three huge guys near her. "Yes… but we need gunpowder and a charge."

Fire blazed the roof, but it was too far for what we needed.

My attention returned to Kek as her demon powers yanked more men off the ground, sending them back into each other and knocking them down like dominos.

Birdie followed my gaze, her mouth parting.

"I think we have the charge." I smirked.

"Fuck a whole barrel of monkeys," she muttered.

I took that as a yes.

"Rosie!" I bellowed out. "Get all the gunpowder you can from your bullets now."

Rosie's eyebrows furrowed, but she didn't question me. Wesley and Killian stepped up closer to guard her as she emptied her chamber, yanking the bullet shells apart and pouring the gunpowder into her hand.

A cry of pain tore my focus from Rosie. I knew the voice without looking, but when I did, my gut wrenched up into my lungs.

"Hanna!"

A bullet went through her hip, dropping her to the ground. My muscles moved before my brain fully registered what had happened. The need to protect her, shield her from any more harm, raced me over there, mowing down the culprits, blasting every bullet I had into their corpses.

"You okay?" I reached for her. "Can you get up?"

A growl rose from her throat, her eyes narrowing like a cat's, ready to attack. I leaned down, and her canines, sharp and pointed, snapped at me.

"Hanna…" I said her name slowly and calmly, my hands going up in defense. "I need you here with me, little viper."

She blinked, her body jerking, realizing what she had done. What she became.

I reached my hand out again.

"I'm fine." She shoved my hand away with anger, struggling to her feet, pain flickering through her expression. I grabbed her to keep her upright. "Get off me. I said I was fine." She pushed away from me, blood dripping to the ground.

"Scorpion, I got all I can!" Rosie took my attention away

155

from Hanna for a moment, trying to ignore the sting of her rebuff.

"Get Rosie over to Kek," I ordered Killian and Wesley. No other time in the world would I be demanding anything from the fae lord, but things were not normal right now.

"Kek!" I called over to her, waiting for her to look at me. "I need you to send that gunpowder up." My head flicked up at the burning roof.

A slow, terrifying smile cut across the demon's face. She understood.

Gunpowder plus fire equaled the only escape we had.

Another cry hit my ears as a rifle spear went through Lukas's arm. Warwick, Caden, and Ash were already wounded before we even arrived. We were going down quick.

Wesley and Killian fought to get Rosie to Kek, the blue-haired demon meeting them halfway when a rumble vibrated the ground. My focus followed the noise, terror freezing me in place when I saw two tanks rolling past the troops, coming for us, several guns besides the main cannon pointed at our group.

"Kek, now!" I screamed.

With her mind powers, Kek blew the powder in Rosie's hands toward the roof.

The tank's cannon was turned to face us, the soldiers inside probably not caring if they took dozens of their own men out as well, as long as they got us.

My gaze followed the powder, watching it drift to the flames. Kek let it drop.

"Duck!" I yelled out too late.

Boooooooooom!

The blast pushed out searing heat, scorching my face as the pressure tossed us all up into the air like rag dolls. My frame tumbled to the ground, rolling across the pavement into the grass, too stunned to feel any pain yet.

My ears rang, everything sounding far away, my mind jumbled, but I knew I needed to get up. This was our only chance.

"Hanna?" I hollered for her, though I could barely hear myself. Standing up, I saw hundreds of bodies laid out, most with melted faces or no longer in one piece, some on fire.

Fuck.

"Hanna!" I bellowed louder.

"Hey! Come on. We have to go." Wesley darted into my view. Rosie, Killian, Kek, Lukas, and Ash were with him.

"Go!" I yelled at him, motioning to run. I wouldn't leave without her.

Warwick carried Birdie, her face burned from the blast, with Caden following behind, retreating before more guards started moving in, taking over for their dead brethren.

Panic caught in my throat when I spotted blonde hair, pieces of it singed black.

"Fuck! Hanna!" I scrambled over bodies to her. She laid half underneath a corpse, and I pushed it off her. "Hanna... wake up." Fuck. Fuck. Fuck.

I shoved her again. "You can't die on me, little viper. I know you want to kick my ass too much." She didn't move. "Hanna!" Terror cut through me. The memory of losing Maddox was still so raw. I couldn't lose her. I knew I wouldn't recover if I did. I barely knew or liked the girl, but everything in me wailed like a storm, furious and ready to slaughter the world.

The stomping of new soldiers' feet grew louder as the tank rolled closer. The regime was moving in.

"Hanna." I shook her violently, reaching for the link with Brexley, for any power that might hum in my veins to help Hanna. "Please. Wake. Up!"

Her eyes bolted open, her mouth opening in a gasp for oxygen.

157

Relief almost sank me down through the dirt, the ache in my chest loosening as I watched her eyes dart around, then land on me. The moment they did, something skimmed against my chest, like she was peeling it open.

"You okay?"

She nodded.

"Come on." I yanked her up. Soldiers started to get through the arched gateway, moving around the tank. "We've got to go." I got her up to her feet. "Can you stand and run on your own?"

She bobbed her head again, dazed, but her feet were solid enough under her. Tugging on her wrist, we took off into the park, the trees creating thick shadows, hiding us from our enemies. I picked up the pace. Soon I realized she was no longer beside me.

Snapping around, I spotted her standing there, gazing back as more and more of the faux-fae army moved in, the flames still crackling over the castle roof and grounds.

"Hanna?" I whispered hoarsely.

She didn't respond. Her hands flexed and unflexed, her chest heaving.

My stomach twisted, dread washing over me. Somehow, I understood, without knowing how. A battle was raging inside her as if a part of her felt tied to them. They were like her. Her kind.

"Hanna…" Once again, my voice was low and soothing. "Hanna, please turn around and come with me."

Her hand rolled into a tight ball, her muscles twitching.

"Hanna." I stepped closer. "You are not one of them."

Her head shot back, her body defensive.

I forced a soft smile to touch my lips. "Come on, little viper. You know you'd rather stay with m—us." *Why did I almost say me?* "I'll give you plenty of chances to kick my ass and punch me in the face."

158

She swallowed, as if she was fighting against her instincts, then gave one more glance back at the regime before she turned to me and started to run, her wounded hip only slowing her a bit.

The bleeding had already stopped, and I felt if I had the chance to look at the bullet wound, it would be healing. Something that certified she was no longer just human.

We had all seen what had happened to those who took the pills firsthand. What they turned into. But she ran next to me, covered in blood, wounds, soot, and algae. I promised myself I would do whatever the fuck it took to stop it from happening to this amazing woman.

And promises were binding.

Chapter 15
Caden

Our group tore through the dark streets of Savage Lands, getting as far away from our enemy and the base as possible before we spoke. Birdie was back on her feet, though moving a bit slower. Most of us were injured in some way, but we didn't stop, following the one who seemed to take lead without even wanting to.

Hate coursed through me as I watched the back of this head, inches above everyone else, weaving us toward a destination. Even Killian didn't fight when Warwick started moving us through the streets. Though, if we followed or not, I'm not sure he cared. He was set on his location, and we either kept up or fucked off.

What had happened earlier was growing louder and louder in my head. My instinct and actions. What it felt like when I was battling. Killing. I had always been a good fighter. Top of my class. But this was different. This was like it thrummed through my veins, pounded my heart, and took over my body and mind. The need for revenge. The desire to destroy every enemy I had and burn this world to ash. Anger was never a trait of mine. I had been a very happy-go-lucky kid. My frustration with my father or vexation with Brexley's antics fizzled out in moments. Now that rage was what filled my lungs and fed my appetite.

Well, it was one of the things.

Killing and fucking. Those were the only things on my mind now.

I'd had my fair share of sex, but I can't say I was aggressive. It wasn't really my style. It just happened, the girl usually pushing it more than I wanted because most of the time, I secretly wanted to crawl into bed with Brexley.

Whatever essence Warwick gave me, it was a craving I could barely breathe around. It dominated and controlled. And it wasn't slow and tender. It was brutal and bloodthirsty. Denying it was pointless, but accepting it felt even worse.

What my father wanted, what he thought was a failure… had worked. I carried some of Warwick's essence.

The Legend. The Wolf. The killer.

Merited or not, I fucking hated Warwick for it. I detested the man before, but now I had this tie to him, a connection that was unrelenting. A need to protect him when all I wanted to do was kill him myself. It could be quiet, or it could roar like thunder, but it was always there. And I felt no peace now.

"Szar." Ash puffed next to Warwick as we rounded another corner, jogging down an alley that smelled of dead carcasses, piss, and trash. Everywhere you looked it was even more rundown—garbage, bullet holes, and burnt-out buildings. I had never been much outside the walls of Leopold before I was taken by Sarkis's army, but even I knew this area within Savage Lands was the most dangerous. "Haven't been back here in a long time."

"Like you'd remember anyway." Warwick scoffed, stopping in front of an unmarked door. He peered around before knocking. After a moment, he knocked again. A

161

scraping sound jolted me to a peephole being opened at the top.

Warwick's mouth didn't even open before it slammed shut.

"Hey, asshole." He banged on the wood again. "Open up."

"Kurwa." Fuck! A Polish accent hissed through the door.

There were a few beats before the locks unbolted and the door swung open. A big, burly man with a reddish-brown beard wearing a stained apron waved us in. His scowl lined his forehead and bald head, his meaty hands appearing like they could snap all of us in half. He was about my height, but the man had an aura that said *do not fuck with me.*

"Hurry the hell up," he growled, his head popping out and checking the alley before he slammed and locked the door behind us. "What am I, a fuckin' halfway house now?" He motioned to all of us, landing on Warwick, peering around as if he was searching for someone. "Already moved on from the girl? Knew you couldn't stick with one pussy." He folded his arms, taking my attention to the gore-covered apron. The odor of blood and meat wafted through my nose with sharp intensity.

"You think I would be here unless it was an urgent situation?" Warwick grunted, stepping into the man's face. Though he was shorter than Warwick, I had a feeling this guy could hold his own. "And I warned you, Gawel, if you spoke like that again about her…" Warwick reached for his throat.

"Whoa!" Ash leaped between the two men. "Step back," he ordered Warwick; his green eyes locked on his buddy without an ounce of fear. "Take a breath." He was probably one of the only people who could get away with telling Farkas what to do.

162

"Ash." The man, Gawel, addressed the tree fairy. "Shouldn't be surprised to see you still running around with this asshole."

"Good to see you too, Gawel," Ash replied evenly. I couldn't tell if he meant it or not.

Warwick finally let him go, inhaling deeply, but his glare still burned into Gawel.

"We need assistance," Warwick replied through his teeth.

"There is no way I'm letting you guys downstairs. Things are precarious enough right now. There are spies fucking everywhere. We've heard the bombings from here, and rumor is that the fae side has taken over, though some say it's HDF."

"It's both," Ash replied. "Sort of."

"Both?" Gawel's eyes squinted, bouncing between him and Farkas, searching for the lie.

"We don't have time to explain." Ash glanced back quickly at Lukas. "But just know Savage Lands has been claimed by an Aneira disciple."

Gawel's nose flared, anger flickering in his eyes when that name was mentioned. I didn't know much about the old Seelie queen, except she had been a tyrant. Wanted humans to be killed or enslaved. She also hated the Unseelie, thinking them lesser than Seelie fae.

"We need a place to hide tonight." Warwick's lack of patience leaped over Ash. "We will also need transportation to get us out of this city by dawn."

"For all of you? By dawn?" Gawel scanned all eleven of us, his head wagging. "Impossible."

"Figure it out." A snarl rose up Warwick's throat, and I could feel his anger trigger mine, tightening up my shoulders. His energy bounced around me like a ball, as my body absorbed it, my muscles twitching to fight again.

163

As if she could sense the tiny shift in me, feel the potency coming off me, Birdie peered over her shoulder. A graze of her eyes glided down my frame, accelerating the verve of my fury. She drove me crazy. Always fucking there, always taunting me, challenging me, and I wanted it to go away. *Her* to go away. Stop making me feel things I was ashamed to feel. She was fae, and even if I no longer completely saw them the way I once had, it didn't mean my principles changed about who I'd be with.

Humans—that was who I was *supposed* to be attracted to.

But with just a glimpse of her heated gaze, the way she teased me, my dick had other ideas. It wanted nothing more than to slide deep into her, pounding the fuck out of her. I had jerked off to that fantasy a dozen times, but I always felt disgusted with myself. Dirty. Wrong.

"You will have your cut, Gawel." Ash once again stepped between him and Warwick. "We just need it for six."

"You will get more for each one you can get," Warwick rumbled, sounding more like a threat than a barter.

Gawel's jaw clamped down; eventually he nodded. "Follow me." He turned for a dark hallway, the scent of dead animal carcasses sharp in the air. Knives, saws, and hooks lined the passage he took us down. This place was a butcher's shop, but I had a feeling it wasn't just animal meat he hacked up in here.

Gawel led us to another door which was hacked out from the neighboring wall and had expanded his space into the building next door. He swung it open and ushered us into the pungent, noisy room. We were surrounded by the stench of manure and musty straw, the sound of snorting pigs and bleating lambs.

Gawel lit a lantern, the space glowing with dim light. It

was much larger than I thought. Once a storefront, most likely with flats above, it had since been burned out. The windows were boarded up, the ground layered with straw as a few pigs and sheep inside wood pens paced around, not realizing this was their final stop before death.

"You can stay in here. There is an upstairs, but the only heat will be near the animals." My father had us study old history books from long ago, when people would put animals on the ground level and build their homes above to warm the main room of their home. It stunk, but better than freezing to death. "I don't think I have to tell you to stay fucking put." He hooked the lamp onto a post. "I'll get you some food and drink."

"And some bandages and rubbing alcohol," Scorpion piped up, looking at Hanna briefly, her hip barely bleeding anymore.

"And clothes if you can." Ash signaled to the lot of us, probably already heading toward hypothermia. "Thank you, Gawel."

"Yeah." The grumpy man huffed before turning back for the main building, shutting the door and leaving us alone. It was the first moment we had to breathe. The first chance to process what had happened tonight.

All I felt was rage. My emotions were balanced on a blade's edge, and when I slid off, it would get bloody.

Warwick paced, his hand running over his tied-up hair over and over. When his agitation grew, so did mine. A sound I had never made before, a sort of growl, hummed in my lungs, rattling my vocals, my eyes going back and forth over the spot he walked.

"Now that we have a moment, we need to go over what happened this evening." Killian took the lead. "What we learned inside HDF."

My head jerked to Killian. Rosie was at his side, pulling off the damp backpack and unzipping the pouch.

"First, I need to know everyone got out safe," Killian said.

"Yes." Ash nodded. "We got everyone out. Barely, but Mykel is taking them to a safe location."

"My mother?" My voice was hoarse and clipped.

"Yes. She's with Mykel. She is fine." Ash assured me.

My head lowered in relief.

"How do we find them? Do we know where they went?" Birdie wiped at the drying blood on her hands.

"Right before I went on the mission, I told Mykel of a location. If anything happened to me, I had another safehouse near Csehvár. He would head there."

"So we catch up with them tomorrow?" Wesley pulled off his soaking jacket.

"Head wherever the fuck you want." Warwick's stopped, his eyes glancing at Scorpion. "I'm heading to Ukraine."

"You found her, didn't you?" Scorpion's spine straightened. "I thought I felt it. Did you see her?"

Warwick's chin dipped in a yes.

"Where is she?"

"All I know is she's in Ukraine." Farkas's voice went even lower. "Tracker was there."

"What?" Lukas exclaimed. "Tracker? How? Why? How?"

"He was in a Ukraine military uniform. Istvan has to be there."

"But where exactly is she? Is she okay?" Ash's concern was written all over his face.

A flash of jealousy burned through me. Warwick, Ash, Killian, and Scorpion all were waiting on a breath. All for *my* girl. She was supposed to be mine. I was the one who held her after her father died, who died when I thought she did on that bridge. I had always been too scared to cross the line. To tell her how I felt.

To disobey my father.

Now I was too late.

"Tracker was there when I linked with her. She was hiding from him. I couldn't tell where exactly she was... she cut me off too soon. I need to find her now." Warwick's muscles were so tense, ready to bolt the moment Gawel found him a motorcycle.

"She was spotted in Ternopil," Killian stated, jerking everyone's head to him.

"What?" Warwick rumbled, stomping closer to him.

"Kalaraja. He's working with Sonya and Andor. He has people out there, and when they realized she wasn't with us, they went searching. There have been sightings of her. If he knows, others will."

"Tracker will find her," Lukas spoke up. "He wasn't called Tracker for nothing. Mykel had him trained since he was twelve."

"Great." Ash rubbed his head.

"To confirm what Scorpion had heard—it's true. The king and queen have sent their bounty hunters." Killian swallowed. "To kill her."

A snarl vibrated the room, Warwick's frame expanding, magic crackling through him like a dark cloud, taking over every inch.

I felt every ounce of his wrath pound against my skin, my own absorbing it, rolling in it, responding to it. Violence coated my tongue.

"Warwick." Ash placed his palm on the Wolf's arm. "Calm down. You can't help her like this."

167

Warwick flicked Ash's hand off like a fly, his chest heaving with ferocity, his voice barely coming out human. "No one fucking touches my mate."

Mate.

One word detonated inside my brain. All I saw was red. All I wanted was to kill.

The girl I had grown up with, who every male in this room seemed to be willing to lay their life on the line for. And I was no different. Brexley was *mine*. The girl I had teased and loved. The girl always pushing and testing me. The *woman* Farkas swept in and took. Something in me understood what mate meant. It was beyond any human notion of commitment, marriage, or love.

It was forever.

I hated him before. I wanted to destroy him now.

A roar pierced the air, and I barreled for him, seething with everything I loathed him for.

Reacting faster than I expected, he whirled on me, a fist slamming into my jaw, tossing me back on my ass.

"Caden!" I heard a woman yell, but my brain spun, the embarrassment flipping to a frenzy in a second.

Darkness.

Death.

Power.

Magic.

My body couldn't handle it, the explosion of sensations, the high of magic. Nothing in my life had ever come close to the abundance flooding my veins. The power of my rage was loud. It screamed into my muscles, roared through my blood, and shredded the back of my throat as I leaped for the man, our forms colliding with brutality. He was my nemesis in every way, but I now had this link to him, one I would never be relieved of, forever punishing me.

My own prison.

I didn't care if some of my hate should be directed at my father. He did this to me. I had been violated. Demeaned. I wasn't enough for my dad. Ever.

He turned me into this.

A fae.

I had known the moment I sucked in air back in the lab that something was off. I was no longer human, but an animal like the human zombies my father created. Full of rage and death.

The Caden before was long gone.

"Back off, junior." Warwick's knuckles dove into my gut, bending me over. Everyone was watching, but I could feel her eyes on me the most, adding to my humiliation. "I'm warning you."

"Fuck you, Farkas!" My punch cracked across his cheek, stumbling him back. Not hesitating, I lunged forward, my foot kicking into his leg as I went to punch again.

"Oh, mini me thinks he can take me on?" Warwick spat on the straw, our fight stirring the animals into a frenzy. "Bring it, captain one-pump." He grinned, blood coloring his saliva, before his punch slammed me back into the post.

"Stop!" Lukas tried to move in, but Ash laid an arm across his chest, his head wagging, telling him no.

"You hate me because of this?" Warwick motioned between us. "How the fuck do you think I feel? I was forced. It's my essence in your system, ripped from me. I don't want it with you any more than you do."

"We finally agree on something." I swung, striking his kidney, before he darted back, a sardonic smile growing on his face.

"Or is this about Brexley? The fact you didn't want her until you were already engaged. Safe. Convenient. Just admit it, Markos. You only wanted her when she no longer wanted you."

"Fuck you!" I punched and weaved, moving in closer. "You know nothing about our history."

"History," Warwick repeated. "Not present. Not future. She was never meant for you. I saw that the night you finally kissed her up on the roof of HDF. There was nothing there."

"What?" I jerked back, feeling blood trailing down my face.

"I was there that night, through *our* link. Watching two people with no chemistry fumble and grope like pre-teens. It was pathetic." He smirked. "And you want to talk about history? Kovacs and I go back far longer than you, douchebag." His arm went out, crashing into my nose, blood spurting everywhere. His foot hooked my ankle and flipped me onto my back with a thud in seconds. He leaned over, his fingers clutching my chin painfully. "You ever come at me again, I will fucking kill you. This was out of respect for *my fucking mate*. She still likes you." He spat with a snarl. "But don't challenge me again. You're nothing but a baby fae in diapers. And I'm the motherfucking monster." He let go, growling before he stomped away.

Eyes bored into me, and the embarrassment of getting my ass kicked so easily only fired me up more. I wasn't stupid enough to go after him again, but if I didn't get away, I'd be killing someone else. I might not be Warwick's level of legend, but I still had it, and I knew I could easily execute someone. The soldiers from HDF earlier, some I even recognized, I cut through like butter.

And I *loved* it.

Scrambling up, a rumble echoed in my chest as I took off up the stairs to the gutted flats above. There were no walls or much left, but it gave me space away from everyone. Room for the blistering mortification and rage to expand. My legs gobbled up the length of the building until my boots rammed into the foundation wall, my fist connecting with it in a loud roar.

Over and over, my knuckles cracked and smacked against the surface, feeling no pain. Blood smeared as bits of the plaster crumbled down. I felt so much anger that I wanted to explode. I had no control over what was happening to me. Though I felt a dark part was always there, and I reveled in it. Felt free for the first time in my life.

This only set me off more. The hurt, grief, and rage swallowed me. I was taught all my life to hate fae; they were soulless monsters. Somewhere along the way, my father's desire to be superior twisted him up so much—brainwashed him—that he turned us into a Frankenstein's monster version of them.

He turned his own son into something he conditioned me to despise.

Red liquid painted the walls, dripping to the floor, a bellow roaring from me, the sound of my flesh and bone hitting the wall.

"Caden!" My name rang through the room. A tiny figure grabbed for my arm, cracking into the red haze I was in. "Stop!"

I didn't know if I could. There was so much rage in me, and I couldn't lessen the pressure inside enough.

"Stop it!" Her voice pierced the veil, her strong grip pulling my fist away from the wall, putting herself in front of the spot before my hand came down on it again.

"Fuck!" My arms jerked back, realizing I almost struck her. "What the hell?" I seethed, my teeth gritting. I saw this tiny woman, her jaw tight, her stance ready to challenge me.

Her face was still half blackened from the earlier explosion, cuts and bruises covering her. "I almost hit you."

"I hit back." Birdie's white-blonde hair was up in a high ponytail, still wet from the lake. I felt an urge to wrap my bleeding hand around it, staining the light locks with my blood. The need to yank hard on it until she submitted spread like fire through my lungs. I would never admit each time I looked at her, something deep in me reacted.

It wanted.

Birdie was nothing I normally would ever be attracted to.

With her heavily lined eyes and red-painted lips, she was dressed in all black like some dark angel sent down to destroy. She was aggressive, blunt, and drove me up the wall. Most of the time, I wanted to strangle her.

The other part of the time… was where the darkness lay. The depraved, immoral part of me bubbled up. It longed for her to hit me back, to feel her nails cut into my skin as I fucked her so hard she could no longer move. I wanted to blame Warwick, say this came from him, but it had always been there, pushed far back behind what was righteous and respectable. I was the model of a good, decent man and future general.

That Caden was the one being pushed back now.

"Go away," I growled at her, my shoulders twitching back, her presence only adding to the aggression hammering through my veins.

"No." She slipped farther in front of me, the blood on the wall spreading and coating her hair and clothes.

My blood.

My chest heaved, my dick hardening as a possessive growl rolled through me.

"I am warning you." I tried to lock my feet in place, to

not move to her. Though I was afraid if she ran, I would go after her anyway. "Leave now."

"Or what, pretty boy?" Birdie slanted her head, her voice taunting me. "You think I'm afraid of you?" She snorted like that was the stupidest thing she'd ever heard. "Of what you are *becoming*?"

I jolted at her words, sucking in sharply through my nose. Her scent filled my nostrils, tightening my balls. Sweet, but a touch of spice too... just like *her*.

"You're just starting to become interesting." Her light blue eyes held mine, provoking me. "Less breakable, and a lot less vanilla."

My brows furrowed, my chest pumping up and down. "Vanilla?"

"Most humans are, but you seemed purposeful in being an idea of something. A self-righteous boring carbon copy of what your father wanted."

"Watch yourself..." I stepped to her, my height and physique towering over her, sparking her eyes. I could feel the heat coming off her, her sexual energy licking my skin. My cock twitched, pulsing with a need I couldn't even explain, sweat dripping down my back.

"You probably had the blandest sex, didn't you?" She peered up at me, her voice thick, only upping my anger at how easily she could make me forget everything I believed in. "Be honest with yourself, Caden. You can blame whatever happened to you at that lab all you want. And I'm not saying your emotions aren't out of control... but this is the most real you've ever been. You crave the debauchery. The darkness. You want the violence. To give yourself over to the feral and depraved."

"I said watch yourself." Impulse raged through me, my hand wrapping around her throat, slamming her harder into the wall, my body pressing into hers. "Shut your mouth."

173

"Make me, pretty boy." She lifted her chin, her own chest pumping. I could feel her nipples harden against my chest, my cock carving into her stomach, trying to burrow through the layers and bury inside her. My muscles trembled with savagery, the sensation so strong that I could no longer think.

I just wanted. Except for that tiny part that still told me this was wrong. Dirty.

"I know what you need." She swallowed as my hand pressed down harder on her throat. "It's too much, isn't it?" Her hand wiggled between us, rubbing at my rock-hard dick. I hissed, my body reacting in contradiction to my mind, grinding into her. "You feel like you're going to explode." Fuck, did I. All the time now. "Fae have to release the extra energy that builds up from magic. It's why we're so horny all the time." She tugged at my jeans, unbuttoning them. I didn't stop her. I didn't move away. I stayed locked in place, her small hand not hesitating as it gripped me, causing a loud groan to heave from my lungs. A simple touch from her, and I felt every barrier crumbling.

"Pokol." Hell. She gasped, her hand rubbing down my length, struggling to wrap around. "Fuck, you *are* huge." She blinked. "I didn't believe her."

"Who?"

"Brexley. The girl who you *think* you love but actually don't. You just miss her being in love *with you.*"

My shoulders wrenched back. Her claim was like an arrow to my gut, hollowing out my chest and surging thunder through me. I pulled away from her, feeling myself grow and expand as the storm surged inside.

"Shut. The. Fuck. Up!"

"Tell me I'm wrong." She pushed off the wall, taking back the space I put between us. This girl was unrelenting. Fearless.

"Get the fuck away from me. You know nothing."

"I see it much clearer than you do. You are so used to her being there, fawning over you, being the girl in the background you could always count on but never chose."

Anger heaved through every molecule of my skin.

"I'm warning you."

"Like I said, pretty boy, I'm not scared of you." She got right in my face. "You're angry because you know deep down, I'm right."

My head wagged, my nostrils flaring.

"Then tell me I'm wrong." She shoved at my chest hard.

"Stop," I grunted.

"No!" She punched at my torso, scorching heat flaring through my bones. "Tell me I'm wrong." She shoved at me again. "Tell me!" She hit me again. "Say i—"

Something snapped inside me. "SHUT UP!" I bellowed, my hand clutching her hips. Her legs wrapped around my waist as I rammed her hard against the wall, shoving her into the crumbling plaster, my blood smeared behind her.

My mouth crashed down on hers. Claiming hers with rough, unrestrained need. My hips slammed into her, crushing her harder into the wall. Birdie groaned, her mouth hungry, her hands frantically ripping at my clothes. "Take your rage out on me. Use me. This doesn't have to be anything more." She bit into my lip until I tasted blood. "I want pain... make me bleed too."

Fuck.

Her dark pleas roared every fiber of my being to life, hitting me like a tsunami. She tapped into my deepest desires. Every barrier snapped in half, a feral noise coming from my throat.

Bucking my hips into her, I clutched her ponytail, wrapping it around my hand before tugging it hard. Her head slammed back into the wall, her pussy pulsing against my stomach as she groaned.

There was nothing else but her. That sound wrapped around my dick and latched on. I wanted to never hear anything else but her moans.

My mouth took hers again; my tongue prodded her mouth, inhaling her, consuming, deepening our already desperate hunger.

"Caden…" She clawed at my jacket, tearing it off before yanking my shirt over my head, biting and nipping at my mouth and neck, the damp clothes dropping to the floor. She finished unbuttoning my pants, dropping them to my ankles, her hand gripping me hard. "Fuck me. Now."

Her words and action drove straight to my dick, pulsing it to painful levels. There were no thoughts anymore except for getting inside her.

Reaching for her top, my hands shredded the fabric in seconds.

"Shit." Her chest surged, her eyes wide at how easily I had done it. Somewhere in the back of my head, I knew I shouldn't… the human me wouldn't be able to, but the thought barely registered as I peeled off her bra, my eyes taking in her breasts. Small, but fuck, were they perfect. My tongue slid over one, sucking, as my hands yanked off her pants and shoes.

I didn't hesitate as my fingers thrust into her pussy.

"Fuuuck." My eyes flickered back at her wetness. It dripped down her leg, my two fingers easily sliding in.

Her hips thrust against me as I pumped in and out. "More! Stop being polite, pretty boy." Her palm wrapped around my neck, squeezing.

The zing exploding through me shattered any last inhibitions I might have been holding. The pounding through my cock turned me into an animal.

Ripping her underwear, I shoved her higher up the wall, her bare skin rubbing through my blood on the wall as I spread her wide.

I plunged my dick into her pussy.

A bellow howled from me, my legs almost collapsing underneath me, my body jolting as I slammed into the hilt.

The most unbelievable pleasure sizzled every inch of me. I had never felt anything like it, my head spinning so bad I had to plant my hands on the wall next to her head to keep steady.

"FUCK!" Birdie arched her back, clawing at my shoulders, blood bubbling under her marks, heaving as my cock stretched her. "Oh gods!"

"You're so fucking tight." I pulled out, shoving back into her again, causing a growl from me. "Shit!" My body took over, wanting to be deeper. To own all of her. I had no control.

Birdie gaped, her hips slamming back into mine, both of us frantic with need. I pounded her into the wall, no reprieve as she cried out, giving it back to me with as much desperation. I could feel the magic pulsing between us with every thrust, threading the air, intensifying everything. Magic was a distant concept to me growing up. It was there but had nothing to do with me. Now it hummed through me, powering my drive and taking me to a high I never knew before.

It was like tasting flavor you never even knew existed, and now you could never go back. Everything would be flavorless and dull in comparison.

Bits of the wall crumbled to the ground as I hitched her legs up higher, grabbing onto her shins, opening her wider as I plowed deeper into her.

"Caden! Oh gods!" Her tits bounced, wrapping my

177

tongue around her nipple before nipping it with my teeth. I felt her pussy squeeze around me. "More. Fuck me harder!"

With a growl, I pulled out, twisting her around. I flattened her into the wall, clutching her ponytail and rearing her head back as I drove my cock back into her pussy.

"Fuck!" we both cried out, the sensation not lessening. If anything, every time I went deeper into her, it only got more intense.

"Take it out on me. I want your rage." She curved her head to the side, her nails digging into the wall, running her fingers through the blood there. Her back was coated in it, her hair dyed red.

Something about that tipped me over the edge.

All the wrath inside me, all the pain and hate—she became a target for it all. For the truths I didn't want to see and the lies I wanted to believe. Birdie became the punishment and penance.

Our brutal sounds echoed through the empty room. I couldn't get deep enough; I couldn't seem to have enough, not able to find my resolution.

Snarling, I yanked her off the wall, taking her to her hands and knees. My body raged; the need to destroy everything was zeroed in on her. I had never put a girl in this position before. The old Caden felt it was vulgar.

The darkness in me seemed to come alive the cruder it was. Liked it. Reveled in it. And the girl under me liked it more.

"Yes! Fuck me." Birdie slammed back into me as I tugged on her hair, fucking her ferociously. I snarled and hissed, wrenching her hair harder, our rhythm brutal. My fingers slipped over where my cock plunged into her, spreading through the wetness dripping from her and rubbing through her folds to her core.

178

A low deep moan curved her back, her arms trembling. A sensation washed over me, something deep inside, my voice not even sounding like me. It was possessive. Demanding. "This is fucking mine." I pinched at her clit. "No one else's."

"*Baszni!*" She went on her elbows, my dick hitting deeper.

I hissed, sweat dripping down me, my balls tightening.

"Fuck! I'm going to come." She dug into the floor with her nails, her back bowing.

"No." I wrapped my hand around her neck, drawing her body up with mine, her back pressed to my torso, taking her even deeper and harder. Holding her in place as I punished her. "Do you understand? No one else fucks this pussy." I bit at her ear.

She gritted her teeth, her walls constricting around my dick.

"Birdie," I growled, squeezing down on her neck.

"Yes. Fuck, yes… No one else, I promise." She cried out. Her head twisted to the side to peer at me. "Now choke me and make me come."

Blood roared in my ears. My fingers clamped down on her fragile neck, my teeth biting into her as my other hand rubbed through her.

Her body jolted, and a strangled scream tore through the room, her pussy clamping down around me as she came, her body locked down so hard a thread of pain danced through me.

Nothing in this world, or any other, felt so unbelievably good.

The walls vibrated with my roar as I released inside her, coming so hard I lost my hearing and sight. All my senses were gone except for her. For how this felt. The magic slammed through me, wrapping around my cock as I continued to empty myself in her. Her body shivered, another orgasm ripping through her, intensifying mine. I never wanted it to end. I never wanted to not be inside her.

"Fuuuuuuccckkk!" Another roar tore out of me, the bliss almost overwhelming as she jerked and cried out with me. We slumped to the ground, my body falling on hers, pushing against her tight hold on my cock, forcing another piercing moan to rattle the room.

Several moments passed. Our sweaty bodies lay where we collapsed, our lungs drawing in huge gulps of air. She sucked in, feeling me still coming inside her. How was that possible? How was I already hardening again just looking at the scrapes on her back and my blood tainting her skin? Why did I already have the desire to flip her over and start again?

As the high started to drop me back to earth, the realization of what I did, what I said, and who I did it with crept in.

Holy shit. I just fucked a fae. And all I wanted was to do it again…

Fighting the urge, I rolled off, pulling out of her, watching my cum ooze down her thighs. I didn't want to admit that it took everything in me to not roll right back on and be inside her again.

I blew out a breath, rubbing my face, no longer knowing what to say. Movement next to me popped my head back up. Birdie stood, her legs wobbling, but she walked back for her clothes.

"What are you doing?"

"Getting dressed." She grabbed for her shredded shirt, frowning. "I'm taking yours." She picked mine off the floor, not even looking at me.

"Uh. Yeah." I was stunned by her nonchalant attitude.

Every girl I had ever been with, I had to gnaw my arm off to get away. They trailed after me for weeks, asking for another "time" together.

This girl couldn't get away fast enough.

What just happened between us? I couldn't even try to find words for it. I was still coated with her, cum dripping down her leg, and I was reeling.

"So, umm…"

"Let's not make this a big deal." She hopped back into her pants, pulling on my damp shirt, covering up the marks I made on her body, the blood still smearing over her skin.

I hated it.

"We both got what we wanted. You feel better, right?"

"Yeah." I didn't realize until she asked how much I did. All the anger I had was diminished. "Thanks."

She shrugged again, stepping into her boots. "Like I said, it's why fae fuck all the time. Magic builds up and needs a release." She swiped up her jacket. "No biggie."

Why did that feel like a punch to the gut?

"Yeah, great." I stood up. "Glad we're on the same page."

Her gaze rolled down my naked body, her teeth biting into her bottom lip. Just that made me harden again, the look spearing heat through me.

She shook her head away from me, clearing her throat. "Okay, well… it was nice." She turned to head back toward the stairs.

"Nice?" That was the last thing I'd call it. Nice was dull. *Boring*.

She peeked back over her shoulder at me, a smile hinting on her puffy lips.

"Not so vanilla, pretty boy. Though I still feel you're not really letting yourself go."

"What?" I guffawed, my eyes bugging out, shocked by her response. My dick was raw, and from the way she walked, I knew she was beyond sore. "Seriously?"

"You're too scared because you know once you do, you'll have to accept the truth."

"And what's that?"

"You aren't human anymore." Birdie strolled away, her figure gobbled up by the shadows and darkness, leaving me standing there with her parting words.

A spurt of anger smacked into my ribs, heating my face. Because I knew she was right.

Chapter 16
Warwick

"Bitzy! Be careful… that one wakes up biting."

Chirppppp.

"I never said I liked it! That was a total misunderstanding."

A groan boiled up the back of my throat, my lids squeezing together, wishing the voices were a dream.

Chirrrrrpp. The imp slurred.

"Lies!" A foot stomped into my ribs, and my lids flew apart, seeing the tiny figure on my chest.

"Fuuuck," I muttered, my eyes slamming closed again.

"Master custard launcher!" Opie cheered. "You're awake."

"No, I'm not," I grumbled, turning on my side, feeling him scramble to my shoulder to stay upright.

"Yes, you are."

"No, I'm not."

"Then how am I talking to you?"

"You're not. Fuck off."

Chhhhiiirrrpp!

"I did not fuck myself off already… twice."

Chhhhirp!

"Okay, four times," Opie huffed. "Again, that was a total misunderstanding! The wool was just itchy there."

My eye twitched. It was too early for this shit.

I had barely gotten any sleep due to paranoia we'd be found. My mind also relentlessly went back to Kovacs, wondering if she'd been caught. It took everything I had to wait for Gawel's return instead of running out into the night, heading for Ukraine to track her down.

Though I could feel her, she was still able to block me, which drove fury through me like nothing else. The only reason I hadn't lost my shit was because I knew if Kovacs was in serious trouble, I would know it. I'd feel it in my bones. She marked her way through every fiber, branding herself through me. Which made me the one she should actually fear.

The moment I found her, she would pay.

"Warwick, your pets are annoying me," Ash grumbled from a few feet away. "This one is freaking me out."

Taking a deep breath, I pried my eyes open again to see Bitzy sitting on Ash, her head tipped to the side, staring at him like he was a god, her prong fingers petting him.

Chhhiirrp! She blinked slowly at him.

High as a fucking kite. And by the poppy buds circling her head like a crown, I had no doubt what she was on.

I peered at the figure on my shoulder. Opie was shirtless, with sheep wool for shorts. He also had a poppy crown, but he had straw in his, spiking up in points. Butcher paper served as a cape, and his cheeks, eyelids, and lips were stained red, his beard braided with more poppy buds.

A sound vibrated in the back of my throat. "Don't tell me that's blood."

"No, of course not!" Opie gasped. "I'm 99 percent sure it was red dye."

"Red dye in a butcher's shop?"

"Okay, maybe 70 percent sure."

"Did you find it in near-dead animals?"

Opie's face twisted with slight disgust. "I'm sticking with a strong 15 percent."

Snorting, I scoured at my face again, sitting up, trying to wake myself up.

"Go away. I don't have any mushrooms." Ash waved at Bitzy to move.

Chirpppp... She batted at his hands, giggling.

"That is so fucking disturbing." I reached over, plucking Bitzy off Ash, making her twitter and squeak like she was on some amusement ride. "You are cut off." I took the crown of opium off her head.

Her lids narrowed, sobering in a blink. *Chipchirpchirp chirpchirpchirpchirp....* She heaved in a gulp of air, her middle finger flying in the air. *Chirpchirpchirpchirpchirpchirp!*

"Ohhhhh." Opie blinked at me with fear and horror. "You know what she does when you take her happy medicine away?"

Yeah. I did. Setting her down, I tossed the crown back at her with a relenting sigh.

"Softy." Ash snorted, sitting up. "What would Brexley say?" Ash tsked, shaking his head. "Giving in to your kid's demands. Not very parental of you."

"Shut the fuck up," I muttered, pinching my nose. The fact that I was even in this situation, waking up to an imp and a Brownie sticking fingers in places I didn't want to think about, and not killing them, told me all I needed about how much that woman had changed my life. Looking at all the figures asleep in the straw scattered across the room, I realized it applied more to just them. I wouldn't have been here at all. As a lone wolf, I already had my pack of Ash and Kitty, my sister and nephew. I didn't want, need, or care about anyone else. Yet here I was.

"When I find you, Kovacs..." I growled in my head, knowing she couldn't hear me, but maybe she'd feel my wrath.

Darkness still leaked through the boarded-up windows, but I sensed dawn was arriving. The animals were stirring, getting ready for their breakfast, which was most likely their final one. Rising, my body already itched to move, to get the hell out of this city. We'd been here too long.

After Gawel came back with clothes and food, locking us in for the night, we settled down and discussed what we had seen at the old prison and what Killian and Rosie had learned at HDF, going through the files they stole. The ones on top were more of this Dr. Rapava's insane theories, but down a few files were the building plans for the lab in Kyiv. Located in the Podil's'kyi district, it was at least ten times larger than the one here. Caden had visited Kyiv enough to know this location was close to the river, train station, and palace. A perfect collection of industrial and abandoned buildings to create an army underground.

When the little prince himself finally returned after his tantrum, he was much calmer. From what we all heard and felt, this place echoing everything, the dickhead should be more than placated. And of course, I got more insight than most.

"What's wrong, Farkas?" Scorpion smirked at me from his spot in the hay, Birdie's cries reverberating down to us, their energy riling up the animals.

"Nothing." I paced back and forth, their magic wrapping around my cock, burning me with more rage, blistering me with excess energy.

186

I needed Kovacs now.

"Someone getting a little firsthand knowledge of someone else's love life?" He shredded a piece of straw before plucking it in his mouth and chewing on the end with a smirk. *"It's a bitch, isn't it?"*

I glared at him.

"Welcome to my world, asshole."

Fuck. If this was permanent, I would kill captain one-pump within a week.

The connection was different from what I had with Kovacs. I could feel his energy, recognize it like my own. I never had a blood brother, but that's what it felt like. An annoying twin brother you could sense and understand without even looking at them.

I resented what he was to me. I hated that he took magic from me, loathing this need I had to protect him.

The door banged open, my body rising instinctually. Gawel's huge form filled the doorway, his gaze going straight to me. I had known him a long time. The guy never showed much emotion besides annoyance. Today I saw a flicker of alarm cross his face, which moved me straight to him, Ash at my side.

"What?" Apprehension prickled over my shoulders, rolling them back.

"There is word that there are already checkpoints on major roads in and out of the city, and troops have spread through the Savage Lands, killing anyone who tries to fight back. They've been raiding homes and assassinating anyone they consider a spy."

"Fuck." I ran my hand over my hair, wrapping it up.

"And you." Gawel nodded at Killian, who had stepped in beside me. "Are her number one bounty."

"How much?" I asked.

Killian's head jerked to me, his lids lowering.

"I'm just curious." I shrugged.

"Like I trust you not to turn me over for free." Killian lifted his lip.

"You have a price on your head too, Farkas." Gawel flicked his chin at me. "I might turn you both in."

"And I might just slip regarding an illegal opium den downstairs, operated by someone who also runs a drug operation through his meat orders."

Gawel's jaw locked, his eyes tapering.

"What I thought." I scoffed. "Did you find what we needed?"

"Took a lot of fucking favors, which I'm putting on your tab, but I found six bikes at your request." Gawel huffed. "Can't say how great they are, but it was the best I could do. They're in the abandoned building down the alley."

"Get them going," I shot to Ash. He instantly got the group moving, filling bags with the last bits of food and drink. Ash picked up his bag, and I dipped my chin, lowering my attention to it, asking for him to make sure two sub-fae were inside. Ash and I knew each other so well, he understood exactly without me opening my mouth.

He nodded, trying to hide a cheeky grin in response to my unspoken question.

"Shut the fuck up," I muttered.

"Didn't say anything."

"Didn't have to."

"It's okay to admit you're becoming a softy."

"Said the guy carrying them on his back."

"I don't want to deal with Brexley's wrath." Ash pulled on the backpack with the two stowaways inside. "Now *she* actually scares me, you big ol' teddy bear."

"I will kill you."

Ash chuckled, then turned his attention back to the butcher. "Thank you, Gawel." Ash dipped his head in appreciation. It was always Ash who did well with dealing with people in our past business endeavors. The charmer. He smoothed shit over while I was the one who would threaten your life if you didn't pay up, and Kitty was the brains. That woman knew how to run a business, and we had many of them back in the day.

Gunfire thudded off the buildings only a few blocks away, reverberating through the plywood-covered windows.

"You have to go now," Gawel growled, pulling a key ring from his pocket. He jogged to the far wall, unlocking a sliding wooden door used to bring in the animals. Another round of shooting popped through the pre-dawn morning, scrambling the eleven of us out the door.

"You got everything in place if things go down here?" I asked Gawel. For operations like this, we always had precautions in place. No matter what, it could never be discovered. Not in one piece, anyway.

"I do." He nodded, tension lining his forehead.

"Be safe, friend." Ash stopped next to him, everyone else sprinting out.

"You too." Gawel peered at both of us as we stepped out. "Now get the fuck away from here." He slammed the door, with us barely on the other side.

"You sure you two aren't related?" Ash smirked at me, already taking off for the hollowed-out structure down the passage from us.

Running after him, the brittle air snapped at my lungs. There wasn't a breath of wind, nothing to drown out our movements, every tiny noise resounding with clarity. We had no time to warm up the bikes or even check if they all worked. Once a single engine revved, we would draw attention to ourselves.

189

I grabbed one singly. I would be the lone rider. Everyone else would have to double up.

"Rosie!" Wesley motioned for the redhead to hop on with him. I wasn't sure, but I thought I saw a moment of hesitation, her eyes sliding to the side to where Killian was, but then it was gone. She bounded behind Wesley, wrapping her arms around his waist.

"Come on, my liege." Birdie cut around Caden like the two hadn't just fucked each other's brains out, tugging on Killian's arm. "You're with me."

Caden didn't respond, but I felt his anger spike, rankling my own, the surge of possessiveness and rage. Caden's jaw almost cracked, but he kept his expression blank, watching the tiny blonde like he was about to kill or fuck her. Possibly both.

I knew that feeling all too well.

Kek crawled on with Lukas, Hanna with Scorpion, leaving Ash and Caden together.

Ash shot me a look, murmuring, "Great, I get the mini you. Like the original isn't enough to deal with."

"Revenge is a bitch." I grinned cruelly back, then peered around. "We ready?"

The group nodded.

"Follow me. If you get separated or fall behind, you're out of luck. Stay off all main roads, be diligent and ready to fight. Head back to Killian's safe house if you lose the group. Got it?"

They all nodded again.

"Okay." I took a breath, my foot slamming down on the kick starter of the bike. The engine popped and thundered, the others following in a succession of growls and bangs. The noise of six bikes starting at once, their engines and styles older, were roars exploding through the brick building and reverberating through the city.

Without a word, I tore my bike out of the crumbling building and down the cobblestone alley, already knowing that we had sent up a flare of commotion, drawing any soldier in a nearby radius right to us.

Five motorcycles pulled in behind me, following as I cut out of the alley, peeling out onto the street, heading for the fastest way out of town.

Bellows shouted in the air, and gunfire sliced through the rumble of the engines, pinging the ground near us. A truck rumbled up fast behind us, the driver trying to keep up with me while the passengers shot at us. All I could do was move us faster through the city, weaving and twisting. Every choice I made, every alley I zipped us through, could have been the wrong one. All our lives depended on my decisions.

A shell pinged off my rearview mirror and shattered it into pieces.

"Fuck." I turned the bike down another lane, my head whipping around to make sure all were still behind. Air halted in my lungs when I saw the blazing headlights from two armored trucks coming up on us, silhouetting men with guns holding onto the sides, shooting at us.

"Go!" Ash waved me on.

Gritting my teeth, I pressed the gas all the way down, the bike jerking and sputtering, trying to adjust to my demands. The streetlamps were no longer lit in this area, the sun still an hour from rising.

There was only one way to escape—becoming ghosts.

"Turn off your headlights!" I shouted back at Ash. He nodded, screaming the same sentiment to Lukas riding behind his bike.

One by one, their lights went off, plunging us into shadows. The only light was from the truck locked on us, their bullets nipping at our tires.

191

We had to get out of their line of fire.

Turning us down another tight lane, weaving through the trash bins and passed-out drunks, I heard Ash yell out, whirling my head around.

Lukas had stopped the bike, Kek climbing off.

"Kek!" Ash slammed on his brakes. "What are you doing? Come on!"

The rumble from the truck vibrated the ground, its headlights flooding her with light, gunfire popping the air.

"Kek!" Ash bellowed again.

She lifted her head, her eyes black. A huge dumpster slid across the pavement right before the armored truck, their brakes screeching to a halt.

The demon pulled in every bin near her, building a wall, blocking them from entering the alley, her power dropping the temperature of the already chilly air.

Blocking the truck didn't stop their bullets.

One cut through, nipping her arm.

"Kek!" Ash bellowed, about to leap off his bike, but Lukas grabbed her, pulling her into his chest. There was a moment I saw Lukas whisper to her, his mouth brushing her forehead. Her body snapped back, breaking her from her trance. Slowly she nodded, both of them climbing back on the bike.

The truck rammed into the barricade, trying to break through, someone ordering the soldiers to go down the lane next to ours.

"Go! Go!" I peeled out of the passage. I didn't want to waste the limited time Kek gave us. I surged out onto a main street, the motorway only yards away.

Yells and gunfire rang after us as I sped the group up the ramp and away, their trucks too far back to give chase.

In the darkness, the six bikes tore through the last bit of

night. The only tell was the roar of the engines, our group becoming ghosts, slipping away from the capital, leaving our city in tatters.

We barely made it out, as our home had fallen under the reign of a tyrant.

Danger behind and peril in front of us.

No place was safe anymore.

Only the battle for our lives.

Chapter 17
Killian

The fire crackled and popped up into the starry night, the flames the only source of heat, every breath a pillow of icy vapor from my lungs. While most of the group huddled close to the bonfire, eating the minimal dinner we had and trying to stay warm, I stood back, my blood boiling.

We had driven most of the day, getting as far from Budapest as possible. The back roads might not have been guarded by troops yet, but they took much longer, especially with the rough roads and beat-up motorcycles. Several of them broke down, needing to be fixed along the way. Thanks to Wesley's mechanical skills and his redheaded assistant, we made it to this forest at the border of Hungary and Ukraine by dusk.

I could even hear the bitterness in that statement in my own ears.

A laugh, which was light and husky at the same time, tinkled through the air. The sound wrapped around my dick. It heaved fury through my veins and locked my fingers into fists, turning my head to the very pair I was thinking of.

The fire danced off her silhouette, licking at her hair as

194

if the flames thought they belonged there. She turned her head to Wesley, her fingers grazing his hand, her head tipping back, exposing more of her neck as she laughed.

"Faszkalap." Dick hat. My teeth clamped together and my chest pounded, feeling like it was punched every time she reached over and touched him. Watching her climb on the bike behind him, her thighs clamping around his all day... I never wanted to kill anyone more in my life... because he was an asshole, *not* because I liked her. I mean, she was smart, funny, strong, and fucking stunning, but she drove me insane. She pushed back on everything. They were actually perfect for each other. Both annoying.

Plus, in my position and being who I was—a fae lord—I could never be with a human. Especially not an actress or ex-prostitute. It wasn't done. We could never be together, even if it was allowed. She was human. She'd grow old and die, and I wouldn't do that to myself.

What the hell I'm I talking about? I shook my head. Why was I finding reasons not to be with her when I didn't want to be with her?

Wesley let out a chuckle, leaning in closer to her. He reached up, brushing a crumb off her lip.

A deep growl shook through my spine.

"Better make your move, my liege." An elbow knocked into my side, Birdie saddling up next to me, an amused smirk on her face, her gaze on Wesley and Rosie. "Wesley's a really good kisser and great in bed..."

My head jerked to her, an eyebrow raised.

She shrugged one shoulder. "It was a long, long time ago after a night we almost died. But he's got game."

I turned my head away from her, lifting my chin.

"I have no idea what you are talking about."

"Please." Birdie rolled her eyes. "Your dick energy for

195

her? It's off the charts. You stare at her all the time. When you guys are near each other, the room about explodes."

"You are seeing things. We don't even like each other." Her lips pinned together in a smirk. "Sure."

I wagged my head. "You're wrong."

"I'm never wrong about two people wanting to fuck."

"Does that count for last night too?" I replied evenly back.

She sucked in sharply, shuffling her weight. "I was taking one for the team. He needed to calm the fuck down. He was being a dick, and I needed to be dicked."

"Mmm-hmmm."

"Nothing is going on between us. It was just sex. It was a one-time deal." She folded her arms. Her cheeks blushed, her teeth nipping at her bottom lip as if she was recalling every moment with Caden.

"Sure." I used the same mocking tone back on her. Birdie shot me a glare.

"Well, take my advice. If you want her, go for it. You never know. We might all die tomorrow." She nudged me again. "Wesley is already stepping up, so you better decide now, *lord*." Birdie strolled away. I watched her walk behind where Caden sat, knocking the back of his head. He jerked around, his anger already firing up to the surface. She flicked her head toward the forest we were camping in, then sauntered into it.

Caden sat long enough I thought he wasn't going to respond to Birdie's clear invitation, which broke her one-time deal claim, but he rose, muttering something about taking a piss, and wandered in the same direction as her.

They weren't fooling anyone but themselves.

Well after she was gone, Birdie's words still rang in my head, stirring up feelings I never wanted to feel again. Love wasn't ideal for leaders, and it certainly wasn't meant for me. I had mistresses, not lovers, and Rosie was too close in the circle to just fuck and walk away from.

The thought of treating her like a prostitute, the very thing she was forced to be because of her ex-husband, made me sick. Screwing her and walking away? *No.*

I just would stay away.

Scouring my face with raw frustration, another grumble whistled through my chest, hating how sick I felt at letting Wesley have her.

I felt off.

My magic still hadn't fully come back since my time in prison. I couldn't sleep, and tension crawled over me like bugs. Seeing my city fall to Sonya was harder than I'd ever let on. I feared I would never get my reign back, that I had been beaten for good. Budapest was now a dictatorship. It made me face how little I had done before, how content I was with the status quo. You don't realize what you have until it's gone. All I wanted was another chance to make Hungary the free and beautiful country it once was. To open parks, restaurants, and theaters again, to have no divide between fae and humans. Sonya made me see I was a leader before, but not a good one. My ego and insecurity about my past made me blind. Too satisfied with the title and not the actual job.

Now I wanted nothing more than to fight for my city, for the people. To deserve another chance to lead this country.

My gaze drifted back up. Wesley's lips grazed her ear, whispering something. His mouth was only an inch away from hers, his gaze going to her lips, his head leaning in to kiss her.

Logic played no part, my body reacting on pure impulse as I stomped to her, my hand wrapping around her bicep. "I need to speak to you for a moment," I grunted.

197

"What the fuck?" Wesley jolted at my sudden intrusion. I could already feel chagrin heating under my skin, my actions shocking even me, but I didn't give myself time to think about it, yanking Rosie to her feet.

"Now." I dragged her with me.

"Killian!" she sputtered, her feet moving to keep up with me. "What the hell are you doing?"

I didn't have a fucking clue. Reason and sanity were trying to tap in, but the storm of my wrath kept them at bay. I marched us around the bikes and into the crest of trees away from the group, only the moonlight slipping through the branches.

"Killian. Stop." She tugged at my grip.

Twisting her around, I pushed her up against the tree, forcing her to inhale roughly.

"Stay the fuck away from him."

"What?" Her blue eyes sharpened, lowering on me. "No."

I moved in closer, pressing her back harder into the bark. "Yes."

"Why?" She lifted her head, challenging me. There was not an ounce of fear in her face, and the demented part of me wanted to change that. To make her understand who she was dealing with. To obey.

Almost all fae feared me.

"Because," I snarled.

"Jealous, *my lord*?" Her accent slipped around my cock like a noose. My jaw slammed shut to stop a groan from spilling out of my throat.

"Not at all." The lie was like an arrow. It was the same sensation I had for another girl, her heart set on another man. One I spent years trying to beat. To become everything he was and more.

I swore I would never feel that again. Never feel the consuming jealousy, anger, and hurt. I promised myself I would never love again. My only goal was wealth and power. I would never be that miserable fool again.

Centuries passed, and no one conjured any genuine emotion from me, no matter how hard they tried. I was dead inside. I enjoyed Brexley and was attracted to her, but felt no urge to fight for her, snap the neck of a guy just for being near her. Touching her.

Now life sparked in my chest. The feel of her body pressing into mine spiraled terror through me.

I grabbed her chin, forcing her to look at me.

"I said stay the hell away from him." Every word was a threat, my glamour dripping off me, weighing on her like a command.

Her mouth parted, her eyes glossed over, and her breasts rubbed against my chest with every breath.

"Screw you," She spat, ripping through my power, fighting it.

I burned with humiliation at my weakness. My magic was so feeble a simple human could resist it.

My nose flared, my grip on her tightening, my body ramming hers back into the tree. "Is that what you want, Rosie?" I dragged my nose up her neck, feeling her shiver under me. My cock, hard against her stomach, dug into her skin. "Or are you, Nina? Do you know who you are anymore?"

She struggled for a moment, my hold locking her in place. "Like you should talk. Who are you, Killian? Are you the fae leader or a penniless pirate, in love with a girl who didn't love you back?"

"Shut up."

"You don't think I know how that feels? I thought my husband was my world until he ripped it from me, breaking me into pieces and then making me believe it was my fault. He turned me into a whore, not the one at Kitty's, but the one he took everything from, leaving a trinket for me instead of love."

My fingers dug deeper into her skin. I fought the urge to track him down and kill him in the most painful way possible.

"You think love is weakness. I believe it is strength." Her hands slid up to my hips, her touch causing my breath to falter. "I still want someone who loves me with everything in his soul. I still want to have babies, a home, a career, family. I blamed Vincente for so long, but it was me who was blocking my own happiness. Giving him too much power. I won't let him have that control over me ever again." Her fingers trailed up to my arms, pulling the one away from her face. "I won't let *any* man." Her expression tightened, her voice dropping. "So, either you give me a reason right now or get the hell out of my way and don't *ever* intervene in my life again."

Terror tore through my chest, forcing back the words telling her to stay with me, that I wanted her. Nothing would come out.

Nothing.

Her head turned to the side, her lids fluttering, trying to hide the hurt.

"That's what I thought," she snapped, shoving me back. She pushed past me, marching toward the campsite. I knew she was serious. If she walked away, there was nothing left for me.

A deep panic coursed through me. The idea of letting her walk away screamed in my soul. Something beyond possessiveness nipped at my subconscious, but I didn't have time to think about it. Once again, all sanity left my body, the urge plunging over me like a spell.

"No." The word barely exited my mouth as I grabbed her arm, yanking her body back into mine. My hands clasped her face, my mouth slamming down on hers.

Holy shit.

The moment my lips touched her, it was like an electric shock to the system, my entire body jolting with the energy, feeling it throb through my dick, down to my soul.

"Killian." A groan broke from her lips like she felt the same things, turning my mind into static.

"Say my name again." I was frantic and needy.

"Killian…" She moaned my name, making me lose every thread of sense.

"Fuck." Grabbing her hips, I lifted her up, her legs wrapping around me. I slammed her back into the tree, her figure curving and rubbing against mine, her hands raking through my hair as she consumed me. Her tongue licked mine, sucking on it until stars popped behind my lids.

Everything snapped.

I was no longer the fae leader who sat with kings and nobles, wined and dined with the elite, or went to the theater and sipped on brandy.

I was the Killian who, at the age of four, could only fill his belly if he was able to catch his own prey. I was so starved that I'd tear into the raw animal flesh, warm blood dripping down my chin, devouring what I had been deprived of for so long.

Hungry. Raw. Desperate. Merciless.

And Rosie gave it back as if she had no control either, her nails tearing at my clothes, her hips rolling into mine, needy and frantic.

There was no thought except the need to be inside her. My mouth devouring hers, I yanked at her pants, unzipping them enough to slide my hand inside.

She was dripping wet and pulsing with need. I moaned as I slipped into her.

A noise bubbled up her throat. "Oh gods." Her mouth parted as I pushed inside her, stroking her pussy, making her claw at my back. "Bloody hell," she groaned. "How does that feel so good?" I know she didn't mean it as an insult. The woman had a lot of sex, probably growing numb to the average act. This was elementary to her, but her body pumped against my fingers desperately. "Oh gods... *Killian*."

Hearing my name made me almost come in my pants, my mouth taking hers again with a ferocity I had never felt before. I needed to claim. To mark. To own.

"Rosie?" Wesley's voice flittered through the trees, freezing us in place. "Hey, Rose... where you at?" The urge to kill him, calling her Rose like they were intimate, gurgled up my throat.

He stepped into the forest, only yards from us.

"Shit," she whispered. Her legs loosened from me, and she dropped to the ground, her eyes wide with panic as she zipped her pants and straightened her clothes.

"I'm coming."

I blinked, seeing her trying to hide all signs of what we were doing out here.

"What the hell are you doing?" Wesley's voice tightened, his senses probably picking up on more than he was ready to admit.

"Nothing." Her voice pitched higher. "Just talking. I'm ready for that drink now. Come on." She strolled over to Wesley, motioning for him to follow her out, but he didn't move, his eyes locked with mine. Anger bristled along his jaw line.

He knew. At least he knew it was more than talking.

Part of me wanted to smirk and taunt him, but seeing the

fear in her eyes, the worry of him finding out, snapped everything back to reality.

What the fuck had I just done? With her? A human.

The weakness of losing control, letting some woman once again have that power when she clearly didn't feel the same, unsettled me. But only for a moment.

I was no one's fool.

I would take her advice; I would never let another have control over me again.

Placing my fingers in my mouth, I sucked off her taste and strolled by them, my arm brushing hers. "She was right. It was *nothing*."

Chapter 18
Scorpion

My eyes flew open, my body jerking awake, apprehension washing over me. My lungs took in a stilted breath as I peered around the shadowy campsite, searching for an attack or the reason for my sudden rousing.

Dawn hinted at the sky. The flames from the fire were down to embers, still giving off heat, though it couldn't combat the freezing temperatures, the possibility of snow lingering in the air. We had to stay off main roads and away from any inns or lodging. Too easy to track. But camping in winter with only a fire and a few wool blankets to keep us warm was brutal. We all huddled close, practically in the fire, resting as much as we could while Killian and Warwick took shifts keeping watch.

Lifting my head, I noticed Killian was down on his blanket, but Warwick was nowhere to be seen.

Another trickle of anxiety dripped down my throat, my neck craning to look over my shoulder at the form lying next to me.

Or was supposed to be.

Sitting up, my unease rose higher. "Hanna?" I

whispered, searching the forest all around, thinking she might have gotten up to pee.

I got no answer.

Climbing to my feet, I assessed my surroundings, my breath billowing in front of me as my adrenaline spiked, heating my body. Perspiration dampened my neck, sliding down my back. There was probably no need to worry; Hanna could take care of herself. But I couldn't shake the warning in my gut.

Where the hell was Warwick?

Yanking my gun from my holster, I crept away from camp, my intuition tugging me into the forest. Dawn inched closer, the sky turning from black to a deep blue, deepening the shadows still clinging to the trees. Alert and ready for anything to come at me, I continued to slip farther into the woods, listening for any footstep or voice. I was sure to hear Hanna before she heard or saw me. I kept quiet. Calling her name would only give away my location if a threat was near.

Less than a mile from where we camped, hums of vehicles and murmurs of faraway voices buzzed in my ear, drawing me forward and intensifying the siren wailing in my gut. The shouts became clearer, sharp, like orders. The ground vibrated from heavy vehicles.

Coming to the edge of the forest, there was an old road. On the other side, some brush and bushes, before it gave way to vast farmland. Open, flat, and bare.

But the field wasn't empty.

"Bazdmeg." *Fuck.* Dread plunged to my feet. My mind barely absorbed what I saw when a hand came around my mouth. A bellow caught in my throat as I was yanked to the ground.

"Trying to get caught?" A deep voice snarled at me, my head pivoting to the side to see Warwick.

"Motherfucker!" I hissed. "I almost shit my pants."

"Probably not the first time," he rumbled, his massive build squatting lower behind the brush. "You waiting for them to ask you for breakfast before shooting you in the head?"

"I wasn't standing out in the open," I spat. Not that anything I did was good enough for the almighty Legend.

Shouts yanked both of our attention right back to the field. Tanks, cannons, and temporary housing dominated one side, while the middle was filled with hundreds, if not thousands, of men and women wearing military uniforms.

Soldiers.

Dressed in Ukraine garb, they all had a yellow bandana tied around their arms.

"Oh fuck," I whispered when I realized what it was.

On the bandana was a patch. Istvan's symbol for HDF, the letters tilted, making up a triangle shape. The same emblem the girls had to sew on uniforms in prison.

It no longer represented just the Human Defense Forces; it was also a symbol of power. Of human purity.

Though ironically, not one soldier here was purely human anymore. They stood like robots, waiting for an order. Autocrats didn't seem to mind hypocrisy or blatant lies if it got them what they wanted in the end. If they could sell to the masses through fear and righteousness, they would back your cause no matter how untrue it was.

Fear was a powerful weapon. It turned people blind, ignorant, and violent.

"Wishful thinking that Istvan would retire after his loss at the prison," I muttered, glancing over at Warwick.

"Not looking like it." His gaze was locked on them, taking in every nuance and detail. "And Markos doesn't seem to be hiding his plans."

We were south of the main motorway between Ukraine and Hungary, but any spy could easily find them.

"Istvan will be obliterated if he thinks this troop will supersede Sonya's." She had far more manpower.

Warwick's head wagged. "I think this is just a holding area. They're waiting."

"For?"

"More." He replied. "Markos's ego won't take another loss; he'll make sure he has more than enough fighters."

"Which takes us to Kyiv." I bobbed my head.

"We destroy the lab, we destroy his ability to make more soldiers."

"While Mykel takes Sonya's out."

"Let's hope." He shifted back on his toes. "We also have to make sure that no matter what, he doesn't find Kovacs or the nectar."

Game over if he did.

I licked my lip, not wanting to ask but not able to help myself. "I feel her again."

Warwick grunted.

"It feels different, doesn't it?"

His chin jerked to me, then away.

"Before I could feel the buzz, sense her. But this is..." Fuck, this was uncomfortable talking about, but if anyone could relate, it would be Warwick. "She feels more guarded. As if she's being shrouded. But on purpose." I inhaled. "She's stronger."

Warwick's head tipped back just a hair, but from that action, I knew he got the same thing from her. A power she was learning to control.

"We need to get the hell away from here." Warwick didn't address what I said, but I knew him enough now to know I got my answer anyway.

"Yeah." I nodded, my feet shifting back in the dirt, ready to run for the tree line across the street until something in my peripheral stopped me dead in my tracks.

Terror clotted my throat, horror dancing on my tongue, locking me in place for a moment. Warwick hissed out something next to me, but I heard nothing, fear blocking out anything but what I was seeing.

Hanna.

Her body was stiff, her focus on the army. She walked toward them as if they were singing a siren song. I had seen her like this before. Seen the pull she had to the faux soldiers.

With every step closer, she could be seen. Captured. Shot.

"What the fuck is she doing?" Warwick started to rise, ready to go after her. A growl mounted from deep within. The thought of him touching her took over me, driving me toward her with no other deliberation—she was mine.

Crouching low, I scrambled behind her, my hand wrapping around her mouth. She let out a squeak as I took us both to the ground, my body covering hers, listening for any signs we had been seen. My heart thudded in my chest, every molecule listening and waiting, but with every second, no shouts or bullets came.

Exhaling, I kept my hand still over her mouth, anger bristling from me. I looked down at her. "You move when I tell you to, got it?"

Her blue eyes were alert and wide with horror. She nodded against my hand. I peeked my head up, looking at the enemy base.

"On the count of three. You get up with me and don't look back," I ordered.

She nodded again.

"One… two… three." I climbed off her, keeping low,

208

my hand wrapped firmly on her arm, not letting go as we both scrambled back for the tree line, running as fast as we could. We stopped a few yards in. Sucking in gulps of air, Hanna leaned back into a tree, bending over her legs, her expression twisting into grief and terror.

Warwick snarled, his footsteps pounding toward Hanna.

"No!" I leaped between them, shoving Warwick back. "Go back. I'll deal with this."

Warwick's nose flared, ready to snap my neck in half.

"I will deal with this," I repeated firmly, my chin lifted, ready to fight him if I had to.

His heated aqua eyes slid from me to her, then back to me again. He nodded once before taking off toward camp.

My back to Hanna, I took in several breaths, terror still knocking around, adrenaline twitching my muscles. All my fear thumped through my heart, coming out the other side as anger. Slowly I turned to her, the rage crawling up my throat, ready to whip her with it, blackened to ash on my tongue.

Hanna slid down the trunk of the tree, her hands covering her face, guttural sobs racking through her.

"Hanna." My chest splintered open, and I scrambled over to her, my knees dropping into the dirt. I pulled her into my chest. Her wails went so deep, they were lost in her throat.

"Shhhh." I wrapped her tighter, rocking her back and forth, my hand threading through her hair. "I'm here."

Her fingers dug into me, her thin frame shaking harder as she let go. This woman had gone through so much in the last few months. Being kidnapped by an opposing group would have been enough for most, but what happened in Vĕrhăza—watching both her parents be murdered right in front of her, the mental and physical trauma, the abuse, and the starvation was beyond what most could endure. I had never brought up the times the guards pulled her away or

209

what they did right on the factory floor. I couldn't imagine what it took to get up every day.

To also deal with what Markos did to her. He took her humanity. We had seen how the pills changed her old classmates. The monsters they turned into in the Games.

She was becoming one of them.

Slowly. Painfully. Cruelly.

Though all I saw was strength and beauty.

"I-I can't... I can't d-do thi-this," she choked into my jacket, her cries turning from frantic to hopeless, tearing through my heart.

"Yes, you can. I will figure it out." I kept my voice steady as if it was a fact. "I promise."

Hanna pulled away, agony streaking her face, which hollowed out my soul.

"No." She pushed away from me. "You won't. You can't promise me something you have no control over. You can't do anything. You don't know what it's like... to slowly be losing yourself every day. I won't turn into one of them... I *won't.*"

"Hanna." I reached out.

"No!" She hit my hand again, another sob contorting her body, feeling like a dagger to my own. "I can't trust myself anymore." She waved in the direction of Markos's camp. "I couldn't stop myself. I could have been seen." She hiccupped and gasped. "I am a threat. To you... to the group." She shook her head. "I have to go... far from here."

"No." A deep growl hacked through the air, my body crawling over to her, clutching her wrists, tugging her closer. "You are not going anywhere. You are staying here. You are staying with *me.*"

A tiny gasp hitched her throat, her watery eyes finding mine, searching for an answer I wasn't sure of myself. I just knew every fiber of my being I would not let her go.

"I'm telling you this once, little viper. You aren't going anywhere without me." I tugged her closer, feeling the dominance surge from me. I had lived centuries, had a lot of lovers, and one time I thought I found my mate, but nothing came close to what I felt now. I would slaughter anything that stepped into this forest and tried to hurt her. I would destroy anything that got in my way, and if she ran, there was nowhere she would go that I wouldn't find her. The overwhelming sensation curled in my chest, making me feel dizzy.

"You can't fix this, Scorpion." Her eyes pleaded with mine. "I am only a danger to you all. And it's only going to get worse." She sniffed, pulling her chin up. "You need to promise me something else."

"Anything."

"When it's time... you will kill me."

As if a tsunami crashed down on me, yanking me up and away from her. "What?" I stumbled back.

Wiping her eyes, Hanna got to her feet, standing strong. "Please, if you care for me at all. You will do this. I won't become a monster."

"No." I gritted, fury bubbling off my skin. "Fuck no. How dare you even say those words?"

"I will kill everyone here without thought or concern. All my friends. Everyone I care about. You." She gulped back emotion. "You have to promise me. Don't let me become that. *Please*."

Her pleas felt like an actual knife to my chest, bending me over, pain shredding through me. "No..." my voice croaked, my head shaking, staring at the ground. "I won't do it."

"Scorpion. Look at me."

I couldn't.

211

"I said look at me."

Her voice was my own siren song, my body obliging her. Locking down my jaw, my eyes tracked as she stepped up to me, her hands cupping my face.

"You said you'd do anything."

"Not that," I ground out.

Her hands dropped away, but her gaze on me didn't relent.

"Right now, all I see is a badass woman." I stepped into her, my frame looming over hers. "Who has the instincts of a wildcat and can tear into meat with a fierce hunger." My hands slid over her cheeks, clutching the back of her head hard. She let out a tiny huff, her eyes tapering like that cat was being summoned. "You only took one dose. This might be all it is."

"And if it's not?"

One side of my cheek lifted, my thumb wiping away her drying tears. "Then I better start taming this pussy now." I yanked her into me, not giving her any time to react before my lips were on hers. I was attacking, inhaling, and devouring the mouth I had fantasized about for far too long. Even when she was our prisoner, chained up and being a pain in my ass, I couldn't stay away. Taking watch every chance I could, assuring myself it was because I wanted to torture the pretty, pampered blonde human from HDF. She was spoiled, ill-trained, and too confident for her own good, and I convinced myself I hated her sharp tongue and even sharper teeth. Though I jerked off every night to images of our hate sex, her mouth around my cock, still handcuffed to the wall as I hammered into her.

Somewhere along the way, my hate turned into something completely different. I saw nothing but strength and fire in her, nothing but depth and beauty. She fascinated me, challenged me, angered me, and made me want to fight the world to keep her protected and close.

There was nothing I wouldn't do to make sure of that.

My tongue slid deeper into her mouth, and I tasted the salt from her tears, only making me want to replace all her pain with pleasure.

"Scorpion," Hanna groaned, meeting me with the same ferocity, her hands hooking my belt loops, pulling me closer to her. Another groan came from her when my hard cock pressed into her, wanting to burn through the layers and feel her heat wrap around it.

Desire rode over me with desperation. I no longer cared that an enemy army was only feet away and our group was probably waiting for us to ride the hell out of here. I couldn't pull away from her.

"Hanna." My voice was hoarse, giving her an out, willing her to stop me because I couldn't.

"Make me feel something other than pain and fear." She tugged harder on my pants as she lowered herself back to the ground, taking me with her. My body covered hers, our kisses becoming deeper, needier.

Shouts and gunfire from the base close by only made Hanna rock into me harder, ripping my jacket off and tearing my sweater over my head. Her mouth covered my chest, sucking on my nipple.

"Fuck!" My dick turned to steel. Adrenaline moved like lightning through me as I rid myself of the rest of my clothes. We didn't have much time. But the outside threat raised the intensity. The demand.

Stripping her, my mouth was back on hers as I lowered my body over hers, our bare skin sparking like flames as it touched.

"I need you now." She rolled into me, my dick sliding

213

through her folds. "Oh gods..." Her head curved into the leaves over the ground. "Scorpion."

Next time, I would take my time. I liked it rough, and I preferred it kinky, but right now, my only thoughts were being inside her.

"Watch me," I growled, leaning on one elbow and gripping my dick. Her pussy was wet and dripping for me. "I want you to watch my cock plunge into you."

She moaned, her legs widening as she went up on her elbows, her pupils dilated, her nipples hard.

I pushed in slowly.

"*Akarlak.*" *I want you.* I hissed; she was so fucking tight. My eyes stayed on her as I pushed deeper inside her, watching her expression as I filled her.

"Oh gods!" Her body jerked, a loud moan heaving from her mouth. I moved fully over her, slamming all the way in, my hand covering her mouth as she screamed. Her core throbbed around me, clenching and adjusting to me.

"Hanna." My eyes rolled back in my head, the sensation overpowering me.

"More." She slammed her hips up into me, sinking me deeper. Sucking in, I thrust in deeper, her body rolling and moving with mine.

With every move we made, louder groans came from us. The intensity was like nothing I had ever experienced before, and my past was full of fantastic sex with thousands of different partners over the centuries.

This? This sunk into my very being, drilled into my veins, and coated my skin. It owned me.

"*Bazdmeg!*" I hissed, driving in harder, our tempo picking up, sweat dripping down my back as I plowed into her. Her hands cupped my ass, spreading me, her finger rubbing through and into my ass, hitting nerves which made

214

me almost buckle, before slipping forward and gripping my balls from behind. She bit into my neck, a cat-like growl coming from her throat.

A moan tore apart my throat, and my head reared back, baying. She matched my viciousness, upping my drive like a madman. Cries of my name bellowed from her under my unrelenting drive, her wetness echoing off the bark and sky, her nails cut into my back, her groans sounding more and more like a cat.

Gripping her throat, I stared down into her eyes, watching them darken as I fucked her harder. The ground rumbled as tanks moved over the land across the road. Pulling out of her, I flipped her over, making her flat with the ground, the earth shaking as I crawled over her, pushing back into her.

"Scorpion!" Her nails tore into the leaves and dirt, feeling the tremor rattle through her body, against her core and into mine.

My hand lifted, spanking her ass. "That's for almost getting caught."

"Oh gods! I'm going to come."

"No." I spanked her again, getting closer to her clit. Her body shook under me. "Not until I tell you, little viper."

Tanks and vehicles could be heard getting on the road only yards away from us, quaking the ground, going through us like an electrical current. My dick rammed into her as I rubbed her clit again.

A yowl spat from her lips, and she bucked against me. My girl was all feral. She clawed back into my thighs, her nails raking up, tearing into the skin, teetering me off the ledge.

"*Vedd a cum!*" *Take my cum*. I ordered, feeling my balls squeezing. She cried out, her pussy clamping around me, milking me so hard, I couldn't stop my release if I tried.

215

Roaring, I spilled into her, my hips still slamming into her, pushing in as far as I could.

Hanna screamed, another orgasm tearing through her, squeezing me harder.

Most people experience their own orgasm, but it was as if I could feel hers as well. The strength of it exploded more pleasure through me. There was nothing like it. It was a high I couldn't find words for and a feeling in my gut I didn't want to consider.

It was several moments before I came back to myself, my body slumped over hers, both of us gasping for air, her pussy still pulling every last bit from me.

My head swam, my body feeling like it had been wrung out and buzzing with drugs at the same time.

Hanna sucked in air, staring off at nothing, her muscles twitching under me. Her eyes were still dark, the wild cat not far from the surface, which hardened me inside her again. This girl was far from the missionary type I figured she was.

"That was..." The words stopped, unable to find a sentiment for whatever just happened.

Hanna didn't move or respond, her lungs gasping.

"Hey." I lifted some of my weight off her, brushing back hair from her eyes. "You all right?"

She blinked, her expression dazed.

"Hann—"

Louder shouts came from Markos's camp. This time I felt the urgency in their nearness, the possibility someone heard us. Felt us. We needed to get the hell out of here.

"We've got to go, little viper." My dick slid out of her as I pulled back, and I instantly wanted to go back in. Take her again, this time slower and painstakingly.

Reaching for her, I helped her up, both of us covered in dirt, leaves, and sex. Quickly, we got dressed, knowing

216

everyone at our camp was probably ready to kill us or had already taken off. She turned to head for our group, but I grabbed her arm, stopping her, her silence bothering me.

"You sure you're okay?" I stepped up, plucking a leaf from her hair. "Did I hurt you?"

"I'm fine." She nodded, but something in her detached tone prickled at the back of my neck. "We better go."

I nodded in agreement, both of us jogging back, but the whole time, I felt that what just happened between us took her farther away from me, not closer.

The moment we came upon our camp, I could feel the restless energy and ire. Warwick waited on his bike, boiled in restless, agitated energy. Probably outvoted to leave us behind.

"Where the fuck have you been?" Birdie shouted, her arms flying as we ran up. Her anger and worry slipped off her face into shock, her mouth forming an O shape, taking in our appearance and most likely our smell. Her gaze moved up and down both of us. "Are you kidding me?"

"Don't," I muttered, wanting to shield Hanna from scrutiny, to take all the blame.

"Seriously?" Wesley laughed sardonically, his head shaking. "Because right now with the enemy only feet away was a good time."

Hanna's head bowed, her cheeks flushing pink.

I shot Wesley a look, grabbing the handlebars of my bike and throwing my leg over. "Let's just go."

Warwick instantly revved his engine, taking off, Ash and Lukas right behind.

Hanna climbed on behind me, holding onto my waist, but I could feel the distance. The regret. The desire to be anywhere else but with me. To run away.

It pissed me off.

217

My throat tightened, struggling to swallow, a realization turning into fear. Because for the first time in the many centuries I had lived, keeping sex separate from my life and never getting together with anyone in my circle, I *didn't want* to run.

Chapter 19
Warwick

From the moment we crossed into Ukraine, the wolf took over, the Legend who wanted to hunt down his prey and destroy it. End the torture she was generating.

I had been beaten, burned alive, gutted, electrocuted, tortured, and still nothing compared to this.

The tease of her. Feeling her sporadically through the day, buzzing through my system, a whisper, a glimmer in my peripheral, a moment I could almost link to her before she pulled back.

So close, but yet so fuckin' far away. The times before when our connection was burnt out, she didn't seem to have control over when it came back or how to cut me off if I pushed in. It felt different this time. She had control, and no matter how much I tried, she kept me out.

And I didn't like it one fucking bit.

I couldn't do anything except push the group to keep going. There was no good time to journey across Ukraine. Daylight was easier for us to maneuver through the badly maintained back roads, but we were also easier to spot. Night would leave us vulnerable to bandits, traps, and unforeseen problems on the road. Taking the back streets prolonged our journey by hours, but the main motorways were far too dangerous for us to chance. If Istvan was moving his army to the border from Kyiv, they would be using those. Tanks and trucks couldn't handle the small, crumbling, potholed lanes.

We rode all day, getting close enough to Ternopil I wouldn't stop even when the sun had long set, entering the time of night where nothing but debauchery was left to sample. The group was freezing, exhausted, and starving, but with my mood, no one challenged me. The idea Kovacs could be only miles away from me blanketed me like an obsession. Controlled me. Pushed me harder to reach our destination, even if the possibility she was still there or the rumor of the last sighting of her was wrong. It gave me something.

My bike slowed as we entered Ternopil. Once one of the biggest cities in western Ukraine, a beautiful, thriving city, it was now another victim of the population divide between the extremely poor and rich. The wealth went only to the elite, who stayed on one side of the city; the poor and suffering stayed on the other side of the river. As if they were kicked out like rabid dogs.

We got glares and suspicious glances from those still out at this time of night, the upper class staggering from one gambling establishment to another.

A shiver walked down my spine. Every single person I saw was human.

"I think I smell something fishy that way." A tiny hand tugged on my ear, pointing toward a park in the southeast part of the city. Opie perched on my shoulder, Bitzy on his back, the pair acting like my compass as we rode through town. They were how I located Kovacs's exact spot when she was at Povstat. Though my instincts pointed me toward this place like I had my own GPS signal to her, as if she had pulled me in herself. I knew what that meant. The instinct went beyond the link we already had. And though I had uttered the word out loud before, it still pressed down on me with panic. It was something I never expected or wanted. Until her. There was no fear of accepting it, but of losing it.

Mate.

My natural inclination was to barricade against it. Run away from it. But all I did was run straight to her.

"I mean, it's not fishy, fishy—like day old rotting fishy, but like fishy you had a couple days ago still lingering about. This is more like a whiff of fishy. Like fish-whiffs or maybe fish-fluffs."

"Shut up," I muttered.

Chirp!

"Not sure you could consider that finger food. Though your fingers have been up—"

"Shut. Up. Now." I growled, snapping my teeth at them. *Chirp! Chirp!* Bitzy shoved her finger in my face. She had been in a mood since coming off her opium high, and Ash didn't have any mushrooms. She sat on his shoulder and chewed him out for an hour.

"There, Master Beef Bazooka!" Opie jumped up and down, pointing to the entrance to the National Revival Park. "I smell our Fishy odor coming from there."

Turning in, I pulled up to the curb, the rest of the group stopping behind me. There were no lights or activity, only an eerie quiet and foggy darkness creeping over the rundown park. My gut knew I was looking for a shadow here, but the draw to check it out, to find any morsel of her, swung me off my ride.

"Something feels off. You sure we're in the right spot?" Climbing off his bike, Ash peered around. Caden stood right

221

behind, his mood crisp and palpable. My short temper seemed to incite his. Or it might have been the blonde getting off her bike with the fae lord.

My eyes locked on a paper leaflet hanging on a tree at the entrance. My boots clipped the surface as I strolled over to it, plucking it off. The back of my throat tightened. "Circus Mystique. Where your darkest fantasies come true." Underneath the lettering was a silhouette of a shadowy Ferris wheel and a circus tent.

A flicker of memory from when I linked with Kovacs the night before teased my mind. The same picture and writing style were branded on the side of a wagon I saw.

"Yeah." I breathed out, shoving the piece of paper at Ash. "She's with them."

Kek and Lukas moved around Ash, peering over his shoulder. The two of them orbited him like the sun.

"Wait." Kek clasped her hand over her mouth, laughing. "Brexley ran off and joined the circus? Seriously?"

Lukas let out a chuckle, his head shaking.

"Sounds about right." Ash couldn't fight his own amusement.

"Yep," I mumbled to myself. "That's my girl."

"The last performance was last night." Lukas pointed at the date printed on the bottom.

My head twisted to the park, dread sinking in my stomach. I took off running, my legs eating up the pathway as I headed deeper into the park. As if I hurried, I could catch her. Wrap my fingers around the ends of her hair and yank her back to me.

"Warwick!" Ash yelled after me, but I heeded nothing.

"Whoa, whoa big man!" Opie clutched onto my jacket, holding on. My feet slowed as I came upon a clearing, bins filled with food, parchment from treats and sweet popcorn covering the ground. You could see a grass field ruined from stake holes, where a tent used to be assembled. It was vacant now, leaving only ghosts of what was here just hours before.

"Fuck!" I bellowed into the sky.

"Easy now, boy." Opie patted my neck like I was some mare.

"Do. You. Smell. Her?" I gritted through my teeth. Everywhere I looked, remnants of a carnival were left, but the troupe was long gone.

Opie tilted his head, sniffing the air. "I really smell her that way." He pointed behind me.

The rest of the group had barely caught up with me when I ran off again, following the Brownie's nose to an old rusty Ferris wheel behind a group of trees.

Before Opie even spoke, a zing of energy ran over my skin, pumping life back into my chest. A growl curled in the back of my throat. I could taste her magic on my tongue, feel it nudge against my bones, lick at my skin. Familiar and fucking powerful.

"Shit." Ash came to a stop beside me, his eyes widening.

"You feel that?" I peered at him, and I saw the rest of the group arrive out of my peripheral.

"Yeah. The energy here is insane." He nodded, his attention going to the trees and brush nearby. "Whatever magic she's stirring… it's potent. It's confusing nature."

"What do you mean?" Scorpion came up beside me. The way he shifted on his feet, peering around, I understood he was feeling her too. Not as strong as I was, but Brexley had left a mark here even Ash could pick up on.

"Her magic goes with and against nature." Ash's gaze went around. "Life and death, but not always equally."

Kovacs walked in the middle, conjuring both sides of the spectrum. No fae should be able to do that. Only Druids

223

born as natural obscurers could get even close, and even so, they couldn't do what she did.

She was neither fae, Druid, nor human.

She *was* the Grey.

"Oh! That's what I smell." Opie snapped his fingers.

"What?" I asked.

"Death."

"As in ghosts?" They did follow her.

"No, it's more pungent than that." Opie tapped at his nose.

Chirp!

"Yeah." He nodded at Bitzy. "Like corpses."

"Corpses?" I repeated.

"Or more like bones." Opie tapped at his nose. "Not that I know what bones smell like."

Chirp!

"I don't know what boners smell like either."

Chirp!

"That's a total misunderstanding!" Opie exclaimed. "I was merely curious."

I rubbed my fingers back and forth across my forehead. The need to find her, get to her before all the other things hunting her did, was eating away at me.

"Kovacs," I growled her name through our quiet link, turning for the parking lot, my determination set, not paying attention to anything else.

Dumbass mistake.

Clickclick. The sound of multiple guns priming to shoot clacked through the air, halting me in my tracks. Instantly, I felt Opie and Bitzy disappear from view.

"Well, look at this." A shadowy figure stepped out of the shadows, his voice firing wrath down my limbs. "It's all my old friends together again." The slice of light from the moon glowed off the man, a snarl lunging up my throat. Dozens of soldiers stepped up with him.

"Except you. You I will gladly put a hole through." He pointed his gun at me.

"Tracker," I snarled, the Wolf heaving under my skin, pushing out, ready to snap his neck.

"Put your weapons on the ground and kick them to me," Tracker ordered, his minions robotically stepping closer to us, ready to fire. "Now."

None of us moved.

"Last warning, Farkas."

"Fuck you."

Pop!

His gun fired, nicking my ear. Blood dripped down onto my shoulder, where Opie had been moments ago.

"I meant to miss you," Tracker sneered. "I won't next time."

The group slowly placed their guns down on the ground.

"I said now, Farkas," Tracker snapped, motioning to the claw I had on my back. Begrudgingly, I unclasped it, lowering it to the pavement. His guards moved in, confiscating the weapons.

"See how smoothly everything goes if you comply?" Tracker smirked at us.

"Fuck you, you traitorous asshole!" Lukas spat. "How do you sleep at night? You are the reason everyone at Povstat is dead. *Children*. People who considered you a friend. Innocent lives. How could you?" Lukas rushed forward, but Ash and Kek grabbed him, holding him back as a dozen more soldiers stepped out of the woods, their weapons on us.

"How could *I*?" Tracker motioned to himself. "Mykel had us living like rats. Hiding. Cowards. He was the one who lied. How many of us died for him, but nothing ever changed?

As if fae and humans could ever live together happily. It was all a lie. At least here I'm doing something of honor. Ridding the world of vermin."

"Coming from someone no longer human." I glared at Tracker.

"I'm something even better." Tracker held up his chin. "A new race. One superior to the half-breeds and fae here."

"*Eszem azt az ici-pici szívedet!*" *I'm gonna rip your heart out and feast on it!* Lukas fought against Kek and Ash, but they held him in place.

"You'd probably like that, wouldn't you?" Tracker glowered at Lukas. "I knew you always had a hard-on for me, you sick fuck. Watching me all the time. Made my skin crawl." He spit at him. "You disgust me."

I sensed Ash before he even moved. His fury whisked through the trees, snapping branches. "I'm gonna fuckin' kill you." Ash moved, but Lukas grabbed him, now being the one to hold him back, whispering in his ear, trying to calm him down.

"Repulsive." Tracker wrinkled his nose at them. "Though I count this as my lucky day. When I got a call that some shady fae characters had come into a human-established town, I didn't think I would get so many of you together. Like a gift… and it makes my job so much easier. Every one of you on his most wanted list, shoot on sight." His eyes danced over me, Killian, and Kek, stopping on Caden. "Except for you. Your father didn't seem to think you were worth mentioning at all. Think he was gravely disappointed you and your whore mother weren't killed in the Games."

Caden's wrath bubbled at the surface, fists closing, veins straining against his skin. He was ready to spring for Tracker. A growl filled my throat directed at Tracker as I stepped in front of Caden, blocking him from doing something stupid.

The magic that had once belonged to me was now also firing through his system. And I could sense it. The urge to defend and protect him like he was my little brother crawled up my spine, spreading my shoulders out like a shield.

I fucking hated him, but I also would kill anyone who got near him.

"Hanna." Tracker tilted his head at her. "Markos had higher hopes for you. You know you are one of us. You do not belong with them."

"Fuck you." Every syllable sounded like a struggle out of her mouth.

He grinned. "You join us today, we welcome you with open arms, no questions asked. It's where you belong, and you know it. We can give you more of what your body craves. You want more, don't you? You think about it more than you'd ever let them believe."

Her hands opened and closed, her jaw gritted, not denying his statement.

"You'll change your mind," he replied confidently, turning back to me. "So, this is how it will go then. I kill everyone but you." He wiggled his gun at me. "You take me to Brexley, where I take the nectar, and then I'll shoot you two together. Sound good?"

"Minus everything you said, and insert I shred your body into pieces and gut you like a pig, and I'm all in," I rumbled, stepping forward, my expression twisting up into a sneer.

"That's not how this works anymore, *Wolf*. Fae are no longer top dog." He swung the muzzle of the gun to another. "Gonna start with you. Think of the medals I'll get for killing the *fae lord*." Tracker pushed down on the trigger, a bullet heading straight for Killian.

"No!" A scream tore through the night, Rosie's figure

227

smashing into Killian's, pushing him out of the way. Blood spurted out of her side, her body jerking as the bullet drove through her ribs.

"Rosie!" Killian's bellow got lost as chaos exploded around us. Caden and I moved as one, barreling for the guards. The others rushed right behind us.

Pop! Pop!

Shells tore through my clothes, cutting into my flesh, only causing the beast to roar louder in fury. Swiping up my claw weapon, I whirled around, slicing through a guard. Caden grabbed the end of a guard's rifle, slamming it back in his face. Bones and cartilage snapped, the man dropping back to the ground as he took the weapon from him, turning it on another. Like we did back at the castle, we moved together, each knowing what the other was going to do, synced in rhythm. He shot and I swung.

Birdie and Wesley took on more beside us.

Tracker retreated, yelling for his soldiers to kill us. The dozens I saw before seemed to multiply, coming from the shadows all around us.

It wouldn't be long until they gunned us down. No matter how powerful, there were only so many bullets your body could take before it could no longer heal itself.

Another bullet drove through my arm, weakening my hold on the claw as I sliced and cut through a handful of fae soldiers. Wesley shouted in pain, dropping to the ground. Lukas was hit right after.

"No!" Anger bubbled inside, energy roaring through me, reaching out in pure instinct.

I felt her before I saw her.

My head jerked toward the sensation of her power. Her shadow was only feet from me, her dark eyes wide with horror as she took in the scene. Our attention locked on each other for a moment before another bullet burned across my skin.

"Use me!" Kovacs screamed at me. Not even giving me the chance to respond, Brexley shoved her magic into me. The power boomed inside my bones, spilling into my veins and locking in my muscles. It took over, a fire burning in my chest.

Life.

Death.

The current of adrenaline unleashed the legend, making me experience magic like I had never known before. Feeling every color, every sound, every smell. She consumed my body and surrendered all of it to me. And every part of me welcomed it. Wanted it *all*. Craved it.

And I took.

My movements were faster than a blink, my war cries barely making it to their ears before I cut and sliced through the throng of officers. They were drugged and too stupid to run. They marched to their death, painting my face with their blood. One after another, their bodies dropped, some completely in half. The faux-fae were fast, but with Kovacs, I was faster.

"Pull back!" Tracker's order hit my ears, the guards retreating. A growl curled out of my chest, and I toward Tracker. He needed to die.

He fired back at me, and I blocked every one of them, seeing the shot before it even hit. His eyes widened with terror. Taking off at a sprint, he ran for the parking lot. His men followed suit.

Lunging to run after him, my legs faltered. Brexley's power left me with a snap, my knees slamming down on the ground. My hollowed-out chest heaved with the sudden loss. The connection we had for a moment was burnt out, leaving me gutted. Like part of me was missing.

"Ash! Help!" Killian's cry pulled my head over my shoulder. A few crowded around Killian. He sat on the ground, Rosie's head on his lap, his hand continuously brushing at her face as blood gushed from her side. It took me a second to see her chest still rising and falling, but in jerky movements.

"Fuck." I got to my feet, stumbling back for them. My body swayed, needing to sleep. Between my multiple gunshot wounds and the power share with Kovacs, it took everything I had to keep upright.

Though all of us were wounded, we would heal. Rosie was human. She would not.

"I can patch her up the best I can, but we need to find a clinic or supplies." Ash leaned over her. "I need cloth."

Wesley kneeled over Rosie, opening his mouth to speak, but it was Killian who acted first.

"Here." Killian ripped his jacket and shirt off without hesitation, tossing the shirt to Ash. "Do whatever. Just help her."

Ash worked quietly for a few moments, tying off her wound and covering it to slow down the bleeding while Caden and I stood guard, watching for the troop to return.

"I can't do anything more here. We need to get her help soon." *Or she will die.* I could hear the sentiment he left off. The truth.

Rosie was going to bleed to death.

Killian lifted her in his arms as he rose, his own bullet wound in his arm dripping down his leg. "Then we find her help." It was not a suggestion; it was a command.

We started to move, heading for our bikes when Scorpion stopped.

"Where's Hanna?" His head snapped around, his question making us all peer around.

"Wasn't she right next to you?" Birdie asked.

"Yeah." He nodded, a panic jerking him around, searching for her. "She was right next to me until…"

"Until what? Where is she?" Caden demanded.

"Until the soldiers ran." Scorpion went still, his eyes jerking to the parking lot. "Oh gods, no." He took off, sprinting toward the entrance. "Hanna?" His bellows rocketed into the sky. "Hanna!" Pure dread soaked her name as I jogged after him into the parking lot, halting in my tracks.

Scorpion stood in the middle of the empty lot. Hanna's pack lay on the ground at his feet. Discarded.

His head bowed like he had just lost everything.

"What the hell? Where is she?" Caden bounded up, his aggressive energy smashing into Scorpion.

"She's gone." Scorpion's voice was low.

"What do you mean she's gone? Where did she go?"

The fae lashed out like a scorpion tail, his hands clutching Caden's throat. "She left with them!" He raged, shaking Caden. "Because of what your fucking father did to her. He turned her into one of them," Scorpion belted, his muscles clenching and ready to punch someone.

"Want to hit someone? Hit me." Stepping between them, I knew it would not end well for either if Scorpion and Caden got into it.

For a moment, I could see Scorpion wanted to, but he turned away with an aggravated, gutting bellow. And even though Scorpion and I weren't linked without Brexley, I felt his pain, his helplessness.

I knew it well.

A wet cough came from behind us. Killian tried to sit Rosie up on a bike, putting her in front of him, his arms caging her in as he took over the bike. She was awake, but barely.

We had to go.

"Come on." I motioned for Caden and Scorpion to move. Caden reacted instantly, going back to the motorcycles, but Scorpion didn't move.

I could see the debate in him, whether he should go after Hanna instead.

"You can't do anything for her right now," I muttered just to him. "You will only get yourself killed." I licked my busted lip. "We will get her back. I guarantee I will be by your side to do it, but there's nothing you can do right now."

It took a few more beats before Scorpion picked up her pack, looking at me. "She's mine."

"I know." I nodded, understanding his meaning. "We'll get her back."

He exhaled, then turned with me, both of us jogging back for our rides.

Tearing out of the parking lot, my desperation to find Kovacs escalated even higher. There were so many hunting her.

I had to reach her before them all.

Because Kovacs *was mine*.

Chapter 20
Brexley

"That's it. Open yourself up to them," Esmeralda spoke, but it was Tad I heard, his encouragement egging me on. She was completely in a trance, letting Tad use her body. Ghosts, I had learned, were not easy to communicate with through dialogue, like having a conversation with a living person. They used their own means to express themselves—images and one-word whispers. My powers allowed me to see Tad more clearly, and it was far easier for him to use Esmeralda to speak.

"You must learn how to block and receive their energy. To use it for your own." She strolled around me, her demeanor patient and softer than the actual woman.

Sweat dampened my forehead, contradicting my frozen fingers and toes. The late afternoon had done nothing to warm up the December temperatures, and it was already dropping again. We had taken off the moment they tore down camp and made our way to the next town to set up for the carnival tonight in the town of Zhytomyr, still thriving only because it was a major transportation hub from the capital city Kyiv, which contributed to a higher number of Ukrainian soldiers in this area.

Jethro never confronted me about the event in Ternopil. His stance on keeping me protected like family didn't seem to need more explanation. The Master had declared it, and everyone accepted it. Well, not everyone. Zelda hated my guts even more. After their vardo was ransacked, she sneered at me when I was near. It didn't help that Esmeralda had taken to me, spending extra time helping me with my magic and not her own granddaughter.

Jethro knew I was wanted, my identity exposed. He kept me hidden in the back of a wagon under blankets as the caravan came through town, officers stopping them for paperwork. Most of the places we'd been through in Ukraine were mainly human, and they looked at the circus as freaks. Entertainment to distract them from their horrible lives for a night, but not welcome by society in general. In most places, the troupe was not allowed in many establishments and shops.

"Brexley, concentrate," Tad griped, pulling my attention back. Bangs of metal and shouts could be heard once again in the background as they reassembled the tents for tonight. The park we were in was set against the Teteriv River, with a neglected children's playground, Ferris wheel, footbridge, and flat area at the bottom for the carnival to set up and welcome patrons.

Reverting my attention from the commotion below me, across the river, I could sense a graveyard not far away, the inhabitants seeking me out like a beacon.

Shutting my eyes, I drew them to me, my skin prickling with their energy. The box with the nectar was tucked under my pelt on the bench, taunting me. Every day was more and more of a struggle not to touch it, to pretend I didn't hear it calling to me, tempting me. It wanted me to use it, and I craved the high, the unadulterated power I had that night of my escape. Each time I touched the nectar, it seemed to come out of me with more force.

"You are no match for it if you can't even command your *own* magic." Tad had scolded me earlier when he noticed my attention going back to it repeatedly. My head bowed at the insult, knowing it was true.

"We need to destroy it… it's beyond dangerous. This tiny substance is the most powerful thing in the world. Think of the damage it can do." Andris's words tickled the back of my mind, the sound of his voice plunging through my heart.

I was working hard, but I was still far from where Tad wanted me to be. "Do not bend to its seduction, my girl. Power is a potent force. It corrupts those of strong wills with the weakest of minds."

"But…" I swallowed. "How can it corrupt me? I mean, isn't it part of me? My familiar?"

"That's what makes it even more dangerous," Tad replied. "What I couldn't see when I was alive."

"What?"

"That *you* are a part of *it*. Your essence is in it." He pinched his lips together, his expression grave. "But girl, it only takes."

"That's not true; it gives me its power. I have felt it." My stomach sank, recalling what I did to him with the power of the nectar—to all those people outside the prison.

"And what happens to you after?" Tad tilted his head, a white eyebrow curving up, giving me a moment to think before stating, "it leaves you depleted."

Emotion closed my throat. "Because magic is a balance."

"Exactly." Tad dipped his head. "Your magic should be a balance with nature, not something that bleeds all the life from it. And through you, it takes from Warwick and Scorpion. I see the binds that tie you three, your link to the

235

nectar. It's becoming more and more unbalanced. It will kill all three of you if you keep going down this road."

Tears prickled at the back of my eyes. I wanted to defend the nectar, to protect it… justify it. But I couldn't; I had seen what it could do.

"You are enough, Brexley," Tad said softly. "*Just you.*"

His sentiment had stuck with me all day, giving me the drive to push back my need for the nectar. When did the very thing I craved become the toxic part of me? Tipping me over the edge, sliding into the darkness.

"Pay attention." Esmeralda tapped me on the head, bringing me back to the present. "Now tell them what you want." She voiced Tad's directive. "Give them an order."

Exhaustion thumped a headache between my eyes, but I took a deep breath, my lids shut, my barrier slipping down, letting the ghosts seek me out.

The moment I did, hundreds of them swooped in, their shades brushing my skin, the buzzing of their energy and indistinguishable voices throbbed in my head, whipping at my nerves like a blender.

A cry broke from my lips. "Back off!" My words were garbled under the flood of them continuously coming at me. The first time this happened in the church, I buckled under the intensity, but since the unrelenting training Tad was putting me through day after day, I had grown stronger. Like working out a muscle, I could take more and more weight on, sharpening my responses, and giving me more stamina.

The weight of death across these lands, the helplessness and sorrow of each soul, was sometimes crippling. The suffering across this area seemed endless.

Digging deeper, I tried to calm the panic bubbling up. My knee-jerk reaction was to shut down and retreat from their overwhelming energy.

Wind swept off the river, snapping across my face. A crackle rumbled in the cloudy sky, a flicker of lightning, and energy hummed around my body, heating it from the inside out.

"Stop." The demand came from deep in my gut, low and calm, but it cut like a knife. The ghosts shifted back, hovering close, but not one touched me. "You do not touch me until I say. Do you understand?"

There were no words spoken, but the buzz in the air and the flicker of the fire lamps below told me they did.

"Good," Tad spoke through Esmeralda. "Now they must feel your intention. Ghosts can perceive things mortals cannot, but they are not conscious of it. You have to draw the line between losing yourself and giving enough to them that they understand what you desire."

This was where I kept failing. The line between was so thin it only took one extra drop to tear through and fall over that edge. It was a pinpoint to stand on. I either took too much from them, losing all ability to control myself, like what happened outside the prison, killing innocent people without understanding, or they took too much from me, sucking all energy and life from me, slowly killing me.

The ability to hold them was waning, upping the desire to reach for the nectar to give me more strength, like a shot of caffeine.

On top of it, I had to work diligently to block my link to Warwick and Scorpion, feeling them brush at the seams, wanting in. I couldn't. Not yet. I had to get stronger so I wouldn't siphon from them or use them as a backup battery.

I bit down on my lip, concentrating on letting my magic seep out to the ghosts, absorbing and directing them. The power hummed in my soul. The thing I feared and craved at the same time. It was forged and constructed from death—

237

my mother's, the queen's, Warwick's, Scorpion's, and the wall between the Otherworld and Earth.

Death came from my bones. It was in my DNA, and the moment I was born, it gave me life. It made me who I was today.

The Grey.

My muscles shook as I struggled to walk the line between life and death, between light and dark. There were moments I felt that sweet spot, a place where I no longer had to work for it. It was automatic, before it again came crashing down.

Today, the spirits glided around me, and I felt my own shade reach out, separating from me. Joining them.

Oh. Holy. Shit.

A gasp hitched up my throat, the buzzing growing stronger as it clicked in. Something hadn't even thought of now made perfect sense. It wasn't so different from what I had with the boys. I could be physically in one place, but my shadow was with them.

A touch of apprehension tapped at my chest, but I ignored it, letting my shade join the ghosts, communicating and leading them in a way I could not before.

"You're doing it!"

My shadow turned around, seeing Tad before me. His shade was as real to me as the man once was.

"Tad!" I cried out, tears burning the back of my lids. Even if he wasn't actually alive, my heart didn't see the difference, but the man was different.

Tad was no longer hunched over. No curse crippled his spine and ached his bones. He appeared at least twenty years younger, glowing with vibrant, warm light. His blue eyes danced with happiness, his energy like a cozy blanket, which only drove a knife through my gut.

"Don't." He shook his head. *"I do not blame you, my girl. You should not either."* A warm smile spread over his face. He reached out, clasping my hand in his, my skin buzzing.

A sob caught in my throat, his touch spilling my tears down my cheeks.

"How can you not?" I still didn't understand how he couldn't hate me. Fear me.

"Like I told you, you freed me. I am no longer confined to that broken shell." His hand rubbed mine, sending electricity into my veins. His smile curled coyly. *"I've been waiting for you to get here. To this point. You amaze me every day."*

"What?" I sucked in. *"You knew I had to let my shadow connect to you?"*

"Well, not to me precisely, but to the spirit plane. After seeing what you and Warwick could do, your spirits going between each other on another plane, I thought it might work here too."

"Then why didn't you just tell me that?" I could feel my energy dipping in my real body. Where Warwick and even Scorpion were effortless to link with, this wasn't. It wasn't unnatural; it just took much more work and concentration to stay in the space between life and death.

"I tried the best I could, but I realized you had to get here on your own, to understand. To let go of your fears and guilt. I could tell you, but you would not understand until you did it yourself."

Through the air, Zelda's voice pierced the connection.

"Bunică!" Grandmother! Her call carried to where we were, slicing through the spirit plane like a knife, Tad's shade vanishing, crashing me back to my body. My head twisted to Esmeralda, and she stared at me like I had grown five heads.

239

"*Bunică*, I've been looking for you everywhere. What are you doing up here?" Zelda stomped into the rotunda we had been working in, shooting me a dirty look, continuing to her grandma. "You know you shouldn't be out in the cold like this."

"I'm fine." Esmeralda barked, her gaze still on me.

"You are not fine. You shouldn't be out here doing… whatever this is." Zelda grabbed her fingers, a frown burrowing into her beautiful features, snarling at me with an accusatory look. "Your hands are freezing."

"Stop smothering me." Esmeralda tugged her arms back. "I'm not a child."

"Really?" She once again glared at me, then glanced back at her grandma. "Could have fooled me. Up here smoking and drinking like a teenager." She tsked. "You know you shouldn't be doing any of that."

"Gods, you are such a pain in the ass." Esmeralda rolled her eyes, puffing on a smoke she held in her fingers, wiggling her very worn bunny slippers. "Let me have the little joy I have until I croak… which I thought you'd be happily waiting for."

"Stop it." Zelda inhaled and exhaled loudly. "We're opening soon. You need to get warmed up, get dinner, and get dressed." She tugged the blanket around her shoulder tighter, swiveling back for the path, her lids narrowing on me. "Stay away from her." She leaned in with a sneer. "I don't know why Jethro deems you worthy enough to protect, but you aren't one of us. I *see* through you. You are going to cause nothing but misery and devastation here." With that, Zelda headed back for the carnival.

"She is just like her mother." Esmeralda shook her head, stubbing out her cigarette. "Another nagging bitch." She huffed, moving for the exit. "But she's not totally wrong."

My chin jerked up at her sentiment, her scrutiny drilling into me.

"You aren't one of us. From what I just witnessed, you aren't one of anything, are you?"

I stared at her, swallowing.

"Yeah." She nodded, a strange chuckle huffing from her. "I had a feeling." She shuffled out onto the pavement. "Time for me to go blow sunshine up asses, telling them I see fortune and love in their future… what a crock of shit," she muttered, heading down the hill to the circus tents and wagons. Leaning on the railing, I gazed over the park. The sun had set, and the firebulbs were lit, giving off a spooky, romantic glow to welcome guests for a seductive night of emptying their wallets for just a whisper of joy and the possibility of another life.

Taking in a deep breath, I longed to reach out to Tad again, but exhaustion ran through my body like a train. The hours of working with Tad and Esmeralda stole most of my energy. I barely got any sleep after last night, knowing Tracker was out there looking for me. They somehow found out I wasn't with my friends in Budapest and knew enough to track me down to this group.

An awareness grazed at the back of my neck, whipping me around to the nightfall creeping in around me. The sensation of being watched shivered down my spine. I saw nothing but darkness but could feel in my gut something *or* someone was out there. Watching. Waiting.

Darting out of the pavilion, I prepared to hear footsteps or feel someone coming after me, but nothing came. The feeling still didn't leave me, the whisper of something at my back propelling me for the protection of the brilliant lights and people below.

Hunger drew me out from the seamstress wagon where I had been holed up all night, knowing it was better to stay far from the public venturing through the festival. Markos probably had my picture spread far across the country with a bounty on it. A single sighting of me could hurt Jethro and his people, and I wasn't willing to do that to them.

Waiting until the circus closed, I slipped from the last wagon in our camp, heading for the tent I knew had food and drink for the entertainers' post-performance.

The bitter cold had me hunkering down in the fur I had wrapped around my shoulders. The firelights along the path flickered, the smell of sugar still hanging in the air, remnants bursting from the overflowing trash bins. Voices and laughs floated from the big tent at the end, filled with the troupe coming down from the buzz of the show.

"Laura." A deep voice came from the dark shadows passing through the carnival, a tall, built figure stepping out.

"Bazdmeg!" I yelped, swinging around to see the Master himself slip from the shadows like he was part of them, his piercing gaze watching me intently. "You scared me."

Jethro didn't respond, his attention fully on me, sparking energy down my skin. He was still dressed in his costume, his top hat tipping lower on one eye. Jethro was intense; he absorbed the space around him, though he felt like he could disappear in it just as easily. His presence was captivating. Alluring. Pulling you to him, giving you no choice, and you didn't want one.

"We can be frank with each other, right, *Laura*?"

Air huffed from my nose. "Think we both know that's not my name."

242

"Indeed." He dipped his head in agreement, strolling closer. "We are all misfits here. Many of us come from pasts that could endanger our futures. There are things we don't want to get out. This world is an unforgiving place, giving nothing, especially to those who don't fit into society, whether fae or human. This troupe is where you can start over, become whomever you want. Though some pasts have found their way here, I have always held strong to the idea that we protect our own."

Swallowing, I kept my eyes on the enigmatic man, trepidation curdling in my stomach.

"You are not the normal misfit, *Brexley Kovacs*."

Hearing him say my name out loud poured scalding heat down my throat. Not moving or responding, I waited for the axe to fall.

"We protect our own here. But when does one outweigh all the other lives here?" He lifted his brow. "The risk of them digging deeper into us, finding things which should stay buried…" Every word was smooth and held no emotion, making it hard to decipher what he was feeling. "Wrecking a vardo is nothing we haven't dealt with before on a normal raid. We are quite used to being targeted by police." He folded his arms. "However, I don't think you fall anywhere near normal. And I don't think they will stop coming for you, will they?"

"No." Shame lowered my head, my tongue swiping over my bottom lip. I was putting all these people in grave danger.

"Coming for you or what you carry with you?" He nodded to the box I had strapped to me, never leaving it unattended.

Impulse brought my hand to the box protectively. My body went on defense until the heaviness of his question hit me. My eyes met his.

"It is growing stronger. Soon fae from all around will be able to feel it… sense it."

"What?" My mouth parted. "You can feel it?"

Jethro's eyes shot down to my hands, a muscle in his jaw twitching. "I'm not exactly normal among fae either." His suggestive tone hit my chest like an arrow. He clearly sensed I wasn't right, but what was he? "This magic grows louder and stronger every day. It won't be long until others pick up on it too, bringing them straight to us."

It was why necromancers had guarded over it for so long, eclipsing the power coming off it, hiding it from the world. And I carried it around, thinking it was safe with me when I was only empowering it, growing its voice from a whisper to a song.

"I will leave."

"This city is infested with officers." Jethro shook his head. "We only have one more day here before we move on. Wait until we get closer to Kyiv. It will be easier to disappear from there."

Or it would lead me right to the viper den.

"I think you will be safe until then." He tapped the brim of his hat. "Goodnight, *Laura*." He winked, slipping through the heavy shadows and disappearing.

I didn't move, suddenly realizing the peril I carried in my hands, a beacon to bring in anyone who felt its power. Everywhere I went, I was a threat, a danger to my friends, to the troupe here. More and more, I realized the danger of this nectar. Of thinking I could hold on to it even if I didn't use it.

Stepping back to the wagon I stayed in, I no longer wanted to join the group. Their merriment and laughs carried to me, making me feel even more like an outsider—one that could destroy the life they had built for themselves here.

I took two steps before I felt Warwick, the link between

us yanking my shade from my body and pulling me to him. Suddenly, I stood in a familiar woodsy area, a circus poster lying on the ground as men in Ukrainian uniforms stomped over it, spraying bullets at a dozen figures. My eyes found the man leading them.

Tracker.

Dread trapped a scream in my lungs.

Feeling the magnetic pull, my heart lurched into my throat, my attention going to the man who stood a foot above all others.

Warwick.

His aqua eyes burned into me, feeling him in every fiber of my being, my heart surging with emotion.

A cry of pain filled the air, and I stood helplessly while Birdie and Wesley got shot. In the distance, there was already a body on the ground.

Rosie.

Terror took over, my eyes popping back to Warwick.

"Use me!" I screamed, still feeling my body back at the circus. I let go of my mind being there, ramming myself into Warwick before he could even respond, giving him everything I had.

Our bond fused, blistering with heat, exploding with magic. I could feel him grip on to it, pulling from me. My body was on fire as he consumed and seized from me. There was no difference between us, my shadow rubbing over his soul, sliding up into his muscles, locking down in his bones, giving him power.

A roar cut through the air as Warwick swiped the claw weapon, severing two soldiers' heads before they could even understand what happened.

The Legend came alive. I could feel him in my veins, see the sparks of color behind my lids. He didn't ask politely or shrink back from taking too much. He shredded through what I offered, sinking in deeper, taking more as he sliced through the throng of officers.

My energy was already limited from my training earlier; my knees dropped to the ground with a grunt, the box tumbling from my hands. The wave of magic pumping into him burned through me quickly, and I could feel him demanding more. I slumped over, the link starting to flicker.

No! My mind wailed. Not now. He needed me. Needed my strength, my magic. There were still too many to defeat.

The box lay within my grasp. The nectar inside would give me the unbridled magic I needed for him. Magic he could feast on.

I stretched my fingers, reaching out, my energy waning every second. Grasping the box, I unlatched it. I could feel its pulse, the energy within it wanting to be used, craving my touch as much as I craved it. The tips of my fingers almost grazed the surface.

"No!" A shoe pressed down on my hand, pain zapping up my nerves, breaking my link with Warwick like a fuse. A cold darkness replaced the connection between us. The moment my shadow pulled away, my physical body heaved with air, my face in the dirt, spots impeding my vision.

Turning my head, I saw Esmeralda standing over me, tranced, her eyes glazed over, her voice monotone, not sounding like herself. But it wasn't Tad, either.

"Fire. Death. Ruin… they follow in your wake. It cannot be controlled. The more you take from it, the more it will take from you. Until you lose more than your mind and soul."

Her words were the last I heard before everything went black.

Chapter 21
Brexley

"Brexley Kovacs." The familiar otherworldly voice spoke into my mind, prickling my body with magic. "The girl who challenges nature." The fae book repeated the same sentiment to me every time. "Terrible things happen when nature's laws are broken. Though, within the terrible, greatness can be found. Power to drain and consume the wrong." The book paused. "You are not the only one in this story who defies nature, who should not exist. It is only together that you can right nature's balance."

"What do you mean?"

My head spun, my body flipped and rolled through the pages, nausea rising until my feet were on solid ground. All was hazy and distant, nothing really solid or clear, as if this scene wasn't actually written yet, just a vague idea being outlined.

I could sense burning buildings, the sky lighting up with explosions, dead bodies covering the ground at my feet. Terror pumped at my heart, feeling in this moment the world was on my shoulders.

I was failing.

Power I couldn't fight was draining me, and though I could feel Warwick's presence anchoring me, it wasn't enough. A figure stepped up on my right. No features I could make out, except she had the same long dark hair as mine, a man standing behind her. It was a warped version of Warwick and me, like looking through a funhouse mirror at myself. She reached for my hand. I felt my own power sizzle in my veins, like I was giving myself the power to keep fighting.

To win.

Before I could really lock onto the moment, the images vanished, the book tossing me back into the darkness.

Air surged from my lungs. My lids flew open as I sat up with a gasp. My pulse thumped painfully in my ears as the remnants of my dream evaporated from my mind but hung heavy in my chest, clinging to me and clawing at my heart.

Rattled, I took in the wagon I slept in, the layers of pelts over me, the musty smell from them drifting into my nose. The silence in the darkness ran a chill up my spine, contradicting the sweat pooling at my back. Taking deep pulls of oxygen, my muddled mind tried to recall what I last remembered before going to sleep, why I felt terror pitching in my stomach, telling me something was wrong. That my panic was warranted.

My pulse picked up as I dug through the furs, letting out a breath when I found the box with the nectar next to me.

Yet the dread didn't fade, the alarm in my chest jangling between my ribs, my brain rolling back to the moments before everything went black.

When I was with Warwick...

It struck like a bullet…

"Oh gods. Rosie!" My hand flew over my mouth as the memory of her on the ground became clearer. Blood gushed from her side, her lungs struggling to draw breath into her human body. Even if the rest were fae, there were only so many times they could be struck by fae bullets before their blood was poisoned. Before they would die too.

Did I give enough to Warwick? Did Tracker come back and finish them off? Was it too late for me to find or help them?

Reaching out for Warwick through the link, I came up empty; we burned through our magic. Anxiety itched under my skin. I wanted to move, desperate to know how Rosie was, how they all were—to be able to help them.

Peering down at the box laying innocently beside me, I was overcome with the need to hold the substance, let it fill me with magic, tapping up my own as I took from it like Warwick took from me. It would be so easy.

"Fire. Death. Ruin… they follow in your wake. It cannot be controlled. The more you take from it, the more it will take from you. Until you lose more than your mind and soul." Esmeralda slithered back into my head, her glazed eyes staring vacantly down at me, threat in her declaration. It curled around my throat, forcing me to swallow, sinking into me with teeth, cutting through my gut like razor blades.

I had already caused death and ruin. It was why I ran. Whether it was fate or even Tad who led me here, I was learning to utilize my powers so I wouldn't hurt or kill people I loved, taking innocent lives in my wake.

My heart thumped as I lifted the lid. It was such a small, unassuming substance; it didn't seem possible an ugly lump that fit in your palm could be so powerful. It was *part* of me. I could learn to control it.

249

One touch? Just enough to reach out to Warwick, just enough to see they were all right.

I knew one touch would never be enough.

No. I growled at myself, the craving making me restless. Not able to sit still, I tossed off the layer of pelts. Shoving my feet in my boots, I yanked a blanket over my shoulders and grabbed the box, exiting the wagon.

Only a few firebulbs were left burning during the night along the path, flickering shadows and creating movement that kept you on edge. Far from dawn, the dead of the night rubbed the sparkle off the carnival, leaving it more frightening than magical. As if the glamour was ripped away and you saw the true face underneath.

Clouds skulked over the slice of moon shining above, the cold air biting at my skin as I headed away from the camp, up toward the rotunda, through a woodsy area. Winter had left the tree branches bare, their limbs like skeletons, bony fingers reaching out for you.

A shiver ran through me. Pulling the blanket tighter, apprehension wiggled through my shoulder blades. I paused for a moment, recalling the eerie sensation I felt the evening before up here.

The notion of being watched.

Hunted.

My eyes darted around. The last of the dying leaves rustled in the wind, and the squeal of metal from the rusty Ferris wheel pierced the heavy air, deepening my breaths. My senses coiled. My heart hammered. Eyes burned into my skin, stalking me. Every second felt like my last, waiting for something to attack. Soldiers would rush in and strike fast, giving no time for the victim to react. Only animals and fae hunted like this—shadowing their prey and waiting for the perfect moment to pounce.

Kill.

I could sense it in the atmosphere. Death was coming for me.

Though it didn't know…

I was death.

The wind gushed through the park off the river, and I swear I heard a growl, the sound so low, it could have been my imagination, but every hair in my body stood on end.

My fingers fiddled with the latch on the box, ready to seize the nectar if attacked. Every breath boomed in my ears, my entire body twitching with the need to run.

A branch snapped, whirling me around, a cry filling my throat. My fingers grazed the nectar, my eyes sure they picked up on a black mass moving for me, when the air popped and roared with motorcycles, whipping me back around.

My hand flew up, shielding my eyes from the sudden glare of headlights, every nerve firing with fear as a handful barreled toward me, their brakes squeaking to a stop. Fright clotted my senses, my brain trying to catch up.

"Master Fishy!" I heard a voice sing out to me. "See, I told you I could smell her! You owe me, mushroom man."

Chirp!

"Okay, you really owe Bitzy. But I need to inspect the product first. You don't want to know what happens when she has mushroom and cocaine together."

"O-Opie." Tears rushed to my eyes, the sudden emotion hitting me like a punch, my attention swinging across the group still rolling up. Each one made my heart leap in my chest; the ache of missing them surged up my throat in a dry sob.

"Brexley!" Ash was suddenly there, sweeping me up in a hug, my heart surging at seeing my best friend.

But all I could feel was *him*. I turned my head toward the magnetic pull, and a pair of aqua eyes sliced into me.

Fuck.

I sucked in sharply. The buzz at seeing him never seemed to lessen. Tangible danger billowed off him, the threat licking at my skin. It ensnared me in his trap, seizing me whole, with no hope of escape. Even though everything told me to run, I would go to him always.

Bitzy and Opie sat on his shoulder while he watched me from his bike. Anger, resentment, hurt, and fury glowed in his eyes, darkening the aqua color, telling me it was not a threat—it was a promise.

The commotion caused me to turn from him, my eyes catching a figure slip off a bike and fall to the ground.

"Rosie!" Killian shouted, following her down to the ground. "Wake up! Rosie? No!" He curved his head. "Help!"

Wesley leaped off the bike he was on, crouching on the other side of her.

"Fuck!" Ash spun away from me, shoving Wesley out of the way, kneeling next to Rosie, feeling her vitals.

"I thought you said she'd be okay?" Killian shot at Ash.

"I told you I did my best with what that ransacked pharmacy had left." Ash snipped, focusing mainly on her, tearing off her red-soaked bandage, the wound leaking more blood. "It should have slowed the bleeding, but she's human, Killian. She doesn't heal or respond like we do."

Panic and fear I had never seen before streaked across the fae lord's face.

"Heal her!" he demanded. "She cannot die."

Die?

Rosie?

The woman had been through so much. She was a survivor and always came out stronger, yet she was still so kind and loving. One of my dearest friends.

Her human body was failing her.

I could feel her death whisper around me, her chest barely moving, her soul beginning to lift free of her physical form.

"No!" I barreled in, my hand slamming down on her torso as if I could keep her spirit inside, block it from escaping. "Don't give up on us." A strangled cry pulled from my throat, and I dug deep inside for my powers. A sick panic rushed over me as nothing came, taking me back to when we lost Maddox. How I could do nothing but watch him die.

I would not let that happen to Rosie.

The box in one hand, my mind not thinking beyond anything but saving Rosie's life, I flung open the lid, reaching for the nectar, my other hand touching her.

"No! Brexley, stop!" A shout tore through the night. Dressed in a heavy wool nightgown, gloves, and bunny slippers, Esmeralda came running for us. But it wasn't Esmeralda who spoke. I could feel Tad, hear him, his spirit taking over the tiny woman.

"Don't do it!" Tad's eyes looked out from her face at me, head wagging fervently.

"I have to," I barked. "I won't let her die!"

"She human! You will char her from the inside out. Her system can't handle that level of magic going into it like that."

"I did it with Andris. I saved him."

"No, you went through your shadow via a connection with Scorpion." Tad placed his hand on mine, stopping me from touching the nectar. "You didn't use it directly on him; otherwise he would have died from the abundance of your magic in his system. As a human, she's too weak to handle it. Also, you have grown in power, my girl. You will fry her."

Tad was right. I had been miles away when I saved Andris, and it took all my energy to push my magic through

253

my shade to him. My shadow was a buffer, filtering my power.

My gaze met Esmeralda's in a gutted panic. Tad looked back with sorrow. "I am sorry."

I could hear Killian yelling at me, freaking out as Rosie took her last breaths.

"Feed it to her!" Killian's words finally penetrated my mind.

"What?" My neck snapped to him.

"It's why it was stolen from me! Why Croygen wanted it!" Killian's desperation was frantic. "To give it to this human girl."

I blinked in shock.

"The nectar was said to be a lot like fae food." The memory of Andris came bubbling back, hope exploding through my body. Fae food turned humans "fae-like," though you could never leave the Otherworld again after you ate it. When the barrier between the worlds dropped, the fae food was lost. People had been searching for something like it.

The nectar still held the magic of the Otherworld, probably the only substance left in the world that did.

Holy shit.

"Give it to her!" he pleaded. "Save her!"

"Oh my gods…" I reached out, touching the gloves covering Esmeralda's bony hands. My bare hands couldn't touch it without it wanting to fill me with magic. I was too afraid to chance it right now.

"Feed a tiny bit to her." I shoved the box at the seer.

"What?" Ash jerked to me in shock, but I stayed locked on Tad. His eyes grew wider, hope filling them, his head bobbing as if he came to the same conclusion I did.

"No!" Ash wagged his head.

"It's like fae food," I explained to him. "It will heal her."

"Just know she won't be human anymore," Tad warned.

I didn't know Rosie's stance on fae or human if she had the choice. I didn't give a fuck. No one did. Her life was the only thing that mattered.

"Do it!" Killian roared next to me.

Esmeralda's hand shook, touching the nectar. A small flare colored the shell brighter but didn't react much as her covered fingers tore a pea-size bite from it.

Rosie's breath stopped.

"Now!" I ordered Esmeralda. Killian tipped Rosie's head back, opening her jaw right when I hit the seer's hand, dropping the small morsel in her mouth and down her throat.

Everyone held their breaths, the world pausing as we waited for something to happen, to feel her soul tether to her body again.

Nothing happened.

Silence screamed like a banshee, grief creeping up on everyone as we realized we were too late.

"No." I shook my head. It was supposed to work, right? Rosie couldn't die.

"Rosie…" Killian's chest rose and fell, his fingers curling around her face, his eyes wild, like he was ready to set fire to the world and happily watch it burn. "Wake. Up." He shook her limp body. "Now!" he demanded. "You are not fucking leaving me." He shook harder. "That's an order!"

"Killian…" Lukas tried to pull him back, but he thrashed against him, shoving Lukas back, moving closer to Rosie. "Wake up. Do it to piss me off, fight me, annoy me, I don't care… but you cannot leave me, Nina."

Hearing him say her real name broke something in me, sorrow surging from me like a tsunami. Once again, I failed… another loss… another body to bury and add to the tally.

"Noooo!" Killian boomed, leaning over her, his lips touching her forehead.

A gasp tore through the air. Rosie's eyes burst open, her body jackknifing up, knocking Killian back on his ass.

Rosie wheezed, her lungs sucking in oxygen, her eyes darting around. She was scared and confused, but the moment she locked eyes with the fae lord, she took a real breath.

"Holy fuck" Kek uttered, pulling Rosie's gaze from Killian back to the group.

"What's going on?" Her brows furrowed. "Who are you?" She stopped on Esmeralda, then curved her head to me. "Brexley?" She scrambled to me, hugging me. "You're okay."

"Are you?" I leaned back, searching her face. She was Rosie, no zombie version of her or faux-fae syndrome. Just Rosie. Though I could feel magic coming from her, sense she was different.

Holy fuck, it… *worked.*

"Yeah. I feel great, actually."

"You don't remember being shot?" Wesley inched closer to her.

She swiveled around, peering up at him. "No… Wait. Yes." She nodded. Her blue eyes widened, her gaze snapping down to where she had been shot, tugging up her top. Blood crusted around it, but the wound appeared to be at least a week old, not hours.

A tiny noise came from her. She pinched an object off the ground, holding it up—the bullet that had been buried in her gut. Her gaze went to Killian, who sat there like he was made of stone. His expression went blank.

"I don't understand."

I let out a crazed, happy laugh. "We have a lot to discuss."

"That we do." A man's voice turned the entire group behind us. Many drew their guns, ready to shoot.

Jethro stepped from the shadows, his gaze drifting over everyone, giving nothing away, no reaction to the weapons on him.

"Jethro." I stood up, placing myself between him and my friends. The ruckus we made probably woke up the entire troupe.

"You're past has tracked you down, I see," he observed, his body still almost one with the shadows.

"Sort of, but… They aren't the bad past."

"Let me guess, they need a place to stay tonight?"

I wondered if he regretted picking me up off the embankment, wished he just rolled on without me. His troupe, their lives, had been in constant threat because of me.

"I wouldn't dare ask you."

"But you hope I offer," he replied, his voice smooth, with a touch of danger. "Like I told you, I have a weakness for the outcasts. We have a couple of wagons some can shelter in. The rest I can offer blankets and a place by the fire."

"Thank you." I bowed my head. I owed this man so much.

He dipped his head in return and slipped back into the darkness.

"What the hell is that thing?" A screech jumped me to Esmeralda. Tad was gone. The woman stared down at the imp sitting on her knee, flipping her off.

Chirp! Bitzy sang, wiggling her middle finger at Esmeralda in a hello. A nice one. Bitzy had to be high.

"Get this thing away from me."

Chirp! Did the imp actually grin at the bitter old lady?

"That's Bitzy. I'm Opie." Opie appeared on her other knee, making Esmeralda scramble back, getting to her feet.

257

"Well, that was rude," Opie huffed.

Esmeralda peered around like she finally realized where she was.

"Who the fuck are all of you?"

The metal of the rusting Ferris wheel squealed in protest as a breeze gusted off the river, fog creeping over the ground, circling around me, dampening the already chilly air. Still a few hours from dawn, the night was at its most bewitching.

It took a while to get everyone settled, promising we would catch up in the morning. Rosie accepted the fact she was now fae with relative ease, though I wondered how long that would last until the shock wore off and the reality of what happened to her set in.

Lukas, Ash, and Birdie hugged me, but I still sensed a bubbling resentment toward me under the surface, a quiet anger waiting to lash out from each of them. Caden, Scorpion, and Killian were standoffish, making me feel a greater divide between me and the eleven who had arrived. They all shared a bond, life and death situations, and struggles. I did not. I didn't blame them. I had run away. Abandoned them. Killed people they knew and loved.

There would be no forgiveness for that, but I hoped in time they would come to understand why I had to leave. My journey was meant to bring me here. To this troupe, to Esmeralda. Without her, I wouldn't have Tad. I wouldn't have learned so much about separating my powers from the nectar, finding myself. Though I still had so much more work to do. Everything still seemed so fragile, as if one tiny crack could destroy all I worked for.

Leaning over into the icy river, I washed Rosie's blood

from my hands, distant murmurs coming from the bonfire in camp. I needed a moment. The adrenaline rollercoaster from almost losing Rosie rattled me. Sucking in a deep breath, the cold air filled my lungs, and I tried to clear out the nerves bouncing around.

My body froze.

Prickles danced up the back of my neck, wrapping around my throat.

My lids squeezed together briefly as every cell in me came alive, aware of each molecule in the air and how he took up so many of them.

Warwick Farkas.

I hadn't expected seeing him to almost bowl me over. The buzz of joy, fear, happiness, and guilt.

We had yet to speak, to acknowledge each other. The moment had arrived, and I wasn't sure I was ready.

Violence, anger, and vengeance incinerated my skin, drilling into my spine like a hammer.

Our link was dampened, but I could feel him engulf me in his presence. His wrath.

Rising, I kept my chin high. Warwick had stayed in the darkness as we settled into camp, though there was never a second I didn't feel his penetrating gaze.

Stalking me.

Lying in wait.

Hunting openly.

Slowly, I turned around. I should have prepared myself better. Air sizzled down my throat as I sucked in, my chest locking up.

His 6'7" frame loomed at the edge of the tree line shrouded in darkness. Only aqua eyes burned through the fog and shadows, punching through my gut.

I was tough. A force. I could kill in a blink, but in the

259

face of this man's dominance, I would let him burn me to the ground.

We stared at each other, threads webbing in the air, emotion crackling in the space between us. There was no one else. Nothing else. Even without our link, I could feel his rage, the hurt he buried underneath, the fine line he walked between wanting to love me and kill me.

"Warwick—"

"Shut the fuck up, princess." His voice scraped along the dirt, climbing up my legs and slithering between my thighs. He stepped out from the trees, his gaze narrowed on me, his entire body throbbing with energy, making him fill up every available breath of air. My eyes devoured him. Dirty, bloody, and battle-worn, he was the most carnal, wild, virile man I had ever encountered. There were no half-measures with him. When he took, he took it all.

My mouth opened again to say something, but he let out a low growl.

"I will tell you when you can *fucking* speak." He strode up to me. His aqua eyes tracked me, his nose flaring as he inhaled, his jaw cracking as he reached up to my face, zapping electricity through my veins. My lungs tripped over themselves when he gently trailed his fingers down my cheek, his eyes softening for a moment, like he couldn't believe I was really here.

Then it was gone.

A snarl ebbed up his throat, and he roughly seized my neck, his thumb tipping up my chin, his gaze hardening, rage coming from his pores. His shoulders expanded, wrath bringing the Legend to the surface. There was no point in apologies, no use in begging for his forgiveness.

Nor would I.

My eyes met the Wolf's, the man famous for coming

back from the dead and seeking his revenge, slaughtering thousands with calculated cruelty and no remorse. The man who people considered death himself.

And I was his maker.

I did not challenge him, but I didn't bow down either. He would never apologize to me if roles were reversed, nor would I to him. This was what I had to do. I would not be sorry.

His chest heaved as my gaze burrowed into him, sensing no regret, no remorse. Our stances clashed like waves against a rock, unrelenting and unbreakable.

His grip on my throat tightened, his thumb digging into the soft spot under my chin. "You think I can't break you, princess?" he growled, yanking me into his body, his physique vibrating with anger.

Blinking, my mouth parted to speak.

"I may not be able to sense you like normal or feel the bond, but I know your expression, Kovacs. I know how you think." He snarled, his mouth so close to mine, heat beaded up the back of my neck, plunging down into my core. "And I will break you."

"Just try, Farkas," I whispered hoarsely back at him. He jerked at the sound of my voice, his ribs knocking into mine.

"I told you not to fucking open your mouth. Unless it's to wrap around my cock." He pulled me in so close, his nose knocked into me, his mouth brushing mine. His nearness almost broke me. His touch, his smell, the feel of him pressing against me built a sob in my gut, realizing how much I had missed him.

Sensing my need for him, he yanked me back, his lip lifting, staring down at me. His anger was too vivid for him to allow me any comfort.

I was to be punished.

261

His blue-green eyes darkened as he let go of my throat, grabbing my arm and hauling me with him. His large steps forced me to double mine, taking us farther away from camp.

Stopping right at the Ferris wheel, its human birdcages creaking and swaying in the breeze. He whipped me around to face him, his voice thick.

"Strip," he ordered.

Inhaling sharply, hating and loving how violently he could make my body react had my pussy pulsing. He'd trained it to sit, wait, and beg.

My gaze never leaving his, I yanked off my jacket, pulling my sweater over my head, leaving me in my sports bra.

"I said strip, not a striptease." Though his gaze trailed over my bare skin hungrily, pausing on the scars marking my body from the trauma we had gone through. The moments we survived together.

Kicking my boots off, I wiggled out of my trousers and socks, leaving me just in a bra and underwear. A noise rattled in his chest, his eyes sliding over every inch of me. Though I didn't feel cold, I shivered, the freezing temperatures melting against my heated skin.

His boots nipped at the tips of my toes, his palm brushing up my arm, causing more goosebumps to pimple my flesh. His frame loomed over mine, eclipsed and engulfed, so easy to consume and swallow me whole. I wanted him to. Whatever he was going to do to me, I craved it.

His fingers moved to the elastic hem of my bra, hands scraping over my nipples. My mouth parted, my body pulsed, wetness seeping from me.

Fuck. I forgot how easily Warwick could rob me of all logic.

As though he realized his touch was too gentle, he

grabbed the fabric, ripping the sports bra off me in a single rip, his warm palms covering my breasts, kneading them roughly and flicking at my nipples, creating gasps from my throat.

He muttered something under his breath before he stepped away.

"Get the fuck on your knees, Kovacs."

Once again, I kept my gaze glued to him as I lowered myself, anticipation skating over my nerves. My breath picked up as he reached for his pants, undoing the zipper and sliding them down his legs. His massive bulge was no longer contained in his boxer shorts, the tip of his cock pushing out, dripping with pre-cum. My pussy pulsed, clawing with the need to feel him thrust inside me. The need hit so hard my head spun, a small cry popping off my tongue.

Warwick clutched my chin, his other hand pushing his boxers down, stroking himself. "You don't get relief until I say. You understand?"

I nodded. The sound of my heart thumped in my ears, my mouth craving his taste.

"Take off your panties. I want to see your desire leak down your leg while I fuck your mouth."

Bazdmeg. Heat swathed my body, trembling my muscles. I pulled off my soaked knickers, the cool air licking between my folds. The contradiction of the freezing temperatures against my hot skin only increased the sensations running through me.

Warwick wound his finger through my hair, gripping the back of my head with a sharp tug, tipping my head back. I didn't hesitate; I licked the tip of him, tasting, feeling him jerk as I wrapped my tongue around him. I took him into my mouth as far as I could, sliding him down my throat.

"Fuck!" Warwick seethed, his fingers digging into my

scalp. Painfully slow, I licked and sucked, feeling the pulsing vein in his cock tighten against his skin, pumping blood faster. "Ko-vacs," he growled, slipping between anger and pleasure, his hand pushing his cock down deeper. My nails dug into his ass, bringing him closer as I picked up my pace, a hum building in the back of my throat.

"Fuck!" he spat. "Fuck." His grip on my hair was constricting, triggering wetness to drip from me; my need grew so sharply that it felt almost painful. His hips pumped, pushing in so deep that my eyes watered, and my throat burned.

He wanted retribution. To punish me. And I wanted more. To be the one who would bring him to *his* knees.

Sliding my hands down his ass, I cupped his balls, rolling and tugging on them, the vibration in my throat deepening.

"Fuuuucckk!" A roar echoed in the night. His grip twisted through my hair, yanking on the strands, sending desire straight to my core. My pussy throbbed so hard, and I ached for relief, sensing my own climax coming along with his. I reached down, rubbing through my folds, ebbing the ache, our groans filling the air.

"No," he ground out, wrenching my head back, pulling away from me, forcing me to look up at him, his eyes burning with lust and fury. "You *only* get relief when *I* say."

Hauling me to my feet, he rammed me back into the Ferris wheel, the cold metal bars of the carriage pressing into my spine, the shock causing me to gasp. Stripping off his jacket and t-shirt, his ripped torso pulled my focus, distracting me. The urge to touch him, to feel every muscle and scar under my fingers, to trace his tattoos with my tongue, had me reaching for him.

A snarl lifted his lip as he cupped my wrists with one

264

hand, yanking them over my head. Using his t-shirt, he tied my arms to the carriage bars, stretching my naked body out, shooting a thread of exhilarated fear through me, feeling my vulnerability.

Getting out of his boots and pants, Warwick stepped up to me, his breath slipping over my skin, tantalizing every cell in my body. Two fingers slid up my inner thigh, grazing across my folds.

"You will pay, princess." Brutal savagery reflected in his eyes as his fingers parted me, sliding through.

"Oh gods." I moaned, the frosty temperatures upping the intensity of every touch, my back arching, my hips opening wider as he continued his intentionally slow movement through me.

"Fucking dripping for me," he rumbled, a nerve in his cheek twitching like it took everything to stay in control. "Your pussy miss me?" He rubbed harder, his fingers teasing my entrance.

"Fuck… yes." My legs opened wider, my hips bucking into him. My body was angry at me for going this long without him.

"How bad does it want my dick sinking into it? Fucking it so hard and deep?" His fingers teased me but didn't go farther.

My head was a blur of need, no longer able to think past anything but him. The world could crumble down around us, and I wouldn't care as long as he was inside me.

"Warwick…" A plea broke from me, clamoring for his touch, for the feel of him.

"Whose pussy is this?" He circled my entrance, pushing in just a little more, then pulled away.

A growl caught in my throat, my arms tugging against their binds. "Mine." I glared at him. "But I'll let you live inside it from time to time."

A smirk tipped his lips, his eyes glittering. "Wrong answer, Kovacs."

He went to his knees. Grabbing one of my legs, he pulled it up on his shoulder, parting me wide. He didn't tease, his tongue driving straight through me, nipping at my clit, jolting my body with a loud cry. The action was so intense, the air stuck in my throat, my vision clouding at the sides.

"Fuck, I forgot how good you taste." He gripped my thighs, diving into me like a man on a mission. A mission to break me.

A scream filled my chest, coiling strange noises from me as the force cascaded down on me, drowning me.

A breeze weaved around us, licking at my skin, feeling like hands pinching at my nipples. My bound arms thrashed, trying to break free, needing more, needing to run my fingers through his hair.

He cupped my ass, pulling my other leg onto his shoulder, taking me completely off the ground. My spine pressed hard into the bars, stretching me more. There was something about being completely in his control, allowing me to focus on every sensation in my body and its response to Warwick, the nonexistent line we had between danger and safety. Between violence and love.

We were gray.

Sweat coated my forehead as my climax climbed, hitched cries falling from my lips. Everyone could hear me, and I didn't care.

"Oh gods… I'm going to come." My thighs squeezed him harder, trying to make him go deeper.

Warwick dropped my legs with brutality, his mouth leaving me as he stood up, punching cold air into my lungs.

A cruel smirk curled his lips as his tongue licked me off them.

"Baszd meg." My chest heaved, pain throbbing through my core.

"I told you that you'd be punished." Retribution weaved angrily around his words, a whisper of his emotions slipping through my soul. It loomed under the surface—his hurt and fear, the fact he missed me. That was not something Warwick knew how to deal with.

Love.

It all jumbled into wrath. Death. Vengeance.

And I was the target.

He untied the t-shirt, flipping me around and retying my wrists above my head again, yanking my hips toward him. A trickle of trepidation filled my bloodstream, increasing my need for air and heightening every sensation in my body.

His palm came down on my ass, echoing through the air. A choked cry tore up my throat, fire sparking through every vein, heat bursting into my cheeks and down my throat.

I thought I would hate it. Feel demeaned. But as he spanked me again, my nipples became painfully hard, wetness dripping down my leg, my body shaking with overstimulation.

Holy fuck.

When he came down again, it was closer to my pussy, making me buck like a wild horse. Everything in me became desperate. Violent. The bars on the carriage groaned, the t-shirt ripping as I writhed against them. His mouth skated up the back of my neck at the same time I felt a hint of his lips nipping at my clit. His shadow grazed me.

"Warwick." His name was beyond an entreaty. It was an order. The air crackled with our energy, our lust raining down on the earth. A rumble of lightning hinted in the sky. Ghosts buzzed around us, feeling the intensity grow.

"Is this wet, dripping pussy mine, Kovacs?" He bit my

ear, his hand smacking my bare ass again, rolling a choked sob through me. My orgasm was on a knife's edge, tears trailing down my cheeks. One finger dipped into my ass as he spanked again. My legs bowed.

"Is it?"

"Yes!" I belted out. "Gods, yes. It's fucking yours, Farkas!"

A deep growl rattled his chest, one hand wrapping around my neck, the other parting me. A sob wrenched up my throat as the tip of him slid through me, taunting my entrance.

"Warwick!" I reared into him, desperately trying to get him deeper, my teeth clenching together. "Fuck my pussy now."

"I thought it was mine." He squeezed down on my neck at the same time he thrust deep into me.

For a moment, I had no understanding of reality. I heard our bellows knock into the clouds high above, my body going into shock as I felt every massive inch of him slide in, filling me to the point of pain. I wanted him to break me, to hurt so good, I never wanted to return to reality again.

He pulled almost all the way out before he pushed back in again, slamming me into the bars with a loud moan.

"Fuck, princess." His voice broke, emotion leaking through, twisting my head to peer at him. Our eyes met. We didn't speak, but we didn't look away as he plunged in again, spinning my head to the point I could barely stand. My arms taking on more of my weight, I pushed back into him.

"Harder. Fuck me harder."

Determination locked his jaw, his grip on my neck tightening as he rammed into me so hard my feet lifted from the ground, pressing my body against the passenger cage. He drove in deeper, running me up and down the bars, my folds parting through the cool metal, rubbing at my clit as he railed into me.

Noise and cries pitched from my chest, no longer feeling part of this world. If enemy troops descended, coming to slaughter us, we still wouldn't stop.

This was the highest bliss, feeling him inside me, having him back, knowing this was my forever. Him and me, no matter what we came across or what we had to fight.

Whispers of our bond were there, a shadow of my tongue tasting his skin as I licked up his thigh, causing Warwick to suck in air. The hand at my neck pulled me tighter to him like he couldn't get close enough. His dick thrust in harder, rubbing me harder into the metal, imaginary fingers pinching at my nipples.

"Warwick!" I felt my climax barreling for me.

"Come, princess," his husky voice ordered.

Color exploded behind my lids at his command, free falling off a cliff into uninhibited pleasure. The bliss so pure it could be mistaken for pain. My pussy ruthlessly clamped around him, taking no prisoners. I could feel him in every fiber of my being. Possessing. Claiming. Calling ownership on him with no apologies.

"Fuuuuuuccckkk!" Warwick ripped at my binds, freeing my arms, his erection so hard I felt it throb like a heartbeat.

Pulling out of me, I cried out as he tore open the door to the carriage, towing me in with him. Taking the seat, his enormous frame barely fitting, he grabbed my hips, yanking me back down on his lap, straddling him. He thrust his cock back into me, slamming his hips into mine with a brutal force, grazing every nerve.

Lightning cracked, spirits zooming around us, our energy bursting through the atmosphere.

"*Sotet démonom.*" He growled in my ear, biting at my neck.

My eyes rolled back in my head, my body jerking like I

269

was being electrocuted, another orgasm ripping through me as he plunged in again and again. A roar bellowed as he emptied himself inside of me. Blackness took over my sight, my ears ringing. The only feeling was his hot cum branding me—taking me away from all space and time.

Then I was struck with flashes of us strolling across blood-soaked ground, dead bodies scattered at our feet, fire burning behind.

The Grey and The Wolf.

The link between us sank in with teeth, crashing another wave through us. Air ceased in my lungs, everything blinking out for a moment. Only the feel of his arms wrapping around me, crushing me against him, keeping me upright, brought me back to myself.

Our chests heaved together, and I nestled into the crook of his neck, hiding in his hair. I took a deep breath, taking in his scent. Peace and calm centered me. I realized I hadn't felt that since I left him.

"*Baszd.*" His voice was coarse and raw.

I leaned back, our eyes meeting. We watched each other silently for a few moments before he reached up, his hands cupping my face. "Don't ever fucking do that again." I could feel no more anger. His walls were down, showing me his truth. "Whatever it is, we're in this together." He tipped his forehead into mine. "Okay? You don't run. Not from me."

"I almost hurt Simon."

"But you didn't."

"I killed Tad and *hundreds* of others. Innocent people. I could've harmed you and so many more."

"I've killed thousands. Many who were innocent." His thumb slid over my bottom lip. "That might be a deal breaker for some, but remember, we don't play by the same rules. We are survivors. We live in the gray. Like I said, if we have to swim in blood and climb through death… we will." He ran his hands to the back of my jaw. "You think you can hurt me? Bring it, Kovacs. That's my fucking foreplay."

His sentiment fizzled heat through me, which popped his eyebrows up, his cock stirring inside me. "The fact that death and my pain turn you on… damn… I definitely found my match." His gaze burned into me.

I tipped one eyebrow up back at him.

"Fine. *Mate*," he rumbled against my lips. "Happy?"

"Ecstatic." My mouth grazed his. "I love you."

He let out a deep growl. If there was a last wall Warwick was keeping up, it crumbled. He gripped my face roughly, pulling me to him, his mouth claiming mine hungrily, possessing every last bit of me, burrowing the connection deeper between us. I could feel his other mouth licking up my spine, ghost fingers curling around my breasts as his real one gripped my hips, grinding me against him, his dick hardening inside me.

He didn't need to say it back. I could feel it surround me, penetrating my soul. I knew how he felt about me. But as our bodies started moving together again, the carriage squeaking in protest, I heard a whisper brush my ear.

"Same, Sotet démonom. In every fucking color."

Chapter 22
Killian

"Here are some extra blankets." Lulu, a petite woman barely coming up to my waist, held up several pelts for me, her American southern drawl pulling my attention from the pair near the fire.

"Thank you." The crisp reply was all I could get through my clenched teeth. Every muscle in my body was rigid and ready to snap. My magic crashed against the surface of my skin, ready to explode. Turbulent and chaotic.

The impregnable noble leader I'd been for two decades had suddenly become brittle and corroded. Nothing had been the same since Věrhăza. My control, the persona I put out to the world, who I had become—everything was hanging on by threads. As if the suits I wore were only costumes, but I could no longer act in a performance.

"Well, I'll just place them right here for ya, sweetie." She cleared her throat, setting them near me. I realized I was just staring at her, my mind somewhere else. "Anything else I can get you?"

"No," I clipped. "Thank. You." Every syllable was a struggle, as if I spoke too much, it would grind what was left of my sanity into dust, letting the mounting fury inside free.

"Well, can I say, it is an honor to meet ya. I never, in my wildest dreams, thought we would have a fae lord bunking with us." She curtsied, her hand tapping at her heart. "Such a handsome one too. It is truly a privilege. I'm happier than a hog in mud." She winked before striding off.

I almost wanted to laugh. Here was a woman from a different country respecting me and revering my role better than the one who was from here.

My gaze shot back across the bonfire, the flames shimmering off her shiny red hair. The luminosity around her wasn't subtle; it blazed like sunshine, and I could see and feel it with every fiber of my being. It wrapped around my cock, squeezing it tight.

Rosie was stunning before, but the fae essence running through her veins now made her porcelain skin glow and illuminated her already bright blue eyes. Everything about her caused my chest to seize, rendering all logic moot and digging into the foundation of my being. The gaping hole I had felt when I thought she was dead. The terror of losing her.

I had whispered to her the entire journey, begging her to stay with me. *To live.* Now, all I felt was burning rage and embarrassment. Not only for feeling those things but letting everyone see.

For forgetting who I was.

There was no doubt everyone could see I cared more than I should have or wanted to… and once again, she had chosen the other man.

My gaze stalked Wesley as he moved around her, touching her repeatedly. His knuckles brushed her cheeks, his fingers slid down her arms, he palmed her lower back insistently. He hadn't left her side since we came down to the

273

encampment. He hovered over her, smiling like a fool, attending to her every need, barely giving her an inch of space.

The place around me bustled as the leader, Jethro, had gotten some of his troupe to set us up in the extra wagons or bedding by the fire, providing food and drink. Some kindly opened up to us, offering what they had, while others glared at us as intruders, which I understood. In this world, it was hard to trust, and I keenly knew that those you let in could stab you in the back without warning.

My past with Kalaraja and the great pirate Croygen had taught me that lesson long ago.

Staying far away from the others, my attention went over the camp. Ash, Lukas, and Kek were drinking tea by the fire, the three of them in their own world. I didn't know how serious any of them were about each other, but the energy coming off them went beyond lust and beyond simple friendship. They just worked, as if each one offered what the other one was missing. Lukas was more reserved, while Ash was more open to physical touch, and Kek was far blunter and more vocal. All three looked so giddy around each other, smiling, laughing, having their inside jokes, and sly shared glances.

It was like a knife in my chest. A jealousy I tried to cut out of myself and never experience again.

Not able to look at their bliss, my attention drifted to Birdie, who might try to give me advice but was awful at taking her own. Both she and Caden acted like the other one didn't exist, though they both watched each other, then looked away when they were caught. Scorpion had taken off into the forest, his mood darker than mine. The loss of Hanna hung over the group, with no time to fully understand it. We had been too caught up with Rosie to comprehend what had happened. I hadn't known Hanna well, though fighting for our lives together in the Games, and going through Věrhăza together, turned us into a fucked-up family. I had no doubt we would go after her. I was afraid, which I think Scorpion was as well, that she wouldn't want us to save her. That it would be too late. She would be one of them.

A laugh yanked my head back to the redhead like it was a conditioned response. She nodded at whatever Wesley was saying, a cup of steaming tea in her hands. Her eyes slid to the side, her face turning toward me, appearing like she was searching for something. Wesley's fingers touched her face, turning her back to him, his chin dipping down, murmuring something in her ear.

Her eyes widened slightly, peering up at him. Wesley cupped her face, his lean, tall form moving closer to her, a sensual smile on his lips as his hungry gaze ran over her, about to kiss her.

The last of my strength cracked. Blistering rage colored my vision, searing through me. The need to destroy what I considered a threat had my muscles tightening, ready to fight and kill. Protect what was mine.

My attention locked on Wesley. I took several steps before I realized what I was doing.

She wasn't mine. That life wasn't meant for me. I halted, my fists crunching the bones in my fingers. My body shook, overwhelmed with the drive to take out all competitors.

How I became a lord.

Wearing a nice suit let people forget how cutthroat and ruthless I was, the blood staining my hands, and what I had done to get to where I was.

Instead of slicing Wesley's throat like I wanted, I turned away, barreling away from the group, my wrath bubbling up like a kettle. My ears rang with my boiling blood, hearing

275

nothing but my pulse. My breath billowed in front of me as my feet sprinted through overgrown woods. Years of neglect had nature creeping back and taking over.

Forced to stop at a dead end where a small groundskeeper's house sat abandoned, covered in weeds and brush, a frustrated bellow tore from my throat, spilling out my anger. Snapping off a branch, I swung it in my hands like a samurai sword, hacking at the brush. The years of training in Kenjutsu and Kendo moved my body with brutal precision. The hours Kat and I would practice on deck with Master Yukimura were the only thing that centered me, reining in my temper. It was all I had to hold on to when I felt everything else was falling apart. I had done it every morning in prison before the alarm went off. With the iron collar ripping me apart inside, it was the only thing that kept me going. To keep fighting when my body wanted to succumb.

I continued hacking at the thicket. Thorns and branches sliced into my hands, nipping at my face. Blood trickled down my cheek, dripping off my hands, but it only fueled the urge to let my barriers down and let the world feel my fury.

To drown in it.

"Killian!" My name rang somewhere in my head, her voice teasing me, mocking me. Not giving me a moment of peace. With a cry, I stabbed harder, my palms ripping across the rough wood.

"Killian, stop!" A figure moved into my peripheral, a hand grabbing my arm. My body went into defense, swinging around to the attacker, primed to strike.

Her blue eyes were wide, her throat bobbing, but she didn't move away, her stance challenging my own.

Rosie.

I blinked out of my trance, stumbling back.

She stared at me, peeling me down to nothing. Her

276

steady gaze created more emotion to boil in my veins. Different, but just as violent, just as crushing.

"What are you doing here?" Glancing at the empty path behind her, I took another step back, feeling my barriers build back up, trying to pretend what she saw was ordinary and certainly had nothing to do with her. "Surprised your lover let you out of his sight." A snarl slipped through my pretense, layering another level of shame on my chest at letting her see my feelings so clearly. "Better go back. He'll be looking for you."

"And if I did?" Her nose flared as her eyes leveled on me. "You wouldn't do anything, would you?"

My brows furrowed, her response not what I was expecting.

"Why would I?" I glared. "You two are perfect for each other. And now that you are fae"—I waved over her glowing figure— "you seem to be adapting well to it."

"Are you taking the piss right now?" Her English accent thickened in her anger. "I can't believe you." She stomped up to me. "I haven't had time to even contemplate what happened. The fact I died. That I'm no longer human. I don't know how I feel about any of it. What to think or even how to come close to accepting it. So no, I can't say I am *adapting*. And I'm certainly *not* all right. The only thing I do know right now is I almost died. And there was only one person who kept me holding on to life." She held up her finger.

"I swear, if you've come here to tell me Wesley is—"

"You! You wanker!" she burst out, her hands flying, shoving at my chest. "Your voice the entire ride here... I clung to it... it kept my heart pumping. And when everything was fading away, it was your voice I heard calling me back. You saved my life. Not just because you knew about the nectar, but..." An infuriated sob hitched from her throat. "It

277

was *you* I felt gripping my soul and keeping me rooted to the earth." She pushed me again, stumbling me back into the wall of the house. "I can suddenly feel you *everywhere*. Under my skin, in my head. From the moment I came back…" She stepped back from me. "And you stood there like a *coward*."

"Excuse me?" I pushed off the wall, using my body to loom over her, though she didn't flinch. No one had ever called me a coward. *Ever*. If they had, they wouldn't live long after.

"You heard me." Rosie lifted her chin, not backing down. "You are so afraid. Afraid of feeling, afraid of living. Afraid of letting anyone in. Probably mad I am fae now because you no longer have an excuse to walk away, acting like you are some hero for doing it."

My head tipped back, her accusation arrowing my chest.

"You paint yourself as the victim so you can stay in your safe bubble. I'm sorry that girl hurt you, but we've all been hurt, Killian. That's life." She shook her head. "I've already lived a life where someone's insecurities and ego took precedence over me. Where I was tossed aside and treated like a pet. I have fucked for money, and I have been raped for revenge. I will not be that girl again. I want someone who will fight for me. Who loves me more than his own issues. Who could give a fuck about right or wrong when it came to me. And if Wesley is that man, then I guess you're right. I *should* return to him." She turned away from me.

Rage-filled terror plunged into my system, tearing down every one of my walls, showing me the only certainty I knew.

Her.

Not the fear of her, but the fear of losing her. Of watching her happy with someone else when I knew she was mine. I could feel it in every fiber of my being, screaming from my soul. I sensed the weight when I first met her, saw her on stage, but I shoved it away. Ignored it. Now it roared through every molecule of my body.

The mere idea of her in Wesley's arms, kissing him, moaning *his* name, colored my vision red. How did I ever believe I would have been okay with that?

I would have killed him.

Lunging, I grabbed her arm, yanking her back to me, a possessive noise vibrating in my throat. My muscles quaked, but I was trying so hard to keep myself in control, afraid I could hurt her.

Her blue eyes went back and forth between mine, her hand slowly reaching up and touching my face, her fingers sliding through the blood on my cheek. "It's not only me who pretends to be someone else for a living."

"What are you talking about?"

"This character you are trying to portray. He doesn't fit anymore, if he ever did. He only keeps you confined. I see you, Killian. I see the passion you keep inside. All the hurt, pain, anger, and violence. We are the same."

"You are nothing like me," I snarled. "What I've done…"

"What *you've* done?"

"You fucked people… I've *killed* them."

"Do you know why I am so faithful to Kitty? It isn't just the debt she helped me get out of, giving me a home and a family. She helped cover up a murder."

"What?"

"I shot one of my rapists in the head. He came into Kitty's one night looking to get his dick wet. He didn't even recognize me. I took him upstairs… and I shot him. Kitty helped me drag out the body and get rid of it."

I blinked against a swell of fury at the idea any person

279

ever made her suffer. I wanted to bring him back to life just so I could kill him again.

"I have blood on my hands too, and I don't regret it for a moment. The only regret I have is letting Vicente control me for so long, even after he walked out. You are letting her do the same to you." She stepped right up to me. "I don't care what you've done. I don't care who've you killed. Your seedy past. Or the fact you are a lord or have money. I don't give a shite, Killian. It means nothing to me. I just want *you.*"

Air burned down my esophagus as I sucked in sharply, my chest heaving.

"Rosie…" I rasped out her name, our mouths almost touching. A rumble of thunder rolled over our heads, though I could see no storm in the sky. Lightning flashed, the air thickening with sexual energy, only igniting my nerves with more desire.

"Nina," she whispered. "I want to hear you say my real name. Just once."

My dick hardened to the point of pain. "Nina…"

She sucked in sharply, the sound breaking my last reserve. Grabbing her head, I crushed my mouth to hers, a hungry groan growling from my throat as if I had been starved all my life of the one thing I wanted. Like this was what I had been searching for all my life. I tipped her head, deepening the kiss, my tongue sweeping deeper into her mouth. Claiming and searing.

She moaned, her fingers dragging roughly through my hair, tugging me closer, making me lose my mind. I had kissed many women in my time, some amazing, some okay. Sometimes it was a means to an end. To get to the sex. Get off. Leave. Rinse and repeat.

Kissing Rosie shredded everything I had ever experienced before, and her lips demanded just as much back from me.

"Killian…" she gasped against my mouth, and I knew she was feeling the same. Whatever this power was, it was making me forget everything but her. Nothing else mattered. Nothing in the world would stop me from being with her.

She rubbed my cock, shooting sparks up my spine, as my mouth took hers again, wanting her to forget every other man who ever had the privilege of tasting her lips. I grabbed her ass, lifting her up, her legs circling my hips as I pushed her up against the cabin. Her hands tore at my jacket. "Fuck foreplay. I need you inside me. *Now.*"

I wanted nothing more, but her pleasure meant more than mine. I didn't want to be another male on her list. The endless stream who came running back to her but never cared about her, who never made her special, making her their first and only priority.

"Too bad." I pulled her bloody, ripped sweater over her head. She had lost so much weight in prison, but her body was absolutely perfect to me, whatever it looked like. My hand trailed over the still-healing scar from where she had been shot earlier. The marks of her past dotted her pale white skin. I wanted to know every story of them, how she got them. There wasn't an inch of her skin I didn't want to explore and worship.

I slid my hands over her breasts, feeling her nipples harden under my palms. After reaching back to unhook her bra, I squeezed and massaged them, smearing my blood over them like I was marking them as mine.

"Perfection." I swallowed before taking one in my mouth.

A hitched breath snapped from her, her body arching into me as my tongue flicked and sucked on her nipple.

"Killian." She drew her nails up the back of my neck as I moved on to the other.

"I want this to be all about you." I dropped to my knees. My fingers skated over her hips, slowly dragging her trousers and underwear down and taking off her boots. I licked my lips, staring at her naked body, her eyes glittering with desire. "Watch me." I kept my eyes on her as my mouth grazed her thigh. Her head tipped back into the wall, but she didn't break eye contact, a shaky sigh expelling from her lips.

My fingers dug into her thighs, spreading her legs wide for me, lifting a leg over my shoulder. My mouth skimmed her pussy, the tip of my tongue just hinting at her folds.

"Bloody hell," she croaked. Her hips bucked forward, putting a sinful smile on my lips. Pinning her down with my arm, I peered up at her.

"I've wanted to taste you for so long." I nipped at her thigh, biting, making her jolt at the contact before I soothed it with my tongue.

"Killian." Her nails dug into my scalp.

The feel of her tugging on my hair fueled me like a fiend, and I licked through her, sucking on her clit hard until she let out a long, primal moan.

"So fucking incredible." I gripped her tighter, opening her wider to me. She was like nothing I had ever tasted before and was now the only one I'd want.

"Bloody hell." Her hips rolled with me. "Oh gods!" She gasped, almost as if she was in shock. Her body responded with verve, clenching around me almost instantly. I couldn't stop my male pride, the sensation in my gut that she could never pretend with me. Her legs were trembling without me even fully entering her.

I slipped two fingers inside her, pumping them as my lips tugged and sucked at her clit, and she let out a scream. I let go of any ego, giving her everything. Hearing her pleasure only turned me on more. I feasted on her pussy, listening for every cry of pleasure, learning her body. Though I felt like I already knew it; some strange connection understood how to please her without prior knowledge.

Electricity danced across the sky, tapping against our skin. I could feel the familiar energy, knowing it wasn't just us adding to the intensity in the air, spilling down on us. Brexley and Warwick's energy was too intense not to recognize. It added to our pleasure, their desire and magic on top of our own, making pre-cum spill from my tip.

"Killian?" She scratched at my back. "*Please*. I need you inside me!"

I could only growl in response. Her demand was too much to ignore, no matter how badly I wanted to taste her orgasm. I wanted to feel her clench around me more. Standing, I kicked off my boots. She was swift to undo my pants, like she had it down to a science. She shoved them over my hips, her hand sliding into my boxer briefs, wrapping around me, producing a loud groan from me.

"Holy shite." She tried to wrap all the way around me. "Like, holy shite… I felt you hard before, but my *lord*." She lifted a brow. "You would think I had seen it all in my line of work."

"Bigger than you're used to?" I pressed my hips into her touch, using my body to tower over her.

She bit down on her lip, lust coloring her cheeks as she rubbed me harder, robbing me of breath. "Think I can handle it."

"Have to warn you. Once you ride a fae lord… you don't come back."

"I won't be riding a fae lord." She rubbed her thumb through my cum, then took it to her mouth and sucked it off. "I'll be riding you, *not* the title. And that's a ride I might want to stay on."

A hiss slid through my teeth, my hands heaving her

thighs up around me, feeling her heat wrap around my dick as I rammed us back into the cabin.

"But I *am* a fae lord. Can't have one without the other. I have power and magic most do not."

"You think you can hurt me?" She rubbed her wet pussy over my cock. "I am a lot harder to hurt now. But I dare you to give it your best shot, my *lord*."

My title coming off her lips cut the last bit of logic from my mind. I became the kid who fought for food, the pirate who killed for coin, and the noble who tortured for power.

I hitched her higher up the wall, giving her no time before I thrust deep inside her. A bellow tore from me, her scream piercing the air. Energy crackled down my spine, bursting through me, charging me with magic I had never felt before.

"Bazzzzdmeg!"

Nothing in my long life could touch what I felt, overwhelming my sensations and nerves so much I had to halt for a moment, my legs dipping.

"Oh gods!" Rosie's mouth parted, her nails cutting through my skin, which had me more desperate. Pushing in deeper, I still was not completely in. Nerves burned with heat and pleasure, her cries filling the air. "Deeper!"

I pulled out, pushing back in so deep and hard that I felt her muscles lock up, her eyes rolling back in her head, a guttural noise ascending from the depths of her toes.

"Shitshitshit!" The feel of her tight and wet around me, gripping my cock like a fist, stole my breath. It was unbelievable, like I had been searching for this all my life.

Another crack of lightning danced across the sky, swelling my cock. "Fuck!" My hips drove into her, shoving her up the wall higher.

Brexley and Warwick's energy sparked at my nerves,

284

like I could feel them fucking as well, only adding to the intensity. I had been a part of several orgies in my time, high on something, but this was on another plane.

Raw. Brutal. Violent.

They crashed together into visceral pleasure.

This was the most real and alive I had ever felt in my life… with someone I never wanted to let go of.

"Harder!" Rosie matched my intensity. The sounds of her wetness, my dick pounding the fuck out of her, echoed through the trees. Her hands sank to the cleft of my ass, making me jolt as she pressed down on nerves there. A choked bark drove from my lungs, my muscles burning. My vision blurred, making me savage.

I lost all control.

Swinging us around, my dick still thrusting into her, we went to the ground. I spread her legs wide, placing them over my shoulder and plunging even deeper. Her gasps and cries pitched as I drove into her like a freight train. Sweat and blood covered our bodies.

Movement in my peripheral popped my gaze up for a moment. In the trees, half covered in shadows, I saw Wesley. Watching us. I didn't know if he just walked up to look for her or if he had been there for a while, but when our eyes met, something primal took over.

"Oh gods!" she bayed, her pussy clamping around me.

I wanted him to know who was fucking her, who was making her scream. Claiming her with everything I had, our hips bruising from the force, I rubbed her clit as my mouth covered her nipple, which I already knew were sensitive, nipping and tugging with my teeth. "Nina," I breathed out.

Rosie's cry pierced the air, her body almost convulsing under me as her pussy bolted down on me, milking my orgasm from me with as much brutal force. My head tipped

285

back in a roar as I filled her, detonating another orgasm from her. I lost all time and space, something latching onto me, yanking at my soul as I emptied myself into her with a cry— staking my ownership inside her.

My ears rang. My mind was lost… my world had flipped.

I collapsed on her, my muscles giving out completely, my chest heaving. She was still locked around me like she wasn't ready to let go either.

Slowly, I went up on my elbows to not crush her completely, but she tightened her legs around me, keeping me deep inside her.

"Shit," she whispered.

I peered into her bright eyes, her expression between utter bliss and pure shock. "What?" I ran my hand over her face, pushing back the strands sticking to her skin.

"I had an orgasm." She gaped.

"Two, if I recall." I leaned down, kissing her.

"You don't understand… I haven't had one from…"

"From what?"

"From vaginal sex… like *ever*."

"Ever?" I sputtered, my mouth gaping.

"I was so young with Vicente. I didn't understand… and then after…" She again let her sentence die, a flick of pain in her eyes.

"After" was her being used as a warm body to fuck, nothing more. They got off, not caring if she did.

Cupping her face, I brushed my mouth over hers. "Then I guess I have a lot of work to do to make up for that."

Her chest sucked in air, her eyes searching mine.

"Come on." I started to sit back, sliding out of her, making her shiver. "It's freezing out here. Let's get you warmed up." I took her hand, pulling her up with me.

286

"We can't go back to camp." She shook her head. "He'll see us together, and… he's a good guy."

My gaze went over her shoulder to where Wesley had been. The spot was vacant now.

"Oh, I think he already knows," I smirked.

"What?" She blinked up at me.

I tugged her frame into mine, my need to be back inside her already hardening me. It would only be moments before I would be diving back in. This was new for me, this feeling of never wanting to stop. There was no limit when I would have enough. She broke something in me, and I could never put it back. She was in. Taking over.

I was mistaken when I said she'd never go back once she was with me. It was her. The moment I met her and she gave me grief, I should have known I was done.

"I didn't say anything about going back to camp." I laced my fingers in hers, heading for the cottage, sensing no fae locks or spells. Easy to break into. Hopefully there was still a mattress in there.

Hungrily, I took in her naked body, still dripping with my cum. "I've only just begun with you."

Chapter 23
Brexley

"I told you not to put that in your mouth."

Chirp!

"It might be feral!" Voices stirred me from a deep sleep. still too weak to move, I nestled back in the solid warmth wrapped around me, trying to ignore them. "You could get rabies! Gangrene. Foot-n-mouth disease!"

Chirp! Chirp!

"I'm sure plenty of dirty feet have been on that, and now you're putting it in your mouth." Opie's pitch fluttered my lids, causing a disgruntled groan from my mouth. I dug my head into Warwick's arm, trying to block out reality, my eyes burning from exhaustion.

We probably got an hour of sleep, and that was because I actually passed out. Warwick was not even close to being done punishing me, spending all night going between tortuous and slow to hard and brutal... and every second, I begged for more.

Especially when his shadow joined in.

Fuck. What he did to my body last night. I could hardly move, though I felt like I could run across the country with the magic pumping in my veins. There probably wasn't a town in a fifty-mile radius that didn't feel the ground shudder every time we climaxed. The ghosts hissed in my ears, lightning zapping overhead, rumbling the earth.

Every time he thrust inside me, our bond latched on tighter, twining and knotting to the point I couldn't tell them apart much at the end. He felt as solid when I rode his face at the same time he fucked me from behind.

I stirred against him, feeling the need for him to enter me again, leaving me gasping and panting.

"Master Fishy, you're awake." Opie trotted up my arm. I frowned. Well, that kind of killed the mood. Though deep down, I smiled with glee. I had missed this so much. Walking up to them. I didn't realize how much they were part of me until I didn't have them. "We were getting really bored waiting… it seemed like forever."

Bored. Nothing good ever came of them being bored. My head jerked up, my eyes opening to see what damage they did.

Opie was only inches from my face, a beaming smile taking over his normally grumpy features. "Fishy!" he sang out. "Do you like it?" He stepped back, twirling his latest outfit, full of bobbles and tassels.

Oh fuck.

I recognized Zelda's costume material instantly. Cut into a turban headdress, towering high on Opie's head, the gold coin tassels clinked every time he moved. He wore white feathers the horse riders wore in their hair on his frame. He fanned them out into an almost see-through short dress, laced together in front and back with sequins and coin tassels. Bitzy was still on the ground, staring into space, draped in tassels and sequins like a Christmas tree. More of Zelda's wrap made her booty shorts.

"Shit." A laugh gurgled up my throat. The woman already hated me.

"You don't like it? It's shit?" Opie's face fell.

"No!" I shook my head. "I love it. It's one of your best."

"Right?" He swung around again.

Chirppppp. Bitzy tried to hold up her middle finger but couldn't.

"What's wrong with her?"

"Oh, she went mushroom picking this morning."

"Mushroom picking?" I peered at her, seeing her sway. "You know some are poisonous, right?"

"She'll be fine." Opie waved her off while she fell onto her back, blinking up at the sky with a strange giggle.

A groan vibrated into the back of my neck. "This was why I tracked you down," Warwick muttered against my spine. "To give you back your pets. They're all yours again, Kovacs."

"Pets?" Opie huffed, stomping his foot. "You weren't calling us that when we led you right to her. When we were getting important information for you about Halálház, with that zombie farm, and that blonde woman... though can I say she may be evil, but her style... Oh, I could roll naked in her shoe closet all day." He sighed.

"Zombie farm? Halálház?" I curved to look at Warwick, trying to keep his jacket covering me. We passed out right next to the Ferris wheel, which was used for more than just tying me to. We laid on our discarded clothes as bedding, his jacket and heated body as my blanket.

His eyes closed, his head resting on his arm, he took a breath, finally lifting his lids. His sharp aqua eyes stumbled my breath. The man sometimes felt too much for this earth. Like he couldn't be real.

The soreness of every muscle in my body told me he was not only real, but *mine*.

290

"You have a lot to catch up on." He watched me, a serious tone knotting my stomach. We only cleared the air between us last night, which I still think he wasn't completely done with. We didn't venture much into what was happening, besides my uncle and others being safe and in hiding. Something told me it was worse than I was imagining.

"Before you start yelling, know there is nothing any of us could do about it right now."

Inhaling, I sat up more, already feeling triggered. "Tell me."

He sighed, running his hand over his face.

"Hanna is gone."

"What?" My head jerked in confusion. "What do you mean, gone?" I flushed with shame after suddenly realizing that in the commotion last night, I hadn't thought about why she wasn't there, figuring she must have stayed back. "Where is she?"

"She's with Tracker."

"What?" I fully sat up. "She was taken? Why didn't you tell me? Why aren't we going after her?"

"Because." He drew himself up, his mouth flat. "It was her choice."

"Her choice?" I sputtered. "What do you mean by that?" I bounded up, taking his jacket with me.

Ire furrowed his brow as he followed me to his feet.

"You haven't been around, Kovacs. You don't know what she's been going through. She is not the same. The pills are changing her... she's becoming one of them."

Horror. Fear.

"No, she's not!" I batted back, hearing the anger at myself because I hadn't been there for her. I hadn't known this. She was one of my oldest friends, and Warwick knew more about her than I did.

"We'll go after her... believe me, Scorpion won't rest until we get her back." Warwick scoured at his face, waking up.

"Scorpion?" The bond that had been fusing back to him during the night tightened like a rope, linking me to him in a blink. I suddenly stood in front of him across the campsite from where I actually was. He sat on his own, staring at the fire with vacant eyes, as if he had lost everything.

"Scorpion?"

His mouth pressed together but gave me no other response. He was mad at me. Mad at the world. It was more than that—overwhelming grief and helplessness which had nothing to do with me.

"Oh. Wow." My eyebrows popped up, a notion hitting me over the head. I could feel it coming off him; he couldn't hide it from me. *"You really care about her."*

He jerked his head to the side, lines denting his forehead, not looking at me.

"Fuck," I breathed out. *"You love her."*

His jaw clenched, his hand running over his face, head slightly shaking as if he was trying to deny it.

To himself.

"We'll find her."

His gaze finally met mine.

"We won't lose her."

"Might be too late," he muttered.

"We will get her back." I crouched down, forcing him to look at me. *"Whatever it takes."*

He huffed through his nose, his shoulders easing a bit. He snorted, his head shaking. "You know you're naked here too, right?"

Sharp yells and commotion nearby snapped my link to him, my head swinging to Warwick as two men's voices grew louder from camp. I couldn't make out their words, but one was angry. Challenging. The other was threatening and defiant.

"That sounds like Killian," I commented.

"Fuck," Warwick grumbled, grabbing his pants, his tone telling me he knew what might be happening.

"Who's he fighting?"

"Probably Wesley."

"Wesley? Why?"

"You've missed a lot, princess." He hurriedly shucked on his pants.

I dropped his jacket, scrambling for my clothes, reacting to Warwick's response. I could only find my trousers and sweater.

"Cover your eyes, Bitzy. We got massive eels and blowholes out free in the wild." Opie pretended to cover his eyes but peeked through his fingers. "I was wrong. That's a *sperm* whale."

Chirppppp!

Shoving my feet in my boots, I ran after Warwick toward the uproar, my gaze landing on Wesley and Killian toe-to-toe, Rosie only feet away, slightly behind Killian.

"Kurva anyád!" Wesley shoved at Killian's chest, forcing me to suck in, shocked to see him assault the fae lord. "You are a fucking piece of shit!"

Killian's chest expanded, a nerve in his cheek twitching, but he didn't engage.

"You didn't want her when she was human." Wesley rammed at him again. "But she's okay to fuck now that's she's fae?"

What? My mouth parted, my gaze darting to Rosie.

Killian and Rosie?

A strangled noise came from Killian as he lurched for

his assailant, fists and arms tangling as they both struck out, punching and kicking like two kids on a playground.

"Whoa!" Ash tried to jump in, able to grab Wesley, while Warwick pulled Killian back, blood leaking from their lips and noses. "Both of you calm down."

"Tell him to stay the fuck away from her." Wesley pointed at Rosie, trying to wiggle free of Ash's hold.

"No," Killian snarled. "And she *came* to me."

"You are using her. The moment you're done, you'll throw her away like trash." Wesley spat at him. "You don't care about her. It was all for your own ego. You saw me last night. Purposely made sure I knew you got her first. Put on a little show for me, didn't you?"

"What?" Rosie's attention snapped from Wesley to Killian.

Killian's jaw strained, his glower set on Wes.

"You were there?" she asked Wesley, but I knew it wasn't really a question. Her cheeks flaming with heat, she turned to Killian. "And you knew?"

Killian's gaze dropped to the ground for a moment, his feet shifting.

"Oh." Devastation flickered over her features, taking a step back. "I see… So I was a game. See if you could take me from someone else if you just snapped your fingers?"

"No." Killian yanked free of Warwick's hold, moving to her. "That wasn't it at all. He had nothing to do with it."

"But you made extra sure he knew you were the one fucking me?"

"*Szar!* He's the one who found *us*. I wasn't trying to do anything. Don't act like you weren't there, that all that happened last night and this morning wasn't real." He took another step, almost pressing into her. "Did I get possessive? Yes. Did I want him to know you are mine? Fuck, yes. That

294

every scream and moan was for me? You better believe it. And I am not sorry about that."

She sucked in, pink spreading from her cheeks, flushing her neck. It was then I noticed how brightly she was glowing and shimmering. The fae magic was still settling into her system, though I could sense it was far more than that, as if a thousand invisible webs connected her to Killian.

Killian and Rose. Scorpion and Hanna. I had missed a lot.

"Just wait until you hear about Birdie and Caden." Warwick's shade mumbled against my neck. The man standing feet away smirked hungrily at me, somehow knowing what I was thinking.

I almost choked, my attention darting to the pair who stood as far apart as they could, but I noticed dirt and leaves in Birdie's hair and fresh bite marks along Caden's neck.

What the actual fuck?

The other four I could almost wrap my head around, but Caden and Birdie? He was so strict and by the book. She was the total opposite. Plus, he had such a prejudice against fae. Though the more I looked at him, the more I sensed something was not the same. The boy I knew growing up was different. Now, he carried an energy I had only seen in one other before…

"Eszem azt az ici-pici szívedet!" I'm gonna rip your heart out and feast on it! Wesley's voice snapped me back before I could process my thoughts, his form tearing from Ash and leaping for Killian. The fae lord pushed Rosie behind him, going for Wesley.

"If that fist gets any closer to her, I will gut you right here," Killian bellowed, grabbing Wesley by the collar and shaking him. "You want to fight me? That's fine. But don't ever get near *my mate* again."

Rosie and I inhaled sharply as the words punched through the air, freezing Killian and Wesley both. Killian's throat bobbed, his chest heaving as if he couldn't believe he just said it and not knowing how to respond to it either.

Silence rained down on the group, no one knowing what to do. The tension between Wesley and Killian only grew with every second.

"Okay, that's enough." I finally stepped in, pushing Killian back.

Wesley's face went from rage to utter pain. His eyes flicked to Rosie as if he was hoping she would refute it, say it wasn't true.

She didn't.

I hadn't been around to see how this all happened, but it was clear Wesley cared about her a lot. I felt horrible for him because his feelings weren't returned. She was one hundred percent taken, and I couldn't have been happier for them, but that would have to wait.

"We have more important things to discuss right now. Personal matters have to be put on the back burner," I addressed the group.

Wesley snorted, stepping back, his head shaking. "Funny, because I think it was pretty personal when you killed a slew of people and then ran away, leaving us high and dry."

My lungs sucked in, his words punching me in the gut. I could see Warwick moving toward him, ready to put him down, but I put my hand out, wagging my head.

Peering around, all eyes shifted away from mine. Their nonresponse was an even louder accusation.

They all felt the same.

My head dipped, my arms folding over my stomach. "I know." I swallowed. "I ran away, leaving you all with the aftermath. I killed people you might have known or cared about. And then I ran away." The declaration struggled to get off my tongue, the weight of my crime sitting on my chest. "What I did was unforgivable. And I understand why you all are mad at me. Possibly can never forgive me."

"Mad?" Scorpion piped up, his teeth grinding. "Oh, we are past mad. Try terrified, worried, furious."

"And hurt," Ash added, his head titled, his green eyes soft. "None of us knew if you were okay. Why you left—"

"Because she needed to." A voice twisted everyone around to the old woman walking up, her pink bunny slippers flopping around. "I led her here."

"What do you mean, you led her here?" Confusion crossed Caden's features. "Who the hell are you?"

Esmeralda winked at me. "Who I am and who you see are two different things."

"What?" Birdie shook her head. "What does that mean?"

"*Szar*...." Ash stepped back, his mouth opening. "I thought something was off last night, but I didn't have time to focus on it." He glanced at Rosie. Because we were too busy trying to save her life. "I knew the aura felt familiar. That there were two energies in her. But how is it possible?"

"She's a true seer and has druid blood in her, making her one of the few I can use as a vessel." Esmeralda motioned to herself. "And she had kindly allowed me in... well, kindly might be overstating it."

I snorted.

"What are you talking about?" Kek peered around. "What am I missing?"

Ash scoffed, his face still in awe, his voice a throaty whisper. "It's Tad."

"I'm sorry, what?" Kek choked. Most of the group had similar responses.

297

"Tad?" Killian moved closer, his brows furrowed in a mix of hope and anger, as if he was terrified to believe what Ash claimed. *"Lófasz." Horse dick. Bullshit.*

While everyone observed the old seer, I saw Tad's blue eyes sparkle, his aura taking over until all I saw was him. Tad smiled warmly, taking slow steps to Killian, taking his hand with a soft pat.

"I'm starting to see the true leader emerge, my dear boy. What you perceive as failings or cracks in your armor are your strengths. Flaws aren't weaknesses. They make you real. A better ruler. But only if you accept them as part of you."

Killian yanked his hand back, critically regarding the old woman.

"Ah, still not convinced." Tad pressed his lips together. "At the cabin, there was a night you thought I was already asleep. I saw you sitting by the fire. You keep a token of *hers*. Of the girl you hold on to. The dark-haired girl who haunts your heart."

Killian stepped back with a jagged huff.

"You use the idea of her to keep yourself protected. To not let anyone in. But she was never meant for you, Killian. She was your childhood. A security you hold on to. It's time to let her go." Tad's gaze darted back to the woman behind Killian. "Because you have met your match, my boy. So *do not* screw it up." Tad turned to the rest of the group, his lightheartedness falling away. "Brexley had to leave to prepare for what is ahead. Her journey was separate from yours. I sense the future, see bits and pieces, and it is dark, full of death and devastation. Every single person is important to this war. Every soul and body could turn the tide—" Esmeralda abruptly jerked, expelling Tad from her, but her eyes became even more hazy and faraway, her voice low and chilling.

"It is coming... Fire. Death. Ruin. You could be the savior or the destroyer. The villain or the hero. Dual fires burn brighter." She cleared her throat, shaking her head, looking around as if wondering why we were all staring at her. "What?" she snarled at us, lighting up a joint. "Why are you all staring at me like that?"

None of us replied. A sense of unease ran through the group. We all knew she was talking about me.

The fire crackled and popped, the low murmurs from around the firepit drowned out by the music, cheers, and squeals coming from the circus tent in the distance. The night was clear and cold, and I shivered under the fur pelt, shifting closer to the massive male heat source next to me. Leaning against his arm to keep from falling over, I was completely spent after the day of catching up, sharing information, and planning. Learning about everything I had missed out on left me gutted and depleted.

My soul ached hearing Budapest had fallen to Sonya. How fast a dictator could take over. And to know Lieutenant Andor, a decorated military soldier at HDF, helped make it happen to save his own hide. In his quest for more power and money, he sold his soul and his country to the devil. It sounded like Romania had as well.

Out of everything, Hanna was the most upsetting. I had known the pills were affecting her, changing her, and I hadn't been there for her. I doubt anything would have been different had I stayed, but it didn't take away my guilt.

Responsibility. Guilt. I carried it like a suit of armor. Even being here, putting Jethro and the troupe in danger, had me on edge. We planned to leave in the morning and head to

299

Kyiv, but until then we stayed in the campsite, away from the busy carnival full of people until then. Many of the circus troupe were not happy we were here, but Zelda was the loudest about it, her brother standing next to her, eerily watching us. She snipped about stuff of hers disappearing, something about us being bad omens and how we would be the downfall. Thanks to Opie, at least part of that was true.

The feel of eyes on me from across the bonfire drew my attention away from my thoughts and to my old best friend. Caden's gaze burned into me, his shoulders hunching around his ears. His expression was blank, but I knew him well enough to know when he was upset. Once again, the sensation of magic, of something different about him, prickled at the back of my neck. The flames reflected off his familiar eyes, but nothing else felt like he was the boy I once knew.

His nose flared, his glance darting to my fingers wrapped around Warwick's arm, Farkas's hand absently rubbing my leg. Caden's head wagged before he shot up and strode away, heading into the darkness, his energy grim and fuming.

Automatically I started to rise; the urge to run after him was instinctual.

"No." Warwick's hand clamped down on my thigh.

My head snapped to him, bristling from his order. "No?"

"Caden is not…" Warwick crunched down on his molars. "He's not stable."

"What does that mean? Caden would never hurt me."

"He's not in control of himself right now." Warwick stared at the fire.

"What aren't you telling me?"

He rubbed his face, exhaling through his nose. "It worked."

"What worked?"

"The experiment." He turned his head to me. "Caden has some of my essence."

"What?" I jolted, blinking rapidly.

"Yeah, daddy did a number on us both," Warwick grumbled. "It took me a while to admit, but I felt it almost from day one. And now I can't get rid of captain one-pump. We have a bond."

"Bond?" I stared at Warwick in shock. Istvan's experiment worked? That meant Caden was not only fae, but was like Warwick? "What kind of bond?"

"Not like ours. I just know things he knows. I can sense him, his moods, if he's in trouble. I guess it would be like having a twin brother. I feel it. And right now, he's jealous and angry. So stay the fuck away from him."

"No." I stood up. "Caden is my oldest friend in the world. If he's hurt, I want to be there for him."

"Even if that hurt is because of you?"

"Me?"

"He thinks he's still in love with you."

In love with me? At one time, those were the only words I wanted to hear from him. Now they were the last. My love for him was young and pure. That was no longer me, and it was definitely no longer him either.

Without a second thought, I spun in the direction Caden walked off.

"Princess." Warwick's shadow stepped in front of me, growling deeply. Ignoring him, I walked through him. His magic penetrated every nerve in my body, almost causing me to stumble to the ground, buzzing my veins with energy. Inhaling deeply, I pushed on, following my instincts toward my old friend. Warwick didn't follow, nor did his shadow, but I knew he'd be right there if I needed.

The darkness engulfed me the moment I stepped away

301

from the bonfire. Heading the opposite way of the circus, I slipped into the trees, feeling his pull. We had been so in sync for so long that I would always find Caden. I was drawn to the boy I knew better than anyone and the man who carried the same magic as my mate. Seeing his figure, his back to me, my new awareness picked up on his frame.

Caden had always been in shape and ripped from training, but now I noticed there was more to him. Like Warwick, he seemed to expand in his rage. Magic crackled off him so much that I wondered how I had never noticed before.

The boy raised to despise fae had been made one by his own father. The man who had dumped him and Rebeka to start a new family, tossing them away like trash. All Caden wanted was to grow up to please Istvan. To gain his father's approval. To be the son Istvan always wanted.

Caden was now all the things Istvan required, and it still wasn't enough. Istvan only wanted a mini version of himself, and Caden had always been better.

"Caden."

"Go away." A growl vibrated back to me.

"Think you know me better than that." I folded my arms, easing closer to him. "Did I ever go when you told me to?"

He huffed, his head going back and forth. "No. You'd annoy me until I gave up."

"Exactly." I came up behind him, nudging him with my elbow excessively like I used to. Drove him up the wall because he'd want to stay mad, but I would see a smile break over his mouth the more I did it. Badgering him until he cracked, turning his sour mood.

"Brex. Stop." He shifted away, turning to me, his mouth clenching. "We aren't kids anymore. Things are different now. I'm not the boy you used to know. That kid is gone."

302

"No, he's not." I tilted my head. "He's still there."

"He's gone." Caden snapped, ire glinting in his eyes.

"You may feel lost right now. Hurt, angry, betrayed… but Caden, magic doesn't change who you are inside. You're still the guy who wiped my tears away when I missed my dad, who jumped into the river to save my stuffed dog when I dropped it. Who pranked our teachers and filled the pool with foam? Who got me ice cream when I first started my period? That guy is the real you. The man Istvan wanted wasn't real."

"None of me is real anymore." Caden stabbed at his chest, his shoulders heaving. "I'm not even a true fae. I'm just a knockoff of *your* man. A pathetic, watered-down version of the great Warwick Farkas. I can't even be my own in that. I wasn't enough for my father as a human, but I'm an even greater disappointment as a fae." Grief and pain weaved thickly through his rant. I could say nothing to take away what Istvan did to Caden. I couldn't imagine the pain he had to feel, but I wanted him to see past Istvan. To see the man I always knew.

"How do you think it makes me feel seeing the girl I've loved all my life choose the *true* Legend? To be bonded to him. To not only watch you two together but to sense how he feels about you. To look at your face and know how much you love him." He pinched his nose. "I was the one you wanted once, and not only have I lost you, but I've lost everything…"

"You haven't lost me." I held up my palm when his head jerked to me. "Maybe you don't have me in the way you imagined, but I will always be in your life. Will always love you." I tucked my hair behind my ear. "But be honest with me, Caden. Do you really love me or the idea of me? The security and the safety of what I represent to you?"

"What the fuck does that mean?"

"Your whole world has just flipped over. Hanna is gone. HDF has fallen. Your father is not the hero you thought. He turned you into the very thing he conditioned you to despise and left you and your mother to die in that ring." I took a breath. "All the things we were taught to hate, the version of the world we were conditioned to think was the only right way. It's *all* wrong. Look around us. Almost all our friends and allies are fae. I can understand if a part of you wants to hold on to something familiar. Safe."

"You think I'm lying? That I don't love you?" He glared at me.

"I didn't say that. But I want you to really think if it's love. You never loved me enough before, Caden. You never chose me when you had me."

"Fuck you."

"Am I wrong?" I tossed out my arms. "You were going to marry Olena. I was nothing more than a future mistress to you."

"That was not what I wanted."

"Yes, it was!" I yelled. "I was right in front of you for years. And *now* you think I'm the one. I call bullshit. I think you are just scared to let go of who you used to be, that life, and let yourself be what you are now. You are *not* a watered-down version of Warwick. You are *not* less than. You may have some of Warwick's powers, but you are *not* him. You are *you*, and I think that man is not in love with me, but with someone else if he just got his head out of his ass. Someone who has challenged and provoked and frustrated the hell out of you—but I've never seen you more alive."

He stepped back, his chest rising in defense, already knowing where this was going. To a petite blonde who could kick both our asses.

Before Caden could respond, a branch snapped in the

distance, jerking us to the noise. An eerie sensation washed over me, pricking alarm bells at the base of my neck, my skin rising with goosebumps. Caden's body stiffened, his shoulders rolling into a defensive stance, clearly picking up the same vibe running through the still forest.

I felt it grow near with every beat of my heart, the silent woods ringing with warning, telling us danger was coming. Silent. Deadly. Not even a cricket dared to make a sound.

We were being hunted.

My shade stretched out for Warwick right as gunfire cracked like fireworks across the night sky. The sound ricocheted from behind me, whirling me toward the camp.

Shouts boomed; shots blasted.

"Kovacs!" Warwick's shadow bellowed in my ear, and for a second, I was with him, seeing dozens and dozens of Istvan's soldiers march down the hill and out of the darkness, rushing for the campsite. And leading the pack was…

"Tracker," I muttered, Caden's head jerking to me.

"Stay where you are," Warwick growled in my ear, but my legs were already cutting across the terrain, heading toward the real man as more gunfire popped off.

There was no way I would stay put. My fight was with them.

Yanking out the gun I carried on my hip, with Caden right next to me, we ran straight into the fire.

Chapter 24
Brexley

Bullets sprayed into the campsite, tearing into the wagons my friends were hiding behind, chunks of wood splintering like daggers as Caden and I leaped behind the closest one, scrambling up with Birdie, Scorpion, and Wesley.

"This asshole really needs to die." Birdie double fisted her favorite guns, shooting at the army coming at us, but it was Scorpion firing like killing Tracker was his only goal. His expression was pure rage; his blame focused on one man. Scorpion's emotions were like gasoline spilling over the ground, ready for the match to strike.

What happened to Hanna was all Scorpion zeroed in on.

Leaving Caden with them, I darted to the next wagon, diving between Ash and Warwick, their bodies on the ground, firing back from under the vardo.

"I told you to stay put." A growl rose from Warwick's throat, and he glared at me.

"And do you see how well it goes for you when you tell me what to do?" I wriggled between the two men, pointing my gun at the army coming at us.

Warwick snarled, his head shaking.

"Plus." I glanced at him. "Know this. In coming for me, you made a mistake."

His head craned to me; his brows furrowed.

"You're mine forever now, Farkas. I'm not setting you free again. We are in this together. We fight together. We die together.

His eyes darkened, his shoulders expanding, his head leaning into mine. "*Know this.* I wasn't *free* until you, *Sotet démonom,*" he muttered for only me to hear, his mouth brushing mine. "And we fight, fuck, and survive together. Whatever it takes."

"Whatever it takes," I whispered back before his lips quickly claimed mine.

"Hey, you two horny freaks, can we focus?" Ash huffed, refilling his weapon. "Kind of in peril here."

"Foreplay for us," Warwick muttered, turning his attention back to the legion advancing on us. "And you have no room to talk about being a horny freak."

Ash grinned, his head bobbing. "Fair enough."

Bang! Crash!

A bullet shattered the widow of the vardo we were hiding under, dropping glass down on us.

"Make it easier on yourself, Brexley. On your friends." Tracker's voice boomed through the night, the music from the circus tinkling behind him. "I will let them all live if you hand over the nectar. We know you have it."

A fist knotted in my chest, making it hard to swallow.

"They don't have to die for this. Just surrender yourself now."

Warwick snorted, Ash laughing out loud. I could hear Killian, Rosie, Kek, and Lukas behind the wagon on our other side snicker. All my friends disregarded his directive.

I was probably the only one who didn't laugh. I was so sick of people I loved getting hurt to protect me.

"Don't even think about it, Kovacs," Warwick's shade grunted in my ear.

"Last chance, Brexley," Tracker taunted.

"Baszd meg." Fuck off, Kek yelled out. *"Egy szemétláda vagy."* You are a douchebag.

"Oh, Kek…" Tracker purred. "You're one of the first I can't wait to put down like the monster you are." He swung out from behind a tree, holding a shiny new semi-automatic. The bullets shredded across the wagons, ripping off the wood, spraying underneath, ripping up the grass and dirt. We scrambled back for safety, seeing the spots we had just been destroyed in seconds.

"Szar!" Ash hissed.

We had all kinds of guns in the east, but this was a top-of-the-line black market machine gun. And Tracker had one, which meant Istvan had the means to get them.

"Fuck." Warwick yanked me farther behind him, getting us behind a wheel, firing back while more and more soldiers moved in. The handful of us had no chance against the army coming at us.

A group of soldiers held torches, moving in on the wagons, ready to light them all on fire, starting with one that held animals inside.

"No." My heart squeezed, tears burning under my lids as I watched the spare horses not being used in the circus tonight flick their heads and stomp, kicking violently in terror. The wild tiger yowled in fear, pacing frantically.

Tracker was going to let them be burned alive.

Something black and sleek moved behind the men surrounding the cages. The glint of moonlight reflected off what looked like blades going down its back. *What the fuck is that?* When I blinked, it was gone.

"Last chance, Brexley," Tracker threatened, his finger on the trigger as he ordered his men to set the camp on fire.

Before my mouth opened, a choking sound came from one of the soldiers, his eyes wide in fear, blood gushing from his neck.

One by one, the men with the torches dropped to the ground as blood sprayed from their throats, their deaths happening so quickly they didn't even scream.

We couldn't even see what killed them.

For one moment, no one moved. Something prickled at my neck, my gaze finding red wolf-like eyes burning through the darkness, sending shivers through my body. My intuition told me not only did it kill those men, but it was what had been hunting me.

It was coming for me.

Scorpion yelled in fury, darting from his hiding spot, his gun spraying down whatever was in his way, his eyes locked on Tracker. His wrath set on the man he felt took Hanna from him.

"Fuck!" Warwick leaped out, knowing how fast this could go south. Ash and I followed suit, taking advantage of their moment of confusion.

Gunfire volleyed around, ringing in my ears. Tracker pointed his machine gun at me. Warwick roared, moving in front of me, ready to take the fire. Tracker's finger curled around the trigger; the power of the weapon would shred through Warwick, flaying him wide open.

Killing him.

The notion of losing him, of watching it happen and not being able to do anything to stop it, triggered a rage so deep, a love so pure, there was nothing I wouldn't do. He was carved into my bones; every cell declared him mine.

It was a drop of a pin. A single match released into a tank of gasoline.

My magic burst from me like a volcano. Wind howled

309

off the river, spinning and slicing over the land like a hurricane, taking on my fury.

"Attack," I ordered. Ghosts moved around me, heading for my target, making my hair fly around my face. A flicker of lightning charged over our heads, the ground vibrating with a rumble. More and more spirits came, lining up like a troop, marching forward on my command. Under my control. I could feel the weeks of training tightening my rein on them. The power I had in controlling them. It took so much energy from me to have them physically interact with the living, the effort already making me dig deeper, straining to keep my rule.

"Fuck!" Tracker stumbled back, his gaze darting around, searching for the invisible attacker. "What the fuck?" Tracker retreated farther as the spirits ripped the gun from his hands, tossing it into the fire. Terror widened his eyes, his gaze going to me. "Whatever you're doing, stop!"

I smiled, pushing the ghosts harder at the soldiers. "Kill."

My invisible soldiers took my order.

Tracker's body jerked back as deep scratch marks bloomed with blood covering his face, then grabbed his chest. The ghost twisted at his heart.

My magic was waning. It was getting harder to keep them all on my plane, interacting with the living.

The buzz from the nectar hummed on my hip where I kept it. It wanted out. It craved more. I could feel the power calling to me to set it free. Every second, my own magic faded. The connection with Warwick and Scorpion would be gone again. And I would be empty.

It didn't have to be that way. I could just use a little of the nectar... just a touch.

I reached down, unlatching the box.

"No, stop!" A voice cut from the side, whipping our heads in the direction.

Esmeralda stood there, her arms up, her face twisted in panic, but it was Tad's gaze on me. "Don't do it, Brexley!"

Pop! Pop! Pop!

Gunfire speared into her torso, her body jolting as a guard pulled the trigger. A shriek burned up my throat watching her small petite frame collapse to the ground. In the distance, Zelda and Leander screamed out, running for their grandmother.

Everything flipped, putting it in slow motion, where all my senses were no longer in color.

All I saw was black. All I felt was darkness.

Anger. Guilt. Grief.

It was too much. Another death. Another hole in my heart.

My gaze darted to Tracker, to the soldier who fired at her. I wanted to feel their deaths. To experience their pain.

"Kovacs?" I heard Warwick call to me as my hand opened the box and wrapped around the nectar, letting it take over.

Energy discharged through the atmosphere, crashing against every mass in its wake. Bodies flung to the ground, and screams echoed in the distance as lightning cracked down from the sky, scarring the earth.

All my training evaporated, the power in my hand too strong for me to fight. With the nectar, I felt invincible like a queen who hungered for supremacy with black magic which reigned dominant.

Right. Wrong.

Light. Darkness.

Hero. Villain.

None of it mattered.

311

I was pure power. Nothing equaled me.

Crack! The zap of lightning glowed in my peripheral, becoming brighter, the cries muted as my soldiers attacked, slicing through Tracker's men like lambs to slaughter. I could feel myself pull more and more from the nectar. Or was it pulling from me? I didn't care. The line of balance grew smaller. My hunger craved more. The high was intoxicating.

"Ko-vacs!" Warwick's shade bit at the back of my neck, trying to reach me. *"Stop!"*

Tracker dropped to his knees, his wild gaze meeting mine, no longer the zealous soldier of General Markos. The one hiding his fear in arrogance. The guy who once loved Ava but let his insecurities lead him down Istvan's path. Weak-minded, he allowed himself to be controlled, which is why he became a tyrant.

Pathetic.

The ghost clenched down on his heart, and Tracker's eyes widened. The spirit squeezed until it burst. His body shuddered, sorrow and devastation watering his eyes, pleading, then they glazed over. His frame dropped to the ground, his eyes wide open, staring at me like he had seen a real-life monster.

Me.

"Brexley!" Warwick's voice called to me, my name piercing me like a balloon. I stepped back from Tracker's dead body with a sharp inhale, his eyes staring up in horror like Tad's had.

Oh my gods, what did I do?

I was the villain.

The nectar fell from my fingers, my lungs struggling to draw in air, panic strangling them.

"Be here with me." Hands clasped my face, aqua irises pulling me in. *"Sotet démonom."* Warwick's voice plunged me back to Earth, anchoring me. My senses sharpened, drawing my attention around me.

Horror almost dropped me to the ground.

Beyond the ring of dead soldiers my ghosts had murdered, flames billowed high into the air, bathing the entire area in light. Screams of fear and pain hurdled from the large circus tent. Horses, tigers, and people ran from the inferno.

Members of the troupe tried to get everyone out to safety as the magic-induced fire raged hot and fast, catching some of the food wagons nearby on fire, destroying everything in its wake.

"Oh gods!" A cry cut through my chest, my feet moving toward the fire, feeling the heat burn at my skin.

"Go! Run!" Hank waved for people to get out as the fire neared him, using his body as a shield between the person and the flames.

"Hank!" I cried out, his gaze meeting mine. Half of his face was covered in singed ash. Behind him, I could see the stands, people climbing over each other to get out. And in the middle was Jethro trying to get people to safety.

Some of the carnies were rushing to the river with buckets, trying to lessen the flames, but they were consuming everything faster than the carnies could move. The fabric of the tent was deteriorating, the stakes keeping it up, burning and snapping.

"Jethro!" My voice barely carried through the noise of the flames and the screams of the people.

The instinct to save him lurched me forward right as the tent buckled. Arms wrapped around me, keeping me in place, my gut wringing as Hank scrambled forward, rushing to Lulu and their kids, getting away as the top came down.

Jethro was still inside.

"Nooooooo!" The scream bellowed from me, hope

burning up along with the lives still inside. I bucked and thrashed; Warwick held me tighter until I felt all the energy drain, leaving me limp and sobbing.

The carnies continued to try to put out the fire as sirens wailed, growing louder and closer.

"We have to go," Warwick muttered in my ear.

My head shook, my voice lost.

"You can't do anything for them."

"It's my fault," I whispered, my soul too heavy to carry. I thought I had grown, that I had trained enough, but one touch of the nectar and I destroyed everything. I let it take over me.

I hurt everyone who got near me.

"Getting caught by the police now won't bring them back." He squeezed me into him. "Don't give up on me now, Kovacs. I need you."

My head turned to him, the honest vulnerability he expressed sending more tears to my eyes.

"Whatever it takes," he stated firmly.

The sirens from the police and the firefighters pierced the air, the flickers of light coming through the trees as shouts and orders descended the hill.

"Come on." Warwick gripped my hand, pulling me the opposite way.

"The nectar?"

"I have it," he replied, pulling me into the dark woods, the police barreling down the steps to what was left of the carnival. Smoke billowed from what was supposed to be a fun, thrilling night. Instead, the ruined wagons and half-burnt vardos turned into a grave for some.

It's all my fault.

The fire was mostly put out, but the damage was already done. The lives were already taken. Because I couldn't control it. Tad warned me. Esmeralda did too. Of course, I didn't listen. I thought I could handle it like I had before.

Something had changed. It felt so much stronger. As if it was growing in power and control too.

All I did since I found the nectar was cause death and devastation. Andris was right. This much magic shouldn't exist. No one, including me, could contain it. Though the idea of destroying it also created panic in me. Like I would lose a part of myself.

Warwick circled us far around the edges of the park, trying to get to the motorcycles they hid at the entrance. The trees absorbed most of the outside noise, the woods engulfed with darkness.

A sensation stabbed up my spine, forcing me to suck in, my head snapping behind me. Alarm stung my skin and clenched down my chest. It was the same sensation that came upon me earlier with Caden. The same fear I felt when my eyes met that creature in the woods.

Warwick stopped, his neck swinging around, his eyes darting to every dark shadow. He shifted slightly in front of me, a growl vibrating in his throat. The Wolf expanded through his shoulders, his back curling in defense.

"Don't move," he muttered into my ear; our link was used up with the nectar.

"What is it?" I mumbled back.

Warwick's nose flared, taking in the air. "I have no idea. Not something I've come across before."

My hand went to the handle of my gun, ready to grab and shoot, my gaze flying everywhere, not sure where the threat was coming from. All I knew was it was there.

Ready to kill.

"Whatever the fuck you are, I wouldn't," Warwick rumbled, his body seeming to grow bigger. "You might think you bring death... but we *are* death."

315

For a blink, I thought I saw red eyes peer through the brush at my right as I heard a crack of twigs from our left.

A low growl rushed adrenaline through me as the enormous monster I saw earlier was suddenly in front of us.

A gasp blew out of my lungs as I stared at the outline. The largest animal I had ever seen stepped from the bushes. It looked like a cross between a wolf and a panther—black as night with knife blades lined down its spine. Its red eyes latched onto us. Terror froze me in place as the massive creature took a step, its long, razor-sharp claws cutting into the earth. It was designed to kill. To attack in silence.

To slice the head off a man without warning.

"Fuck," Warwick muttered, his expression awed disbelief.

A low growl throttled in the beast's throat. Its focus latched onto Warwick, and its hind legs looked like it was about to pounce.

My hand whipped out my gun, my finger ready to pull the trigger and shoot until that thing was a bloody corpse.

"Eli, stop!" A woman's voice cut through, the beast instantly stopping, but a deep growl snarled from its fanged teeth. "Don't!"

A girl ran up, stopping beside the huge beast. Something right away made me wrench back. She reminded me of the girl I saw working in Carnal Row who had split features. This woman had one bright greenish yellow eye, a high demon color, the other a violet blue, which was a high pure-blood fairy color. Her black hair was streaked with red like flames were burning through her strands. It wasn't her unusual looks that took me back. There was something about her aura, the magic she put off, which felt so familiar it sent chills up my back.

She watched me with the same reserved curiosity. "Who the hell are you?"

I blinked, not ready for that response.

"And who the fuck are you?"

The beast next to her snarled, his paw padding at the ground. Warwick snarled back, inching farther in front of me.

"I heard the rumors your king had Dark Dwellers working for him, though I didn't believe it until now," Warwick spoke to the creature. "Thought it was a story to create fear and panic."

"We don't need to be a story to cause fear." She stroked the creature's head, causing flames to dance in its eyes. "We are fear."

"Dark Dweller?" My lungs fluttered. I had heard about them. They were killers in the Otherworld. Hired mercenaries. One of the most feared species but were considered almost extinct, with only a handful left.

One was the Unseelie King and the Seelie queen's personal bounty hunter.

"You came to kill me." I lifted my chin in a challenge.

"That was part of it," the girl replied. "But the primary task is to—"

"Take the nectar," I finished for her.

"That's not going to happen." Warwick rolled his hands into fists. "Sorry you came all this way for nothing."

The beast snarled, his enormous paws stepping closer.

"Eli." She stroked his neck, muttering something in his ear. He rumbled, stepping back into the shadows. Along with the sound of bones popping, a low groan came from the spot the great beast blended into, but when he stepped back, a man of about 6'4", ripped, gorgeous, tattooed, and naked, stood there.

"*Azta...*" *Wow.* I blinked, unable to look away from the man's physique. Warwick looked over at me, one brow cocked.

I would pay for that later.

"Put the weapon away, Dragen." The girl rolled her eyes, grabbing sweats from the bag on her back and tossing them to her partner.

"Didn't say that earlier, Brycin," he muttered, yanking on the sweats, winking at her. She shook her head, a slight smile curling her lips.

Then her gaze came back to me, studying me like I was a bug. "I'll ask again. Who the hell are you? How were you able to do that?" She motioned in the direction of the circus.

My shoulders bristled. "Do what?"

"That wind… the lightning. That fire you caused…" Her head wagged. "You shouldn't be able to do that. Not like that. Why could I feel it? Like it was mine?" She shook her head. "So I will ask again. Who the fuck are you?"

Warwick's shoulders twitched, a noise coming up his throat. "Let me get this straight. You're here to kill her and you expect her to answer you? I don't think so."

Eli countered Warwick, stepping slightly in front of the girl, a warning coiling in his throat. "If she wanted you dead, you already would be."

Warwick scoffed in humor, though everything in him was strained, ready to act. "I'd like to see you try, dweller. I think you'd find it wouldn't be our bodies left behind in pieces." Warwick was bigger than Eli, but if he was in his dweller form, Warwick might not be able to fight him. And without knowing who she was, I still could feel her magic, the power bristling at the seams.

What freaked me out was it felt familiar. Like something I already knew.

As if the same magic was in us both.

A gust of air stepped me back, my mind going to a conversation with Tad I had so long ago. *"Every person has a special signature of magic, and every family has one too. Aneira's magic is part of you; her family line is in you."*

I remembered he said Aneira's sister, Aisling, had the power of fire. Her daughter would carry the same magic, the niece of the old Seelie queen. The one I had seen when the fae book took me back to the moment Aneira died. It showed me that for a reason. The same girl before me now stood next to Queen Kennedy as Aneira's head had been cut off.

When I had been just outside being born.

With Aneira's death, the last part of the wall between worlds fell.

"*Megbasz,*" I whispered. "You're Aneira's niece, Ember."

Her mouth opened, shock fleeting over her features before it dissolved2, hidden under a neutral mask.

"Yes? Why?" Her grip tightened on the sword at her belt.

How did you even start to explain our connection? But standing in her presence, it felt like I met a half-sister I never knew I had. A family member you knew without knowing. A lot of our magic was alike, coming from the same family line. Though hers was genuine and mine was unnatural, siphoned from a queen who didn't want to let go and a mother who would do anything for me to live.

"You're a fucking Dae." Warwick inhaled, his shoulders rolling back. "King Lars's daughter."

Her lids narrowed. "You have a problem with that?"

"What's a Dae?" I glanced between them. The name sounded slightly familiar, but it wasn't like I was brought up knowing every single kind of fae out there, only the main ones.

"Offspring of a high demon and pure fairy," Warwick replied, cautiously watching her. "They were highly illegal in

319

the Otherworld because of the blend of powers. Most would go insane because the mix of magic was too much to handle."

"Oh, she's insane, but not because of the magic." Eli grinned down at her, making her shake her head. "The Dark Dweller in her keeps her somewhat rational."

"Let me guess, you're talking about your dick and not the fact I actually am a dark dweller too." Ember nudged Eli.

"Wait. You are also a Dark Dweller?" Warwick's head wagged. "How is that possible?"

"She's a super freak." Eli lifted his brow, hinting at more.

"I kinda have one of those too," Warwick's low voice said near my ear.

"The Seelie queen, my aunt, had a problem with anything more powerful than her. Druids. Dae. She had them annihilated. I'm probably the only one left."

My mouth opened to tell her I was pretty sure I had seen another, the girl in Carnal Row, when a buzzing sound caught my ear.

"My lady! My lady!" A small voice cut through, turning me to something flying toward us. Squinting, I saw what looked like a blonde pixie, but instead of wings, it had a motorized contraption letting it fly. He was dressed in an old pilot suit with a cap. Another pixie zoomed in behind him with dark hair, wearing jeans and a Woody Woodpecker shirt.

"Uh, girlie… it's time to go. That ugly cracker-hole is here."

"Seriously? Crap on ashbark, that guy is getting on my last nerve." Ember tightened her ponytail. "Been on our ass since we left Budapest."

"I'm the *only* one who gets to ride your ass, Brycin." Eli smirked, causing her to smile and blush, their shared look one of complete love, respect, and adoration.

"Budapest?" Warwick stiffened.

"Who?" Though I had this weird feeling I already knew.

"He was once known as Hazem… but I think he goes by Kalaraja now," Ember replied.

What I feared.

"Fuck." Warwick ran his hand over his head. We both knew he was using the bounty hunters to lead him right to us.

And they did.

A bullet zipped between us, splintering the wood only centimeters from my face.

"The whole killing us thing," I glared at the pair, already pivoting on my heel. "It's gonna have to wait."

Chapter 25
Warwick

Bullets splintered the wood off the trees, raining chunks down on us as we darted away, flaring fury through my limbs. Running went against my DNA. I fought. I killed. I got hard when the blood of my victims dripped down my arms. I used to seek it, desire it, crave it like a fiend. That wouldn't go away, but I never had so much to protect before. My life before consisted of revenge and death.

Now I walked next to death and never felt more alive.

Nothing would take her from me.

"Go!" I barked at Kovacs, waving at her to go, tucking the nectar in her pocket, needing them to get to safety.

"No!" she shot back.

"They're after you, princess, after the nectar." I crouched behind a tree, shooting back. "Don't let them get it."

Her gaze held mine for a bit before I saw her head dip, understanding what she held went beyond us. What would happen if Kalaraja took it back to Sonya or Istvan got his hands on it?

I saw what happened when it was in Brexley's hands.

The power it gave and took. It felt toxic. Treacherous. I could feel it trying to push me out. To possess her. It took all my strength to break through... to fight for her to come back to me.

Brexley turned to run as Ember, Eli, and I stayed to fight, dozens of men coming at us, spraying us with gunfire. Eli swore under his breath, ripping off his sweats as his body shifted back into his Dark Dweller form, blending in with the darkness, the razors on his back ready to slice a man in half.

Death screams and gunshots filled my ears from the direction Eli went. More coming up on me, I leaped out, my elbow slamming into a guard's face before my gun fired into his head, spraying his brains out on the dirt. Fae had gotten used to fighting like humans, guns becoming the easy, lazy way of fighting. Once, we battled with swords and fists, with honor and true skill. Watching your enemy's life draining out of him as your sword dug into his guts... I missed those days.

Slicing and shooting at every figure moving toward me, a cry filled my ear, crawling down my spine and chilling my bones. It wasn't loud, but it hit me like a train, calling to every fiber in my body.

Brexley.

Swiveling around, I bolted toward her, hating that our link was gone, not knowing what was happening to her. Terror clogged my throat, my breath locked, my boots slamming the earth.

Through the trees, I spotted her standing still, Kalaraja pointing a gun at her forehead, his hand out, waiting for her to hand over the nectar.

Fuck no.

Before I could reach either of them, Brexley ducked and twisted, her fist smashing into his gut, stumbling him back, then knocking into his nose, spewing saliva and blood from his mouth. Her knee rammed up into his face, knocking him on his ass.

Fuck, that was hot.

A blast boomed through the trees from the circus area below, fire blasting high from the tent, flames eating up everything inside, including anything flammable and toxic, causing explosions.

Figures moved hurriedly up the hill near us. My shoulders lowered with relief seeing Ash leading the pack, the elderly woman, Esmeralda, in his arms.

Ash's gaze met mine, our expressions mutual.

We needed to get the fuck out of here.

"Esmeralda!" Brexley shouted, running to Ash as we moved for the motorcycles parked close by. Ember and Eli jogged up after us.

"There are too many." Eli yanked on his sweats.

Between Tracker's soldiers and Kalaraja's, we were far outnumbered.

"Go! Go!" Ash waved everyone to hurry as he and Scorpion propped the old lady on the back of Ash's bike. Blood still oozed from her wounds, but she acted like it was just a cut, batting the men away to stop coddling her. I had to give it to her, the old bat was tough as nails.

A bullet scraped my arm, the metal sizzling at my skin, jerking my head in the direction it came from. Kalaraja hobbled forward, his weapon pointed at us, soldiers flooding from the woods behind him.

"Kovacs!" My hand wrapped around hers, yanking her to the motorcycle as more shells volleyed at us. Her thighs locking down on mine, she returned fire as I pressed down on the gas, bolting us forward, following the rest of our group. The dweller and Dae were right behind us on a bike they stole from Tracker's men.

The bikes sped off over the worn asphalt, plunging us into the darkness away from the scorched circus and the various parties trying to kill us. Keeping our headlights off, the engines roared through the streets like an animal you couldn't see but could hear coming for you.

With no time to talk, I pointed us toward Kyiv, making it outside the city limits in only three hours, using back roads. There was no doubt the closer we got to the city, the more troops we'd run into. My theory only mounted as every train going by us headed west, filled with army troops, equipment, and tanks.

"What the fuck?" Brexley whispered behind me as she watched carriage after carriage zoom by.

"Istvan," I muttered. "He's lining up troops at the border. Getting ready to invade Hungary."

"*Szar...*" she muttered under her breath. "So much of me wants to let them fight it out among themselves while we all escape to Unified Nations." She sighed into my back, her warmth seeping through my clothes.

"You won't."

"Fuck no," she replied huskily, making my dick ache for her. "Istvan needs to be stopped. He'll keep creating armies until no one can stop him. I will go down fighting, and I will take him with me."

"How about we kill him, and you let me go down on you?" I glanced at her over my shoulder, wishing our link was there so I could slide my tongue through her pussy.

"War-wick." A warning hinted in her tone, seeing in my eyes exactly what I wanted to do to her. The idea of taking her right on this bike had my adrenaline banging through my veins, needing a release.

"I will seriously fucking kill you both if you start this shit right now." Scorpion rolled up next to us with a bark. His mood was darker than mine since Hanna left, which was saying a lot. "I'd cut off my arm if it would untie me from you two."

"Worth a shot." I shrugged. Brexley hit my back, shaking her head.

"Where to?" Ash came up behind Scorpion. Eli's motorcycle revving up on my other side. "We have to stay out of the city until we know what's ahead. They'll be looking for us."

We were probably on every most wanted poster hung all over town, especially Kovacs.

"Brycin and I know of a safe house not too far. An old inn that caters to... let's say... the ones who work outside the law."

"I thought you worked for the king and queen?" Brexley lifted a brow.

Eli and Ember exchanged glances.

"Yeah, and sometimes that means outside of the law *here*," Eli replied. "The Eastern bloc is a hotbed of problems, which need to be managed to protect *our* country. We *bend* the truce we made with the East to get the job done."

"So, this inn is a front? Western sympathizers? Or just spies?" Annoyance threaded through Kovacs's tone.

"My father has eyes everywhere." Ember looped her arms tighter around Eli as they took off in front, leaving the rest of us to follow.

A growl grew in my throat.

"Play nice," Brexley murmured into the back of my neck.

"When have I ever done that?" My teeth clenched as I followed behind, which I never did pleasantly.

They were already too many fucking alphas in this group. This Dark Dweller added another we didn't need. His

326

ego was on par with mine, and there might be a moment when he learned who the real killer was. The true legend.

Outside the city walls, down a deserted dirt road, we stopped at a small two-story inn tucked in the woods. Smoke coiled out of the chimney, hidden from anyone who didn't know it was nearby. It wasn't there to take in vagabonds roaming through; it was here precisely to hide spies.

"Mr. Dragen, Miss. Brycin!" A small gray-haired human man greeted us on the porch when we drove up, clapping his hands together. "It is a pleasure seeing you again."

"Olek." Ember climbed off the back of the bike. The two pixies in her bag flew out of it, heading toward the man.

"Sir Olek." The blonde pixie with the mechanic wings bowed at the gentlemen.

"Oh, Mr. Simmons and Mr. Cal. So happy to see you." He took Ember's hand in his, addressing the pixies before smiling warmly at her. "What a great honor you have brought me on this Christmas Eve."

"It's Christmas Eve?" Kovacs got off the bike, pulling off her gloves, surprise widening her eyes. The holiday meant nothing to me, but seeing her face light up with childlike excitement told me she still cared for the human holiday, which made me shift on my feet. I wasn't used to wanting to make someone else happy. Wanting more for them than me.

"I hope you have room for all of us." Ember peered back at Ash, helping Esmeralda off the bike. Everyone else saw the old woman, but if it was me or because of Brexley, I could see someone else bleeding out of her. The druid let her rest while he kept her body alive, using his energy to heal her. "And we need medical care."

"Oh!" Olek's eyes widened seeing Esmeralda, her clothes shredded from bullets. One of the bunny ears on her slippers was burnt off, and a plastic eye was melted on the other. "Of course, of course. Please hurry! You can take her upstairs to the first room." He waved Ash in.

Ash easily picked Esmeralda's petite frame up, carrying her up the steps and disappearing into the house.

"Come, come!" He motioned us in. "Plenty of room. I can cook you up something warm. You all must be famished and freezing." His English was clear and fluid, but you could hear his Hungarian accent surrounding each syllable.

I ducked coming into the doorway, the inn's ceiling only a few inches above my head. He settled us near the fire as he retrieved everything Ash needed to heal the old woman. Brexley joined them upstairs, needing to be near Esmeralda, a.k.a. Tad, to make sure she would be okay. I knew the weight of what happened tonight would fall down on her later, adding to the burden she already carried. I wanted to take it away, to carry it for her, and for the first time in my life, I felt helpless because I couldn't do something.

By the time Ash and Brexley made it back down, Olek had dished up hearty stew and bread, serving Uzvar infused with vodka, which was a Christmas drink in Ukraine. Not usually with alcohol, but I was glad Olek spiked the fuck out of it for us.

"She's okay?" I spoke to Kovacs, her head nodding as she settled next to me on the sofa.

"Yeah. Tad is still with her, and whatever Ash gave her really helped. She's sleeping now." She slumped in relief, her body fully resting against mine. Esmeralda couldn't counter all the bad that happened earlier, but for this moment, it was enough for her. At least she saved one.

"Can we cut the bullshit now and get to what the fuck happened tonight? Who the hell you two are?" Caden stood up, tossing his dish down on the table, pointing at Ember and Eli. "And when are we going after my father?"

"Calm the fuck down, junior," I grumbled at Caden, turning my fury to the new duo. "Let's start with you two... and why the fuck you are hunting my mate?" I growled, the word slipping out before I could stop it, grinding my back teeth together. It pissed me off how easily it came off my tongue. I wasn't mad that it was true, I just didn't like everyone knowing my business. But if the meaning of those words scared them off her any, it was worth it.

The fae world understood the seriousness of the claim. It went beyond soulmate or wife, husband or partner. It was sacred, and if you knew a pair was mated, like the two I was looking at, you knew fucking with one would rain fury down with the other.

Eli's shoulders lifted, sensing the threat underlying my question, his gaze challenging mine as Ember spoke first.

"There's not much my father isn't aware of. Even if the East is not under his rule, he understands the threat of all these countries vying for power, when governing is no longer the goal but a stepping stone toward dictatorship. He has spies all over, keeping tabs on what is going on." Her eyes danced to Eli, sharing something that went beyond our awareness. "Fifteen years ago, we learned about this nectar. Then it disappeared. Now it has suddenly shown back up at the same time as Dr. Rapava's old formula to create super soldiers." She leaned her elbows on the table. "It's no coincidence, and nothing is taken for granted anymore by Lars. He's been watching this area for a long time. The nectar is his biggest concern. We *know* what it can do." She said it as if they knew more than they had seen here. "It's equivalent to a treasure of Tuatha Dé Danann, which is honestly the last thing this world needs. Too much power for anyone to have. It always ends badly."

Eli scoffed, rubbing his head at her statement. I knew the

history; they had been around a long time to know that the treasures were real. Queen Kennedy was on her throne because she killed the previous queen with the Sword of Light, a treasure of Tuatha Dé Danann. Rumors were that King Lars had found them all and almost lost his throne and his life because he had lost control.

"If put in the wrong hands, the threat is on the world… we can't have that again." Ember folded her arms.

"What does that mean?" Brex sat up straight, her hip pressing into the very object they were talking about.

"We were sent here to retrieve it. Kill you if you got in the way," Ember stated, her gaze unapologetic.

I rushed to my feet, the threat falling from my lips without a second thought. "If you get near her, I will *gut* you and feast on your liver. If you and your puppy here want to get cocky and think you can fight the Wolf, then let's go."

Eli rose at my threat, his eyes flashing red.

"Warwick." Brexley got up, stepping in front of me, her jaw set tight. Her voice was husky and low, probably wishing we could communicate privately. "Stop. I don't think they're going to hurt me."

"You don't know that," I murmured, my gaze darting up to the Dark Dweller and Dae.

"I do." She nipped at her bottom lip and turned back to face Ember. "You sensed my magic. Recognized it. It's why you didn't kill me. You couldn't then, and you won't now."

"You sure?" Ember tilted her head.

"Yes," Brexley replied confidently. "Because you feel the same. We share magic."

Ember took a breath, her head shaking. "How is it possible? How do you have some of *my* powers? I mean, they're mine. I can feel it."

"What?" Eli and the entire room bounced from Ember

to Brexley. "What do you mean, *your* powers? That's not possible."

"Actually, it is." A deep woman's voice came from the stairs. A pair of slippers flopped down the steps, only three bunny ears and two eyes between the two. Esmeralda's tiny form moved slowly down the steps, her body stiff, but she was not in charge. All I saw were the mannerisms and demeanor of the druid taking over.

"In this case, anyway." She gripped the railing, taking the last steps into the living room slowly, just like the old man.

"You should be resting." Rosie reached out to her, helping.

"Don't worry, dear. She is." Esmeralda winked at her, taking her hand, letting Rosie help her walk into the living space. "She will be back to her feisty, grumpy self soon, I'm sure."

"Tad." Brexley went over, hugging them. "Thank you so much for helping her."

"Of course, my girl. Her journey, like yours, is far from over. She is also too stubborn and crotchety to die."

Brexley let out a huffed laugh, both of them smiling knowingly.

Tad shuffled farther into the room near the fire. "It's hell to get old and be so chilled to the bone all the time," he grumbled, shaking his head and perching on a chair.

"What did you mean it was possible for her to have my magic?" Ember returned us to the conversation.

"You might want to sit down, girl." He patted the seat next to him for Ember. "This story really begins the night of the Fae War, which you had a significant part in, if I recall."

Ember glanced at Eli, her head tipping down. "Yeah, you could say that."

331

"Ash, can you look in your bag for me? I think I left something in there." Tad motioned to the backpack he took off near the door. Nothing was in it except for snacks, clothes, and an empty container of mushrooms, which Bitzy had finished within an hour of our journey.

His brow wrinkled, but he snatched up the bag, his mouth dropping open as he looked inside.

"How….?" Shock widened his eyes as he pulled out a heavy book from what appeared to be an empty sack. "How did you do this?"

"Holy shit!" Brexley moved quickly to the table next to Ash, my ass right behind, pressing into her. "That's the fae book. But…" She peered back at Tad.

The power of the book pulsed in the air. Centuries of life stuffed the pages. Fae books were rare, and I never had the opportunity or reason to hold one. Ash was the first person I knew who had one, but it never came up until Kovacs. Still, I had no connection or desire to pick one up. Let's say I was never a kid who read much. I learned hands-on in the streets, but tonight I felt this strange pull, and I leaned closer to Kovacs, peering over her shoulder at it.

"Warwick Farkas…" A whisper brushed across my mind, a buzz in my ear, a deep voice feeling older than time itself, imprinting and disappearing so quickly I felt like I had imagined it.

"I thought I lost it?" Ash, still dumbfounded, peered at the book, then at Tad.

"Dear boy, you can never *lose* a fae book. It goes where it wants to. You should feel lucky it chose to stay with you so long, though I think it knew in time you would return to its family."

"Family?" Ember's brows cinched together.

"To you." Tad patted her hand. "And by default, her too." He nodded at Brexley.

"I'm confused." Ember glanced around, Eli at her side. "I don't have a sister or other relations. *That* I would know."

"Not a blood relation per se, but she's in your family line just the same." Tad motioned for Ash to set the book on the table, opening it up. Energy pulsated in the air, my head swaying at the intensity.

"I don't understand." Ember shook her head.

"Here." Tad grabbed Ember's hand, hovering it over the book, nodding to Brexley to do the same. "I think it will be easier to show than tell…"

He pressed their hands down on the pages. Energy crackled, pushing through Brexley's body and into mine.

"Brexley Kovacs," the old crackly voice spoke. *"The girl who challenges nature's laws, and the man she brought back to life. Ember Brycin, the girl who broke nature's laws for the man who should not have lived."*

There was a pop, and I felt myself fall. Tumble and rolling, scenes from history flashed by so fast that I had to shut my eyes to avoid getting sick. The flicker took me back to the days I was put in the hole, where my senses were blasted and tortured, along with my body.

Everything stopped, and my lids slowly opened.

A deep, twisted knot braided through my stomach, taking every sensation I had twenty years ago.

Brexley, Ember, Eli, and I stood on the dark field, our boots sinking in the red-soaked dirt. The smell of magic, death, and fear scorched the air. The sky crackled with colors, the torn barrier barely there, fully showing the queen's castle behind. Screams and sounds of metal clanking surrounded us. The grass was littered with dead bodies. Instantly I knew where we were. The memories I tried to shove away popped back with utter clarity and horror, burning up my throat.

It was the night the wall dropped.

The night I died.

The night the Legend was born.

My hands rolled into balls with the vividness of being back here, reliving the unbearable pain of being tortured and burned alive. I could almost feel my death happening somewhere on this field—the last breaths I took as a simple half-breed fae before they snapped my neck.

Before my *Sötét démonom* drew me from the gutters of hell and brought a legend to life.

"Crap on ashbark." Ember's voice tugged me from my thoughts, reminding me I was in the here and now.

"The book brought us back to the fae war," Brexley told her.

"I know how a fae book works." Ember stared out at the field, emotion flicking in her eyes. "I just never imagined how real it would feel. Like I'm actually here again…" Tears filled her eyes, her hand wrapping around Eli's. I had no doubt they had lost people they knew in this war. Everyone did.

Everyone here besides Kovacs had fully lived this. We had bled, killed, died, and sacrificed everything on this battlefield to save Earth. Lost friends, family, and comrades. We couldn't save Earth from the barrier falling, which killed thousands of humans, but we did stop Aneira from taking over.

It had everything to do with the Dae next to me.

A scream came from our right, twisting all our heads to it. A woman with dark hair, her belly protruding, gripped onto another woman, who looked similar to her, lowering herself to the ground.

Eabha.

She was plump with life, and she looked so much more like Brexley than I thought. The skin and bones necromancer I knew was a shadow of the vibrant, beautiful woman here.

Her face flinched in pain as she breathed, the baby coming. I now recognized her sister, Morgan, standing before her defensively, fighting with a gray-haired man.

"Shit, that's Tad," I muttered in shock at seeing him healthy, his back straight and tall.

Sparks from the barrier rained down when Eabha cried out, her hands on her belly, her legs parting as the baby crowned.

A crack of light broke across my vision. In that blink, the book relocated us. Suddenly, the four of us were inside, the walls of a castle surrounding us, but I could see the war taking place below through a window.

A gasp came from Ember, her hand covering her mouth as we all stared at her earlier self next to the future queen of the Unified Nations, who stood over Aneira, and a dead body laying off to the side.

"Fuck," Eli muttered, his gaze going to the lifeless form.

His. The dead body was Eli's.

I blinked, turning to him. I could see him staring at himself. An eerie feeling came over me, understanding both of us had died that night.

Both of us should still be dead.

The man who was brought back to life and the man who should be dead.

Both of us with the women who, in some way or another, brought us back from the dead. The strange connection tying the four of us together seemed to wind around us.

A wet cough snapped me back to the figure on the floor. Aneira lay on the ground, stirring awake, blood leaking from her mouth. Grabbing for a sword, she started to rise, coming for the other Ember.

The future queen swiped up an ancient-looking sword,

the blade bursting with a blue glow the moment she touched it. She swung it down on Aneira with a cry, cutting through her neck. Aneira's head dropped to the wood, rolling under the throne.

Magic plunged through the room, slamming through me like a freight train. I could hear both the young and current Ember scream as the book ripped us from that room, taking us back to Eabha. The barrier collapsed just as Eabha gave birth, muttering out a curse. The baby let out a wail as magic plunged into the infant, soaking into it and the substance still coating it.

Lightning struck the earth. Magic burned through my veins.

Simultaneously, Eli and I gasped for air, coming back to life, the women we loved over us.

"Sötét démonom."

Once again, we were tumbling, spinning, before the book spit us out, dropping us painfully back into the present.

My ass hit the floor, Kovacs's frame falling on me, her head slamming into my chest, puffing a groan from my lungs.

"Szent fasz." She grabbed for her head with a curse. "Your chest is harder than a stone floor."

"Not the only thing hard," I muttered, feeling her tight body covering mine. I closed my eyes for a moment, trying to slow the spinning in my head.

"I see the potential for pairs diving. That was a solid 3 or 4." Tiny feet padded over my shoulder, opening my lids with a different type of groan. Opie wore a skirt of strung potato peels, the top of a carrot sprouting from his head, and dill threaded in a layered necklace. Bitzy wore a butter wrapper for a tube top and carrot sprouts on her head.

All items that went into the stew we ate.

The leafy sprout on his head danced around as Opie

peered down at Brexley and me, hands on his hips. Bitzy was on his back, already flipping us off.

Chirp!

"I agree. Form still needs improvement, but the synchronization was on point."

Chirp!

"Well, that is harsh. I said I *see* potential."

Chirp! Chirp!

Grunting, I brushed them off my shoulder, rolling Kovacs and me back up slowly.

"That was rude!"

Chirpchirpchirpchirp! Chhhiirrp! Chirp-chirp!

"Wow, is that even possible to do to oneself? His love plunger would reach, though. It's certainly long enough."

Kovacs let out a groan.

"You guys okay?" Ash leaned over us, helping Brexley to her feet.

"Yeah." She nodded but held on to Ash as I rose, making sure she was stable.

Ash peered at me. "It took you this time?"

I dipped my chin, feeling a gaze burn in our direction from the other side of the table.

Ember's two different colored eyes bored into Brexley; her mouth parted in utter bewilderment.

"That's how you have them..." She struggled to finish her sentence, her head shaking, her focus hopping from the fae book that just kicked us out, to me, then landing on Kovacs.

"Your aunt wasn't ready to go out so easily." Tad closed the book, patting the cover as if he was saying thank you, and looked up at Ember. "Even in death, she wanted her power to survive. Her magic and the barrier's magic, which is your family line, went into Brexley that night. It's how you two have similar magic."

"It's not just similar. I think it *is* mine." Ember glanced at Eli, sharing a look. "Aneira held my magic the night she died."

Tad tipped his head, his brows furrowing. "What do you mean, she held your magic?"

"She was always jealous of my mom, her power of fire and lightning. Of me, when she learned I was even more powerful. Before the war, Aneira ripped my power from me, using it to destroy cities around the world to get the Unseelie king to bow to her. So, when Kennedy killed her, my powers came back to me, but..."

Brexley's head jerked back into me. I pressed my frame into hers. The need to protect her, guard her against the world, was instinctual. Though the woman was stronger than anyone I had ever met.

"Is that possible?" Brexley whispered.

Ember's mouth pinched.

"Magic isn't a solid thing." Tad exhaled, a reaction flickering over Esmeralda's features. "It doesn't transfer cleanly. It will leave residue, or some will decide to stay in the new host. When Aneira died, most of Ember's magic was returned, but some clearly was not..."

Like how mine was with Caden now.

"Meaning—" Brexley dipped her chin, her muscles tensing against me. "What was left of your magic went with Aneira... into me. I actually took some of *your* powers that night."

She swallowed.

"A Dae's magic."

Chapter 26
Brexley

I went numb.

Staring at the group, the only safety I felt was the rock behind me. The man anchored me, keeping me from totally losing it. I was barely holding on as it was. My stomach was still wrenching with thoughts of Jethro—with all those I left. The danger I put them through, the lives I destroyed. Now I find out I was even more of a freak than I thought.

"What does that mean?" My attention bounced from Ember to Tad, needing someone to calm the panic I could hear in my voice. "Does that change me?"

"No. It doesn't change anything, my dear," Tad replied softly. "You are what you are. I don't think any new powers are going to pop up suddenly. You are a mix of many things, and that portion is probably very, very minuscule."

"But I have her fire magic."

"You have her family's magic. Aisling, her mother, also had the power of fire."

"Daes are extremely powerful, right? Don't they usually go insane?"

"Every. Single. One." Eli snorted, grabbing his stomach when Ember elbowed him.

"Not helping," she grumbled.

"On the contrary, woman. I helped a lot. My blood kept you sane. Needed a little Dark Dweller inside you to keep you sane." He winked, and it was full of insinuation. "Though that is sometimes still in question."

"Shut up." She rolled her eyes with a grin. "You're the one who makes me crazy."

"In all the right ways."

"Wait. What do you mean, your blood?" Ash turned to Eli. "You can't transfer blood between fae species. It kills them."

"Tell that to this one." Eli flicked his chin at Ember with a cocky grin. "She took it greedily. Kept begging for more."

"Seriously?" Shock turned to fascination on Ash's face.

"We think Daes react differently to blood transfusions." Ember shrugged. "Since I am the only Dae anybody knows of, it's a working theory." Ember batted her hands. "That's not important. We're getting off track." She tucked a strand of loose hair behind her ear. "So, I want to get this straight… the night of the fae war when Kennedy and I were taking down Aneira, you were being infused with not only the Seelie queen's magic and the barrier's energy, but also mine? How in the hell did you survive that? Just one of those should have killed an infant."

"My mother was casting a black magic spell to protect me." I nodded at Tad. "From him. But I think it helped bounce things off me a bit, absorbed into the shield around me."

"Your mother was a druid?" Ember's voice went up, her eyes widening.

"Sort of." I swallowed, feeling my throat tighten. "My family was stripped of that title after they tried to rebel, but Aneira twisted my grandfather's mind so much that she convinced him to curse his own family line if they went against her. They'd die if she died." I leaned farther into Warwick's warmth, feeling his strength surround me. "And on their death, they would become necromancers."

"I'm sorry…" Ember's mouth dropped farther open. "Did you say necromancers?"

"My mother died just a few moments after I was born. I should have too. But instead, all the conflicting magic merged. Counteracted each other and protected me. Saved me… saved more than me." I shot a look to Scorpion, my fingers threading through Warwick's. "I have the power to bring people back to life. I can also communicate and control spirits."

"Holy fuck." Eli rubbed his face, his hands sliding back into his dark hair as he paced in a circle.

"So instead of reaping souls, you put them back?" Ember blinked at me.

"If I can. It's limited. It has to be within a few moments of their death before their soul leaves."

"And I thought I was a freak." Ember snorted, her head wagging. "You really are a magic mutt."

"Yeah." I snorted, my lips thinning. "And to add to the freak show, the nectar you all are after? That's what saved my life. Took on most of the magic hitting me."

"What do you mean saved your life?" Ember's lids narrowed.

My eye twitched, knowing what their responses would be already.

"The nectar… it's my afterbirth."

Silence.

A choking sound came from Ember and Eli, and I think Caden and Wesley also gagged behind me.

"Oh my gods… seriously?" Ember looked green. "I think I'm going to throw up."

"Everyone needs to grow up." Tad waved his hand, annoyance wrinkling his nose. "It's one of the most natural things in the world, but to clarify, the magic changed its makeup. It is no longer what it was. It functioned as a shield for Brexley, absorbing much of the magic before it went into her. A buffer of sorts. The elements and composition altered the moment magic hit it. No human lab in the world would be able to test it and find its makeup. It's more like ancient, preserved honey. The nectar is now pure organic magic. One of the most magical objects in the world."

"Still." Ember shivered, her tongue sticking out in disgust.

"That's gonna be a fun story to tell someone when we get home." Eli chuckled, grinning at Ember. "And we can't let it anywhere near Sprig."

Ember groaned with humor. "The most powerful treasure in the world being pooped out by a monkey-sprite."

"Think he gets the zoomies now?" Eli snorted. "He really will be a super sprite."

She laughed, shaking her head before a weary sigh expelled from her, like the realization of everything that had happened tonight finally hit her. She rubbed her head, turning back to me, her humor dropping away.

"We were sent here to retrieve and kill if need be. Though tonight didn't go *at all* like planned or what we even considered, and our mission may have altered"—she paused— "the core of it has stayed the same." Her focus was on me, slightly dipping to the small box protruding from my pocket. "The nectar comes with us."

I felt Warwick's energy smashing against my back, and a low growl hummed from his throat. Warwick barely moved an inch forward, his chest and shoulders expanding, before Eli reacted to the threat, green eyes flashing red, his teeth appearing like daggers as he growled back, his body curving in attack mode.

The entire room pinged off each other like a game. Caden came to Warwick's side, his stance identical to the Legend's, like they were one and the same. Scorpion, Ash, and Killian flanked his other side.

In a matter of minutes, this room would be soaked in blood—in death. We outnumbered them by far, but I knew not to underestimate a Dark Dweller or a Dae. They were at the top of the food chain for a reason.

If we killed the demon king's daughter, we would be so fucked.

"Warwick." I put my hand on his chest.

"They're not touching you or the nectar," he gritted through his teeth.

"That's not up for debate." Eli's fingers began to shift into claws.

"You want to bet, pussycat?" Warwick snarled, stepping around me. His and Eli's energy suffocated the room, their physiques ready to collide.

"ENOUGH!" Tad yelled, Gaelic words following. He had no staff this time, nor the same level of power he did when he was alive, but the impact of his magic divided the room like a sledgehammer, stumbling all of us back, separating the two alphas about to attack. "We have enough enemies outside these doors. We don't need to fight amongst ourselves too."

"They *are* the enemies." Warwick's lip lifted at the pair, his muscles locked, ready to jump back in.

"No, they are not." Esmeralda's tiny frame stepped between the two groups, holding up her hands. "For better or worse, we are all on the same side. All the rest is meaningless if we don't come together to stop the true threat. The goals of the king and queen are the same as ours. Stop Istvan and Sonya at all costs. What people seem to forget is we are all connected in this world. If the East falls, the West will be *severely* affected. Their economy will weaken to the point Istvan will try to attack it as well. With his super soldiers, he has a good chance of succeeding. This fight is not only affecting us, but it also involves you now." Tad motioned to Eli and Ember.

"Lars can't declare war unless they outright attack the Unified Nations." Ember shook her head.

"I said nothing about the king declaring war. Though I figured you two would not be able to walk away, knowing of the threat against your nation. Your king and queen. Will you fight with us or against us?" Tad asked bluntly.

Mistrust filled the space, the two sides watching each other.

Ember and Eli barely glanced at each other. A buzzing sensation tickled my skin, and somehow, I knew they were communicating with each other. Not like Warwick and I could, but through a link I knew mates might share. Some fae species could communicate through a similar link, like my mother and her clan.

Ember dipped her head, folding her arms, her words tight, not easing the tension. "We are with you."

Tad peered between us, gauging the unease in the room. The melted bunny slippers seemed so ridiculous in contrast to the tension, and I couldn't help a crazed laugh from coming out. All of this was too much. I tried to remember my life back at HDF, when I was a boring human in love with my best friend, who I thought didn't feel the same. And I thought that was complicated.

Now my best friend was part fae, connected to the man I brought back to life because of powers shoved into me from an evil queen, a cursed witch, and a probably half insane Dae.

The same person trying to kill me now.

344

We all were being babysat by a dead druid, using the body of an old gypsy seer who had been shot multiple times tonight.

"My life." I scoured at my face in utter disbelief, realizing I hadn't even gone into my friends standing around me and all their issues.

"For now, the nectar stays with me." Tad swiveled to me. I stepped back, a growl set on my tongue. The instinct to keep it with me flashed out in an instant.

"Brexley." Tad softened Esmeralda's expression. "You can't be trusted with it."

I took another step back, like he actually daggered me.

I knew he was right, yet I still hesitated. It was mine. Part of me.

"Dear girl, don't forget what happened tonight. Your training worked until the moment you touched it." I didn't forget. The death and destruction. Jethro. More moments that would haunt me forever.

"Well, maybe you should have trained me to handle it," I sneered.

"You barely learned to handle yourself. It is not for anyone to use. You know that." He held out his hand. "It's unsafe with you."

Swallowing, my attention poignantly darted to Ember and Eli.

"I won't let them have it either." He shook his head. "With me, it will be protected. In neutral hands."

A full minute passed, Tad never dropping his palm, his patience with me infinite.

He was right. I couldn't be trusted, and my need for the power, to feel it sizzle through my veins, to take over, was overpowering at times. I had no guarantee I could stop myself next time, risking killing more people I loved.

Blowing out a huge breath, I reluctantly dropped the box in his hand.

He nodded at me with appreciation. "I will watch over it. I promise."

Shifting on my feet, the urge to reach out and snatch it back twitched in my muscles, but the images of Jethro stopped me, knowing he died because I couldn't manage the power.

Warwick's hands wrapped around mine, pulling me back into his frame, giving me comfort and strength. He didn't have to say a word; he spoke with actions instead.

"I think tonight we have had enough revelations and drama. We need a good night's sleep, and we can reconvene in the morning." Esmeralda's shoulders slumped a little, as if Tad's energy was waning as well. "Have fresh minds for our plan to get into the city and destroy Istvan's labs."

"Yes, yes." The owner of the place jumped up, glad the threat and tension had eased. "Let me show you all to your rooms." He waved for us to follow.

He showed Eli and Ember the first room. Just as they stepped in, Ember turned back to me.

"You asked what having my powers meant?" she huffed, not looking thrilled I might have also them. "It means your magic has a bit of a royal fairy princess… and a high *demon* king." She said before she shut the door on us.

I blinked, the realization of who Ember's parents were settling in.

"Fuck." Warwick let out a barked laugh.

"What?" I whirled to him.

"Knew it." He peered down at me with a hungry smirk. "Sötét démonom."

My dark *demon*.

346

A clanking noise from downstairs dragged me from sleep, my eyes burning with exhaustion the moment my lids pried open to the approaching dawn.

The reality of what happened at the circus attacked me once Warwick and I were alone. My soul was too heavy to carry more death. More guilt. But I had to... I was the one who caused all the suffering. I felt wretched thinking about Jethro. What he had done for me. What he had sacrificed.

And I killed him.

I took all the people and things he cared about and destroyed them, then left them there to deal with the aftermath.

"You could not have helped them." Warwick slipped my jacket off me, his tone softer than I had ever heard.

"It doesn't matter." I heaved out a sob. "I should never have put them in that situation. I should have left. It's all my fault. I can't..." My heart felt like it was cracking in half, stealing my breath, my nails tearing at my chest like they would reveal the agony pressing down on my lungs, the disgust I felt for myself. "I-I can't..."

"Then give it to me." Warwick yanked my clawing fingers away so I'd stop hurting myself. "I will carry it for you."

He gave me no time to oppose his offer. His mouth came down on mine, kissing me with desperate need. "Give me your heartache and grief. I want it." His voice rumbled, and he walked me back to the bed. "Take it all out on me."

His mouth was the solace I needed, the air I required, and the relief I craved. I took it greedily. When he stripped me naked and drove deep into me, his determination challenged my pain. Conquering. Taking. Seizing it as his.

Our bodies moved together in penance, our moans our atonement, our shadows finding reparation.

He punished and commended.

Neither hero nor villain.

We lived in the gray.

I felt my screams reverberate through the house before I passed out, my body finally forcing me to sleep. Though only a few hours later, I woke from another nightmare. Fire. Death. Screams. Jethro's burned corpse rising from the ashes, his dark eyes finding mine. Angry. Accusing.

Warwick didn't speak, ask questions, or try to verbally soothe me. He showed me instead, pushing in from behind, taking me so deep and slow, letting his soul brush against mine, our shadows intertwining, seizing more of my pain, my grief, until I was shaking and crying out in another way, my mind and body giving out, letting me rest a while longer.

Until the noise downstairs jarred me awake. Another clatter from below lifted my head. Something felt off, itching at the back of my mind. The room seemed eerily quiet.

Muscular arms wrapped tighter around me, curving me into his huge frame, burying deeper into the bed, an exhaled groan vibrating against my back. "Not yet."

"Something's not right." I peered around, not sure what was bothering me.

"Because we weren't woken up by your annoying pets shoving their fingers in places they shouldn't."

That was it.

"Oh shit…" I scrambled out of his hold, leaping out of bed and grabbing my clothes as another bang twanged from under my feet. As if I had some motherly instinct, my gut told me if they weren't here, then they were probably up to no good.

"Princess…" Warwick growled from the bed, gripping

his erection, sliding up and down, his gaze glossy and hungry. "I wasn't done with you."

My breath hitched, and my pussy pulsed, not at all done with him either. I was about to climb back into bed, straddle him, and ride him until neither of us could see or think.

Smash!

Chiiiiiiiiiiiiiiirrrrrrrrrp!

"Fuck."

The sound of a dish shattering and Bitzy's voice turned me away from him. I ran out of the room and down the stairs, tugging on my shirt and pants as I went. I came to a screeching halt in the doorway of the kitchen, my mouth gaping.

Olek, seemingly oblivious or not caring, sliced dried fruits next to the pot of oats he was cooking, while the kitchen island in the middle was covered in pure chaos.

Naked chaos.

"My wee-bits are flying." The pixie I recognized as Cal lay on the table butt-ass naked in a pile of flour, his hands swaying above him. "Do you see them? They have wings. Big hairy balls with wings."

Chirrrrpp! Bitzy, wearing only a necklace of blackthorn berries, sat next to him, her arms up in the air like she was trying to catch something.

"Watch out, little B, my balls bite." Cal giggled, his arms moving up and down like he was making a snow angel in the flour. "Everything feels tingly."

"Oh gods." I cringed, my fingers pinching my nose. It was way too early for this.

"Fishy!" Opie waved from the other side of the table, dressed in what appeared to be part of an oven mitt sewn into a onesie, his nipples and belly button cut out. He wore a cloth napkin as a cape, and his beard was braided with rosemary, a diadem of blackthorn berries crowning his head. He sat on a juicer like a seesaw, crushing a brownish-white object inside into a cup, getting more bits than juice.

"Are you…" I shook my head, stepping closer. "Are you juicing a mushroom?"

Chirpppp! Bitzy tittered a yes in response, snatching her long fingers in the air. It was scary that I understood her.

"Cal said he wanted juniper juice, and Bitzy wanted mushrooms, so we compromised." He motioned to the cup. "Mushroom juice!"

"Mushroom juice!" Cal belted out in a cheer.

Chiiirp Ccchirp! Bitzy mimicked them, raising her arms in the air.

"Stop grabbing my balls out of the air, imp," Cal shouted and laughed. "Weeee bits are alive!"

Chiiirp!

"You can hear them too?" Cal put his finger to his lips, leaning down toward his crotch. "What are you saying, wee-bits? Speak louder for the room to hear."

"Oh my gods…" A voice came behind me, Ember and Eli coming into the room, the other pixie flying right beside them. "Not again."

"See, my lady, I told you." Simmons buzzed around in a flutter. "I tried to stop him. I did. But you know what he's like."

"Girlie!" Cal sat up straight, calling out to Ember, then pointing at Eli. "Dumb arse!" He turned his finger on Simmons, his Scottish accent getting thicker. "Tight arse." His voice went low with paranoia. "Do you see my balls? They've escaped!"

"How much juniper juice did you drink?" Ember groaned, pulling her sweater around her tighter, looking like she had jumped out of bed in a hurry too.

"Zero!" Cal giggled, falling back down again. "Juniper is my love, but Mr. Fungi might be coming in a close second." He put his finger to his lips. "Shhh… do you hear them? My bits are pure poetry in the sky."

"Great." Eli snorted. "Now the flying barbie doll will be drunk *and* high."

Chhhiiirrppp!

"Oh, crumbling crackers, my hair balls are multiplying! Watch out! They are like an asteroid field." Cal rolled over, trying to swim across the counter away from us.

Chirpppp! Chiiirp! Bitzy plucked at the air in hysterics while Opie bounced on the juicer with a little too much enthusiasm, like he was on a bucking bronco. "Oh, yeah… faster, daddy…"

Chirrrrpppp-Chirpp!

"What! No, I didn't!" Opie almost fell off as he tried to stop, scrambling to his feet. "That is a lie! Total misunderstanding!" He straightened his outfit. "I was only making juice for you."

Chirp!

"It is not like the cake blender incident." He huffed. "That was also a total misunderstanding."

"What the fuck?" Warwick's deep voice came behind me, and I could feel his large hand gliding over my ass and up my back before he even touched me. Our bond was solidly back in place. His body heat scored me as his head came over my shoulder, peering at the scene on the table, a small snort coming from him.

"Wolfy, the Impal-*her*!" Opie sang out, swishing his cape around him. He was high, but not as much as the other two.

Chirppppp! Bitzy wiggled her six fingers at Warwick with a high-pitched squeak, her eyes batting at him awkwardly.

351

"Dive bombing hairy biting ball bombs." Cal scuttled behind a jar, covering his head. "Save yourself!"

"Are you taping this?" Ember glanced at Eli.

"Fuck, yes." Eli had his mobile out, capturing it all, an evil smirk on his face. "After the glue antic he pulled last week? Sweet justice in the form of blackmail."

I'd heard pixies were known pranksters, and it could get bad if it escalated.

"Oh!" Olek turned around from the stove, his hand going to his chest. "You startled me." He tapped at his ear. "My hearing is not what it used to be, I'm afraid." He grabbed the pot of oats, bringing it over to the table, nonplussed by the naked sub-fae on the table as if it was an everyday occurrence. It might possibly be. This place struck me as the kind to have brownies and other sub-fae around. "I will have breakfast ready in a few moments."

"Thank you, Olek," Ember replied. "I will get my naked friend off your table... *once again.*"

"Cal!" Simmons's mechanical wings took him closer to where his buddy was. "Did you hear my lady? You need to get dressed. You swore you wouldn't swim across Sir Olek's table naked again."

"Ahhhhh!" Cal screamed, looking up at Simmons, his eyes wide. He took off running, everything out and swinging. "We're being invaded by motorized nutsacks. Run for your lives!" He dove into a bowl of sugar, trying to bury himself underneath.

"What the hell?" A woman's voice interrupted the mayhem, jerking our heads back around. Birdie strolled in, staring at the scene with disbelief. She absently pulled her long blonde hair back in a ponytail, showing off the finger imprints and hickeys on her neck. Caden was a distance behind her, as if he was trying to act like they didn't come

352

down together. Though I could spot the fingernail scratches and bite marks covering his skin from here. Their energy was palpable. Full of anger, disgust, and lust. I had no idea what really was going on between them, if it was more than sex, if Caden would let it be anything more. He was stubborn, his ideals set, but if anyone could flip his world upside down, it was Birdie.

There was a moment I had a pang of jealousy. Not that I wanted Caden or wanted him to love me. It was more the final door closing on what had been. The death of innocence. The bubble we had been in together. The life I had dreamed of and believed I wanted with him. It would never be the same ever again. Not even our friendship.

"Kovacs..." A gravelly voice scraped up the back of my neck. An invisible mouth grazed through my folds, making my body jerk. My head snapped to the real man, a smirk on his lips, an eyebrow cocking as if he knew exactly what I was thinking and wanted to remind me what I had.

I didn't need the reminder. Warwick consumed every bit of me. Our lives were linked and intertwined from the moment we both gasped for air. When I dragged Warwick from death's grip, claiming him as mine. Even if I wouldn't know him for years to come, I couldn't live in a world he wasn't in. Not for a moment.

I stole a Wolf from the grim reaper and made him a Legend.

From a few feet away, my tongue slid over the top of his cock, his frame jerking at my retaliation, feeling me take him deeper, his fingers digging into the wood of the table.

"Is this my Christmas present, Kovacs?"

I grinned at the real man as my shadow took him fully in my mouth, sucking harder. *"Merry Christmas."*

"Fuck, I love this holiday now."

353

I saw Ember shiver, sensing the change in the air. Eli's eyes flashed red for a moment.

"Will you two take a fucking break?" Scorpion stomped into the room, his sour mood clouding around him, glaring at both of us. The connection to him buzzed at my skin, telling me he could feel every nuance running between Warwick and me. "Or seriously, I will kill you both," he grumbled, nudging past me and swiping up one of the mugs Olek had put out for us. He poured himself a cup of coffee, turning back to us. "We are wasting time. We need to attack Istvan's labs." His attention was set on every one of us with utter conviction.

"Tonight."

Chapter 27
Scorpion

Large maps covered the table, the food shoved to the side as we studied them. Some were of the city, roads, and rail, and some appeared to be handmade, covered in *X's* and hundreds of lines connecting the city like weeds.

"What are these?" I pointed at the webs connecting through the city, which went back to the sixth century.

"Ah." Olek pushed up his thick glasses. "During the Cold War, Stalin had underground tunnels and bunkers built, adding to the catacombs and drainage system already there." Olek traced his finger over the lines from one of the *X's*. His face had shifted, and the kind old man running the keep became intense with knowledge and critical information someone had risked their life for. It was a seriousness people had when they had gone through real life and death experiences day to day. At any moment, you could be dragged off the streets and killed on the mere speculation you were a spy or speaking truths about the government. No proof needed. They turned everyone against each other. Everyone was an enemy. "Most don't realize that under their feet, there is a world that is probably just as large as the city above. A vast labyrinth of systems which connect the city."

"Many of the tunnels are known. Before the wall fell, they even had tourist tours of them." Killian cupped his coffee with one hand, leaning over the table to inspect the map with the other. "Ivanenko would have them not only guarded, but probably in use. Great way to do your dirty work without being noticed." He glanced at Olek, his free hand absently moving from the map to the girl next to him, his hand brushing Rosie's hip as if he needed to know she was there. You didn't have to be connected to them like I was to Brexley to feel the sexual energy and giddy emotion coming off them. It was thick, coating the room like confetti, pissing me off more. Caden and Birdie's hate-fuck mood didn't help either. And my bedroom wall was shared with Ember and Eli; those two seemed to be on par with Brexley and Warwick. And I wasn't even going to get into what I heard coming from Ash, Lukas, and Kek last night.

The inn was full of sex. No, worse—love. I fucking hated it. It tugged at something in my gut. A need to move, to forgo all this bullshit and find her.

My lungs clenched, struggling to breathe, the thought of her drifting out from the back of my mind where I tried to keep her tucked away.

Little Viper.

All I could see was her face in the last moments before she ran off with Istvan's soldiers—the pain in her eyes when she looked at me. I should have known, understood what she was telling me. Stopped her.

Done something. *Anything.*

The guilt and anger I felt for not fully comprehending, not hearing her cries for help, was overwhelming. My ego was too big to think she could walk away from us—from me. But she did.

356

I was mad at her for allowing them that power over her and mad at myself for letting her go.

Would she be here right now if I stopped her?

The restless agitation, the need to tear the world apart, the sensation nothing was right until I found her, pumped air heavily through my lungs. Because I understood what it meant. What she was to me. What I felt the moment I had sunk into her.

It wasn't the realization that scared me, and now that I knew, I might lose it forever. My gut told me she was alive, but she might be lost to me all the same.

"Yes, a lot of the main tunnels are in use. Sources have told me the activity has picked up since General Markos's arrival. Especially the old shipping yard area, which is also close to a government's private rail station," Olek replied, oblivious to the slight snore coming from the sugar bowl, where all you could see was a naked ass and pixie wings. Not one person had sugar in their coffee this morning.

"That's where my father has his labs." Caden nodded at the section Olek was circling. "Shipping out from land and sea."

Warwick rubbed his head, a grumble in his throat. "He will have them well guarded. We probably can't get anywhere close without being seen."

"Not true." Olek wagged his head. "The tunnel system is vast and complicated. Most passages are unused or not even known. I have spent many years discovering and finding passageways no one has used in decades, if not centuries." He stabbed his finger into the map. "The good news is that starting here takes you right to the shipping yard." He pointed at an X and slid his finger to the port.

"Why do I feel that was the end of the good news?" Brexley folded her arms, bearing down, preparing for the bad.

357

"Because not only are these tunnels dangerous—many have died trying to get through them—but they are filled with fae doors."

"Fae doors?" I exclaimed, dread sinking into my gut like a stone. Fae portals were tricky when the Otherworld still existed. Back then, it had been a way for fae to travel to and from Earth and around the Otherworld. But after the wall fell, it created thousands of magical holes, which seemed to have no meaning or structure. They were hard to see, and even fae were falling into them, getting trapped, never to be seen again.

"*Szar*." Ash tipped his head back. "Of course."

"Nothing is easy with us, is it?" Lukas sat down with a heavy sigh, all of us having the same dismal reaction. "The chances of one of us falling in one? Getting lost? Can we take that chance?"

"Well, good thing you have me." Ember's half smile turned from Eli, sharing some inside joke, to us.

"What do you mean?" Wesley asked her.

"I happen to be a master at fae doors."

Choked laughs sprinkled around the room.

"No one knows how to use them anymore. They lost all meaning when the wall fell," Killian stated.

"I think that's why she gets them." Eli scoffed. "She and my brother are the only two I know who actually understand how to work them. I think it's because they're both mentally ill."

"You're putting me in the same category as *Lorcan*?" Ember rammed her fist into Eli's arm playfully. "I will so get you for that one."

Lorcan Dragen was known here because he was the mate of the Seelie queen. The scandal of a Druid queen and a Dark Dweller lover had rolled through the east with intrigue and shock. The mated pair defied the odds, even having twins, a boy and a girl.

"Bring it, Brycin." Eli winked at her, then glanced back at us. "She's not lying. She really does know how to work them. It's how we can get around the countries and travel so easily unseen."

"Though please avoid them if you can help it. They will waste a lot of time if I have to keep searching for you guys." She set down her mug. "I can stay in front with Simmons and Cal. They are good at seeing them too."

"At your service, my lady." Simmons tugged on his jacket with pride, beaming at Ember, hovering right near her ear.

"Okay, say we can get into the lab." Warwick tied back his hair, his forehead crinkling. "How do we take it down?"

"I think I can help with that." Olek dipped his head, waving us toward a broom closet. He pulled open the door. Leaning down, he lifted a stone slab, which seamlessly appeared as part of the floor. Underneath was a staircase leading down underground. "Follow me."

Trailing after him, we all stepped down the creaky wooden steps, venturing into a dank, chilly basement. He reached out and pulled on a string. Dim light brightened the small hidden room enough to see what he concealed below.

"*Ó, hogy baszd meg egy talicska apró majom,*" *Oh, may a wheelbarrow of small monkeys fuck it.* Birdie breathed out in awe. "That is a lot of distraction."

Our figures moved like shadows in the night, our dark clothing blending in with the brush and trees, heading to a spot we had stared at all day on a piece of paper. The only sound was the hum of Simmons's wings flying next to Ember, which could be mistaken for crickets or insect wings. The entrance to the underground Olek had circled for us was obscure and hidden, probably only known to him and his "scouts."

The cold temperatures prickled my nose and cheeks, my lungs aching, but it made me alert. I had almost lost my shit waiting in the house all day, my need to do something—act, move, do anything but sit and stare at maps, going over the plan again and again. I couldn't stay still. I couldn't concentrate, a pull I couldn't describe tugging at my chest. And it only seemed to be getting worse with every passing hour.

Ash, Lukas, Kek, Birdie, Caden, and Wesley slunk around me, while Brexley, Warwick, Eli, Ember, Killian, and Rosie were slightly ahead of us, climbing over broken chain fences and trampling through weeds and overgrown plants. The late hour left the motorway near the site absent of horses and automobiles.

"By the GPS, it should be about here." Brexley's whisper floated softly through the dark, though I could feel and hear her without her even opening her mouth. The link was locked in place again, and from the energy in the air last night and how many times I had to jack off because I could feel them together, their bond was winding deeper. It never bothered me like it did now. I never saw the reflection of what I didn't have before. It was an utter loneliness I felt in my soul.

That was before *her*.

Now it was pure torture. I was more restless and agitated, wishing I could sever my link to them forever.

Would this be my life? The third wheel in *their* love story? Feeling everything I couldn't have, being reminded of everything I wouldn't experience. Would I always be tormented with the happiness that was lost to me before I even had it?

Why let me taste something and take it away? It wasn't supposed to be her. I never wanted a mate, especially not a mouthy human girl. Did I know deep down that night we took her prisoner and chained her to the wall that she would be my demise? The spitfire who did not back down or express fear at my threats. She bit back with words and teeth sinking under my skin and poisoning my soul with her smell and taste. When did the thought of living in this world without her become agony?

A grunt snapped through my teeth, and I rubbed my forehead, trying to shove her out of my thoughts.

Focus on the mission.

Killian, Eli, and Warwick hacked through the underbrush, the light from a flashlight glinting off metal underneath.

"There." Ember pointed to the covered manhole. Warwick kneeled, gripping the top. He easily pried the heavy lid off, letting a hiss of stale air out. Brexley directed her flashlight into the hole, revealing a ladder heading down into a narrow cement room.

"All right, boys. Go check it out." Ember wiggled her shoulder where Cal sat, still pouting that neither juniper juice nor mushroom juice were being provided on the trip.

"Be my honor, my lady." Simmons buzzed for the opening.

"No way, girlie." Cal wiggled his butt deeper into her shoulder, staying put. "There are probably spiders and rats down there. You know what happened the last time? That rat tried to mate with me. Uh-uh. No way."

"Do it, or I glue your dick to your asshole," Eli grumbled.

"Ha! Unlike *your* monster, mine won't reach." Cal huffed, folding his arms like he won, then slowly realized what he asserted. "Oh, wait…"

"You said it," Eli huffed out a laugh. "Now get your ass down there, barbie—"

"I'll get you juniper juice." Ember cut Eli off, speaking to Cal. "A sink's worth."

"Tub!" Cal retorted. "That rat almost penetrated me. I'm scarred for life!"

"Okay, a tub." She nodded at him.

Cal huffed, climbing off her shoulder, his wings flying him to the manhole with a grumble. Simmons followed him in.

Ember winked at Eli. "Trap them with honey, not salt."

"Why am I afraid that you even saying the word honey will cause a sprite to suddenly pop out of nowhere?" Eli ran his hand over his head. "Like summoning a demon."

"Hey now," Kek spoke. "You can't summon a demon, but we do *come* on command." She grinned at Ash and Lukas. Ash lifted his eyebrow with a knowing grin while Lukas blushed, staring down at his boots, a soft smile hinting on his lips.

Yeah, I had heard them last night too. Let's just say by the way the walls were shaking, I was shocked that old house was still standing in the morning. Wesley had taken it as well as I had, knowing one of those rooms held Killian and Rosie. He had slept outside in the small storage barn.

"Her pets are at least *trained*," Warwick muttered to Brexley. "Yours shit, eat, destroy things, and pass out. High out of their fucking minds."

Chirp! Bitzy flipped Warwick off from Brexley's shoulder. She sat in a pack on Opie's back, both dressed in black, with cat masks with spaghetti noodles for whiskers.

"I take offense to that too." Opie's voice caught the air. "We don't destroy things. We create masterpieces. We make dull things better."

"I'm not sure the fae book would agree." Ash retorted, his bitterness over that incident still clear. Though I think he was hurt the book didn't take him in last night, picking Warwick and Eli instead.

What no one knows was I went too. It wasn't physical like with them; it was more like a movie in my mind. I watched myself die and saw Maddox running for me, screaming. Magic funneled through me with a zap of lightning, knotting me back together. Taking that first breath, I recalled images flashing through so quickly I couldn't make them out. They melted away, never to be thought about again. This time I saw them more clearly. I didn't really believe in all that fate crap, but last night, when Hanna's face flickered in my head as I came back to life, knowing she wasn't even born yet, I wondered. Like roots of a tree, the bond connected me to Brexley, who would lead me to my mate. It was as if somehow, Brexley or the magic foresaw what I would be, who I was meant for, and saved me. That it wasn't happenstance at all.

I could have died on that patch of grass, my life no more than a memory to some, growing dimmer in time. I would never have known her. Never have understood the power of loving someone. Fighting for someone. Dying for someone.

"She might be lost," Tad-Esmeralda had whispered to me before heading upstairs to sleep last night. "She has not forgotten. Not yet. But time is slipping her further away. I can't see if she is gone for good." He patted my hand. "I want to believe there is hope. You were brought back from the dead by magic. Maybe it's you who needs to do the same for Hanna."

"I don't have that kind of magic." I shook my head. "Brexley does."

"Magic isn't always a spell. Love can be the greatest magic of all."

His words stuck with me all night. I was hoping to speak with him again to get more insight into what he meant, but whatever energy Tad used to possess Esmeralda had wiped both of them out. She slept all day, not even stirring by the time we set off earlier, leaving Olek to watch over her, the nectar tucked under her pillow.

"All clear, my lady." Simmons whirled out of the hole.

"Clear? There were a dozen rats and a million spiders just in the first chamber." Cal shivered, brushing at his arms. "That one was giving me sex eyes. Though, can you blame it? Who wouldn't want a piece of this marinated beefcake?"

"Beefcake? Try pickled twinkie," Eli snorted.

I barreled forward, irritated by their slow response, practically pushing people out of the way to go down first. The thin metal ladder whined against my weight as I descended, dropping into the tight space, my flashlight igniting the low passage in front of me. The sound of trickling water came from the room beyond, pulling me forward. One by one, everyone followed me as we ventured deeper into the tunnels, passing underground rivers and old bunkers built in the Cold War to areas that went back to when this capitol was founded. The reeking stench of vermin and river water filled my nose, and the tight spaces were coated in spiderwebs and mummified bugs.

"Oh goodie, more tight underground places we have to squeeze through." Ember's breath pumped in and out as she tried to calm herself. "You'd think by now I'd be over my claustrophobia."

My gaze darted to Brexley, sensing her anxiety spike,

364

knowing that being underground brought back her time in prison. It took most of us back. Vĕrhăza would be something we lived with daily. It would never be forgotten, a deep scar marring all of our souls. Being buried far underground, tortured, beaten, starved, and assaulted. Not seeing the sky or breathing fresh air, knowing we might never be free or glimpse a tree or bird again. Fighting for our lives, our sanity. The memories hung around, waiting to pop back up and attack.

Gritting my teeth together, I pushed forward, following the passage inching us closer to our destination, without any other thought than the need to move faster. An itch in my soul, a drive making me want to cut through the tunnels with my bare hands.

"Scorpion! No!" Ember grabbed my arm, yanking me back. I stumbled backward, almost falling on my ass.

"What the fuck?" Ire prickled up my spine, my head whipping to her with confusion.

Her head flicked to the spot I was about to barrel through. "Look."

My lids narrowed, and it took me several blinks to notice the disparity in the air before us. A wave of magic veiled by the darkness. Sucking in, I stepped back with fright.

Fuck. I had almost walked right into a fae door.

I was so consumed by my anger and the need to move forward that I didn't even see it. If Ember hadn't stopped me, I would have gone in… been lost forever.

Though oddly, a part of me was tempted. It seemed fitting. I was always searching, never finding—in perpetual torment. Lost. Alone. I had been fine with that. Accustomed. Preferred it, actually. Saved a lot of drama and nonsense.

I had grown up alone, an accident between two people who despised each other, and hence me. At seven, I watched

365

my father murder my mother and then kill himself, forgetting or not caring I was sitting right there. I was of such little thought to him.

Whoever said blood was thicker than water was full of shit. My real family was found outside the bounds of any DNA. On the streets, with other unwanted kids like me. Where I found Maddox, Birdie, and Wesley. And when we joined Sarkis's army, we felt we had a home for once in our lives.

I would kill and die for them, though I never completely let my wall down.

Now what had been normal and comfortable filled me with dread and anxiety. As if I finally touched the sun and was put back into the darkness. It gripped my soul, cut and burrowed in until I couldn't breathe.

"Scorpion..." Brexley's shade whispered in my ear as if she could feel every emotion running through me. I knew she couldn't, but she knew me enough now to sense the turmoil, the fight. I hated it because I had grown accustomed to her presence, the feel of her there, depending on the connection.

Two women had pushed past every barrier I had, giving me no choice. One saved my life and the other my soul.

Murmuring a quiet thanks to Ember, I circled widely around the fae door, shaking off the adrenaline still coursing through my veins. I needed to get it together. Not do stupid shit because my brain was scattered all over the place.

Ember took over the lead, with the pixies scouting out fae doors with her. Eli and Warwick were right behind, seeking enemies. I couldn't rid myself of the edginess as my boots nipped at their heels, screaming at me to move faster. Time was running out.

For forty-five minutes, we made our way through the

tunnels, dodging fae doors and edging closer to the heart of the city, when Eli stopped dead in his tracks. His head cocked to the side, listening, his nose flaring. Even with my fae senses, it took me a moment to hear boots hitting concrete, the smell of cigarettes and cheap cologne in the air. Dark Dwellers could smell and hear prey miles away.

Slipping closer, my heart beating in my chest, I spotted seven guards loaded down with guns standing like robots at a tunnel entrance. They had walkie-talkies on their hips and bandoliers draped across their chest. Probably every bullet they wore I had helped make in prison. Would one of those be my demise? It was comparable to digging your own grave.

Eli's eyes flashed red, his fingers shifting into claws. He glanced over at Warwick, and they nodded at each other as Warwick drew a long, serrated blade from his sheath. Gunfire would draw attention and echo down the corridors. We didn't want to let them know we were here.

I didn't even see the Dark Dweller move, his body almost blending in with the shadows as Warwick crept closer. The two of them didn't give the rest of us time to fight alongside them. We only heard the sounds of throats slashing, gagging screams, and bodies dropping.

The seven guards went down, either guts pooling out along with their still-beating hearts or heads rolling over the ground.

"Bazdmeg." Fuck. My hand still on the blade I was about to yank out, I blinked at the two guys splattered with blood, to the dead guards still gaping in the throes of death. "Good thing my dick is big, or I'd have a serious complex right now."

Warwick snorted, wiping off the remnants of blood on his face with his shoulder.

"After this long, that still gets me hot." Ember winked at

367

Eli, going up on her toes and kissing him, blood still on his mouth.

"So, it runs in the family, huh?" Brexley smirked, her heated gaze on Warwick. They pulled me in on their link, making my dick hard.

"Fuck no." I shook my head, pushing between them, snapping the connection. "Keep it in your pants, Farkas. Physically and mentally," I growled, stepping over the dead bodies and picking up more ammo and guns.

"Second that." Ash adjusted himself, grabbing a case of bullets off a dead guard.

The group traveled quietly up the passage, the tunnel growing wider and bigger as we went, sounds traveling to us from a distance, before we turned a corner. The path led to a massive underground bunker.

"Holy shit," I muttered, slipping behind a wall and peering into the large space. Holy shit didn't cover it. The size alone was more than I expected down here, but what was in it almost dropped my jaw to the ground.

Tucked behind the cement barrier, I observed the scene ahead, my lungs tightening with the deep awareness we were in over our heads. Most of us understood what Istvan was capable of, the grandiose narcissistic ideals he had of himself and what he could do. The further he fell into the inflation of his own self-importance, the higher and crazier his plans would be, except he made them come true.

The expanse of the underground chamber widened my eyes, noticing the newer built area that housed a handful of tanks, trucks, and trains, which idled as smoke billowed from the train's smokestack, ready to head out. He didn't have his men going to the train station; he had built one to come directly to him. Hundreds and hundreds of men and a handful of women of diverse ages and types were spread over the space doing various jobs, dressed in the same gray military uniforms Tracker wore. Each had a patch on their shoulder, which reminded me a lot of the HDF symbol the women had to sew on in prison, except these had FHF.

"First Human Forces," Caden muttered next to me, his hard gaze forward. "I have seen it before. I found drawings of it in my father's office when I returned."

Markos's stamp.

Whether known or unknown to Ivanenko, Markos had already taken over Ukraine. His brand was on everything in this room. Istvan marrying Olena made this an easy transition, pushing the old ruler into the background as Istvan and his wife took over. He had the future leader of this land growing inside his bride. Ivanenko was probably smart enough to understand that if he wanted to live, he needed to play along.

The hiss of the trains filled the vast space like they were getting impatient waiting. Soldiers loaded two trains with huge wooden crates while another group filled their trains with weapons and soldiers.

"I guarantee he has the pills in those." Brexley pointed to the boxes they loaded in, looking to Caden and Lukas, who nodded in agreement as if they had seen them firsthand as well. It only confirmed what we already feared—Istvan had this place completely operational, and probably for longer than we had calculated. He had been planning this takeover for a long time.

"Doesn't anybody learn from history?" Ember frowned. "Dr. Rapava's attempt at making a special race didn't fare well for him or his experiments."

"I don't know, Brycin," Eli replied. "Over twenty years later, and we're still trying to hunt down the rest of Zoey's freak offspring. They've learned to hide and adapt better than we imagined."

"Zoey's freak offspring?" Brexley tipped her head. "Who's Zoey?"

"She's a seer Rapava used to create a special breed of monster fae. They were stronger, smarter, and almost impossible to kill. We've been hunting them for years and still haven't been able to track them down."

"My father has read and studied everything Rapava did." Caden's teeth gritted. "He noted his successes and failures and made improvements on them."

"Nothing compared to what the Stone of Fáil did," Ember muttered, and I could tell there was a long, painful story connected to that, but she didn't expand on it.

"What you're saying is these things are already out there?" Brexley's mouth pinched, motioning to the soldiers.

"They are far worse," Eli replied. "Exceptionally smart. They aren't mindless at all."

"Let's hope those groups don't meet up someday." Ash blew out a heavy exhale.

A tall, lean, blond man strode out, pulling our attention. His uniform was tailored and darker, showing his higher rank among the other soldiers here. Medals and patches lined his arms. His arrogance dominated the space, his chin high. A twisted pleasure illuminated his eyes as he looked upon the mindless drones moving efficiently around him.

Brexley sucked in sharply.

"Captain Kobak," Caden grunted. He had a white-knuckle grip on his gun, anger and hate echoing off him like a radio station.

"Calm down, junior." Warwick's low voice weeded through us, directed at Caden, clearly sensing Caden's emotions through their connection.

"Who is he?" Ash asked.

"My first HDF teacher," Caden snarled through his

teeth. "Let's say he enjoyed pushing the limits, putting the weakest student with the strongest and forcing us to beat them until they were in a coma. He was taken out of that position when a kid died because of it." He glanced at Brexley, her lips pinning together in a shared moment. It wasn't until I saw Birdie secretly reach out to him, her hand touching his lower back, that his shoulders eased down, a breath exhaling from his lungs.

"He's found his perfect role now." Kek lifted her lip, her eyes darkening. "Just the kind I like to show who's the bitch."

"He was there at the marketplace that night." Brexley turned to me. "He was picking up the captured fae for Istvan's labs."

I was already in the market, stealing supplies, when Brexley came tearing through, the HDF soldiers after her. I never got to see him. My mind flickered to the memory of that day, our escape, Maddox still alive, fighting next to me.

"Brexley. Look." Caden's voice was low, teeming with alarm, his attention going to a short, balding man waddling out to Kobak, a clipboard in his hand.

A growl vibrated from Warwick, his shoulders rolling forward, vile rage pointed at the fat man.

"Dr. Karl," Brexley sneered.

"Where he is, my father will be near." Caden's demeanor altered at the mention of his father, his gaze focusing down to a point on Dr. Karl.

Our eyes tracked him as he handed papers to Kobak, then turned back, heading for a door across from us. He typed in numbers, pressing his thumb to a keypad before the door opened, shutting quickly behind him.

"We need to get in there," Brexley stated. "That's where the labs will be."

Our plan had been to split up. One group, Brexley,

Warwick, me, Ash, Lukas, and Caden, were to locate and destroy the labs. The other team, Ember, Eli, Killian, Rosie, Wesley, Kek, and Birdie, were on guard, setting bombs everywhere they could, waiting for us to return before we blew this entire place like a volcano.

It was a very loose plan. Everything could go wrong, and most likely would.

A train whistled with the pills, pulling out, heading for its destination, spreading the fae essence further and wider. Being near the river, there was no doubt that Istvan was also distributing the pills through cargo ships.

Not only was he getting richer, but his power was spreading like a cancer.

"Lars doesn't even know the extent of this place." Ember licked at her lips. "How far Markos has gone." She peered over at us. "This is a direct threat to Unified Nations. This place has to come down."

"It. Will," Caden retorted, his attention on the door like he could see through it and find his father somewhere behind it. "Even if I do it myself." For a moment, he glanced back at Birdie. No emotion showed on his face, but when their eyes met, the air charged around us before he whipped back, gripping his gun. "It's time." He darted out, scrambling to the next barrier to hide behind, setting the mission in play.

There was no turning back now.

"Here we go," I muttered to myself. Inhaling deeply, I crept out from behind the wall, the rest of the first group close behind me. We darted to a stack of wooden crates, bringing us closer to the door. My heart thumped wildly in my chest, knowing how easily we could be caught. Every breath attached to my pulse, fear coating my throat, adrenaline zapping through my muscles. I had been in a lot of life and death situations, too many to count, in which I barely made it out, but something amplified tonight's mission, the sense of dread turning in my stomach. It was like we all knew the chances of pulling this off, being so outnumbered, and getting out of here alive wasn't even in the cards. That our fate was to cripple Markos as much as possible while Mykel picked up the baton back in Budapest, the one to finish the war because we gave him the chance to do so.

My finger on the trigger, I peered out, my eyes focusing on the door. Another man in a lab coat tapped at the keypad, the door opening and closing quickly behind him.

"There's a coded lock," I whispered to my group, tucking back in when a small troop marched by. Terror plunged through my lungs when I saw one twitch his head our way, ready for the acknowledgment of our presence. Seconds ticked by, and nothing. Swallowing, I peeked back out, the unit already absorbed into the other mindless soldiers. "And a fingerprint entry."

"Fingerprint? How do we get past that?" Lukas hissed.

"Seriously?" A tiny voice pitched in my ear, whipping my head around to see Opie climb onto Brexley's shoulder from her backpack, Bitzy in her rucksack, her middle fingers up, her eyes peering at us like she couldn't handle our stupidly. "Oh, peasants... Your continued lack of intelligence astounds me." Opie pulled his kitty mask tighter across his face, the dried spaghetti noodles wiggling. He motioned to the Ash. "Hey, mushroom man..." He nodded to his hand.

Ash lifted an eyebrow but put out his palm, Opie strolling onto it before he lowered him and Bitzy to the ground.

"See, Bitz? You *can* train them." He waved Ash's hand away, strolling like a noble past our legs. "You all think so small and forget small things can do very big things."

Chirp! Bitzy whirled her fingers at us with a glare before

Opie took off. My eyes could barely track them until they reached the door. Scaling up to the keypad, they poked and tapped at the panel. From here I could see the red flash on the screen, denying them access.

Sub-fae were good at unlocking magic locks, but not computer ones.

"Shit," I hissed, looking around to make sure no one had noticed the activity, the red flashes feeling like a beacon. My body froze when I saw the door start to slide open. It would only be a second before whoever was on the other side would see Opie and Bitzy. My gaze darted to the man stepping out, waiting to see his attention pull down to the keypad, my heart in my throat. The man stepped through, continuing without a flicker in their direction. I blinked, realizing they weren't there anymore. A scuttling behind the man's dark shoes drew me to the pair rushing for the closing door. Opie threw his body in the opening, the door hitting him and stopping, leaving it pried open enough for us.

"Brownie pancake." Ash chuckled, nudging Brexley, sharing something none of the rest of us did. "Not very magical, but gets the job done."

A howl of a train whistled down a tunnel to us, pulling attention from the soldiers for a moment.

"Now!" Brexley ordered, already leaping out of our hiding space, darting for the door. Warwick and I were right behind, our guns pointed opposite ways, covering the areas someone could come from. Brexley took only a second to check behind the door before swiping Opie and Bitzy up and slipping through.

The rest of us followed like water through a gap, the door hissing shut with a clink behind us. We entered a bunker-style chamber, feeling like we had stepped back into the old world before the iron curtain fell. I could see curved ceilings, with water and electrical lines running along the side of the cement tunnels. There was no place to hide, our boots softly padding down the corridor toward the door at the end where an intersection of passages made a T.

Murmuring voices stopped us in our tracks, two soldiers coming down one side of the path, stopping in front of the doors, speaking Russian in low tones.

Air held in my lungs, my muscles locked tight, I felt like I could disappear into the wall, none of us daring to move an inch.

I saw one of the men turn to the keypad, his fingers about to type, when he stopped, his head curving to us instead.

Fuck.

His eyes widened in shock, his buddy swinging around. "Intruders," he yelled in Russian, grabbing for his gun.

Warwick and Ash reacted in unison, their figures were brutal, but their movements were almost a dance, cutting between the men in a blink. Warwick struck out, slamming his fist so hard into one that the officer flew back, cracking his head against the wall. He dropped to the ground limply, his neck clearly broken. Ash whipped the other one off his feet, knocking the air from his lungs as he hit the cement, gasping and struggling for air.

"You will not make a sound." Ash stood over him, pointing his gun at his head, speaking fluently in the man's native language. "Or you will end up like your friend." He nudged him with his foot. "Get up."

"Po'shyol 'na hui!" Fuck you! The officer spat at Ash.

Warwick growled, grabbing the man by his neck and picking him off the ground.

"Type in the password," Warwick commanded.

"No." The man stuck out his chin in pride.

"Do you know who I am?" Warwick tilted his head,

squeezing down harder on his neck, bringing their faces inches apart.

The officer swallowed, a nervous tic twitching under his eye.

"You do." Warwick grinned, baring his teeth, appearing even more menacing. "You've heard the stories, what I can do. Let me tell you, they are greatly *under* exaggerated. No one talks about how my victims piss and shit themselves, pleading and groveling for mercy… but the more you fight back, the slower I rip your lungs out and flay them open. I will slice out your intestines and force you to eat them."

The officer's teeth gritted, trying to hide his terror. Being face to face with the Wolf was the stuff of nightmares for many; his legend struck fear in the hearts of his enemy. Just his presence alone had most groveling in seconds.

This one was trying to be tough, but we smelled the urine, seeing it darken his pants and trickle down his leg.

"Type the code in." Deep and menacing, Warwick's order almost had the man in tears. Shaking, he reached out, putting in the password and placing his thumb on the screen.

Beep!

A green light flashed, unlocking the door. It skated open to another small outer chamber, another layer of security before you could get to whatever they were protecting.

An officer stood guard by the door, a gun in hand, ready to defend. Their gaze far off, their body stiff, waiting for an order like a mindless zombie.

The world stopped.

My lungs shut down, my body freezing in place. Everything flipped over, burying me underneath.

Bazdmeg…

The guard was Hanna.

Chapter 28
Brexley

My mouth opened as her empty gaze took us in, my shock locking me in place. They had seen her decline; I had not. The girl who stood before me was gaunt, lifeless, and only a shell of the girl I had grown up with.

"Hanna," Scorpion muttered her name, snapping her attention to him. There was a moment when she spotted Scorpion, a flutter of something, air catching in her throat, her blue eyes widening.

"Hit the button!" The officer Warwick held prisoner shouted at her. Like that was the switch, anything familiar about Hanna was shut off, her expression becoming stone.

Hanna swung her gun to us as she leaned back, reaching for a black button next to the door. I knew whatever that did, the moment she hit it, we were done. Everyone would know we were here.

"No!" Scorpion leaped for her. With one hand, he grabbed the barrel of the gun, twisting it out of her grip as his body collided with hers, the gun tumbling to the ground. She twisted, hissing like a wild cat, her fist cracking across his cheek, snapping his head back.

A jolt of fear punched at my lungs, seeing my friend turning feral. I had not seen this side of her before, and it terrified me.

Scorpion shook his head, blood leaking from his lip. He dove for her with a hungry growl as she kicked out, her boot hitting his side. He grunted, continuing for her, though I could tell he was trying not to hurt her. She swung out for him, mimicking how a leopard or tiger would fight in nature. He twisted around her, his hands grappling at her wrists, pinning them to her sides. A yowl rose from her throat, causing a chill to sweep up my neck. Scorpion wrapped his arms around her, yanking her back into his chest, pressing him firmly into her, his mouth grazing her ear. "Stop, little viper."

She stopped. Her lungs heaved, her body curving back into his like he was her only anchor to the world. His breath fluttered her hair, her lids closing briefly. It was at that moment I saw it. It wasn't just a bond between them, two people growing closer because of circumstances. My link to Scorpion highlighted what he felt.

What she was.

Holy fuck…

He exhaled in her ear. "That's my wildcat."

Her eyes popped open instantly at his words, the moment gone. Her nose wrinkled with fury, her body thrashing, slamming her head back into his with a crunch.

Pain and anger ignited Scorpion's eyes, clamping his jaw together. His grip on her tightened like a cobra while blood leaked out of his nose. "Hanna."

The Hanna he was trying to reach had slipped away, her lip curling, her teeth snapping.

Scorpion yanked her away as Warwick took his prisoner to the keypad, a deep rattling threat humming from his chest, which struck fear into everyone—everyone but me, it seemed.

I had no doubt something was wrong with me because when he did that, I wanted to strip him bare and fuck him until we both passed out.

The officer hesitated, but when Caden pressed his pistol into the back of his head, his fingers swept over the pad, a scanner accepting his thumbprint.

Click.

The door unlocked, rolling open, revealing what was behind.

Horror. Shock. Repulsion. It cascaded over me, locking my breath in my lungs. I had been expecting something similar to the lab Istvan had in Budapest.

Not this.

The scale of the room turned my blood cold—at least sixty feet wide and going up at least seventy feet. Four levels of individual water tanks took up the entire wall, all filled with men; some had several in one tank. Machines pumped fae essence into them straight from the fae source down below. Rows and rows of tables lined up were filled with various fae, strapped down, their bodies being forced to shift, their essence filling the tubes connecting them to the men in the tanks. These were Istvan's super soldiers. The top tier of his army. His private army. Similar to what Hitler or Stalin had. Istvan was following the fascist formula, wanting to succeed where they had eventually failed.

In another half of the room, the fae were dumping their essence into vials, which would probably be taken out and used to make the pills. That was for the mass of men and women who would be used as disposable foot soldiers.

The fae's faint moans of agony hummed with the machines, showing they were closer to death than life. The room was a buzz of equipment, magic, and suffering. At least ten figures in lab coats moved throughout the room, checking

379

on the experiments, their attention so focused they had yet to notice us.

And Dr. Karl was the head of all of them. His back to us, he scribbled numbers from a monitor on the wall next to the water tanks.

Caden stood next to me, his muscles clenching so hard he started to shake. Fury, disgust, disbelief, and trauma billowed off him. The pain of a son who used to look up to his father, only to find his idol was a true monster. Everything he was raised to believe was nothing but lies, whispered from the black tongue of a devil.

The extent of Istvan's project had at least tripled in size. This was far more than any of us expected—better equipment, more streamlined. I knew Markos would only keep expanding. He'd litter countries with labs, producing these mindless drones throughout the world until he took over cities, then countries, one by one.

"Intruders! Attack!" Hanna's emotionless voice belted out through the room, her mouth wiggling free of Scorpion's hand, bouncing off the tanks as every head twisted toward us. It took them only a blink before realizing their walls had been invaded and pulling out guns hidden under their lab coats.

Istvan wanted to make sure his assets were protected at all times now.

"Wait! Stop!" Dr. Karl leaped out, his arms over the tanks as if he could protect his experiments from the bullets about to be sprayed. "Don't shoot! The tanks will shatter!"

There was a moment no one moved, unsure how to proceed, before Hanna let out a wail, her foot stomping on Scorpion's. She kicked back, nailing him in the groin. He bent over in agony, his arms releasing her enough for her to reach out and flip down a plastic shield, slamming her palm down on another black button on the wall.

Fuck.

EEEEEEEEEEE! The air shrilled with an earsplitting siren, pounding down on us like a hammer, lights flashing through the room.

Chaos exploded in the space.

Bang! Bang!

Gunfire cut across the lab, the armed technicians firing back at us. Caden snarled with rage, his gaze locked on Dr. Karl as the man went scampering off, crouched low, heading for a door closest to him.

An escape.

"No," Caden sneered, running after him. His frame expanded as he descended on the cowering man, reminding me so much of Warwick.

The same fury bubbled through my veins, keeping me right on Caden's heels. We grew up our whole lives with Dr. Karl. He was there for every growth spurt and broken bone. He was the man we trusted and believed in to take care of us.

This was personal.

Caden kicked Dr. Karl in the leg, his round body stumbling to the ground. Karl curled up against the wall, holding up his hands. "Don't kill me."

"Where is he?" Caden reached down, clutching his throat. His power, even if it was a slice of Warwick's, was daunting, making Karl snivel and squirm in fear. "Tell me, *kövér disznó.*" *Fat pig.* "Or I will gut you right here."

"No, please," Karl begged, his eyes watering, his nose dripping with snot. Anything left of the man I thought he was had disappeared. "Don't hurt me."

"Tell me where my father is," Caden clamped down harder, pressing his gun into his temple.

"He just left!" Dr. Karl motioned for the door at the opposite end of the room. "Through there... only a few minutes ago."

"If you are lying to me…" Caden's threat even vibrated through me.

"I'm not! I'm not!" The old man wheezed, his eyes pleading for reprieve.

Caden glanced back at the door Karl motioned to.

"I swear to you. He was just here checking on the latest results. He left only a few moments before you came in."

Caden let out a growl, and without a word, he whirled around, sprinting for the very door his father had gone through, our entrance probably missing him by mere seconds.

The distraction on Caden was enough time for Karl to start to crawl to the door.

"Stop!" My boot slammed him back down again, a cry spewing from him, his hands up by his face as if they could protect him from the gun I had pointed at his head.

"No! No! Please don't kill me!" His round frame tried to curl up like a roly-poly, huffing and puffing. "I watched you grow up. I patched you up and was there for you when you were sick. I was there after your father died. Do you not remember how much I loved you? Cared for you?"

"Loved and cared for me?" My lip lifted as I shoved the barrel into his forehead. He tried to scramble back farther, burrowing himself into the wall, his whimpers growing louder and louder. "*Menj a halál farkára.*" *Go onto death's dick.* My finger pressed firmer on the trigger.

"No… please!" he begged, snot running from his nose. "You don't understand. I had to. Istvan… He made me."

"He didn't make you do anything. You did that all yourself. And you loved it." I reached down, knotting my fingers into his collar, pulling his sweaty red face to me. "You enjoyed testing on us, draining me of blood, standing there while children, fae and human, were tortured and killed in front of you. You are a sick fuck, and I hope you rot."

"Brexley, please!" Tears spilled down his cheeks, and for a moment, all I saw was the man who had stitched up my knee, who was there every time I fell or fought too hard in training. But then he was also the man who turned his back on me, looking at me like I was an animal when they realized I wasn't totally normal.

Bang! A bullet went through his forehead, blood spurting as his eyes glossed over, his body slumping. A cry caught in my throat as I swung around to the assailant.

Warwick stood there, his hate and disgust centered on the dead man before his gaze went to me, softening the moment our eyes found each other.

My mouth opened to speak, my head shaking in incensed disbelief. *I* was supposed to kill him. After all he had done…

Warwick's shadow gripped my face, forcing me to look into his eyes, no longer seeing the dead man I had known all my life. *"If I could take all the weight you carry, all the death, heartache, and pain, I would."* His mouth brushed mine. *"He didn't deserve to be on your conscience, princess. He wasn't worthy of one piece of your soul."*

I gasped, feeling like he was the air I breathed.

Pop! Pop!

Bullets cracked a tank near our heads, hunching us down below the tables as water poured out, cutting off our link.

"Come on!" Warwick's hand grabbed mine, yanking me with him, our forms hunching and keeping out of the direct line of fire. "We need to do this now."

My backpack and Warwick's had been filled with grade-A bombs, the quality and technology coming straight from the king. Olek told us these had timers on them, giving us about thirty seconds to get out before they exploded.

The door we entered started to slide open. My head

jerked when I spotted soldiers already packing the entrance, ready to protect Markos's investments.

"Scorpion!" my shade screamed at him as he shot at a technician with one hand, the other still trying to keep ahold of Hanna. *"The door!"*

He instantly swung to it, seeing a few wiggle in. I could feel his internal debate happen, his emotion simmering through our link.

"Forgive me, little viper." He whirled on Hanna, his mouth claiming passionately, kissing her deeply. Before she could react, he pulled back, pinching her right in the vagus nerve. Her body jolted and crumbled to the ground. Sorrow flickered over his face as he watched her drop. For her survival, he had to take her out of the equation like I had to do to him that night in the Games.

He whirled around, shooting at the enemy coming in, dead bodies lying at the entrance.

"Kovacs?" Warwick's voice shot me back to him, his hand pulling out the small black discs, slapping them on tanks as we passed. "Hurry!"

The gunfire and alarm shrieked through the space like a banshee, dancing on my nerves, my hands shaking as I stuck an explosive to a tank, not looking at the lives inside we were about to take. My gaze went to the fae on the tables, a few hands weakly reaching up for me. Bile burned through my stomach and twisted me in grief when I noticed they weren't just strapped down. They were chained and cuffed.

We wouldn't be able to save them.

"Don't." Warwick's shade stood before me, his gaze burrowing into mine. *"You can't think of that. You have to think of the ones you will save by destroying this place. Their essence is drained. They are too far gone. They would not survive anyway. I need you, Kovacs. With me.*

384

Fighting." His eyes held mine with his unsaid question until I nodded.

The real man flicked the timers on the bombs.

"Ash!" Warwick bellowed at his friend, fighting alongside Kek and Lukas. Scorpion was at the main entrance. Caden had already gone after his father, though that didn't mean he was safe from danger.

"Scorpion?" I shouted at him, feeling every second ticking down my vertebrae as Warwick whirled me toward the door Dr. Karl had been heading for, shoving his dead body out of the way. "Go!"

Everything was set on fast forward but also felt in slow motion, every beat of my heart like the ticker on the bomb.

I yanked open the door, ready to sprint as fast as I could, but my lungs and feet came to an abrupt halt, a cry hitching up my throat.

It was a closet.

"Fuck!" Warwick roared. We had no way out of here. Any other exits were blocked or too far away to reach in time.

Warwick didn't hesitate, shoving me inside as Ash, Kek, and Lukas ran in after us, bullets spraying on their heels, Warwick about to shut the door.

"Wait! Scorpion! Where's Scorpion?" Panic shoved me through the group. Warwick tried to grab for me, but I slipped through his fingers, swinging the door back open, reaching out through our link. *"Scorpion!"* I spotted him barreling for us, Hanna over his shoulder. Every second, I waited for the light to flash and the bombs to detonate.

"Brexley!" Warwick cried out, trying to grab for me, yank me back in.

"Scorpion! Hurry!" My shadow shoved Scorpion from behind, his feet crossing the threshold into the room. The door shut us into complete darkness right as Warwick grabbed me, diving for the ground, his body covering mine.

BOOM! BOOOOM! BOOOOOOOM!

The multiple explosions shattered my eardrums, the sonic wave bursting across my bones, ripping the air from my lungs. Warwick cocooned me under his huge frame, holding me for dear life as the world around us came to its knees. I couldn't see. I couldn't hear. My senses were traumatized by the assault. All I could feel was Warwick, his breath steady against my neck, his body warm and solid over mine. He was the only thing that kept me from falling, twisting and turning into the brutal violence. The tether that prevented me from floating away. He kept me in the gray. Anchored to consciousness.

A few more moments passed before Warwick lifted his head, and I realized it wasn't his body that had blacked out any light. I expected the cupboard we were in to be demolished, only a skeleton left, but it held strong around us.

"You okay?" his shadow muttered against my ear.

Still in shock, all I could do was nod. His exhale was felt inside and outside my body, curling through me with relief. He lifted himself off, allowing me to see the faint forms stirring in the room. The door had buckled at the top, letting a little light seep into the closet. My attention went to the thick door and the reinforced walls.

It wasn't a closet. It was a bomb shelter.

Many underground bunkers were supposed to be made to withstand bombs from above, not from inside. This room had been built to be almost impregnable. Probably why Dr. Karl was coming here—to lock himself inside and wait until the danger passed.

Ash rose to his feet, helping Kek and Lukas, the three of them the closest to the exit. Using his shoulder, Ash shoved at the door. It took a few tries, but it finally cracked open, flooding thick gel-like water into the room, almost rising to my knees.

The substance from the tanks poured out like waterfalls. Sparks danced and hissed off the equipment, the power cords sizzling and popping, flickering light through the vast space. Trudging farther out of our sanctuary, my attention scanned the room, bile coating my throat. It was nothing but devastation and wreckage, but the eerie stillness still buzzed with sounds, ringing like death in my ears. The absence of life shivered over my skin. There were no ghosts hovering close, as if their souls had long ago departed, leaving the skins of their beings behind.

It was a sea of dead bodies and equipment, floating and bobbing in pieces and parts like a shipwreck scattering the ocean. Half the ceiling had buckled, crushing anything underneath. No one survived. Not even the soldiers trying to get in. One body clogged the doorway, not allowing it to close, letting the thick water seep out.

A loud boom shook the ground beneath us. An explosion echoed from the main area in the bunker where our friends were on their own mission. My stomach dropped to my toes.

They wouldn't be that early to set them off unless something had gone terribly wrong.

"Kovacs!" Warwick's voice thundered in my ear, cutting off all other thoughts as his arms wrapped around me.

CRACK!

The rest of the ceiling gave way, coming down and crushing out the light.

Chapter 29
Caden

My boots punched at the ground in rhythm with my lungs. My skin prickled, my muscles on alert. My eyes darting to every dark corner or doorway though the shadows didn't veil much from me anymore. My sight was sharp, perceiving things I had never noticed before. Details and colors I didn't know existed. Until I became fae.

Fae. I will admit that I was not a man with a deep imagination. Brexley had filled that role for me, but never in my wildest dreams did I imagine this would be my life now, that I would become fae.

Was I a hero or a villain? I no longer knew. One time the answer was so clear. Black and white, right and wrong. Human, fae. I was raised to be the hero—the prince—a future king in our world. Leading Leopold, taking over my father's position. It was the blueprint from the day I was born. A role I never questioned, even if I might have wanted something else. I had no choice. It was the *only* path I was given, and I took it on with pride and dedication.

Then my life imploded. Nothing set, the path gone, leaving me out in the middle of nowhere trying to figure out how to get back… or maybe just end it all.

Somewhere along the way, that changed. I no longer wanted to find my way back. Magic hummed through my veins, sharpening my senses, my strength, my mind, and my drive—for food, death, life, and sex.

Fuck. The sex…

My dick thickened even at the thought of it… or maybe it was death. I didn't know anymore. I seemed to get a thrill from both, thanks to whatever my father turned me into, attaching me to the one person I wanted to hate most in this world. He took her from me. The girl I had secretly wanted for so long. He stripped me of hope, chance, of what could have been.

Or what the old Caden wanted.

That was a life I would never have anymore. Maybe Brexley was right. It wasn't her as much as what she represented. The old me. The old life. When things made sense. Pure, innocent, simple.

Safe.

My thoughts and fantasies were anything but safe now, and it wasn't Brexley my mind conjured, hardening my dick to the point of pain. It was a girl who drove me insane, irritating the hell out of me until I could rip her clothes off and bury my dick inside her to shut her up.

I couldn't escape the memory of bending Birdie over the dresser last night, plunging so hard and deep that I no longer could feel the world around me. The image of her straddling me, her small, strong hands locking down on my airway. Riding me until I lost consciousness. The unbelievable high. It was like nothing I had ever felt before.

The instinct to feel disgusted at myself still kicked in along with the idea I had not only fucked a fae once but every night, *multiple times*, until we both passed out from exhaustion.

389

That's all we were. Hate sex. An itch my fae side needed right now. Nothing more. Though, I still couldn't seem to take the edge off needing more. Needing *her*.

A growl crawled up my throat, shaking her from my thoughts, and putting them on the target where they were supposed to be. My father.

Hate spewed up the back of my throat, my chest pumping quicker, my nose picking up a whiff of my father's scent. Emotion colored my vision, the intensity making me want to slaughter everything in my path.

Turning down another passage, my gaze locked on his back, two soldiers on either side.

"Father!" My voice echoed down the corridor, my fury slamming into him. He pulled up short, twisting around. The blue eyes I had looked into all my life widened only for a moment, his focus scanning me, perceiving with a shrewd gaze that I wasn't quite the same anymore. Bigger, stronger. My presence was ten times what it had been before. I would never be at the level of Warwick, but I also wasn't the son he had last seen in the pit. Hoping to eliminate the awkwardness of his old family from his new one.

"Caden." He fully turned around, using the calm, almost patronizing tone he had all my life. "Oh, my boy, I can't believe this. It worked." His focus went over me again, and this time I could see the switch in his demeanor, the spark of excitement in his eyes. The thrill of knowing his experiment on me did not fail. "You should have come to me."

"When?" I growled, slowly stepping closer. His guards reacted to my movement, lifting their weapons at me. "When you put my mother and me in the ring to be torn up by your monsters? Or when you ran off, hiding here, to create more mindless minions? Or maybe it was when you sent your guards to hunt us down and kill us?"

390

"I didn't know you were with them," he replied, not dissuading his men from pointing their guns at me. "If I had known... If I had known it had worked. How magnificent the experiment turned out—"

"What? You wouldn't have tried to have me killed?" My lip lifted, my feet carrying me even closer, my shoulders widening. I felt no fear, though my father *appeared* he didn't either, but I could taste the slight uneasiness of his nerves. He understood he had created something that could kill. "You wouldn't have turned your back like a coward on your first wife and son? We meant so little to you when you thought we couldn't help you. You wanted us out of the way. But now that you see I have turned into one of them? A legend? Now you reach a hand for me again?" Deep grief and raw fury clamped down on me, dredging up from my soul— unbearable pain, confusion, and anger. A father was supposed to love their child, protect and guide him.

Mine had never been warm or kind, but I still thought love resided within his strictness and demands for me to be better. He wanted me to be better, to be a better man and leader. But it was never about that. Only his ego and power mattered. My life was nothing more than a reflection of him. A shallow pond imitating what he wanted.

A robot.

A mindless soldier.

"Caden, *my son*." He stressed the term, hitting it like the words mattered to him. Like *I* mattered to him. That need inside to want your parents' love never went away, especially if it was hard to earn. I worked my whole life to please him, to hear him praise me, to just say I love you once. Unconditionally. But my father only knew conditions, terms, stipulations, and requirements to earn his respect. And for once, I felt like I had it. "Don't you see what this means?

391

What we can do together?" He motioned to me. "What we can accomplish. With you ruling by my side, the sky is the limit for us." His irises sparkled with possibility, looking at me like I was the most precious thing to him. For years I'd yearned for that, to see my father behold me how I had seen Benet look at Brexley, or Andris had. I had been so envious of Brexley and her dad; he worshiped her, would do anything for her. "Let's forget the past, start over, you and I." His gaze locked on mine. "We will take down the fae and rule this country, this world, like it should be."

"Take down the fae?" My hands rolled into balls, gnawing anger nipping at the back of my neck. "I am fae. You are turning everyone into fae."

"Sometimes you have to fight fire with fire." The heavily decorated general stood before me, his chin raised, now having to look up at me. "Of course, there will be exceptions. You are no ordinary fae, Caden. You are not only *my* son but you're constructed from a *Legend*. Now that I know it works. That his powers can transfer. I will become one too. We both can be as powerful as him, if not more so. His status and abilities have always been unrivaled. Until now. You can lure him in, and we transfer his powers to me, and then you can kill him."

"What?" I blinked.

"Don't tell me you don't want his death. I know you, son. You want nothing more than to destroy the man who took Brexley from you… the woman you have loved all your life. The woman who betrayed you, kidnapped you, turned her back on you. You can show her how she chose wrong in the end."

My shoulders jerked back; an instinctual growl caught in my throat. The impulse took over to not only protect Brexley, the girl who had been my best friend for as long as I could remember, but Warwick as well. The sensation crawled up my spine like an insect, burrowing in my bones, even while there was a contradicting urge, a piece of me who still wanted my old life back, to do exactly what my father said, washed over me.

I could have Brexley. I could have more power. I could be the one people feared and worshipped.

I could have my father's admiration.

At one time, destroying the Wolf, killing fae, and having humans take back control of Earth was all I wanted and desired. That time had crumbled away so slowly that I hadn't noticed those goals were not what I wanted anymore. Was it my time as a captive in Sarkis's army? Was it being fae myself, or was it in the strands of long blonde hair, a sweet smile few had seen, a strength you wouldn't expect from a tiny girl, along with brutality she could give and take, and a past with parents that broke her? I liked to pretend she was just a fuck, but I had told her things I had never told anyone, and she had spoken of her past, which was heartbreaking and cruel. Opposite ends of the world, and we found very similar themes in our situations. A common bond. A connection I never thought I'd have with a fae.

I no longer saw fae as the ones without humanity.

Human-ity.

Exclusive. Select. As if only humans could possess a soul or could be kind and loving. Humans created a word to make themselves virtuous. The ones fighting for good. When all I saw was the opposite.

It was bullshit, and I had believed it all.

"You have it all wrong." I gritted through my teeth, feeling my body expand, magic boiling through my veins.

I welcomed it.

Wanted it.

Embraced it.

"It's not the fae who took from me, who turned their backs on me… who *betrayed* me." I sneered. "It's not them I want to destroy." I shifted my frame, towering over him. His soldiers cocked their guns, pressing them into me like that would scare me.

A smirk curled my lip as a low growl vibrated my chest, the sound even making my father gulp.

"You might have raised a boy to fight for you." I snarled in his face. "But you created a monster who will *kill* you." I lunged for my father as my hands wrapped around the barrels of the guards' guns, yanking them out of their grips, flipping them around, ready to shoot.

BOOOOOM!

My feet were torn off the ground, the bomb sending me up in the air as more explosions went off around me, ringing in my ears. I hit the ground, the weapons flying from my hands. Everything went black as billowing dirt clotted my lungs, pain echoing through my bones when cement chunks came raining down on me. I curled up, covering my head and neck from the wreckage.

They did it. They blew up the lab. I just hoped Brexley and all of them were out before those bombs went off.

The debris petered out into a light mist. Blinking, I opened my lids. Darkness and clouds of dust cut off my sight from anything, my eyes watering, my lungs hacking, rejecting the grime thick in the air. Groaning, I shoved off pieces of the ceiling, knowing at one time, every bone of mine would have been broken. But a legend didn't break so easily. Not even a partial one.

"Sir! Come on!" A voice hissed through the haze, my vision clearing enough to see the officer with brown curls getting my father to his feet. While my father struggled, hobbling and limping away, the faux-fae guard almost carried him down the passage.

"Nooo!" The legend part took over. The need to kill, to end his life, was like swallowing down my dry throat. I craved the kill like water, the taste so vivid in my mind it became more than a thirst. The need rocked through me, forcing me to my feet, racing after them. My mind was so focused on reaching my father that I didn't hesitate to push through the thick metal door, following their exit into the main bunker. My emotions overruled years of training, following only the barest of rules, like never run through a door without taking notice and precautions of what could be behind it.

Click. Click. Click.

A row of guards stood there waiting, their weapons out and pointing at me, ready to fire. My feet came to a stop, seeing the dozens of guns aimed at me. I was harder to kill, but not impossible.

I felt anger at my stupidity. My recklessness exaggerated the squawking sirens ringing in the bunker, screaming that the walls had been breached. Guards were running around in the background, reacting to the attack. Nowhere did I see any of my friends. The group that was left out here to set bombs of their own and wait for the signal. I shoved back the panic in my chest, the thought of something happening to them… to her.

"Let me guess. This assault on me was courtesy of your little group. All my work… though you think this is the only one I have?" A flush of vibrant anger ran over my father's features before he got control of them. "I'm disappointed in you, Caden. I thought I raised a smarter person than that. I have given you *every* chance in the world, and you have thrown away each one." My father shook his head at me with a frown, wiping off the dirt from his uniform, his arrogance back in place, forgetting that I was the one with his life in my hands only moments ago. "You are either with me or against me. And it's quite clear which side you have chosen."

I stared, my nose flaring, not rebuffing his conclusion.

Istvan dipped his head. "Then you are useless to me. But I can't say it was for nothing. Just your existence has put Warwick's life significantly above yours. He's who I need. Whose essence I will take while the rest of you die tonight."

Though I shouldn't care what my father said about me, it cut deeply; the little boy in me wanted to please him. Still did. I wanted to hate Warwick for being worthy when I was not. Warwick was not to blame. My father would never find worth in me—because I wasn't him. *Nor do I want to be.* Thinking those words, a strange relief exhaled somewhere in me, letting go of trying to be what my father wanted. Seeing my father in his truth, I couldn't have been more grateful I wasn't like him. Brexley's presence in my life had always kept me from tipping over. Her sway was usually stronger than my father's, keeping me from folding completely under his heavy hand.

Deep down, he knew that, and that's why he never trusted or respected Brexley or me. He saw her influence on me at every turn.

"Tell Brexley I know where the nectar is. It was easy when you follow the ones who follow it."

It took everything I had not to react, to decipher if he was telling the truth or not. Could he have found Olek's hideout? Found the nectar?

"Now I must deal with this mess you created. Just know none of your friends will escape. They will pay for what they've done here." He tilted his head with a cruel smile. "Maybe I make them mindless animals… like Hanna."

396

My teeth ground together; the need to barrel forward and tear him apart flexed my muscles.

"Kill him," General Markos ordered with no emotion.

Sucking in air, everything went in slow motion, their guns rising higher. I waited for the sear of the bullets. The moment they would shred me apart and life would no longer be.

"Noooooo!" A cry hollowed through the bunker, snapping every head in the direction of the voice.

Birdie stood only a yard from us, her cry echoing over her face. My eyes latched on to hers, seeing the fear and panic.

Guns whipped to her, about to shoot at the new threat.

Emotion I had never experienced before flooded me and made me want to run straight to her, wrap her up, and take us far from here. Keep her safe. Not that she needed anyone to protect her. I had learned she could hold her own against the most daunting fae. The impulse wasn't about saving *her*... it was about saving *me*.

I didn't know exactly how I felt about her; I just didn't want this to be the end. I wanted more time.

The terror dissolved from her face, her eyes narrowing, her mouth moving, screaming something to me that looked like "run."

It was the only warning I got before everything went to hell once again, exploding in our faces, twisting us up in the air and flinging us around like dolls.

The bombs out here weren't planned to go off this soon. We were supposed to be far from here.

Cause chaos.

Distraction.

Though nothing ever went according to plan with this group.

This time I felt the explosions through every bone in my body, firing off like an endless stream of fireworks, flinging me back into the iron door, my head cracking back, my eyesight blurring.

The bombs they placed around the space blew up huge sections of crates filled with pills and ammo, a.k.a. gunpowder. It sparked more blasts as the two met, weakening the already old bunker. Pieces of it started to topple from the walls and ceiling.

"Caden!" Birdie's cry slapped me out of my stupor, spurring me to move. Scrambling up, I darted past the slew of guards, all sprawled over the ground, confused but rising to their feet.

"Caden, come on!" Birdie waved me to her, her hand threading through mine when I reached out to her. She looked up, and for the briefest moment, I thought I saw something in them before her brow furrowed again, her hand tugging me, her tiny body yanking me forward.

Bang! Bang! Bang!

Gunshots volleyed all around us, our bodies diving behind a group of crates near the train. Killian and Rosie were there, firing back. Eli, Ember, and Wesley were firing from crates close to us.

"Where are the others?" Killian asked between shots. Birdie yanked out an extra gun and tossed it to me.

"I don't know. I separated from them." I shot back at the guards. "But I know they are alive." It was just something I knew. Warwick was alive. And for once, I was grateful for the connection, to feel his presence in this building.

Metal groaned from the ceiling, a huge piece dropping on a jeep, crushing it. More started to peel away, like dominos.

"We need to get the hell out of here. Now," Birdie insisted.

I couldn't have agreed more, and we weren't the only ones who thought the same thing.

The train's whistle screamed through the building, steam pooling out of the tunnel as it moved out, the conductors forgoing any orders and saving themselves.

Officers blasted at us, their bodies huddling around someone as they headed toward an armored truck, trying to get their leader out safely.

"Fuck. No," I grunted, rising. I couldn't let him escape.

"Caden!" I didn't stop as Birdie yelled for me, my gun up, already firing as they shoved him in the passenger seat, slamming the door.

Another part of the bunker ceiling crashed down, shrieking like a dying animal.

"Go! Go!" The brown-haired guard jumped in the back, waving for the driver to pull out. Tires squealed, reversing, about to pull out. I didn't care the windows were bulletproof, I continued to fire at the same spot, unloading my Glock until it ticked empty.

The passenger side window rolled down, my father's eyes meeting mine. I saw nothing there. I was a stranger. Something easily discarded.

He pointed a gun at me. I stared at him. Waiting for him to just do it. I would not give him the courtesy of looking away or cowering. If he was going to kill me, I was going to look him dead in the eyes as he did.

His gaze slid from me to something right behind me, anger locking down his jaw before a vindictive smirk arched his lips.

Bang! The gun fired.

I waited to feel pain or for my body to at least react, but there was nothing.

A hitched cry came from behind me, and the sound of a body hitting the ground spun me around.

Everything bottomed out. My entire world felt like it was ripped out from under me. Laying on the ground, gasping for breaths, blood pooled around her.

"Birdie!" I bellowed, dropping to my knees, panic taking over. I could hear the truck peel out, my father escaping, but I no longer cared.

The only thing that mattered was her.

My father knew that.

That's why he shot her, not me.

He wanted me to watch her die.

Chapter 30
Brexley

Bang!

The singular gunshot popped in my ears as we came running out of the tunnel, watching a body drop to the ground. An armored truck tore off, swerving out of the way of a falling piece of debris.

My brain took in the fact this room was collapsing on itself, guards running around like rats trying to get out, no one paying us any attention now. All I saw on the ground was white-blonde hair dyed red from blood and Caden dropping to his knees next to the figure, screaming her name.

"Birdie!" I cried out, my legs tearing off across the room, a sickness knotting in my chest as I dodged and weaved as the room started to buckle. My knees hit the pavement hard, falling next to Caden, Ash coming on the other side.

Birdie's eyes moved frantically between us all, trying to take in enough air. I couldn't even see where she had been shot because there was so much blood. Her lids closed a little longer each time she blinked.

"Hell no... you stay with me. You hear me?" Caden was frantic, almost looking like he wanted to cry. "Help her!" he barked at Ash. "Do something!"

"I am." Caden was already tearing at her shirt, trying to find the wound. "Put pressure on it!" Ash ordered Caden. The commotion around us seemed to haze out. "We need to slow the flow of blood. Give me your shirt."

Caden ripped off his coat, yanking his shirt over his head in a second, giving it to him. Ash tied it around her shoulder/chest area, trying to ebb the flow of blood pouring from her.

"We need to get out of here." Ember guarded us, Eli next to her. Their heads swiveled around frantically, watching more trucks and the last train pull out of the bunker.

A crash vibrated the ground near us, another section of the underground crumbling down. We had barely made it out of the labs before it collapsed. The space the dead soldier left in the doorway gave us enough room to escape before the whole thing buckled.

This room was about to do the same.

"Kovacs," Warwick growled against the back of my neck, the real man standing over me, ready to scoop me up at any moment if he needed to. At that moment, when the whole world felt against us, death snatching my friends and family from me like retribution, he had my back. Literally and figuratively. The sensation dug in so deep, realizing something like that went even beyond mates. A trust so absolute... love felt like a foolish word to utter.

We went beyond words.

A howl screeched from above us as if screaming out in pain, a huge section of the ceiling ripping in half, starting to drop.

"Move!" I bellowed, jumping up. Warwick's hand latched onto my arm, yanking me forward as more shrills came from the deteriorating structure. Caden gathered up Birdie, her head falling limply back, no longer conscious, his beefed-up physique sprinting forward. All of us ran for the exit, feeling the ground echo with the weight of the ceiling collapsing, pieces shooting out like darts, cutting into us.

In front of us, Wesley waved us on, climbing into the last caboose of the moving train.

"Give her to me!" Wesley yelled as Caden ran along the train as it was picking up speed.

Wesley leaned over, grabbing Birdie's tiny frame, while Caden leaped on the steps, reminding me so much of the countless times he and I used to jump on moving trains, robbing them of a few trinkets before escaping. How naive, cocky, and entitled we were then. So unaware that one little misstep, which landed me in Halálház, would lead us here.

"Move, Kovacs!" Warwick yelled at me. Ear piercing booms blasted out behind us while more of my friends jumped on the train. Warwick and I leaped for the steps, his hand pushing me up to the highest rung, using his massive frame to engulf me while the shock waves and wreckage sprayed out, the train barely slipping away from the collapsing tunnel. The Wolf pinned me so tightly to the side, his bones bruised mine, holding on for dear life while the train tottered and squealed, trying to stay upright. The wheels sparked against the rails, about to slip off. The pull of the front slammed the caboose back on the tracks, ramming us into the railing. He buried his face in my neck, taking a deep breath as if he was making sure I was safe before he tipped his head back. We both peered back through the dark night, watching the last bit of the structure collapse, crushing every life still left in there.

"*Bazdmeg.*" *Fuck.* Warwick muttered against my head, realizing how close we were to being the ones still in there. Though I had no time to think about the what-ifs right now. Shaking my head, I climbed the rest of the way up, rushing into the carriage.

Ash and Caden already surrounded Birdie on the ground. Rosie stood over them with a torch, giving Ash enough light to check her wound, while Killian and Lukas barricaded the door connecting the carriages, sliding crates in front of it.

"Is she okay?" I came rushing down next to Ash, ready to use my powers or do anything to keep her with us. It wasn't even a question. With a simple glance over at Caden, I realized how significant her life had become. He had the look of a man about to lose his entire world. Even if he wouldn't admit it, the terror, grief, and devastation in his eyes spoke the truth.

"Here." Wesley pulled off his jacket, handing it to Ash to use. Both he and Scorpion hovered over her, terrified for their friend.

Ash wiped as much blood away as he could with the fresh material, inspecting her wound.

"It's a clean shot. Went all the way through." He sat back on his heels. "She's losing a lot of blood, which I need to stop, but I think the bullet just missed anything vital."

"She's gonna be okay?" Caden's head jerked to Ash.

"Yeah." Ash tilted his head, staring down at Birdie. "I want to watch her for a bit and make sure, but she's tough."

Caden heaved, tears prickling my eyes as I watched him curve over her with a quiet, relieved sob.

"She's a fuckin' badass," Wesley said.

"Yeah, she is." Scorpion nodded proudly, though worry still hung all over him.

"If the incident in Belarus didn't take her out, this certainly won't." Wesley looked over at Scorpion, making Scorp puff out a laugh, his head bobbing in agreement. Wesley looked down at Birdie; her light breathing furrowed his brows in concern. Birdie was like a sister to them. They had been through a lot together, more than I knew.

Ash cleaned her up the best he could, using Wesley's cleaner jacket to rewrap the wound before he got up to his feet with a groan.

Lukas didn't speak but reached out quietly, rubbing Ash's arm in comfort, acknowledging all Ash took on.

"Our hero," Kek smirked at Ash with a wink as she leaned into Lukas, her gaze full of hunger, but I knew there was more between them. Kek was not the type to continue to hang around anyone if she didn't really like them. Not even for good sex. She got bored too easily. Something developed between the three of them when I was gone—something deeper than anything I expected.

With Birdie out of immediate danger, an exhale went through the carriage. All of us took a moment to absorb where we were and what had happened. Exhaustion instantly sunk my shoulders down, my hands rubbing at my face, the adrenaline seeping from me.

"We did it," I muttered.

"Barely," Eli responded, running his hand over Ember's shoulder, twisting his hand through her ponytail, playing with it like he was trying to memorize every strand, each one dear to him.

"Yeah, barely," I agreed. "But we still did it."

"Now what? Do we even know where this train is going?" Ember leaned back into Eli like they were each other's charging stations. Something I could relate to. Warwick wasn't touching me, but I still felt him everywhere, his shadow right behind me, offering any energy I might need, while he tore into a crate, displaying the rifles stacked inside.

Killian ripped off the top of another one, holding up more rifles. This time there was no false bottom hiding pills. These held only weapons. Hundreds of them.

"I will bet this train is headed to the border." Warwick picked up one of the rifles, checking it out. "Guns for the army he's building there to attack Budapest."

"We might have stepped up that timeline." Eli broke into another one. More guns.

Eli was right. Istvan would respond to the loss of his lab with muscle. He needed to feel his power again and let everyone know he was in charge.

"Was gonna happen anyway." Warwick shrugged. "I suggest until then we try to rest. It's a long way back to Budapest, and this might be the last time we can." He loaded the rifle, cocking it. "I will stay up and guard... if anything changes, including our direction, I'll let you know."

"No. I will." Wesley stepped up, his gaze drifting toward Rosie and Killian. "I can't sleep right now anyway." I knew seeing them together hurt him; he struggled to be in the same space as their energy sang with lust and happiness.

"We'll take shifts." Warwick nodded at him, holding out the rifle. He didn't fight Wesley's offer, as if he sensed the same thing. Wesley took it, his mouth firming. He moved to the exit, settling in the doorway so he could see the terrain and anything coming at us.

Warwick didn't speak. Taking my hand, he led me to a corner, sliding down the wall and pulling me with him. I snuggled back into his chest, and he wrapped his arms around me, encompassing me in warmth and protection. My heartbeat calmed in the comfort of his arms, his presence soothing some of the torn edges in my soul.

Taking his hand, I twined our fingers together. "Thank you," I whispered. "For earlier." I didn't have to say it. He knew what I was talking about.

He killed Karl. He didn't take that *from* me; he did it *for* me.

There were ones I was going to have to do myself. I needed to do myself. Though glancing over at Caden, still sitting in the same position, staring at Birdie numbly, I wondered who deserved to end Istvan more.

The son he abused, experimented on, turned his back on, and left to die in the Games with his mother. Or the orphan girl he took in because he was the one to murder her father, the girl he experimented on and tortured. The one he tried to marry off to a sadistic abuser to gain more control.

He sold both Caden and me to obtain more power, and it still wasn't enough.

It never was for Istvan.

Caden and I knew Birdie was intentional. Istvan shot her on purpose. As Istvan did to Andris, killing Ling, he wanted to take away the one thing his son might care about. Istvan was always watching, observing, noticing more than others. When Caden called for Birdie in the Games, seeing the fear in his son's face, he knew the fae girl was not an enemy. There were feelings there. Markos wanted to avenge what he felt was the deepest betrayal.

Caden falling for Birdie, *a fae*, was the ultimate disloyalty.

Hurting her was more impactful to his son than shooting him. Thank the gods that Birdie was straight out badass and wouldn't let Istvan win. He couldn't take her down so easily.

The train rocked back and forth, my muscles relaxing into Warwick, the night's events slamming down on me. His arms tightened around me as I curled into him, laying my head on his chest.

I was proud that we did what we set out to do, at least clipping Istvan's wings, though my gut coiled with the truth that the real fight still lay ahead of us. I was terrified as I looked around the train. Some of these people—my family—might not survive.

Tucked up against some crates were Rosie and Killian. She had her head in Killian's lap, his finger threading through her hair, watching her with an expression I had never seen on his face. Ever. Utter adoration. Killian couldn't hide it if he tried. The man was completely in love with her, making a smile grow on my face, watching them together. The high noble leader was stripped down; the facade he kept up, the role he played, even with me, had crumbled with Rosie.

Some might think they had little in common, but they had lived very similar lives, both acting their parts for survival, for power, for money. Their pasts weaved together into understanding and respect. And for once, they could both find who they really were together.

On the wall to my right, Ash, Lukas, and Kek muttered and whispered together, smiling and joking; their interactions were such a unit. Ash was the anchor, but the three of them worked together in a way no one could explain.

Eli and Ember were at the far wall leaning against the crates blocking the connecting door, and though they were practically strangers to me, I couldn't deny that I felt like I had known them forever, especially Ember. Maybe it was the magic we shared, a strange family bond.

Though another bond took my focus, my heart aching as I watched Scorpion bind Hanna to a metal bar, her hands behind her back, her unconscious body slumping against it. I could sense his pain. The agony of knowing this had to be done for her own good still didn't take away the disgust he felt at himself for doing it.

"Scorpion." I reached out to him. His head turned just slightly toward my shade. His mouth didn't open, but his head dipped in a nod, understanding what I was saying

without uttering a single word more. *I'm here if you need me.* He instantly drew back up the wall between us, not wanting me to be part of his struggle.

I understood. Sometimes you just needed to be by yourself and deal with the trauma the only way you could. Being linked to Warwick and me was not easy on him. Even more so when Hanna might be too far gone to save.

Closing my eyes at that thought, I burrowed into Warwick, his heartbeat thumping against my ear like music. The sound of life. His existence was a song I conjured up before I was born and sang the moment I entered this world, beckoning him to be in it because not for one second of my life could I not have him in this world somewhere.

A deep vibration came from his stomach, humming up to his throat, feeling me reach for him. My soul sank into his, twining and gliding through, wrapping myself around like a blanket. Warwick and I were always going to want to fuck each other's brains out, that was who we were, but right then, it was about comfort. About feeling safe and loved for one moment in this fucking hellish world.

"Merry Christmas, princess," he growled in my ear, wrapping his arms tighter around me, using his shadow to blanket me even more in his smell, his heat, his body… his love.

I could feel it in every pore of my being, making me cling to him more, tears stinging my eyes, wanting to stay here forever.

"Warwick…" My voice barely made it out, tucking closer to him, not able to get close enough. The panic, terror, and possessiveness I felt thinking about anyone hurting him, taking him away from me. Nothing would be safe from my wrath, including my sanity.

"Shhh…" His breath filled my ear, his nose nuzzling in. "*Sleep, Sötét démonom.*"

The carriage rocked and jolted as it changed tracks. My lids bursting open, instinct jerking my limbs to move, my hand hitting something and knocking it onto the floor.

"Ahhhh!" Opie's voice cried as his butt hit the ground.

"Oh shit, Opie!" I lifted my head off Warwick's thigh, where I had fallen into a deep sleep. "Sorry!"

"Geez, Fishy, shouldn't we have a safe word before starting the rough stuff?" He rubbed his butt, standing up.

Chirp! Bitzy flipped me off from the bag on his back, glaring at me, though nothing could stop me from chuckling.

"What are you wearing?"

"Don't judge!" Opie put up his palms. "I mean, we have very little to work with here, and wow... the quality is less than par, but you know I can make miracles out of nothing." He swished the shredded packing paper from the crates around him like a hula skirt. Bullets were strung together in a high crown on his head; his chest and face were marked with gunpowder like a warrior. His beard was braided, and his hair was tied in a bun with dark green fabric with smudges of red. Bitzy had a single bullet tied to the top of her head, her face painted with gunpowder, and she was wearing dark green-red shorts. "At least the fabric came pre-tie-dyed."

My gaze drifted to where I had seen that dark green material before. Caden's shirt, the one Ash used to stop Birdie's bleeding, was in pieces.

My cheek flinched; did they want to know the dye was Birdie's blood?

Warwick huffed behind me, a smirk dancing on his lips, his head shaking. "If we run out of bullets, I'm sticking your head into my gun."

"Ohhhh. Yes, please..." Opie's blushed, nodding.

410

Chirp!

Opie blinked, going serious. "No, I meant no…" Opie wagged his head, his eyes open wide. "I don't want that. That sounds aaawwwful." A small purr came from his throat. "And really violent."

Chirp! Chirp! Chirp!

"I did not!" Opie put his hands on his hips. "That was not what I meant."

Chirpchirpchirpppp!

"Take that back. It was a total misunderstanding!"

Chirp! Chirp!

"Oh, don't give me that… like you weren't sticking your fingers in there earlier."

A groan pushed out of Warwick, and I twisted to him as Opie and Bitzy argued.

Warwick leveled his eyes at me.

"You kind of walked into that one." I grinned with a shrug.

"I did."

"How long have I been asleep?" I brushed back my hair, my stomach gurgling with hunger.

"Probably about nine hours."

"What?" I hadn't slept that long in years. "Did you sleep?"

"Some." He shrugged a shoulder, rolling it back as if it ached. I realized it probably did… this whole time I slept, he hadn't moved a muscle, no matter if he was aching or uncomfortable.

"You needed it." Warwick's stare was heavy, his voice gravelly.

"Your fingers were there too." Opie's voice cut through our moment, making me rub my head again. "Don't play innocent with me. You're just cranky because the tree humper is out of mushrooms."

411

Chirp!

Warwick took a breath, tipping his head back on the wall, his eyes never wavering. "I don't even want to think about where their fingers have been," he growled, grabbing my legs and straddling them over his lap, pulling me into him. *"I just want to think about where my fingers are now."* The feel of his imaginary hands gliding through my folds hitched my breath, sending heat sparking through my nerves. His huge hands stayed on my thighs while I felt his thumb rub over my core, his fingers sliding slowly in.

"Fuck." I sighed, my body instantly on fire. My nails dug into his arms as I tried to pretend nothing was happening. He pushed in deeper, pumping harder with a smirk on his face.

"Warwick…" I gritted my teeth, a warning to stop lingering loosely in there.

"What?" He nibbled my ear. *"I want to make you come right here. It's up to you how much they know, princess. How quiet can you be?"*

I peered around, biting my lip. Most everyone was asleep. Scorpion was now on watch, but he sat outside on the steps.

"Fuck, I knew my girl was dirty." He growled in my ear, his ghost fingers pushing in farther, moving faster, forcing me past the point of being rational.

My lids shut, knowing I should stop it. We were all on top of each other in the carriage, but pleasure hijacked me, my teeth clenching together to keep from moaning aloud.

His fantom mouth bit my thigh, jolting me, his real arms holding me in like we were only hugging, as his tongue sliced through my pussy. A cry bubbled up from my throat, his hand covering my mouth, blocking the sound as his shadow dove in deeper, taking my body prisoner. My muscles shook as I felt both his mouth and fingers working me, bliss rolling my eyes back. I couldn't even strike back and level the playing field. He was in full control, my body needing him so badly that I stopped caring who heard or noticed. Most felt our energy anyway.

"*Warwick,*" my shadow whispered hoarsely. "*Fuck me right here.*"

His grip on me became almost painful, though it only made me wetter.

"Don't move," he ordered in my ear, his voice thick and husky.

My muscles locked down, trying not to naturally respond as I felt his cock teasing my entrance, my teeth biting into his neck to keep from crying out.

Like a wild cat yowling, the noise echoed through the car. Panic and alarm lurched me up to my feet, slicing the link and the moment between Warwick and me like ice. Spinning around, my attention went toward the sound.

Hanna thrashed against her bindings, her teeth bared, eyes narrowed, like she wanted to attack and kill.

"Shit!" Scorpion scrambled back in, his arms low as he approached her like a wild animal. "Hanna."

"Fuck you! Let me go!" she seethed, her canine teeth appearing longer than normal human teeth, her pupils dilated.

"Calm down, little viper. We're not going to hurt you."

She flailed wildly, hissing and growling every time Scorpion took a step.

The true horror at what Istvan had done to Hanna punched me right in the gut. They all had been around, watching this happen to her. I hadn't. I knew it only got worse when she went back to Markos. He put her right back on the pills again.

It reminded me so much of Joska and Samu. Seeing

413

them turn feral. Most likely, they weren't even alive anymore. Their brains pretty much melted.

Would Hanna have the same outcome?

She bucked and squirmed, a strange sound puffing from her.

"Fuck." Scorpion rubbed his forehead, shooting a glare back at me. "You two really couldn't keep it in your imaginary pants for a little longer."

"What?" My head jerked, my cheeks blushing.

Scorpion's eyes narrowed, his expression saying, *don't act dumb.*

"We all can fucking feel you two," Scorpion exclaimed. "Me especially… but guess what? So do animals. They can pick up smells and energy better. Her instincts are responding, but the human part of her is confused and scared."

Heat flooded my cheeks as I looked around at everyone, then back to Hanna.

"That's a mating sound." Scorpion pinched his nose.

"What? How do you know that?" I balked.

"Because…" Scorpion suddenly was the one to look embarrassed. "I read up on wildcats." He lifted one shoulder. "I wanted to be able to pick up on things. Understand."

My lids fluttered with emotion, knowing what that meant. Scorpion wasn't going to do that unless he cared. A whole fucking lot. He wanted to be there for her, help, and recognize all the changes she might go through. To be by her side every step, no matter if she could be saved or not. He wouldn't give up on her. I realized how much I missed, but possibly because of my absence, those bonds forged stronger.

"Scorp."

He waved me off, focusing solely on Hanna. She panted

and puffed, her wild eyes watching his every move. Sweat trickled down her face, her skin pale.

"Untie me now," she demanded.

"I can't." Scorpion crouched in front of her, sorrow in his tone. "Hanna…"

She flinched at her name, her nose flaring. I could see her brain calculating and taking in her surroundings.

"They hurt," she pleaded, nodding at her arms. "Please. I promise I won't do anything." Her gaze met Scorpion's. "You said you cared about me. Would never hurt me. I hurt everywhere. You don't understand. I feel like I'm going crazy. *Please, Scorpion.* I need more pills. Please. Just a little. I just need to take the edge off."

Scorpion's jaw ticked, his lids closing briefly. "You know I can't, little viper."

Like he flipped a switch, she lunged forward, her tied arms halting her only inches from Scorpion, her jaw snapping and hissing.

"Fuck you! I hate you!" She kicked and screamed. "I want you dead! I cannot wait to sink my knife into your gut! Rip you apart with my teeth!"

Scorpion stood up. His expression didn't change, though I could sense the hypothetical knife drive through his heart.

"You think I cared about you? You are pathetic!" She wailed. "A disgusting, foul fae! Give me the fucking pills!"

"You know she doesn't mean it." My shadow was next to his.

His gaze still on her, he tipped his head so slightly in agreement, not looking convinced at all.

"She's coming down from a high. She doesn't realize what she's saying."

"I know."

I wanted nothing more than to hug him and tell him it

415

would all be okay, but I didn't know if it was. I had no idea if Hanna was ever going to be all right. My heart ached for him. For Hanna. Losing someone you love was beyond horrendous, but losing your mate…

That's how empires fell.

A squeal pitched through the space, and the train jolted to a screeching stop, lunging all of us forward.

There was a beat when we all looked at each other. All seemed to understand. Our time on the train, the moment of calm we had to regroup…

Just came to an end.

Chapter 31
Warwick

The train jerked to a stop, and my head whipped toward the closed door, which had been left unmanned and unguarded after Scorpion left his post.

I gritted my teeth, traveling to the exit. The cargo carriage had no windows, concealing us from the outside, but it also hid the outside world from us, leaving us blind to the dangers.

The train's whistle blew as I pried open the door just enough to peer out into the early evening. The sun had already lowered behind the horizon. It left enough light to capture the terrain.

"*Bazdmeg,*" I hissed, fully taking in what I was looking at.

We had seen Markos's army building up along the Ukraine and Hungary border, the tanks and soldiers prepping for war. I thought that was the extent of his troops. They would all leave from there to invade Hungary.

I should have known to not underestimate Istvan.

This train had taken us west as I hoped, but not to where I thought. We were in Slovakia.

I had driven through this area a hundred times before. It

was hardly a village anymore, more of a border junction between Slovakia and Hungary, off the 22 motorway, which led you straight into Budapest from the north.

Istvan was surrounding Hungary, coming in on Sonya from the north and east. By the sea of tents filling the field and the dozens of tanks, trucks, and soldiers spread as far as I could see, they were more than ready for war.

"Crap on ashbark," Ember muttered next to me, taking it all in. Soldiers shouted, their figures moving to the arriving train, ready to unload the cargo.

I slammed the door shut, my gaze rolling around the space, knowing we had only one other way out—the door which led to the next car. That was our only possibility to escape. To slip out between the two.

"Move those now," I ordered, pointing at the crates blocking the door. Kek, Lukas, and Ash were on it, sliding them out of the way. "You keep her fucking quiet…" My shoulder bumped Scorpion's, my gaze dropping to Hanna, leaving off the *or I will fuckin' kill her myself.*

His jaw locked, but his head nodded, dropping to untie her, tying a cloth around her mouth. I hoped that would be enough, because if she let out one scream, we were done.

"You got her?" I turned to Caden, though I didn't have to. He already knew what I was going to ask.

He nodded, curling his arms under Birdie's unconscious body, lifting her easily.

Grabbing guns and ammo from an open crate, I tossed them back to everyone before Kovacs and I moved to the door, cracking it open, seeing the camp was all on one side and a forest with some abandoned buildings on the other. I could hear the guards closing in, some already opening the doors to the carriage in front of us to unload, footsteps walking back toward ours.

We wouldn't have enough time for all of us to get out.

"We could really use one of your distractions about now," Kovacs whispered, her voice trying to hide the sheer panic rising inside her, the magic bubbling, feeling the threat, though she kept it in control.

"Well, slap cheese on my ass and call me a cracker." Cal's tiny voice buzzed past my shoulder. "Distraction is my middle name."

"I thought it was Beverly." Simmons flew next to him.

Cal shot Simmons a glare. "Noooo, it's *not*."

"Yes, you were named after your grandma—"

"Shhhuuut. Uuuuppp." Cal jeered through his teeth.

"What the fuck are you wearing?" Eli blinked at Cal, making me notice he was dressed almost exactly like Opie. The same shredded paper skirt, gunpowder designs on his torso and face, but instead of a crown, he had the bullets strung around his neck like a warrior necklace. He also had a small sack around his neck, full of something.

"It's a baked good original," Cal replied. "Plus, it lets my wee-bits hang free." Cal flew out with a half-assed salute, the paper skirt twirling in the air, hiding nothing.

"We will not fail you, my lady." Simmons did a proper salute, following Cal out of the carriage.

"Are they in any way going to help us?" I growled.

"Fifty-fifty chance." Ember shrugged.

"Try sixty-forty," Eli huffed. "And not in the positive."

"Do you need us to help, Fishy?" Opie piped up from Brexley's shoulder.

"Noooooo." Almost everyone responded in unison.

"What?" Opie gaped. "But I have a 90 percent rating of success."

Chirp!

"Okay, maybe an eighty…" Opie replied. "It's a solid forty."

Ash sniggered right as we heard voices at our carriage, the locked door jiggling. Tension expanded through my muscles, my finger dropping to the trigger, ready to shoot our way out of here.

"What. The. Fuck?" A male voice spoke in broken English from outside. "What was that?"

"Pixie dust bomb!" Cal sang out in a chuckle.

"Get away from me, disgusting sub-fae."

"*Sub-lime* you mean," Cal retorted. "And you better be nice. This pixie dust is pure gunpowder I just sprinkled over you, dumbasses. One flicker of flame... whoosh! Fried zombies!"

"Fuck," I muttered to myself, motioning for Killian and Rosie to go while the guards were distracted. "I think I'm beginning to like that flying rat."

One by one, the group snuck out of the carriage, jumping down on the opposite side of where the troop was and darting to the abandoned building to hide behind.

Gunshots rang out, halting the air in my lungs.

"Really? That's the best you can do?" I heard Cal laughing. "You suck, mush-for-brains."

Air exhaled through my nose when I realized the guards were shooting at the pixies and not at us.

"Go." I pushed my hand into Kovac's back. We were the last two on the train. Like a ghost, she slunk out, slipping almost silently into the darkness as I followed. Our link threaded through the night like a protective shield.

I didn't stop once I cleared the field. My pace not relenting, I led the group around the soldier encampment. Crossing over into Hungary, I got us far enough away from the troop to feel we had made a clean escape. Spies were probably everywhere through this area—for both sides. We had to constantly be on guard.

Gulping for air, Scorpion heaved Hanna off his shoulder, where she had been fighting and struggling against him the entire time. She kicked and hissed at him, trying to wiggle free of her restraints and gag.

"Dammit, little viper." He gripped the back of her head, pinning her body against his so she couldn't move. His voice was low and demanding. "Calm. Down."

Hanna's muffled cries died instantly, her body locking up, her chest heaving as his grip tightened in her hair, their gaze fastening on each other. I gave them ten seconds before they were fucking each other's brains out.

"Where are we going?" Caden hitched Birdie's figure up higher in his arms. "We can't stop. This area will be filled with spies. Probably not any on our side." He repeated what I had been thinking, his mind taking in all the information I knew about this region.

"We're about a day's walk from my safe house near Csehvár," Killian spoke, jerking my head up in attention.

Where my sister was. Simon. Kitty.

My mouth opened to respond when a branch snapped in the dark forest behind me. As if we were all synced together, our group spun toward the noise, guns cocked and ready to fire.

"Your sister will be really pissed if you shoot me." A figure moved out of the shadows from behind the trees.

Brexley's arm dropped, her mouth parting in shock. "Za-Zander?"

"Brexley?" A small neigh rumbled in his throat, joy and shock at seeing her.

"Oh gods, Zander." Brexley ran to him. He caught her up in his arms, hugging her tight.

"I thought I'd never see you again," Zander whispered to her. "I can't tell you how good it is to see you."

421

"Same," she hiccupped.

He squeezed her again, his eyes catching mine over her shoulder before pulling back.

That's right, pony-boy, step it back.

"My lord." Zander dipped his head at Killian, nodding at everyone in greeting.

"Zander, what are you doing here?" Killian asked, watching more figures move out of the forest behind him. I recognized most of them from Sarkis's army but didn't know any by name.

"Keeping watch. Spying on Istvan's troops and their movements," he said lowly, all the others staying quiet and in the background. He was clearly the leader of his group. "Mykel has us spread all over. Near Budapest and the borders." He nodded behind us, indicating Istvan's camp. "We've been watching them for a couple days now. We heard the train and gunshots."

"Yeah, that was us." Ash snorted. "Go figure."

Zander waved us on. "It's too dangerous to stay here. Too many eyes and ears around. Follow me." He turned, his faction leading the way as we followed. We stayed alert, guns drawn, while Zander directed us through the forest out to a country road.

His group disappeared into the ravine, the darkness hiding anything beyond. After a few minutes, an engine vibrated, a Hummer pulling up, headlights off.

"Guess they found my underground garage," Killian muttered.

"Oh yeah, speaking of that." Brexley grimaced. "You have fewer motorcycles at your other safe house. And guns… and your bed might be broken."

"Wait. What?" Killian stopped in his tracks.

"Come on," I smirked, swinging the passenger door

open to the Hummer and hauling Kovacs in. We had to pack in like rats. Wesley, Scorpion, Hanna, Caden, and Birdie got in the far back, some more squishing in the back seat, while I put Kovacs on my lap in the front. Some of Zander's men rode outside, their feet on the side panel, holding onto the mirrors with one hand, gun in the other. Zander flew us down the road, knowing at any time trouble could be coming the other way, looking for blood.

The Hummer bounced and shook through dense woodland and rough terrain, making its way up a dirt lane no one would find unless they knew about it. A good thirty minutes off any main road, the Hummer took us through spells, alerting the guards hiding our arrival in the brush. A handful stepped out as Zander came to a stop at a gate. A man nodded, recognizing Zander and his group, opening the gate for us.

The safe house was almost obscured to the naked eye. A large two-story house was built with the same wood of the trees, twining in and around the forest as if it was part of it. It blended into its surroundings like magic. I had no doubt that was exactly what the intent was.

The moment Zander put the car in park, the front doors swung open. Mykel strode out, his expression stoic, pinched with the fear of bad news. He probably expected a declaration of war at any moment.

His gaze was on the horse-shifter, waiting for a report, but it jerked to see Killian exit, then quickly fell on Caden carrying a wounded Birdie out of the car. Scorpion dragged Hanna from the back with them. Mykel didn't bother to ask what happened, immediately reacting to the situation.

"Zander, show Caden to the clinic." He gestured for

Caden to follow the horse-shifter. Mykel's gaze locked on Hanna, watching her hiss and claw like a wild animal. Sweat poured down her pale face, eyes glazed with a fever, coming down from a high. "Scorpion, take Hanna there too."

Scorpion swept Hanna up in his arms, trailing after Caden and Zander. Her yowls echoed after us, leaving a gutted silence between us all.

For a long time, we all watched the space they left behind; the unspoken thought hung heavy between us— Hanna might be Istvan's now.

"Uncle." Brexley finally spoke. Her voice was soft, but it somehow cut through the night like a knife, swinging Mykel's head to her.

"Brexley?" His eyes widened. "You're all right." Emotion I had never seen on his face before crumbled his brows, but unlike Andris, he didn't run to her. Something kept him back, like he didn't know if she wanted him to hug her or not.

Nor did Brexley. She was rigid, her guilt and shame ghosting over me like her shadow for those she hurt that night at the prison break, people he cared about. For running away and leaving us.

They stared at each other, no one making the first move.

I nudged her, pushing her forward, the motion moving her feet toward him, breaking through the walls they had up. His eyes glossed over, his arms opening, and she fell into them with a choke, her agony and pain tearing into me.

"I'm sorry," she whispered. "I am so sorry."

"I know you are." He spoke only to her. The hug was a little stiff, but I could see the love underneath. They still didn't know each other very well, but they were family. The last of it.

She pulled away, her head bowed. His eyes softened,

squeezing her shoulders. Their gazes met for a beat, expressing something deeper than their words ever would, before he sucked in, stepping back, becoming a leader, not an uncle.

"Killian." He bowed his head to the noble fae. "Good to see you. Good to see all of you." He nodded at everyone, stopping short on Eli and Ember. "Who are you?"

"The king's bounty hunters," Killian replied. "We have *a lot* to catch up on."

"That we do." Mykel watched the pair, guarded and untrusting.

"Let's head to my office." Killian strolled to the front door of his house. I could see Mykel's shoulders tighten for a moment, his role here suddenly changing. Though Mykel had been in charge, this was Killian's place.

Everyone traveled after them. Kovacs stood there, not ready to come face to face with all the people she walked away from, all the people who lost loved ones because of her. The endless grief and apologies lying in wait for her.

Stopping next to her, my body brushed against hers, my hand flattening on her lower back, telling her with a gesture that whatever she needed from me, she could have. She had to face it, but I would be there for her in any way she wanted me.

A small smile hinted on her mouth, her dark eyes staring up into mine with a nod of gratitude. She held up her chin and walked in on her own, ready to face her crimes.

We stepped into the house, people milling around through the large family room, into the open kitchen, and out the back doors. Through the sliding doors, I could see tents, tables, and bonfires set up in the backyard.

The kitchen and dining area were filled with seating, and a buffet was set out, people grabbing something for dinner. There were charts on the walls for chores, meetings, and

425

training. Everything was color coded—efficient and meticulous in a way that felt familiar.

A prickle of something, maybe hope, nipped at my gut.

"*Szar...*" Ash huffed, his head shaking, joy brightening his eyes. "Though I shouldn't be surprised." He glanced at me, flicking his head to the corner. "She loves controlling everything."

There at the center, chin high, clipboard in hand, commanding and directing it all...

Kitty.

My lungs tightened at the sight of her, emotion bubbling up seeing her so full of life. The last time we were together, I was lifting her lifeless, bony body off the cot, demanding she not give up. She was depleted. Empty. A shell.

Now she shined in all her glory. Strong, healthy, and beautiful, her wig was up in a sleek ponytail, and she wore tight-fitting cargo pants, heeled knee-high boots, and an off-the-shoulder black sweater.

She was in her element. A Madam. A boss. A director.

"She has this place running tight as a ship." Mykel motioned to her. "I don't know what I would have done without her."

It was where she thrived. Being the director of chaos, bending it to her will until it was in order. When the brothel burned down, she was put in Věrhăza to be tormented and demeaned, and she lost who she was. She gave up on life. This gave it back to her. I could see it as she spoke to people, as she ticked off items with the pencil and told them where to go... Kitty was back.

As if she sensed us, her eyes found Ash and me across the room. A smile twitched on her mouth, but true to Kitty, she quickly flattened it out, pretending our arrival was expected. Almost a nuisance.

Her long strides brought her to us in only a moment. "Of course, as soon as I have this place running to perfection, you two show up to cause trouble." Her mouth twitched at the corners, trying to act annoyed with us.

"Missed you too." Giving her no choice, I wrapped my arms around her, picking her off her feet in a bear hug.

"Warwick, put me down!" She stifled her laugh, rolling her eyes instead. I dropped her back to her feet. She wagged her head at me. "When you return, I know mayhem will soon follow. Things tend to blow up around you." She pointed at Ash. "You too."

I took her hand, kissing it with a wink. "At least I'm consistent."

She huffed, her long lashes fluttering with feigned annoyance.

"You look so good." Ash pulled her into a hug as well. "Glad you're okay, Kit." His voice was sincere and happy. There was no resentment or unrequited feelings lingering. Just pure love. "Missed you."

"Don't call me that. You know I hate it." That was why he did it. A brother razzing a sister. She pulled away with a frown, but her tone and gaze were full of warmth. Genuine. Real. "I must be crazy because…"—she took a breath— "I've missed you too." She squeezed Ash's hand and looked over at me. "Both of you."

We were family. We might annoy the fuck out of each other half the time, but our bond was for life.

"Good to see you looking so well, Madam." Rosie dipped her head, smiling lightly.

"And you." Kitty eyed Rosie with an arched brow, like she saw more than met the eye and was impressed. Kitty would never physically show you, but if you had her respect, you felt it in your bones. "Now, I must get back." She cleared

427

her throat, her shoulders rolling up. "This place falls apart without me." She turned, her ponytail slightly swaying with her walk. All along the way, individuals stepped up to speak to her—to be led by her.

This was Kitty's true love. What gave her life. This was where she flourished.

"Uncle Warwick?" A cry whipped me around, clenching down on my heart as a little boy came running for me at full speed. "Uncle Warwick!" Simon leaped up, and I clamped my arms around him, bringing him up to my full height. His arms strangled my throat, his head nestling into my shoulder, hugging me so tight. "I missed you!"

"Missed you too," I muttered privately, holding him firmer to me.

Eliza stepped into the dining room from outside, her attention landing on me. Her mouth parted before I heard her cry out my name, running for us. Her arms came around both of us, a sigh of relief coming from her, her eyes watering with joy.

"You're okay." She blinked tears back, repeating, "you're okay." She let out a small hiccup, then in a flip, she punched me hard in the arm.

"Ow."

"Damn you for making me fret like that." She hit me again. "We've been sick with worry."

Setting Simon back down, I leaned over and kissed her head with a shrug. "Sorry, sis." My life would never be worry free. Never going to be without danger. You'd think she'd be used to it by now.

"Ugh." Eliza flicked her eyes with sisterly annoyance. "Such a dickhead."

"That is true." Brexley nodded in agreement, high-fiving my sister.

428

"All right." I wrapped an arm around Brex, tugging her into me, nuzzling her ear. "Wait until later… I'll show you how much of a *massive* dick I can be."

"*You think so, Farkas?*" Her shadow rubbed against me, taunting me. "*See, I think you're all talk and very little action.*"

I let out a barked laugh. Kovacs and I were nothing but action. Any time and every place we could.

"Let's go to the office." Mykel addressed us, motioning for us to follow, breaking through the link. "There is much to catch up on."

"Brexley, Warwick, Ember, Eli?" Killian nodded for us to follow, the rest knowing they were to stay behind. Killian's attention stopped on another. "Lukas, I'd like you to come too. You might have insight on Sonya."

"Doubtful, but I will help if I can." Lukas's mouth pinched, his head dipping in accord.

Killian peeked back at Rosie, their fingers hooking together as they walked to the other side of the house, not hiding their relationship. Most probably didn't even notice the subtle action, but for Killian, it was like screaming from the rooftops.

Zander returned as we were leaving, strolling up to my sister, his arm coming around her shoulders. He kissed her, stopping me short.

"Hi," he muttered. "I missed you."

Eliza's cheeks pinkened, her eyes flaring, an eyebrow curving playfully. "Really?"

"Yes." Zander's hand threaded through her hair, kissing her again. "Need me to show you later?"

A growl rose from my throat, my eyes tracking how his hands touched my sister, making me want to rip out pony-boy's intestines and twine him through the chandeliers like streamers.

429

"Wow, big man… come on." Brexley yanked me with her, my attention still on them, wanting to dismember the donkey. "Let them be."

"Why him?" I snarled. "Seriously, out of all the guys, she picked him?"

"Zander is a good man." Brexley twisted back to me, a smile growing on her mouth. "Sexy as hell. And a *really* good kisser."

A deep growl vibrated my body.

"Fuck, woman…" I rumbled, cupping her face and dragging her to me, the instinct to make sure she never thought of that horse-shifter again burning through me. "You will so pay for that."

"I'm counting on it." Her mouth brushed mine, ghost fingers grazing up my shaft before turning away and striding for the office.

Another deep growl chased after her, my dick throbbing at the mere idea of her hands, lips, or pussy squeezing it. A snarl pushed out my nose. Adjusting myself, I followed.

She was right. There was no leash. It was always my own free will. Though the pull to her wasn't much different from one—lead, follow, or stand beside. I would crawl on my knees or level the world to be anywhere near her. To fight with her, for her, next to her. Protect her at all costs.

Entering the office, I shut the door, leaning against the wall. Mykel and Killian both started to go behind the desk and stopped. The two leaders stared at each other. The instinct to be dominant was ingrained in them both. It was who they were. There was a moment I wondered what would happen if their egos collided. Then Killian shocked the hell out of me. He motioned for Mykel to continue, stepping slightly back, sharing the position with the human leader.

Brexley's eyes secretly darted to me, eyebrow curving, picking up on the same thing.

"Did I just see that?" her shade questioned. *"Progress?"*

"I wouldn't hold your breath," I replied, my attention still on them. *"But who knows? I've seen miracles happen."* My hungry gaze swept back to her, moving over her poignantly.

"Clearly, getting his cock ridden hard has relaxed him a bit." My shade nipped at her ear, sliding my fingers through her.

She stiffened, shooting daggers at me.

"Told you you'd pay, princess."

"Give us a rundown of what is happening here." Killian addressed Mykel, pulling me back to the conversation. "Then we'll go into what we have done and seen. And what our next step is."

"Sonya has Budapest and most of the area around in her complete control. We tried to get close enough to Halálház to destroy her labs. We couldn't. She has it locked down tight."

"What?" I punched off the wall. "Halálház is still functioning? She's making more soldiers?"

Mykel dipped his head. "Yes. We lost many men that night. I couldn't afford to keep putting our people in harm's way when I knew it was only a death sentence."

Shit. That meant Sonya had been multiplying her troops this whole time as well.

"We also have another worry."

"What?" Killian asked.

"Romania has been sending her supplies and weapons. They also have troops waiting at the border, guarding it against Istvan or ready to come in. I haven't figured that part out yet, but Sonya has Romania as an ally."

"Romania?" Brexley's mouth dropped. "What?"

Right. It was something we probably forgot to mention… that Sergiu was spotted leading troops for Sonya's new army. A sign of faith from Prime Minister Lazar.

431

"Whatever deal she made, he is more than willing to fall behind her, waiting on her word." Mykel pointed to the map on the desk, red marks and circles all over it. "She has roadblocks and heavy guards on almost every road in or out. She is bringing more and more humans from Prague and Romania, building up her army. All of them under the pill's influence." Mykel scratched at his beard. "Like I said, we tried to get close enough to destroy the old prison, take her primary source out. They far outnumber us."

"And so does Istvan." Brexley placed her hands on the back of a chair, leaning on it. No one was sitting, all of us too tense to sit still for a moment. "The only hope we have is if Istvan and Sonya wipe each other out and we can come in."

"What about the nectar?" Mykel shifted his weight, his focus on Brexley. "I've seen what it can do, what *you* can do with it. With that, we have a chance."

Brexley's shoulders tensed up. "And if you remember, I killed *many* innocent people because of it."

"Many innocents die in war," Mykel replied. "Many are dying now. At least their death would have purpose."

"Tell them that or about the loved ones whom they lost. Those who lost everything because of me." Brexley lifted her lip at the word, head wagging. I knew she was thinking about the circus troupe, of all the people she had hurt. "Plus, I don't have it."

"What?" Mykel jerked. "What do you mean you don't have it? Where is it?"

"It's in safe hands, far away from me." There was a mix of relief and agitation in her stance. She was fearful of it, but she also wanted it, like an unhealthy addiction.

"This is not the time to get conscientious on us. The nectar is the most powerful weapon in this world. And we have it!" Mykel hit his hand on the desk. "You have not seen what is out there, what we are up against." He gestured toward the outside. "We have nowhere near the numbers or weapons they do. I will be blunt and say we are fucked if we don't have some secret weapon." It was fear causing Mykel to lash out. His voice was filled with it, bubbling up in anger.

"We *do* know what we're up against. We know what Istvan has and what *he* is capable of." Brexley shot back. "Don't doubt for a moment we aren't aware of our chances. Of the magnitude of this. I get it more than you know, and I will fight with every ounce of magic *I have* in me." She stabbed at her chest. "But I can't control the nectar. I tried… and failed. It is too much for any one person to handle and all I've done is kill people I care about every time I use it."

Thick silence crammed the air, everyone watching the standoff between the uncle and niece.

"Like I said. I don't have it." Brexley finally spoke, her voice gravelly. "And we have no time to get it."

"Then unless the Unified Nations is coming to fight with us," Mykel squinted at Ember, pointing out he knew exactly who she was. "We are finished."

"Lars can't." Ember shook his head. "The treaty they signed made sure they had no say in what went on in the east unless the war came directly to them. Believe me, I've gone over it with Kennedy and Lars multiple times."

"*This* doesn't *affect* them?" Lukas piped up with shock. "Our country turning to a dictatorship, humans turning to these super faes… that would certainly impact the west."

"Kennedy and Lars would have to wait until they started moving in on the west. Even a touch at our borders and Lars could declare war," Ember replied.

"Sonya and Istvan are too smart to do that right now. They don't want a fight with the UN, not until they are ready." Killian leaned against the desk.

433

"The contract is magically bound." Ember nodded to Killian, talking to us. "It's not something they can just break because they feel like it. My father has tried to find any loophole. That's why he sent us here to retrieve the nectar and kill anyone standing in our way."

Good thing she failed miserably on that one, not that she would have gotten close enough to touch Kovacs. If they had, Ember and Eli would be heading back to the states in small boxes... what was left of them, anyway.

"Though"—she held up her hand—"that's not to say I can't *indirectly* get some fighters here. *Off* the record. It wouldn't be an army..." She peeked at Eli. "But I know a few beasts who might want to fight."

"When don't we?" Eli snorted. "Fuck or kill—that's our motto."

"What a coincidence. That's my motto too." I smirked at Kovacs.

"Lorcan knows the doors," Ember said, more to Eli than anyone else. "He could get everyone here."

"I'll talk to him and Cole." Eli nodded to her plan.

"It's something." Killian folded his arms.

"Hardly," Mykel blew out, rubbing the back of his neck. We all knew this was a long shot, but none of us would sit back. This fight was probably to the death. The Games set in a larger arena. This country might collapse, but there was no doubt that if I had to dig through corpses, trudge through blood, and hack my way through bones, I would get my dark demon out... alive.

"Kapitan!" A pounding on the door jolted us to the commotion. A young man, at least half fae, stepped in dressed in all black, a balaclava pulled up to his forehead. "Sir! Oh, Lord Killian." The kid bowed to Killian, noticing the fae lord's presence.

"Report, Ervin," Mykel ordered.

"We have two people at the gate."

"What? How?" Mykel's eyes widened, understanding that was a bad thing. No one should be able to find this place.

"I don't know, sir. They were just suddenly there. They set off no alarms."

"What do they want?"

"She wouldn't tell us."

"She?"

"Yes, there is an old man and a woman. She told me to tell you..." He swallowed.

"What?" Mykel barked.

"That Tadhgan is here."

Chapter 32
Caden

Life lay like a feather in my arms, and with every stilted breath she took, I wondered if it was my life she was holding on to and not her own.

Ash told me she would be okay. She was strong. A fighter. Until I saw her eyes open and felt her heart steady against my palm, I struggled to fully let myself believe. So much had been taken away already. There was so much agony and grief. And even if the thought wouldn't completely solidify in my head, I understood in my gut that if she decided to bail on this world, there was no coming back for me.

Like a chain she had hold of, she would bring me down with her.

Tension trotted up and down my spine, my boots nipping at Zander's heels as he led us downstairs, dipping below the ground level of the house to a huge underground space. The threat of war in this country, in the Eastern bloc, was never a far-off notion. We lived in the present with wounds from a past still marking the people and buildings like scars, with a future on the horizon set on repeat.

Suspicion, violence, power, greed, pain, death, grief,

436

loss. It lived in our blood, was stamped in our DNA, and molded our behaviors. We grew accustomed to sorrow and suffering. And that was even before the fae came into the mix. We were replaying it all over again, just with different leads.

Though in that suffering, the importance of life, of love, of the family became deeper to us than most. There was no room for bullshit. We loved harder, appreciated more, and tried to live in the moment.

When my father fired that gun, he aimed for what would make me suffer the most. My death might have given me peace, an end to the suffering. That was exactly what he didn't want. He wanted to hurt me. To shove his hand into my chest and rip out what was still beating inside.

My gaze went down to the small fae in my arms, her head sagging, her limbs limp, blood coating her face and body, streaking her white-blonde hair. My heart surged up into my throat, my gut twisting with an emotion so overwhelming it made me dizzy.

Birdie was stunning. Anyone could see that. Though it wasn't her beauty that sucked all the air out of my lungs. I couldn't even explain what it was exactly. What she made me feel. It scared the shit out of me because I knew it went beyond the sex, though that was mind-blowing. It rocked me to my core. I couldn't stay away. I loved her defensiveness, her combative, fierce nature. She challenged me, pushed me, and did not back down. I could see her walls and the armor she wore, and I felt it crack just a little every time I was inside her. Every time we lay together after.

At the safe house, something flipped. I didn't move from the bed after, nor did she. We lay together, touching each other and talking. Finding out more about each other. More that bonded us.

Her parents were so drugged out most days that they

didn't feed or even change her diaper when she was a baby, letting her sit in her own feces for days. Her father even tried to sell her off once to get another hit when she was a teenager. She ran away later, finding her family with Scorpion, Maddox, and Wesley before they became part of Sarkis's army.

I could relate. My father sold me too. To a country he wanted to rule, to a woman he already impregnated, to ensure our family line was rooted forever. Then he tried to make me one of his monsters, a guinea pig to go before him, and when he thought that failed, he put me in the Games to be slaughtered before his eyes.

Her breath faltered in my arms, panic surging from me.

"In here!" Zander motioned us through a doorway, exposing a large room full of cots and medical supplies, much like the setup we had at Vajdahunyad Castle. I was so focused on Birdie I didn't notice anything else as I placed her body on an empty cot, my gut knotting when her chest stopped for a moment. "She needs medical attention! Help her!" I screamed, searching the room for healers. "Now!"

My gaze landed on the one nearest to me, my head jerking back with shock at the woman before me.

"Caden?" Her eyes widened, hope, love, and joy filling them.

"M-Mom?" I gaped. The woman I grew up with, the one draped in diamonds and top-of-the-line fashion. The queen of HDF who was always on, keeping emotions at bay, and me at arm's length, playing her part as the beautiful wife of the General to a T, was gone. I had seen it slowly melt away before I left, but this time I not only saw the difference but felt it in her demeanor.

Dressed in cargo pants, a worn sweater, and dingy boots, her hair was tied up in a ponytail, with no makeup on. She looked tired, but also the most beautiful and real I had ever seen her in my life, comfortable in her own skin.

Emotion flooded her face, watering her eyes, looking as if she wanted to run to me, embrace me, but she took in my expression, my terror, and ran to us.

"Help her!" I bellowed as she came around, other healers running at my entreaties. "Please!"

Two healers moved on either side of her, checking her vitals.

"Do something!" I screamed at them as my mother grabbed my arm, yanking me away from the bed. "You have to heal her."

"They are, Caden. Let them work." Mom pushed me back. I was now a thousand times stronger than her, but I stumbled back, letting her pull me away, my gaze still on Birdie as the healer tore off the clothing hiding the gunshot wound, injecting her with something.

My eyes went to my mom, her brown eyes soft and filled with grief, like she was suffering my pain.

"Do something... she *can't* die." My voice came out weak and broken, revealing my fear.

"I wish I could, but I'm just helping out down here. Mainly with the kids. I don't know enough yet." She rubbed a comforting hand on my arm. "She's in the best hands, Caden."

I swallowed, not able to tear my eyes from Birdie. Mom's attention followed mine to the tiny blonde, then back to me questioningly. I could hear the question she didn't ask. *Who is she to you?*

I would have answered, *I don't know*, but all I could feel swimming in my gut was one word. *Everything.*

I watched the healers clean and sew up Birdie's wound, giving her a painkiller. Her breath was steady, her expression peaceful. My adrenaline nosedived, sinking my shoulders down. I took in a shaky breath, feeling the recoil of emotions.

"Father shot her," I said hoarsely, almost more reminding myself of the truth.

"What?" Mother blinked at me, her mouth parting.

"I thought he was going to shoot me, but instead..." My voice cracked. "He knew. Somehow, he knew."

Grief for me filled my mother's expression, and she pulled me into a hug. She had embraced me many times in my life, but it was always a little stiff and cold, my father berating her, saying it would only make me weak.

This time, warmth and fierce love engulfed me. She didn't hold back, now finally allowed to show her affection for me. My mother had been through hell, but seeing her now, how she had flourished and grown, she seemed lighter, like she no longer had to act a part.

"I'm so sorry, Caden," she whispered in my ear. My arms tightened around her, needing the strength of my mother like I was a little boy. "I am so sorry."

I nodded, my teeth clamping together, keeping back the dam wanting to break.

"She'll be okay." She sounded so sure. "I promise."

The word punched my lungs, feeling the weight of it, the understanding which separated me from my mother now.

She was human. I was not.

Promises by humans were easily broken, something they said to calm and reassure someone, the word almost becoming meaningless. I had done it so many times before, promises I knew I'd never keep. To the fae, they were binding, a contract you had to fulfill. It wasn't until now I really felt what I was. The change in my being that connected me to the guy upstairs. Shared magic bound us with a sixth

440

sense. We'd forever know where the other was—have information outsiders wouldn't be privy to.

Oddly enough, it didn't make me want to tear out of my skin like it once did. Not that I wouldn't hack our association off in a moment if I could, but I stopped hating Warwick.

As I pulled away from my mom, my focus going back to Birdie, I had a feeling the girl lying on the bed had a lot to do with that. She brought peace to my life.

A muffled wail lurched me to a cot along the wall. Hanna kicked and thrashed as Scorpion handcuffed her to the railing, dodging her feet. Her complexion was so sallow and sweaty. Her eyes were wild, her hair a mess.

"Hanna?" My mother gasped, her hand covering her mouth, already running for her old friend's daughter. My mom had watched Hanna grow up and been part of her life for a long time. To see her now had to be a shock; the change in Hanna had advanced so much. "Oh gods, no…" My mom stopped right at her bed, horror making her immobile for a moment, while Scorpion struggled with Hanna's strength.

"Help her! She's going through withdrawals," Scorpion demanded.

Mother jerked herself out of her frozen state, going into action.

"Hold her down!" Rebeka ordered Scorpion, grabbing a syringe.

"What is that?" Scorpion fought to keep her still.

"Just a sedative." She stuck Hanna in the arm, emptying the plunger. "Should calm her down." She spoke and moved with confidence, handling the situation. Rebeka Markos was always good at taking control of situations, but usually for parties and humoring heads of state. She never was there when I was sick or hurt. The nanny took care of me, comforted me, and was there when Dr. Karl stitched me up.

The woman I grew up with wasn't cut out to work in a clinic, to handle blood, sickness, and death.

But this woman was.

Hanna let out a loud yowl before her body slumped into the bed, the drug working through her system, easing Scorpion's hold on her. That's when she started convulsing, her skin slick with sweat.

Another healer came around, an older fae woman. "She needs to be detoxed, get the toxins out of her system." She faced my mom. "Rebeka, get me an IV drip."

Mom acted instantly, retrieving a bag filled with liquid and rolling it over to the healer, knowing what to do as they inserted the needle into Hanna's arm.

"Will that work?" Scorpion asked.

"It has magic-laced salts and electrolytes. It will help cleanse her system quickly," the healer replied, her mouth pinching. "But I don't think that is what you are really asking."

Scorpion and I both gazed down at Hanna with the same worry. She might get "clean," but would she ever be "okay?" Would the pills kill her anyway?

Staring at my longtime friend and what she had become, I felt the weight of my father's actions. The guilt she had lost her parents and herself because of my family. Another victim in my father's pursuit of power. We were both turned against our will and became something else because of my father's greed.

My intuition suddenly flicked on like a blender, jolting magic through my bones. An overwhelming sense of Warwick. Of his alarm. Apprehension.

Danger.

It was instinctual. I whirled around for the door. "Scorpion!" I called to him, knowing he'd follow without question. With fighters like us, you reacted first and asked questions later. "Mom..." I paused in the doorway, glancing back. "Watch her." I flicked my chin to Birdie.

She nodded her head in agreement before I took off, Scorpion on my heels.

The pounding of our feet echoed off the wood stairs. As I reached the ground floor, I spotted Ash and Kek beelining out the front door in pursuit of the others. Scorpion and I raced right behind, my hand on my gun, ready for what was to come.

Shouts and commotion directed Scorpion and me toward the gates, falling in line behind Warwick, Brexley, Killian, and Mykel. My eyes adjusted quickly to the darkness, a torch beaming on the pair on the other side of the gate, causing a gasp to stick in my lungs. A small petite woman with torn bunny slippers held up an old man, his face half burnt.

"Oh gods!" Brexley cried out, pushing past the guards, tugging at the locked gates. "Let them in!"

Killian motioned for them to do what she said. The metal squealed, the two people on the other side barely making it across before they fell to the ground.

Esmeralda held Olek in her arms, both weak and exhausted.

"Brexley, my girl." Though it was Esmeralda's voice and body, I knew it was Tad speaking. "I can't hold on to her much longer. She's so weak." He reached for Brex as she dropped to her knees in front of them.

"What happened?" Brexley touched where Esmeralda's hair had been singed, her concern dropping to Olek.

"They found us." Tad struggled to speak, his words almost lost between Killian's orders for gurneys and healers.

"Who found you?"

443

Esmeralda's dark eyes went up to me, indicating something I felt clenching in my gut.

"And tell Brexley I know where the nectar is. It was easy when you follow the ones who follow it."

"Istvan." I muttered my father's name like a stranger, needing to distance myself from him. He no longer deserved the honor of being called father.

"Istvan found the hideout?" Panic pitched Brexley's tone.

"He had it burned down..." Tad nodded, peering down at Olek. "We barely got out."

"How did you know to come here?" Mykel's attention drifted around as if he was expecting an army to be coming up behind in attack.

"The book," Tad spoke more to Brexley than Mykel. "It showed me where you were."

Ember's attention went to Esmeralda and Olek, seeing they were carrying nothing. "Where is the book? Did it burn up? Where is the nectar?"

"The book... will always find its way," Tad replied, glancing over at Ash. "If I had a guess, I would say it might be tucked away in someone's bag here already."

"The nectar?" Brexley tensed up; terror expressed in every syllable. "Where is it? Did Istvan get it?"

Tad slowly reached inside Esmeralda's nightgown pocket, pulling out an object wrapped in a hand towel.

"No, my dear. I promised you I would keep it safe."

Brexley let out a sigh, relief washing over her face, her hand automatically reaching for it.

She stopped. Her fingers dangled over the item.

"Thank you." She struggled, breathing through her nose. I could tell she was trying to fight the need to touch it. Take it as hers. To hold the power.

"Is that it?" Mykel leaned over, his eyes bright. "I never thought I would cross paths with it again. To be this close. To feel its power again." A flicker of something I recognized all too well went over his features. I had seen the look on my father's face so many times.

Greed.

Desire.

"What that small thing is capable of…" Mykel's hands rolled into fists, his chest heaving, his gaze intense on the wrapped object. I could feel it too. With that much magic, no fae or human couldn't. It prickled at your skin, whispered in your ear, gave you ideas of what you could do. What could be accomplished. Even if your intentions were good, power had a way of corrupting even the most virtuous of minds.

It seemed to sing louder to those who craved authority.

The healers rushed up to us, moving Mykel back, surrounding Esmeralda and Olek and lifting them on gurneys.

"Are you sure no one followed you?" Killian asked while the healers picked up the stretcher, heading them back to the clinic.

"I made sure. I was cloaked." Tad was fighting to keep hold of Esmeralda. "I don't know how they found us. How they knew the nectar was there." Guilt and confusion glistened in her eyes.

Killian clasped Esmeralda's hand, speaking to Tad. "Don't worry about it. You kept it protected and got safely here. Now just relax, my dear friend. We've got it from here."

"Here, my lord." Tad held up the nectar.

"No." Killian jerked back, his head shaking, staring at it like it was a snake. "I don't trust myself. I don't want it."

"That is why the burden falls on you." Tad slurred with exhaustion, placing the nectar in Killian's hands. "How much you have changed, my lord. You are worthy of it now."

445

Killian's throat bobbed, his expression almost torn with pain.

"*You* have the strength to fight it. Protect it with your life." Esmeralda's lids closed, her body going limp as Tad let go of her, allowing her to fully rest.

I stood in place while everyone headed back indoors, my father's sentiment echoing in my head.

"I know where the nectar is. It was easy when you follow the ones who follow it."

Was he talking about us? Who else could follow it?

My gaze went out to the dark forest, thick fog threading through the trees as a howl of wind raced over my skin, spreading goosebumps over me.

Except it wasn't the icy air that chilled me to the bone, it was the sensation of being watched.

Like death was waiting in the shadows.

Chapter 33
Killian

The clock ticked on the nightstand like it was counting down the seconds until everything I knew and cared about was taken from me. What I worked my entire life for, everything I sacrificed, lost, bled, killed, and almost died for.

From the poor kid on the streets fighting for a slice of bread to a ruthless pirate to a lord of a country. I was merciless and powerful. I bit, clawed, and killed for my position, for what I wanted most in this world. The whole reason I became lord was to prove—to my father, Croygen, Kat, *myself*—that I was worthy. To have all the power, bend them to my will for once. Show them how wrong they had been about me. I was something special. They were wrong for turning their backs on me.

I became a leader not for the people, but for my own ego. For confirmation that Kat chose wrong. I was the one she should have picked. I had the role, the riches, the castle, and the power. People bowed to me, carried out every order I commanded of them. I was the one all the girls wanted, fae or human.

I got everything I wanted, and now I felt more unsure

and unworthy of it. All my drive to get here was empty and meaningless. Prison had crumbled the facade I held up, even to myself, taking me to one basic understanding.

Success was nothing if you sat in your castle alone.

It was no longer the girl I imagined long ago who would be at my side when I was finally there.

Never could I foresee that the naive, sweet-faced actress I had seen in that god-awful play, who became a whore to survive in the new world, would challenge me every step of the way and be the one to bring me to my knees.

Opinionated, stubborn, fiery, beautiful, and smart as hell. She cut through all the bullshit, making me see she was the only thing I needed at the end of this war. I could walk away from the title, the money, and the power without hesitation.

Rosie. *Nina*. Whatever she wanted me to call her, I knew I could not live in this world without her.

My eyes flicked to the nightstand, sensing the magic lying in the secret compartment in my drawer. It was such a small object to have such inconceivable power. The energy coming from it was unmistakable. I couldn't deny the draw to it. The compulsion to place it in my hands and let the magic fill me, to end every threat to my future, to the people I cared about.

The old Killian would have done it in a heartbeat. It was what I had desired the most at one time. I pretended I wanted to have it to keep it out of the hands of Istvan or others like him, but was I really any different?

When you have everything, but there is no meaning to any of it, you only want more to fill that hole. It never stops because you are trying to satisfy a bottomless chasm.

An empty carcass.

"No. I don't trust myself. I don't want it."

"That is why the burden falls on you. How much you have changed, my lord. You are worthy of it now."

Was I?

The fire crackled behind me, flickering off the walls of my master bedroom. It was everything a lord would have—a king-size bed loaded with faux furs, leather headboard and sofa, sleek dark wood furniture, and dark beams running across the ceiling. A fireplace, walk-in closets, and an enormous bathroom with a sauna and hot tub.

All for looks and prestige, because I had never once spent the night here. I actually preferred the smaller, homier cabin to either the castle or this place.

Waste was for the wealthy who had nothing to show inside. This was their personality, and we applauded them for it. As a young boy, dirt covering my face, my belly growling in hunger, I would look at the houses and boats of the rich and think someday I wanted to buy it all and show the world I could. That if I had so much wealth, wasting it made me someone worthy…

Fuck, it was all shit. Věrhăza peeled away every veneer I had layered myself with over the years and stripped me to the bone. The irony was not lost on me being put in the very prison I built and made sure it was even harder to penetrate.

Though I would give anything for my friends to not go through that experience, I had to wonder if I would be here now without it,

Without Věrhăza, would I have found Rosie?

Rubbing my head, I sighed, my burning eyes reading the clock. It was almost two in the morning. After dealing with Tad and Olek, Mykel and I had locked ourselves away in the office to speak in more detail about the situation, which didn't leave me in a hopeful mood.

Grunting, I stood up, going to the door, wondering where she was.

"My lord." A woman fae soldier stood outside my

449

bedroom, addressing me as soon as I opened the door. It was something I wouldn't have even questioned a few months ago. No matter where I was, I had guards at the doors, day or night. The threat of assassination from even a trusted employee was on the mind of every leader. And deep down, I had liked it. Again, it proved I was so high up I had to have guards watching me all the time.

I didn't like it here. It felt wrong in this place. Like my position might be worthy, but I no longer felt *I* was.

"Did you need something, sir?"

"No…" I started to shut my door. "Actually, yes. Can you locate Rosie? Bring her here?"

"Yes, majesty."

"Please don't call me that." I frowned. "Call me Killian."

"Not sure I can, sir." She dipped her legs.

"Please try."

"Yes, my lord. *Killian.*" She smiled like a schoolgirl, her cheeks blushing, before she took off, searching for my fiery redhead.

Closing the door, I tugged off my filthy sweater, picking at the platter of food left on the table for me.

"Are you kidding me?" A door slammed behind me, whirling me to Rosie. Her hands were on her hips, clothing torn and filthy, her hair matted from being in a beanie.

Dirty, smelly, and exhausted, she was still the most gorgeous woman I had ever seen. Stunning as a human, but she stole my breath as a fae.

"Are we back to this?"

"What?" I blinked, realizing she was mad.

"Ordering me around like I'm one of your servants or soldiers?" She folded her arms. "I've played the whore for a long time, Killian. Paid my dues… I am finally free. I won't go back to spreading my legs from one owner to another."

"Bazdmeg." I took a step back, offended. "This went off the rails quickly."

"You had a guard *retrieve* me." She stepped closer, her voice rising. "You couldn't come find me like a normal person? Ask if I was ready or wanted to come to you?"

"I'm *not* a normal person." I gritted my teeth, retaking the ground I gave up.

"Oh, right." She curtsied. "How would His Majesty like me to please him this evening?"

"Rosie…" I pinched my nose, though I felt my dick twitch at the phrase. Inhaling, I looked her straight in the eyes. "I was going to come look for you, but sometimes being who I am comes with limitations."

She burst out a dry laugh. "Limitations? You think being a lord is *limiting*?"

"Yes," I growled, moving closer to her. "It comes with a lot of perks, but I have fewer freedoms as a lord than a normal guy looking for his girlfriend." My eye twitched at the last word, not feeling right on my tongue. Girlfriend sounded so young and frivolous.

"Girlfriend?" Her lips wobbled, trying to hold on to her irritation.

"Yeah, that sounded silly to me too." I held up my palms. "And before you take it wrong. I mean you are more than that."

Her blue eyes lifted to mine. Rosie was so strong, but I saw fear flicker in them, both of us scared to death of this thing between us.

I had called her my mate. We had never talked about it, never even brought it up since that morning.

"I'm sorry I had someone get you. I won't do it again."

Her arms were still crossed, but her head nodded in appreciation.

451

"What did I pull you away from at two in the morning?" My hands ran down her arms, trying to relax her.

"Madam. *Kitty,*" she corrected herself, like she was adjusting to calling her just by her first name.

My head shifted back. "Why?" A pinch in my gut had the word come out slow and unsure.

"What do you mean, why? I've known her longer than you."

"Have you ever sat and chatted before? Were you friends?"

"No, but things are different now." Rosie rolled her shoulders, dropping her arms, but I could still feel she was reserved. "We were just talking about what we will do after if this war goes in our favor."

"And?" That feeling grew like weeds in my stomach.

"She wants to reopen Kitty's." She shrugged. "And I might want to help her."

Rosie might as well have punched me. I almost stumbled back, my chest heaving. "I'm sorry, what?" I shook my head. "You want to go back to the whorehouse?"

"Not as one of her girls," Rosie replied, like I offended her. "But as a business partner."

"No… no… fuck no." I wagged my head vehemently. "Can never happen."

"Excuse me?" Her defenses shot up, her blue eyes glittering with anger. "Are you once again telling me what I can and cannot do?"

"Why would you want to go back? You worked hard to get out of there," I questioned, my emotions taking over.

"Yes, and I want a place that protects them better and provides more security and safety for the girls. Prostitution is never going away, as much as I'd love that. It will always have a draw because of the money. So why not make it better for girls like me?"

"You are not one of them."

"I was," she seethed, pointing at herself. "And I could be just as easily again."

"What the hell are you talking about?" I glanced around like I was in some alternative universe. "What do you think this is between us?" I motioned between us as anger stomped up my vertebrae. "What's going on?"

"I don't know." She glanced away, and I could feel the lie on her tongue. "But I am no longer a weak or helpless little girl. I won't put myself into a position where my entire world revolves around you. What if you decide you've had enough one day? All I've done is survive… live by someone else's rules and conditions. Living well or in the gutter on a man's whim. I will stand on my own two feet. Make my own way in this world without any help."

"I am a lord. I can't have my lover running a brothel."

"I will not be *kept* or become a pretty pet you have when you want me, fucking other girls on the side."

A growl ripped up my throat. "You don't fucking get it." She retreated until her back hit the door, my body pressing into hers, looming over. "There is *no one* else." It sounded more like a threat, but I felt a shiver run through her. "You're new to being fae, your emotions are jumbled and overwhelming, but I know you feel it."

Her mouth parted as I flattened myself into her, my erection hot against her.

"If we get out of this war alive and you need time to figure it out or decide you don't want me… I will give it to you," I gritted out. "But you are my fucking *mate*." I clutched her hair, yanking back her head. "And that means your pussy is the only one I want to be in. Every moment of every day. Only you."

Her breath hitched, her eyes glossing with hope.

453

"You didn't bring it up again. I didn't want to assume. It could have been a mistake."

"Red, the only mistake I've made is not coming to my senses faster." I cupped her jaw. "I love you."

A soft cry came from her before my mouth crashed down, kissing her deeply, her nails clawing at my bare chest. The spark was instant, the need like a tsunami.

"You are seriously filthy," I muttered against her mouth. "Let's get you cleaned up." I picked her up, her legs curling around my waist. My aching cock parted her folds, hinting at entering.

She groaned, claiming my mouth frantically.

I rushed to the bathroom. Turning on the shower, I didn't even wait for the water to warm or undress, the chill of the spray clashing against our hot skin, making us both gasp. Our lips claimed each other's hungrily as I peeled off her clothes. My mouth followed my hands as I stripped her bare.

"Killian…" she gasped, pulling my head back up to her. "I need to feel you come deep inside me."

Fuck.

Stripping quickly, I clutched her thigh, pulling it up to my hip, spreading her legs open. "Watch," I ordered as I grasped my cock, positioning it at her entrance. "Watch how I sink into you."

Rosie reached out, her hand cupping my balls, making me groan as I thrust into her.

"Oh gods!" Her nails dug into me, her breath stilted, watching me pull out and push back in slowly, hitting every nerve along the way.

"How does it feel this good?" She grabbed the back of my ass, pushing me in deeper. I could feel her spasm and stretch around me. "I can't believe it feels like this." Her eyes glossed as the shower pelted down on us.

"Because it's us." I nipped her ear as I pushed in deeper. "And it will only get better."

"What?"

"Sex between mates, as I've heard and think we've experienced just with Brexley and Warwick, gets more intense over time, not less." I slipped almost all the way out before slamming in again, causing Rosie to belt out a cry, clicking something in us, turning us wilder and more feral. Her fingers dipped into my ass, pushing in so deep that I chomped down on her neck, pounding my hips harder.

"Fuck!" I bellowed, pumping my hips, hitting a spot that made her arch into me, a sexy noise in her throat.

I couldn't seem to get deep enough. Pulling out, I flipped her around, pressing her against the tile as I drove back in, the angle making her groan loudly. Grabbing a bath sponge, I slid it down her body, stopping at her clit and dragging it through her again and again.

"Kill-ian." She gritted her teeth, the noises she was making causing me to go even more crazy. She pushed her ass out, bending over, sinking me in farther. The different angle blazed fire through me, my climax bearing down on me. She pushed into me, giving back just as much. The sensations burning through me were almost too much, but at the same time, I only wanted more and wanted it to last forever. I pushed her farther over, burying myself in her. The sounds of sex echoed in the room.

"Oh gods!" I could feel her squeezing around me, the magic between us tightening, ready to shred us apart with pleasure.

Once again, I yanked out of her, flipping her around again before picking her up. "Grab the shower head," I ordered. She reached up, holding on as I sunk her body down on mine.

We both shouted. I started off slow, taking her deep and long; my teeth drove into her bottom lip, tugging until I tasted blood.

Something about it made me lose any control I had left. I wanted to look at her when I came inside, feeling her pussy clench around me. I wanted her begging for mercy as I fucked her relentlessly.

"Killian, please… *a társam*," she whispered in my ear.

She broke me and glued me back together in two words. *My mate.*

A roar splintered off the tile, my body turning feral. Pounding so hard, I felt our bones hit.

"Oh gods!" Her pussy strangled my dick so intensely that I almost stopped breathing. My hot cum exploded inside her, claiming everything as mine.

For a moment, I was no longer in my body. I was somewhere on a different planet. I could feel her right there with me. Her soul, her pleasure, her happiness—it only heightened my own.

"Fuck!" I breathed out, my body collapsing on hers.

We didn't speak for a bit, our eyes meeting with awe and shock as we struggled to breathe. Sex had been unbelievable before, but this was even more so.

"Shit." I swallowed, her legs still around me, my cock still inside her. "If that continues to get better…?"

"I lied. I can be a kept woman," she teased, her eyes still glazed, her heart pounding against mine.

"Believe me, I'll do everything I can to prove it to you. Over and over again." I gently put her back on her feet, moving her toward the shower spray. "Once I get you clean and put you in my bed."

Her eyes opened with shock.

"I will never be done with you. I will never have

enough." I slid my hands up her face. "Centuries I wasted. I didn't even know."

"What?

"That I've been waiting for you. Now I've found you. *Now* I realize what loving someone really means. I plan on making up for it."

She looked up at me, her eyes so clear. "I didn't know either, but since the night you came to the theater, I've been waiting for you too."

A lump formed in my throat. "The war will be here, maybe in hours. Is there any way I can convince you to stay out of it?"

"No." She placed her hands over mine. "Because where you are, I am. You're mine, Lord, and I we live or die, we do it together.

"Fuck, can you call me that again?" I pulled her into me for a kiss, her hip already feeling how easily she got me hard.

"Only when you obey," she teased, her mouth brushing mine, then pulling back. "But I'm not kidding, Killian. I'm not going to be some piece at your side. I want to be my own person, have my own interests and business."

"Totally fine. You can do anything." I tugged her face closer. "Just not in a brothel, okay?"

"We'll see." She shrugged, popping up on her toes and kissing me. I quickly bundled her up in my arms, strolling out of the bathroom, our wet bodies falling into my bed together, instantly going back at it.

We talked as if the future was a sure thing. That this war wouldn't impact the plans we were making.

As if death wasn't coming for us.

I would still be a lord in the end.

But as our bodies moved together, we made love like it could all end tomorrow.

Like this might be goodbye.

Chapter 34
Brexley

Dawn was only hours off, yet my eyes had only closed for maybe twenty minutes. I stared off into the darkness, feeling the pull of the nectar calling me. The power in it was growing, gaining more control over itself as if it was mimicking me. If I grew stronger and more dominant over my own magic, it did too. A reflection. Learning. Studying. A life of its own. It still was part of me, and I knew it had no ill intent, though that didn't mean it wasn't capable of horrendous things. I had seen it too many times.

It carried dark magic, the power of a cruel queen, yet it was used to protect an infant. There was nothing purer and more untainted than an innocent child.

A balance

Yin and yang.

One could not exist without the other.

My own magic was a lot, but still just a drop in the bucket from what that object held. It was a danger to all. Even me. Yet, the need to run down the hall and retrieve it from Killian wrestled through my muscles, shifting my legs and arms with restlessness.

Tad had given it to Killian to protect.

Pure raw possessiveness curdled in my stomach, beating my chest with envy and anger.

"You have the strength to fight it. Protect it with your life."

I wasn't worthy or strong enough.

Time was a pitiless teacher. And we were gluttonous students. We gobbled it up, wasted it, wished it away, and then got angry when it ran out, stomping our feet like children, declaring someone else to blame. Demanding we were owed more.

I wished I had trained harder and gotten more control over myself. Maybe then I would have the strength to work with the nectar. But time did not work like a fairytale. So many books and movies I had read and seen had everything fall into place at the exact moment. The happy ending. The hero was ready for the final battle and won.

Life was not like that. It didn't cater to you, to the outcome you wanted. I was not ready for war, but war was ready for me.

"Did I not wear you out enough, Kovacs?" A deep gravelly voice muttered in my ear, an arm wrapping around my middle, yanking me back into his naked body, tucking me into him, letting me feel he was more than ready to try again.

He understood and comforted me without a word after I checked on Esmeralda and Olek, both sleeping soundly as the healers moved around them, attending to their burns and other wounds.

Tad might be using Esmeralda, but she still had a human body that could be killed easily. She needed rest and time to heal.

My gaze had gone across the room to Hanna, Birdie, Olek, and Esmeralda. Shot, burned, and one of them a victim of the pills changing her DNA. In some way, it all came back to me. The weight of my guilt was pushing down on me, making it hard to remember why this was worth it.

"It's not on you, Kovacs." I had felt his shadow even before the real man entered the room. His huge frame stood behind me without touching me, but his shade slipped around me, running over my shoulders like a massage.

"Yes, it is." I didn't have the energy to link back.

"This would be happening with or without you. This is on Istvan. And don't for a moment forget you are also a victim of this. Caden, you, me, Rosie... Rebeka. And thousands more."

My gaze went to the person cleaning Birdie's healing wound. Rebeka. The woman I practically grew up with was glamorous, elegant, and poised. This woman was warm, relaxed, and grimy. She was hands-on, her clothes covered in blood, her face pure of anything but her own beauty. Not a doll or an armpiece. Rebeka looked alive.

Warwick's hand cupped mine, tugging me to follow.

"Where are we going?" I muttered, taking one last look over my shoulder at my friends.

"Shower and bed."

"I can't sleep."

"I know," his shadow mumbled against my neck while he led me back up the stairs. *"You don't think I know you, Kovacs? What you're feeling and thinking? You can watch them all night, hiding the fact that all you want is the nectar. To rip it out of Killian's hands and take it back."*

Inhaling sharply, I realized how much Warwick could see. Understand. Feel.

"I'm gonna get you to sleep, even if I have to make you black out." Warwick's shade nipped at my ear, pressing into me from behind. *"Gonna take two of us, I think."*

And fuck, he made good on that promise, using every surface between the shower and the bed. Both Warwick and his shadow took me so high I forgot anything but pleasure. His body gave me everything until my brain and body shut down.

At least for twenty minutes.

"Princess...?"

I tucked into him, fighting back the tears. "We're not ready." Though what I really meant was *I* wasn't ready.

"No one ever is. War stories are told in ways to glamorize them. Made to be heroic and honorable by history. But they never are. I have been through too many to know. No one is *ever* ready. Even when they think they are. They're horrific, cruel, violent, and most of the time not worth the death and destruction they cause." He brought both arms around me, encompassing me in his safe world. "I used to think fighting for hope and dying was better than living and suffering." He rolled me over onto my back, his aqua eyes burning through the dark, drilling into mine. He settled between my legs, opening up my hips. There was no warning or teasing. His thick cock pushed inside me, forcing a gasp from my lips.

"We were born in battle, Kovacs." He pulled back, thrusting back in again, my entire body igniting with fire, my heels digging into his taut ass with a loud groan. "Made from the blood and bones of war," he growled, driving in with force. "We've fucked, fought, and killed, rising from death. Becoming it." He grunted, keeping up the long, deep strokes, causing every muscle and nerve to tremble under him. "Nectar or not, do not forget who you are. What we are together. And we fucking survive, *Brexley...*"

With my name on his lips, his deep thrusts burned through me, spinning my mind, every letter being carved into

461

my bones like his speech was being engraved upon my soul. I felt my orgasm coming fast, his pace picking up, his teeth gritting as he clutched my jaw, forcing me to look at him.

"You are *The Grey*… and I am *your* Wolf."

My spine arched, my pussy clenching down on him. His roar shook the walls, wind whipping through the room. A spark of lightning flickered as his hot cum filled me, his hips still driving in, making me come again.

"Warwick!" I screamed, my eyes slamming shut as images flashed through my mind—us, covered in gore, walking through a battlefield. Flames, debris, and bodies scattered all over, determination set on our faces, our hands locked together.

The Grey and The Wolf.

Then darkness took hold of me, my consciousness plucked from my body.

"Brexley Kovacs, the girl who challenges nature's balance. Come with me." The old raspy inhuman voice spoke, and I felt the book suck me into it. Spinning and rolling, I fell through the pages, and it spit me out in a familiar room.

"What?" I gazed around the clinic I had been in only hours earlier. This time Birdie was awake. Caden sat in a chair next to her, his hands clasping hers. Their voices were too low to hear what they were talking about, and their expressions didn't give anything away. But I knew Caden better than anyone; the relief in his eyes was obvious. Birdie was going to be all right.

Scorpion was with Hanna. She faced away from him, but her eyes were open, and she stared at the wall, acting like he wasn't there. Her hair was wet, like she had just taken a shower. His damp head was bowed in hopelessness, though the moment I arrived, he glanced over his shoulder to where

I was as if he could sense me. Seeing nothing, his attention returned to Hanna, exhaustion and agony stenciled over his features.

Somehow I knew this was the current time, the book writing the story as we lived it.

"I asked it to bring you here."

I jumped, spinning to see Tad standing next to Esmeralda's bed. Solid and real. At least in here, he was more tangible than everyone else. He glowed with power, with light, love, and life.

"Tad." I couldn't help darting over to him, sighing at the feel of his arms hugging me back, the tickle of his long white hair on my face.

"Oh, it is good to really feel someone's touch again." He patted my back, pulling back with a smile. "I can feel the energy of touch through Esmeralda, but not the actual contact. It is her body experiencing it, not mine."

That made sense. Peering around, I shook my head. "Why are we here? Why did the book pull me in?"

"Because I asked it to," Tad replied, taking my hand in his as if he needed to absorb the sensation before it was gone again. "And it was kind enough to oblige me." He motioned to Esmeralda. "I can't go far. She needs me. Her body is very weak and getting here took a lot out of her."

Pain crunched my brows as I stared down at the sleeping woman.

"Bet she regrets the day I walked into her life," I puffed. "Lost her job, her family, her entire world. All because she was kind to me."

"Kind?" Tad chuckled, peering down at her fondly. "I guess she has her moments. You aren't the only one who disrupted her life." He shook his head. "Don't blame yourself. It was me who drew them to you and you to them. Esmeralda is very rare. Not many people are capable or have the strength for a Druid to take over their body. To find someone else like her was unlikely. I'm to blame for her situation." He squeezed my hand, letting it drop. "Though I think she would want it this way. She might complain, but I know firsthand what is inside her. She's exactly where she wants to be. No one, even me, can force that woman to do something she doesn't want."

I snorted. "That's true."

"Though her part in this is done."

"What?" A bolt of fear jumped up my throat. "She's going to be okay, right? She's not dying?"

"No, no. Esmeralda has many years left in her. She's too stubborn to die, don't you worry." Tad patted my hand. "Though her physical body is too weak to proceed in this war. What she did to get here, carrying Olek, carrying the nectar. Even if she wasn't conscious for most of it, it has taken a toll on her body. She needs to rest and heal now."

I nodded, agreeing. Esmeralda had done more than enough. As the thought rolled around in my head, my chin popped up, my eyes widening. "That means you too, right?"

Tad dipped his head in acknowledgment.

"But we need you. *I* need you," I exclaimed, feeling panic bubble up.

"My dear, I might not be in the form you've gotten used to, but I will always be around. And the stronger you grow in your own powers, the more you will find. I have never left your side."

Tears built up behind my lids. "But not now." I choked. "I'm not ready. I don't have enough control. Otherwise, you wouldn't have given the nectar to Killian."

"You might never have, my girl. It will always be part of you, a weakness you won't ever be able to fight."

"Killian does?"

"Yes, Killian has gained enough power to become the leader he was always meant to be. He no longer wants the nectar. He is the only one who can fight the draw to it." Tad folded his arms in front of him. "Though your uncle is a good man and has a good heart, he does not have that same conviction as Killian. Even Mykel knows deep down he would be weak against the call to it."

"It has grown stronger, hasn't it? I feel it. Like it's growing too."

"You and the nectar are too connected. Something I did not foresee was how it has copied you. The stronger you become, so does it."

I let out a breath, relieved Tad saw the same thing I did, though it scared me.

"What does that mean?"

"I do not know. It only confirms the substance is far too dangerous to be out in the world. Especially around you."

"But it's part of me," I lashed back.

"You cannot look at it with an impartial view. You do not see clearly when it comes to the nectar." He shook his head. "Look at how powerful you are on your own. You are a miracle. A phenomenon of nature. A marvel. Do not think that the nectar makes you whole. It does not. It will only turn you into something you are not."

"So what? We destroy it?" The thought made my stomach turn.

"Can magic like that be destroyed?" He said it in such a way I knew it couldn't. "The only way is to make it disappear. Hide it from even yourself."

"What does that mean—"

My sentence was cut off as Esmeralda's body flung up, her eyes glazed, her voice pitching like an alarm.

"THEY ARE HERE!"

I stiffened, my attention snapping to Tad. He jerked his head up like he was seeing and hearing something I couldn't.

"They have come…" Panic widened his eyes.

"Who?"

"Go, Brexley!" He yelled as the book sucked me back, a cry flinging from my throat as it tossed me back into my body, my eyes bolting open to the room Warwick and I shared.

He sensed something the moment my lids flew up, feeling the alarm slam through my chest, terror stiffening my limbs. I vaulted out of bed, grabbing my clothes as gunfire ricocheted off the mountains and trees outside. The vibration of vehicles shot through my toes to my heart.

I knew who had come. What they were coming for.

Markos was bringing the war to us.

Chapter 35
Scorpion

She stayed facing the wall, staring blankly at it, her body curled defensively away from me. I probably should have left her alone, given her the space she wanted.

I couldn't.

I had tried for ten minutes and then found myself back down here. She was where I wanted to be. Even if she didn't want me here. I knew deep down a part of her did. I knew she didn't want me to give up until one, or both, of us were dead. I couldn't. It wasn't a choice. It was fact. I would go down fighting to get my girl back.

"Do you remember the time you bit me?" I whispered. The clinic was in night mode, most asleep, the night giving way to the morning hours. "You drew blood. That's why I started calling you little viper." The memory made me chuckle lightly. "Fuck, I pretended you drove me nuts, and you did, but I never left, did I? Was always on your watch duty." I recounted the excuses I gave myself and others, why I would take another shift, why I wouldn't let anyone else watch her. "I don't think I stood a chance." I brushed my fingers through her knotted, dirty, blonde hair. Grime covered her face, and she still reeked of herbs and hours of being on that train.

Staring down at her, she hadn't moved a muscle. She was empty. Vacant. My memories of us were getting me nowhere. I was losing her.

I stood before my brain even registered the command, unlocking the cuffs keeping her to the bed.

"Get up." I pulled her up. Her eyes tracked me but didn't fight.

"What are you doing?" A healer hopped over to us, her eyes bugging out.

"Shower?" It was less a question and more a demand.

The healer pointed to a doorway in the back, a worried expression on her face. And I didn't know if it was for me or Hanna.

"Come on." The anger at Hanna, at myself, trudged up my shoulders as I stalked back to the bathroom, yanking her with me.

The healer's protest died as I slammed the door to the restroom, fire bulbs flicking on, bathing the windowless room in a buttery light, taking me back to the first I dragged her from a cot into the showers and forced her to start living again. We had come full circle; the only thing changed was how I felt about her. Then I was still pretending, pushing it back, ignoring what was in my gut.

I couldn't lie to myself now.

The vast room had been built for soldiers and staff with multiple shower stalls and areas to get ready. It was simple, but nicer than most places I'd been in. Compared to prison, this place was a luxury.

I marched us to one of the stalls, turning on the water. "We've been here before, Hanna. You can shower with your clothes on or off, but this time the door stays open. Got it?"

Hanna's narrowed gaze went from the shower to me.

"Decide, little viper, or I will."

Her nose flared, a sign of emotion. She held up her cuffed hands, her head tilting.

"What do you want?" I lifted an eyebrow. "Use your words."

She glowered at me.

"You had enough to say on the train." Even though I understood she was going through withdrawals, her declarations still sliced through me like a blade had been left in my gut, and it kept cutting in deeper and deeper.

The healers told me the drugs should be through her system by now, but she was far from okay. Her brain might be too fried to ever be herself again. The idea made me crazy, and I wanted to push her until I saw life in her eyes. Until I saw Hanna somewhere in there.

She wiggled her arms. "Off."

My heart took a sick leap at hearing her voice. Scratchy, raw, and low, but it was a start.

"You can wash with them on." I nodded to the water, checking the temperature with my hand.

"Not if I want to undress." A purr slunk up the back of my neck, making my body jolt and my dick harden. "Don't pretend you didn't want to watch me last time." She started to unbutton her pants. "I could feel your need to fuck me then. Go ahead, Scorpion, take what you want. I know how rough you like it."

My eyes shot to hers, her blue gaze on me like she was hunting prey. Hungry. *Bazdmeg,* I wanted to kiss her, push her against the wall and forget the fact I knew she was trying to trick me.

Tug at a man's dick, and our brains seem to unravel.

"Nice try." I grabbed her cuffs, pulling her under the spray, the water gliding down, sticking her clothes to her.

469

She smirked as she watched me adjust myself.

"Need help with that?"

I ground my teeth, handing a shampoo bottle to her. At least I had her talking, though now I wasn't sure it was a good thing.

"Looks like you might need this too?" She poured the soap into her hand, running it through her hair, her eyes on me.

My body responded to her; my desire for her had me clutching the stall door, trying to stay upright. It was instinctual, the need to take her. Have her again. Claim her as mine, making sure she had no mistake in what it meant. I had only been inside her once, and it made me feel I was the one going through withdrawals. Craving a drug I would never recover from.

She fully turned to me, her fingers undoing her pants, the shampoo bottle falling out of her hands.

"Oops."

I was already bending down, grabbing the bottle, when I realized my mistake. The tone of her voice was filled with sugary fakeness.

Stupid asshole.

I twisted just as her knee flew up to my face, hitting my ear. I stumbled, my equilibrium tilting, when metal cuffs rammed across my temple and cracked my nose, making me fall into the wall. Her elbows dug into my back as she tried to slip by me. I pushed off the wall to lurch for her, my hands reaching out, wrapping around the cuffs as she started to run. The wet floor and soap slipped her back as I used all my force to yank her into the wall, slamming her head and spine into the tile.

Anger billowed off me, my chest heaving as I moved in under the stream of water, tasting the blood from my nose wash down my lips.

"Bad move, little viper. You keep thinking you can get away from me," I snarled, pushing my body into hers. "Haven't you learned by now that there is nowhere you can go, nowhere you can run, that I won't find you?"

Her body heaved into mine, her blue eyes glittering with hate. I could feel the life in her veins, the desire in her blood. *The hunger.* For a moment, all I saw was Hanna. The girl that fought me at Sarkis's base with fire and passion. The girl who had lost her parents, who had been abused in prison, who had been through hell and back. The girl who fucked me with fury in the woods.

My hands gripped her jaw, my mouth coming down on hers with savagery, my tongue slipping past her lips, ruthlessly demanding entry. There wasn't even a moment of pause as she responded, a deep groan rolling her body into mine, her nails scratching through my wet hair, making me lose my shit. Her thin fingers tore at my pants, shoving them down my thighs as I ripped her tank over her head, wrapping around her cuffs, exposing her bare breasts. I pinned her manacled hands against the wall, my lips slipping over her skin, taking her nipple in my mouth, hearing her moan as I sucked and tugged on it. Her body bucked into mine as I claimed the other.

"Scorpion…" It was so soft, but it hit so deep in my soul. The need, want, and love in three syllables. It turned everything rational off, turning us both into animals. I wanted to taste her, lick her everywhere, explore every inch of her body.

"Fuck me," she demanded, her eyes sharp and bright, her teeth biting my lip until I tasted blood. "I need you."

"Be careful, little viper." I yanked down her pants, shredding her thin underwear. "Cats might bite." I grabbed her hips, and she wrapped her legs around me, my cock parting her folds. "But a Scorpion has a deadly sting." I drove

471

into her, pleasure rippling over me so severely that I had to palm the wall behind her, my legs quaking as the intensity grew.

A frenzied cry, full of pleasure and pain, came from Hanna, her nails digging into my back, clawing at me and cutting into my flesh.

It only made me crazier for her as she gave it back, climbing higher on me to plunge herself harder on me.

"Fuck! Fuck!" I couldn't stay upright, the connection between us too much, my legs taking me down to the wet tile floor, the water cascading on us. The shift in position hit her deeper, and she pushed me back, riding me so ruthlessly that my spine started to tingle. Grabbing her hips, I pulled her up to my head, her thighs locking around my face with wails of pleasure as my tongue and lips sucked, licked, and nipped at her pussy, holding nothing back. My hands cupped her breasts, twisting and flicking at her nipples.

"Scorpion!" I loved her crying out my name, hearing the girl I knew screaming out for me. "Oh gods, I'm coming."

"Not yet." I tugged her off, wanting to come inside her. Sliding her back down my body, I sat her on my lap. Roughly, I held her chin. "Watch me, Hanna." She tried to turn her head, but I forced it back. "I need you here with me. Do not take your eyes off me." My hips lifted, driving back into her, our mouths parting. It felt so fucking good. There was nothing else like it. I never counted on finding my mate, I never cared to, but as I pumped into her, her eyes on mine, feeling what it was like to be inside her, to have her in my life. I never wanted to be without. I understood Hanna was hanging on by a thread, that only intimacy, a moment she could hold on to when all was lost, might save her from falling. I would be her rope, her rock, or her punching bag. Whatever it took. I would be that for her.

With each stroke, I forced her gaze on mine. "What am I to you, Hanna?" Her lids closed as I arched higher into her. "No, look at me."

"Just fuck me," she seethed, trying to move me faster, the intimacy itching at her.

"No." I gripped her jaw harder, keeping my strokes long and deep. "What am I to you, Hanna?" I said more firmly.

"Nothing," she growled. "Just someone to fuck."

Ignoring the strike of pain, I picked up my pace, seeing her eyes glaze, her moans puffing from her chest.

"Watch me," I growled, feeling angry and hurt. "Feel me come inside you." I flipped her on her back, my hand on her throat, keeping her head pointed at me as I pounded the fuck out of her.

Hanna's lips parted in a silent scream, her entire body exploding around me, gripping my dick so hard I bellowed, my seed spilling in waves into her as I thrust into her again.

For one moment, our eyes connected, and the bond between us tightened. Hanna was fully with me, her eyes pleading for me to hear the words she didn't say. I swear it was like her voice sank into my gut, burning into me.

I need you. Don't give up on me.

In a blink, that girl was gone.

Her lids narrowed, and she used her cuffed hands to push away from me, my seed dripping out of her, washing away under the stream.

"Hope to knock me up?" she fumed. "Tie me to you forever."

"Almost all fae take precautions as teenagers." There had been too many problems with humans dying, not able to hold a fae child to term. Nor did we want to get fae women pregnant either. We were a fertile bunch. Tree Fairies had a birth control concoction that could only be undone with

473

another brew. Though I heard with Druids, it didn't work as well.

She stood up, not looking at me, her jaw clenched. I was still leaking down her leg, but it was as if I was nothing but a stranger.

Shutting off the water, I sighed heavily, my body and mind wanting to sleep.

"Come on. Get dressed." I picked up some fresh clothes stacked on the shelf, dressing her in loose pants and a tank. I quickly clothed in extra black military pants and a black t-shirt and ran my hands through my hair. I dragged Hanna back to her bed.

I could feel the healer's eyes on me. I knew she heard us. Hell, the entire house probably did.

Hanna crawled back onto her cot, turning over and facing the wall. It was like we never left this room. The moment in the shower never happened.

I was back to square one.

Leaning over my legs, I rubbed my head with frustrated exhaustion while my body zinged with energy, my dick already wanting more, but I felt so heavy and… sad.

My skin prickled, feeling as if Brexley had walked into the room. I turned to greet her, but nobody was there.

I noticed Caden was now down here, sitting with Birdie, both talking quietly, but no Brexley.

It felt odd, because her energy danced around me, but not even her shadow was there.

Scouring my face, my attention went back to Hanna.

I need you. Don't give up on me.

"I won't, little viper," I muttered. "You're mine."

Hanna's head jerked slightly, her blue eyes staring back, her mouth opening to speak.

I never got to hear her words, what she might have said

in response, before gunfire shattered through the peace. Screams and bellows found us all the way underground, the earth vibrating as heavy engines moved in.

There were no more days, hours, or even minutes.

The war had begun.

Chapter 36
Brexley

Alarms blared, and people ran in every direction amid the gunfire and screams. Everything had turned into chaos. My mind was moving a million miles a minute. I had no recollection of getting dressed or running to the foyer, my hand on my gun, ready to proceed.

Mykel was already in action, pointing and shouting out orders to the army here.

"Brexley?" Ember jogged up to me, her different colored eyes sharp and focused, like she had flipped a switch to fight mode. Eli stood right next to her with the same level of intensity. No wonder they made good bounty hunters; they were intimidating and badass together.

"It's Markos," I said with conviction. "He's coming for the nectar... for me."

"And taking out a fae lord probably wouldn't hurt," Warwick muttered.

"Contact Lorcan and Cole." Ember turned to Eli. "Get them here as soon as possible. We need everyone they can get."

"Already on it." He nodded, tapping at his head.

"Brexley!" My name was shouted again, and I whipped my head to see Killian and Rosie darting toward me.

"Where's the nectar?"

Before Killian could answer, a shrill screech from a speaker rent the air, Istvan's voice barking over it with arrogance and disdain.

"There is no point in fighting. I have this place surrounded. You are outgunned and outmanned, Killian. Unless you want pointless bloodshed for your people, come out." There was a pause. Silence took the house as if we were all holding our breaths. "And Brexley, I know what you are hiding. Bring it to me, or every person here dies. If you try your powers, the children will die first. The hostages I have right now... their brains will be on the ground because of your actions."

Rot took root in my stomach, swishing acid up into my throat. I wouldn't put it past him. He would do it.

Killian's muscles tightened, both of us looking at each other, the weight falling on us. The connection between Killian and me would always be there. An understanding, magic which came from ruling. Even if I had never personally had the experience, it was in my DNA to step up like a queen. To lead. And in that moment, I made peace with that part of myself. To accept Aneira's magic was part of me. To stop fearing it and use it.

Out of all of us, it was really Ember who was the rightful heir to the throne. I never asked her why she didn't become queen, why her friend did instead. Though, seeing her and Eli, I could see being a bounty hunter was the perfect role for her.

Killian and I glanced at each other, then together, we stepped outside, a spotlight shining from a tank, forcing me to hold up my hand to block my eyes. Blinking, I adjusted to the opposing darkness and light, seeing two tanks, armored cars, and hundreds of guards curving around the property, the front gate under the tank's wheels. At least a dozen of our guards, who had been monitoring the gate, were dead. The others were being held at gunpoint.

Killian and I walked down the porch, our own people moving out of our way as we made our way to the demolished gate. Istvan stood between the two tanks, soldiers surrounding him. Air fluttered in my lungs, but I locked down my jaw, pushing my shoulders back, giving nothing away.

"I got your back, princess." Warwick's shade brushed down my spine, giving me more strength with each step. *"Need me, just take."* His strength, his magic, his energy—it was all mine if I required it.

I wanted so badly to use my magic. My body thrummed with desire, but I swallowed the impulse back, not wanting to escalate things.

A smug smile curved Istvan's mouth. "Let's not drag this out. This doesn't have to get messy as long as you give me what I came for."

Snorting, I stared at Markos, realizing I would have been standing behind him at one time. No questions asked. Rationalizing whatever he was doing was for the better. I was on the right side.

Now I was standing in direct opposition.

"I don't know what you think we have," Mykel spoke up behind me.

"Oh, yes, Mykel *Kovacs*." Istvan's glare rolled over him like he was a bug. "Do you know, Benet hardly spoke of you? When he did, it was always in embarrassment and shame." Istvan used words like a knife, twisting and spearing them in your chest. "I can see why. It's sad you think you have the right to be standing here. That you are a player… or have any

478

power. You are nothing now. Your little rebel group has been wiped off the field. Soon you will be joining them." He turned back to me with his icy glare, his arm rising, his fingers tapping at the trigger of the gun he pointed at Mykel. "You want to watch another uncle die in front of you? I suggest you bring me the nectar now."

A whip of wind curved through the trees, snapping branches. A zap of electricity crackled in the air, my fear and anger calling the spirits from the thousands of graves peppering this area. In cemeteries or unknown tombs, ghosts were plentiful in war-torn countries.

"Brexley…" Something tickled at the back of my neck, my name so wispy, I was sure I imagined it, but I knew it wasn't Warwick.

Istvan's gaze went up to where the lightning struck, his tongue clicking. "What did I tell you, Brexley? My finger is faster than whatever you can conjure."

"Want to bet?" I growled, feeling the wind snap at my hair. The spirits swirled in, bowing to my power, waiting for an order.

Pop!

A cry screamed out, whipping my head in the direction of my uncle, my stomach plunging to the ground. Mykel stood there, his eyes wide, his hand going to his ear, blood leaking down his neck.

The man right behind him dropped to the ground, a bullet between his eyes.

"Next time, I shoot your last living relative," Istvan declared. Like with Caden, this was no mistake. Istvan was a true marksman. He would go down to the shooting range in the basement of HDF for hours to "unwind." He would not miss unless it was on purpose.

It was a threat.

479

"Give me the nectar, Brexley, or my next bullet is for your lover." He sneered at Warwick behind me.

My powers hummed in my veins, the ghosts stirring restlessly, some pushing my line and brushing over the soldiers in back, unsettling the horses and men, pulling focus for just a moment.

It was enough.

Warwick moved with me like he knew each step before I took it. We pounced on Istvan's first line as I let the ghosts attack the ones from behind, creating chaos and diversion. Spinning, punching, and kicking, our guns fired. Caden and a healed Birdie were near Warwick. The tie between Warwick and Caden was extraordinary to watch. Their movements were perfectly synced, each knowing what the other would do, taking down men from every direction. Yin and yang. Shooting directly into their heads, making sure the super soldiers were dead.

I felt my energy being divided. I had yet to fully learn to control the ghosts while continuing to fight. It took a lot of me to keep the two going, and with one false move, one moment my focus was not sharp, I could be killed.

A shrill horn blared through the megaphone on Istvan's armored car, jolting the sound through my bones as he did it again.

"Stop!" Istvan's voice demanded. "Or you watch her die."

A woman's whimper gripped at my heart, swinging me toward Istvan. He stood behind a female who was on her knees, his hand cruelly ripping her head back to display the knife at her throat, blood already trickling down.

"Nooooo!" Killian bellowed, the cry guttural and terrified.

Acid burned up my throat and into my eyes.

Rosie.

Everything stopped. No one moved or breathed, watching Rosie swallow, her eyes leaking, but she made no other sound, her expression defiant.

How the hell did he get to her? Did he know who she was? Pick her out on purpose?

I knew he did.

"I'm done asking nicely." Istvan glanced over at Killian. I don't know how Istvan seemed to always know, but he learned of Rosie's importance. A weakness that would bend the lord to his knees. "Give me the nectar, or you will watch her choke on her own blood before I cut through her spinal cord."

"Please, don't hurt her." Killian held up his hands, his eyes pleading. I watched panic and terror take over Killian. The cool, collected fae lord, who never let emotion control him, was gone, his sole focus on his mate.

"Then you know what you need to do."

"Killian, don't." Rosie shook her head, flinching as Istvan's blade cut deeper.

Killian stared at her for a few beats. His gaze swung to me; it was full of agony, but not conflict. This wasn't a choice for him. I understood. If it was Warwick there, I would hand over the world.

Istvan took his pause as hesitation. The blade sliced deeper through Rosie's soft skin, a cry pushing through her teeth while blood cascaded down her neck.

"Stop!" Killian jolted for her, his hand yanking something from his pocket, pulling out a small, wrapped object.

My attention went to the item, my gut twisting, realizing what was about to happen. What we were about to lose. Everything in me wanted to fight, to keep it from Istvan. The world went into slow motion. Killian's shaky hands held out the nectar to Markos. Istvan reached out, tongue sliding over his lip, his eyes glowing with greed. Hunger. Desire. Power.

My mouth opened, but it wasn't my scream which screeched with terror and pain. The sound of metal slicing through human flesh resonated loudly in the air, bodies hitting the frozen ground. Confusion scrambled my head, but my body hummed with recognition, knowing before I did.

One after another, cries of fear and death rose from Istvan's officers from behind him, the darkness concealing the assailants.

"Daughter…" The voice nipped at the back of my neck, sending chills down my skin. It was the same voice that called me earlier.

I stopped, air seizing in my lungs when I noticed the moonlight reflecting off sharp metal scythes. Hooded figures silently slipped out from the trees, descending on Istvan's men, their figures swiftly cutting down people before they even knew they were dead.

They were the stuff of chilling nightmares.

Death's elite soldiers.

Necromancers.

"Mo-mom?" I croaked, picking out her slight frame and scythe, twirling and slicing through bodies, making her way to Istvan. Morgan fought right by her side.

Eabha's head jerked to me, but I couldn't see anything but darkness under her hood. No emotion or life could be sensed from her, though I felt her eyes piercing me. There were no words, but I still seemed to understand. They had been with me the whole time. Watching. Protecting. Waiting. It wasn't Eli and Ember who led Istvan and Kalaraja to us. It was the necromancers. They knew where the necromancers went, the nectar was.

My mother turned away, her sole focus on Istvan. They

had stopped it from slipping into the wrong hands. It was their clan's creed, their mission—to protect the nectar at all costs, and once again, I failed. Not able to keep it safe, and now they were here to save us from catastrophe.

Their entrance gave us the moment we needed. Our group seized the opportunity without hesitation and charged the enemy without hesitation.

"Attack!" Markos demanded, his men lurching at us. "Get the nectar!"

Warwick knocked Killian out of the way, getting the nectar farther out of Istvan's grasp, as he lunged for the guards coming at us.

Pandemonium broke out, magic pumping through my body, calling for my own invisible soldiers. A flash of lightning danced in the sky as wind sliced through the trees, knocking into Istvan's men. My spirits attacked his troops, my mind focused on Istvan as I cut through some of his army, but my energy waned trying to concentrate on fighting and controlling the spirits.

"Burn it down to the ground!" Istvan screamed out the order, motioning to the house as he grabbed Rosie, dragging her with him, using her as a shield to protect him from any shots headed his way. Istvan's troops moved in, lighting torches, some with bows and arrows on fire, shooting them off onto the roof of the house or straight through windows.

Screams of terror and death rang in the sky as fire gnawed at the house, consuming it quickly. The wind I was creating only spread the fire quicker.

"There are still people inside!" With a child on her hip, Rebeka screamed, helping a few patients who weren't well enough to walk on their own. Kids were crying, and people ran in and out, trying to save anyone still inside as gunfire sprayed through the air.

Kitty was getting people out of the house, hiding the more vulnerable from the fight.

The sound of the engines turned over, the tanks moving, jerking my head toward them. What was left of Markos's group climbed into their armored cars, their wheels spinning over the gravel.

"Hanna! No!" Scorpion's voice thundered, cracking through my heart. I whirled around to see him, his expression trying to hide the desperation he was feeling. "Please. You don't want to do this. Not again."

Hanna stood only yards from us, her face blank, but her blue eyes were filled with turmoil as her body leaned toward the faux-fae leaving.

"Look at me, little viper. *Only me.*" Scorpion spoke calmly as the world around us was literally on fire. "I know you're still there. You can fight it. You are stronger than them."

A sob hitched her throat, her head bowing.

"Hanna. Do not take your eyes off me," he urged, jerking her chin back up. "I need you, little viper. Focus on me. Remember how it felt earlier when I was inside you. The connection between us." He inched closer to her like she was a feral animal. "I know you're scared and tired. And don't want to fight it anymore, but please don't give up."

"I-I can't." Her shoulders sagged.

"Yes, you can. You are fierce and strong, and you don't back down from anything." He inched even closer to her.

"I'm not her anymore. I am not one of you. He's turned me into a monster." She sounded resigned. "I just want it all to end."

"No," he growled. "You think I care if you're fucked up?" His own ire shot back at her. "What I've done, who I am... I'm a fucked up, broken mess too." He took another

484

step toward her. "It's why we work, Hanna. Why you need me as much as I need you."

She shook her head, a tear sliding down her face. "You say that now, but what if I turn fully into one of his freak monsters? You saw them. They're mindless killers. My brain is going to dissolve and bleed out my nose. I'm going to die."

"We don't know that."

She gave him a look.

"Well, sweetheart, I will build you the most luxurious crate, feed you steak dinners, and hope you'll let me rub your belly from time to time."

A sobbing laugh came from her.

The vehicles started to pull away, ripping her attention from Scorpion to the troop leaving. The one that called to her, but she didn't belong to.

She belonged with us.

Her feet went in their direction, her body starting to follow.

"No." Scorpion leaped forward, his hand clamping down on hers, yanking her into him. She struggled against him, a cry baying out, but Scorpion wrapped his arms tighter around her, holding her to him as Istvan's caravan rolled out, leaving death and destruction behind. "Dig deep, little viper. Hold on to anything you need to keep you here with me. Just stay with me. Forever."

She sobbed into his chest as if the entire world was breaking, her knees dipping. He went to the ground with her, holding her to his chest and rocking, repeating over and over, "I got you."

The love I experienced through our link, what he felt for her, almost dropped me. He didn't just love her. Hanna was his soul. The person he would destroy the world for. And if anything happened to her…

"Kovacs." Warwick's voice twirled me to him, and I wrapped my arms around him, needing his comfort and warmth. He kissed my head before looking past me to the raging fire, his brows crinkling at the sight.

"Rosie?!" Killian roared, ripping me from Warwick's embrace, finding the man, wounded and bleeding, limping after the already departed caravan. *"Rosie!"* His heart bled out on the gravel, his legs dipping to the ground in anguish as he stared off down the dark road.

Oh gods…

Rosie.

My head jerked around; I hoped she was still here somewhere, but I knew.

Istvan took her.

Hostage. Revenge. To hurt us because he didn't get what he wanted.

I ran to Killian, crouching next to him.

"He took her," he heaved out.

"I know." I held his face, his wild eyes meeting mine.

"We have to go get her."

"We are. We'll get her back," I agreed. I knew Istvan was heading straight for Budapest. This was supposed to be just a pit stop. Get the nectar and destroy Sonya and anyone else who stood in his way.

He may have not gotten the nectar, but he took something vital to us anyway.

Killian pulled the nectar from his pocket, shoving it at me. "You take it."

I sucked in, feeling its power. The need to touch it, top off my own power, set my jaw.

"No," I whispered. "I can't."

Killian's violet eyes lifted to mine. "I am no longer worthy," he snarled. "I gave it up without hesitation for her.

486

And I will again. Even if I knew we'd all die anyway... I'd still do it." He held it out. "Take it, Brexley. I am not strong enough. I would let this world burn for her."

My hands shook as I claimed the prize, dread and tranquility filling me the moment I touched the wrapped object. It was both my savior and my doom.

Swallowing, I tucked the nectar in my pocket, locking my gaze on Killian.

"We will get her back." I grabbed his arm, getting his full attention. "But I need Killian, the fae lord. Focused. Ruthless. Cutthroat. I will not lose you because you can't get your head together. I need you all in. Do you understand?"

His eyes tracked mine, his chin lifting, his jaw locking. "Yes."

"Good." I stood up, pulling him with me. "Because we are going into battle. Not just for Rosie, but to save this country."

"We don't have the numbers," Mykel said, walking up to us. "We have even less now... and we have people hurt. And no food or water." He motioned back to the burning house, reduced to nothing but flames.

"Is everyone out?" Killian asked.

"Yes." Mykel nodded, glancing back at where Rebeka and Kitty were caring for the children and elderly. I spotted Esmeralda and Olek bundled up with other patients and babies against a tree far from the fire, awake and surrounded by healers.

"I have extra food, water, and supplies in my bunker," Killian told Mykel. "Along with more weapons."

"We still don't have the people we need to fight this war."

Mykel was right; we didn't have the numbers. Not even close. Between Sonya's troops and Istvan's, and now possibly Romania, it wasn't even a contest. We were fucked.

487

We had no chance.

"Daughter." A chill bit at the back of my head, darting my head to the seven figures hovering at the edge of the woods. So much had taken my focus from them, though I never forgot my mother had saved us from losing everything.

Eabha's voice was still low, but it was clear, ringing in my mind. We still had that connection, it seemed—at least this close. But it wasn't words she spoke to me. It was images.

"We can let them fight it out first." Mykel ran his hand over his beard in frustration.

"I am *not* sitting back and leaving Rosie with him to wait it out." Killian seethed, gesturing in the direction she was taken. "I will go my fucking self if I have to."

"And get yourself killed too?" Mykel yelled back.

"I don't care!" He got in Mykel's face.

Mykel pushed him back. "Don't be an idiot. *Think!*"

"Stop it! Both of you!" I stepped between them, my palms pushing them apart. "We are going to get her. We're going to fight for our country."

"How?" Mykel motioned around. "We can't! We are not even a drop in the bucket compared to their troops."

"What if I said we could have the numbers?"

"What?" Both Killian and Mykel stopped, peering at me with confusion.

My black eyes lifted, finding the ones across the yard almost identical to mine.

"You have enough weapons here for an army?" I kept my sight forward but spoke to Killian.

"Yes." He nodded. "I have several underground bunkers here with weapons, motorbikes, and cars. Whatever you can think of. It was built to fight against an attack."

"Good." I didn't waver from the intensity of my mother's stare. Her clan stayed in close ranks beside her. "Because we will have the bodies to carry them."

Chapter 37
Warwick

"This is fucking insane, Kovacs," I muttered more to myself, though she heard me just fine through our link. The purr of motorcycles, Hummers, and trucks, filled with weapons and bombs and what was left of our army, moved toward the heart of Budapest. A few horses Markos left behind followed Zander's lead, my sister on the horse-shifter's back, perched high, her expression set with determination, reminding me so much of mother.

They had the same stubbornness.

"Eliza, you aren't going." I had practically stomped my foot when we were gathering up supplies earlier.

"Excuse me?" She tipped her head, her hands on her hips.

"What about Simon?" I motioned to where Esmeralda was reading stories to the children to keep them calm and occupied. While Olek, still hooked to an IV, had some of the elderly folk at a picnic bench, following his steps in creating bombs. The feeble old human was a hell of a lot stronger than he looked.

Morning had come with dreary, cloudy skies, which

only seemed to shadow and highlight the burned-down remains of the house. Everyone had made it out, but like the heavy ash in the air, tension and fear filtered in your lungs with every breath. We all knew what was ahead. What the chances were.

"This is my fight too, *brother.*" Eliza glared at me.

"I can't have something happen to you." I almost seethed, my voice low. "Simon needs you."

"I won't sit back."

"Your son would rather have you alive."

She hissed, stepping back. It was harsh, but I needed my sister to understand. To hear the truth.

"I may not be as skilled as you, but I can fight. And I *will* fight. For this country, for me, and mostly for Simon." She challenged me. "I want my son to have a future. To be proud of his country. Proud that his mother, uncle, and all the people who love him, stood up and fought. Fought for freedom, for others, for what was right." She turned around and strode over to where Wesley, Ash, and Lukas were handing out weapons to all those coming with us.

"Stubborn, pig-headed, and proud." Kovacs slipped up next to me, nudging me with her shoulder.

"Right? She's being impossible."

"I was talking about you." Brexley peered up at me with a wink. "But those traits run deep in the Farkas family."

I sighed, a frown crinkling my brows with the realization that my mate was ten times more obstinate than my sister.

I was fucked. Though I knew that from day one.

Determination and pride weren't just a Brexley or Eliza trait. Strength and fight was bred into the DNA of the people of this land. The Eastern bloc had always been at war, suffering starvation and fighting tyranny at every turn. There was never a day we weren't battling for one or all. We fought, we scraped, and we survived, even if everything fell around us. We had leaders come and go—freedom and democracy always sliding one way or the other. But the people here never gave up. It was all we knew, and we got up and continued to fight.

"Insane, but it's all we've got." Brexley's shade against my ear snapped me back to the present, responding to my muttering. Her arms and thighs latched around me, spearing warmth down my vertebrae. The feel of her, the intangible bonds tying us together, the thought of ever being without her—terror so deep shot through me, locking every muscle down at the idea. I knew without a doubt that wherever she went, I would go too, whether in life, death, or somewhere in between.

Ash drove the Hummer right behind me, Killian forced to take the passenger seat, Lukas and Kek in the back. We had barely kept Killian from going after Istvan immediately, getting himself killed. I had known Killian for a long time. Never once had I seen his controlled, aloof demeanor drop. Torturing or leading, he held the same reserved, regal manner. Ruthless when he wanted something. Always above, always collected. That was until Rosie. For once, there was nothing I could fault him on, because if it had been Brexley instead? No one could have kept me from going after her. The notion that Istvan would have taken Kovacs if the opportunity had been given to him made me want to rip the man apart, but instead he used Killian's weakness to escape.

Caden and Birdie rode on a motorcycle slightly behind us, Eli and Ember on our other side. Scorpion, Hanna, and Wesley were in a truck in the middle, while Kitty, Rebeka, and Mykel drove in a Hummer at the back. The rest of the group were riding horses, in trucks, or on motorcycles. Our group was barely a hundred people now.

Sunset had already dipped the temperatures, the night seeping in, making it harder to be seen but also more difficult to see enemies hiding. It was obvious Istvan had already come through here. Dead bodies of Sonya's soldiers lay where they dropped at all the roadblocks into the city. The eerie quiet was thick with souls still hovering near, crawling against my skin. Through Brexley, I could feel the spirits, as if they had died so fast and unaware that they didn't realize they were no longer living.

Turning off the main motorway, I could see the dome of HDF peeking above the tops of the buildings. So many times, I had looked upon it with hatred. It represented power, greed, and oppression, while the rest of us suffered in Savage Lands. Now it meant something different to me. A symbol of potential, of what our country could be, of what we were fighting for. It belonged to all of us.

We descended into the city, following the wall that had protected Leopold and its wealthy for so long. My skin bristled with magic. The air was thick with unmistakable tension. It was palpable, sticking in my throat.

Caden and Brexley both knew Istvan would bring the fight here. He needed to reclaim his sector, to take back what he considered *his*. To let it go would show weakness. He either took it back, or he'd burn it to the ground. No in between.

I was ready for troops, tanks, and weapons. I had seen it all before. Though this time, when we rolled to a stop at the edge of the wall, I felt every bone in my body go cold.

I wasn't prepared.

"Bazdmeg." Fuck.

From Liberty Park to the river, it was a sea of endless soldiers standing in perfectly spaced rows. Thousands of faux-fae, dozens of tanks, and just as many cannons surrounded Leopold, at attention, ready for Istvan's order.

492

The troops in front were silent, robotic, which pulled your attention toward the back, to those who no longer appeared zombie-like, but *monsters*. They shifted on their feet, sounds gurgling in their throats, looking like predators ready to attack. The unnaturalness of either group crawled over my skin. Istvan was bending nature, trying to control it, changing and manipulating the laws. Humans, in their pursuit of power and money, never seemed to learn that if you messed with nature, it usually fought back.

Guards dressed with Sonya's emblem on their chests lined the tops of the walls along with guns and cannons around Leopold, pointing back at Istvan's troop. This would be a blood bath.

"Andor!" The same speaker Istvan used on us blared through the night, darting my eyes to the tank behind the troops at the gate, his "special elite guards" around him, the ones who were rich enough to be created in the water tanks. Smart. Strong. In control. Making them even more deadly. "Come out and face me, traitor. Though what did I expect from you? You have always been a coward. Weak and pathetic. Always hiding behind someone else's strength because you had none. So scared you bow before a woman. Turn against your own people to save yourself."

The silence lasted for a long time. Istvan wasn't one to speak and get ignored. His ego was too prideful to be slighted.

I heard an order shout through his troop, two cannons rolling closer to the gate.

"You've become predictable, Markos. Your bruised ego is easy to foresee." A voice rang out from the walkway high along the wall. Andor stepped up, examining Istvan from his perch. "It's made you blind to what lurks behind. Your greed and obsession will be your downfall." A smirk twisted Andor's mouth, but it was Istvan who laughed.

493

"Oh, Henrik…" Istvan clicked his tongue. "It is you who could never see the bigger picture, who never understood what it takes to be a true leader."

"Really?" Andor smugness stretched his shoulders back, peering up at a building behind Markos. "You overinflated your skills, Markos. Always have. It is you who has a gun pointed at your head. My sniper is ready to drop you where you stand before you can even blink.

Istvan let out a malicious laugh. "You are such a fool. I am already ten steps ahead of you. So gullible to think he was on your side." Istvan's head lifted, nodding just slightly, signaling his next move.

The recoil of a gun was barely caught on the wind before Andor's body jolted in shock as a bullet drove between his eyes. He blinked in shock, his expression in utter disbelief that he had been caught so off guard. That bullet was meant for Istvan and not him. His body collapsed, falling over the wall onto the ground with a crunch. My head followed the trajectory, going to the top of the building behind Markos.

"Fuck," Killian whispered next to me, his attention on the same thing, understanding what we all did.

Kalaraja.

He had never left Istvan.

The man we thought had turned to Sonya and Andor's side was a spy the whole time. Not that I was shocked at all. I was more surprised Kalaraja had any loyalty to anything. I guess Markos was still paying him more.

"I will kill that sick mother fucker," Killian gritted through his teeth.

I hated Kalaraja. I would love to gut him alive, but I picked up Killian's history with this asshole. I would enjoy it, but Killian *needed* it.

"If I get to him first, I'll save him for you." I glanced at the man who used to be my enemy. Killian looked back at me, a strange understanding coming between us. He wasn't in my family, but we were far from enemies now.

"Thank you." His chin dipped back at me with respect.

"Your leader is dead. Either join me, the true master, or die where you stand." Markos boomed at the army behind the wall.

No one moved. Not a peep of a response.

"Very well." Markos motioned to the men at the cannons. "Proceed."

"Oh, fuck." I twisted around, grabbing Kovacs, screaming at the others to move. I dove behind a building, pulling Kovacs to my chest, the others crowding in around. The boom resonated through the pavement, rattling my teeth and bones. Tucking Brexley in closer, the next one hit with an even louder resonance, drowning out the screams of death on both sides while it tore through the mortar, spewing stone and concrete in chunks, not caring which side you were on. Not that it mattered to Istvan. These troops were created to die, to just be a number to build up armies. To be nothing more than the first line into the slaughterhouse.

Peeking around the building, the cloud of debris thinned out enough to see that a huge section of the southern wall, one which had stood for twenty years, was gone. Destroyed by the very man who put it up, leaving a massive gaping hole into Leopold. It only took a moment for Istvan's men to scream in unison, a creepy warrior cry, running in and attacking ex-HDF troops waiting on the other side. Friends and allies became foes, all killing without any recognition or thought.

Istvan's tank rolled past the wall line, by the Attila Jozsef statue, a famous Hungarian poet, the tires smashing the chunks of the wall into dust, claiming back his territory.

"Rosie." Killian moved toward the tank Istvan was in. I whipped my arm out, slamming him back into the wall.

"We will get her," I rumbled, my glare warning him to get control of himself. There was no doubt Rosie was his mate. I could feel the claim, the tie between them, pulling him to her like a magnet. "Don't get her killed." One stupid move, and either he could die, or Istvan could kill Rosie without a second thought.

Killian's nostrils flared, and his jaw twitched, but I took his nonresponse as an agreement.

"Eli!" A deep voice rumbled behind us, swinging me around, my gun already cocked and ready to kill the man trotting up, a dozen or so people behind him.

"Think that could take me down?" His green eyes went to my gun with a smirk, the same color as Eli's. The guy looked so much like him. I knew he had to be a relation.

"Lorcan." Ember moved to the group arriving. "Never thought I'd say this, but I'm happy to see you."

Lorcan Dragen. The infamous Dark Dweller who was mated to the queen of the Unified Nations. I didn't know much about their clan's history, though I did know Lorcan at one time was on the old Seelie queen's side, but rumors were that he was forced to be a minion of hers.

Another man stalked up behind Lorcan, only slightly shorter, though his air made him ten times larger. The demeanor of a leader.

"Cole." Ember hugged him, moving on to the blond guy next to him. "Cooper."

"What about me, darlin'?" Another tall, fit guy strolled up, though this guy had an easy swagger to him.

Ember's smile took over her face, almost leaping into the other guy's arms. "Could never forget you, West. How's Rez and the baby?"

"Good." A smile glowed on the man's handsome face. "Really good."

Eli turned to Brexley and me. "This is Cole, Cooper, West, Gabby, Nic, Lorcan, Dax, and Dominic—"

"Yeah, I don't give a fuck right now." I brushed off his introduction, pushing past them, my attention on the only thing that mattered. Stopping the madman about to take our country. "Is this all who's coming?"

"Lars couldn't send any of his men without it being a declaration of war from the UN." The man they called Cole spoke. "We might be small in number, but we are as deadly as the tales say." He lifted his chin, challenging me.

"Me too," I replied through my teeth. I had no doubt he knew perfectly well who I was.

"Cole." Eli drew his attention away from me. "I need you guys to take as many off the back. Be careful—Istvan surpassed Dr. Rapava's methods. They are harder to kill and more feral."

"So are we." Lorcan smirked, ripping off his shirt and kicking off his boots. The others followed suit, stripping down to nothing.

"Damn." Kek sucked in, biting down on her lip. "Like *wow.*"

"Kek?" Ash lifted his brow, reaching for her. "Come on."

"Go ahead, I'm good. I mean, if I'm gonna die, this is a good way to go out."

"Agreed." Brexley and Birdie said in unison, watching the almost all-male group get naked, starting to shift into their other forms. My head jumped to Kovacs, a growl tickling the back of my throat.

"Need me to show you who this belongs to?" My shade licked up her thigh, slicing through her. Brexley jolted with a

497

sharp inhale, shooting a glare at me, only making me smirk. *"That's what I thought."*

"Let's move out," I ordered the group, stepping out of our hiding spot and pointing for Istvan's caravan. When I looked back, the Dark Dwellers were gone. Only the guy Nic, who had a patch over his eye, still in human form, could be seen slipping into the darkness. From the intense sexual energy I got off him, the guy was definitely an incubus.

Like we did in Kyiv, we grouped into small clusters. Kovacs, Killian, Eli, Ember, Ash, Kek, Lukas, Birdie, Caden, Scorpion, Hanna, Wesley, and I moved in waves toward Markos's convoy, thousands of soldiers battling in the streets and across the plaza into HDF. My skin felt electric with death, alive in battle, like part of me had come home. Reborn and restructured from violence. Once again, Kovacs and I were on the battlefield, like the day we both took the first gasp of life.

Since we had nowhere near the numbers to fight head-on, we had to be strategic. While the two forces slaughtered each other, we had to get to Istvan. Cut the head off the snake. It would be nearly impossible, and all of this would fall apart if Brexley's plan didn't work.

Mykel and his team had split off when we first entered, placing the trucks full of weapons near the river.

Fuck, I hoped this worked.

Istvan's army clashed against HDF. The air was filled with the sharp clank of metal, the pops of guns, the booms of more cannons from both sides, and the shrill screams of death. It had only started, and some soldiers were already carcasses on the ground. Robbed of weapons and left forgotten.

"Csapassuk." Let's do this. Birdie pulled out two more guns from her waist and thigh, ignoring her healing wound.

The sound of a tank missile zipping through the air, cutting through a strip of Istvan's men from behind, tore all the air from my lungs. The small rocket smashed into another portion of the wall in an explosion of brick and cement. We ducked behind another building, shielding our heads, while tanks and trucks rolled over the fresh dead bodies coming up on HDF. Movement drew our attention to the bridge.

"What the fuck?" Birdie responded, our attention going to the new convoy.

From both bridges on the north and south side of HDF, hundreds, if not thousands of troops, all with Sonya's emblem, came marching up, circling Leopold.

"Holy shit." Brexley gaped next to me, horror filling her eyes. She wasn't here when Sonya had taken over Killian's palace, making her own militia. By the looks of it, Sonya had been a busy girl.

Where did all these people come from?

"Mother." Lukas snapped his teeth. Anger and pain burned in his eyes watching a sleek black armored SUV roll to a stop, surrounded by tanks and trucks.

"That bitch is using *my* car," Killian grumbled.

A man got out of the passenger side. Brexley hissed next to me, both of us recognizing the man playing servant. Boyd.

He jogged to the back, opening the back door. The wannabe Seelie queen stepped out of the car, looking confident and collected, like nothing could touch her. No bullet or blade could get near her, surrounded by some miracle force field. Reminding me of the days when leaders would meet in the middle before they released their troops on each other, treating each other with this strange respect they didn't give their own soldiers.

A door slammed, and another blond man climbed out of the backseat next to her, making Lukas, Killian, and Brexley snarl.

Iain.

"You've wasted your time, Sonya." Istvan was the one to speak out, his voice echoing off the buildings, his figure on the last bit of wall left up, peering down at his challengers. "Unless you want to lay next to your pet?" Istvan motioned down to Andor's dead body.

She barely gave Henrick Andor a glance. "You did me a favor. He had already fulfilled his use and was becoming a nuisance."

"Really? Because here I stand." Istvan motioned to himself and his domain. "Taking back what is rightfully mine. All your soldiers here are dead. And I have troops from the north moving in around the palace to take that too." Istvan's smugness billowed off him, his certainty he was many steps in front of everyone. "You are done, Sonya. Might as well take a knee or die where you stand."

"Oh, Markos." Sonya shook her head like she pitied him. "I almost feel sorry for you. Your incompetent brain and male ego couldn't fathom what it takes to be a true ruler. To spend decades being treated like you're nothing but a side piece, biting your tongue and waiting for an opportunity. To let stupid *human* males think they are the ones in charge when all along, I've been moving the pieces." She tilted her head. "Leon, you... you're both the same. Your weakness is your confidence, thinking nobody could be smarter, better—especially a woman. And the greedier you got, the more predictable you became. Easy to perceive when every move you make is out of pure narcissism." She clasped her hands as if she was slightly bored. "They are already dead." She brushed at her silk top. "They were ambushed by my men. Every one of them was slaughtered. Oh, and the army you had coming from the east? They are dead too." She nodded at a figure who stood next to her like a main guard, his pinched face snarling at Markos. "Thanks to his father."

"Holy fuck." Brexley sucked in. "Sergei."

The little fuck she was supposed to marry.

My eyes shut briefly, realizing Mykel's worry about Romania had come true. Her deal with Lazar gave her more bodies and ammunition to defeat Markos.

We were no match.

We were fucked.

"Thanks to Lazar and our deal." She tilted her head. "You burned too many bridges with your pride and arrogance, Istvan. Turned against those who at one time might have helped you. This is all your own doing."

Istvan stood still, his eyes watching her closely to see if she was lying or not. What he lost if it were all true. The armies he counted on to unseat her were now gone. His plan was failing.

"So, Markos, you are the one who is done." She grinned cruelly. "You might as well take a knee, or would you rather die where you stand?"

Istvan's throat bobbed, his jaw locked, but he rolled his shoulders back, his conceit never backing down. "Your armies will soon be under my rule. You are finished, Sonya."

"Really?" Sonya tipped her head to the side as if she was appeasing a child.

"They are faithful to the hand which rules them. You won't be around much longer." Istvan's eyes went up in the direction where Kalaraja was hiding, his chin dipping in an unsaid order. I could feel us all hold our breaths, waiting for the sniper's bullet to hit its target, taking out one of the chess pieces.

Tick. Tick. Tick.

The seconds went by. Istvan shuffled his feet. "Shoot her!" he ordered.

Still nothing.

501

A laugh came out of Sonya, like bells pitched with cruelty and self-satisfaction.

Two figures emerged from a building. One I recognized as Kalaraja; the other took me a moment, my brain not wanting to register who had a knife to his throat and something against his spine.

"Oh my gods." Brexley choked.

"No." Killian jolted back, his head shaking in pure shock seeing his old guard.

Holy. Fucking. Shit.

"I thought I killed her?" Ash shot at me, his eyes just as wide and full of disbelief. "She should be dead."

That bitch just wouldn't die.

Nyx. The hawk-shifter who still had a deep vendetta against me and my mate.

Nyx was not only alive but now was Sonya's pet. And she had that same stun gun she used on me at the back of Kalaraja's neck, walking him to Sonya like a trained bird bringing back a kill to their owner.

Apprehension crossed over Istvan's face. It was the first time I had ever seen him look scared. His grasp on this country was slipping through his fingers.

"You've *lost*, Istvan," Sonya declared. "The war, your country, your position, and your li—" Sonya froze, mouth parting as her attention went to the river.

The sound of bones hitting concrete sounded like a drum and spiked the air, stabbing chills down my back, forcing oxygen to get stuck in my lungs as my eyes took in what my brain still couldn't believe.

Bodies rose from their watery grave, marching for HDF, hundreds and hundreds of them carrying weapons from Killian's stash.

"Bazdmeg," I muttered. *It worked.*

Every step they took rattled down my spine and shivered my skin. No matter who you were, this would strike fear through your gut.

It was unnatural and wrong.

Screams of terror crashed through the square as the new players joined the battle.

Because this army wasn't alive.

Chapter 38
Brexley

Skeletons strode stiffly up the embankment, loaded with guns. The clatter of their bones shivered through me. The unnerving magic that controlled them tapped against my own bones, feeling both wrong and right at the same time. It was different from mine, but threads I could recognize and feel like they were my own.

A necromancer's magic.

My mother's clan hid in the darkness, but I could feel them, their dark magic controlling the skeletons like marionettes. Moving the dead army toward Istvan and Sonya's troops, striking fear in hearts and minds.

Even knowing the plan, I still wasn't ready for it. The click of bones on the cement hit in unison. Clothes still hung off some, tufts of hair and patches of skin still left on others, their eyeless sockets focused blankly ahead.

The people Istvan had thrown into that river from his terrible experiments were now coming for their revenge.

"Szar," Ash whispered next to me, his mouth parting while more and more paraded in, their bony fingers holding on to a rifle given to them by Mykel's group. "That is so not

okay." The tree fairy shivered, everything about this going against the natural order of life and death.

"No, but it's fucking working," Warwick replied, ticking his chin at Sonya and Istvan.

Horror swamped the plaza, screams shrilling through the air as fear turned into chaos. Rounds of bullets drilled through the night sky; the two enemies turned on the new threat approaching, finding their bullets couldn't kill things that were already dead.

Istvan took off running for HDF while Boyd, Nyx, Segui, and Iain started shooting at the bone army, letting Kalaraja slip away.

"No!" Killian gritted. Rising quickly, he took off after the chameleon.

There wasn't a second of hesitation, and my boots were slapping the pavement after Killian, followed by everyone else. We were a unit. A family. We moved together, ready to kill and die for each other.

Boyd twisted around, sensing our approach, his eyes widening, then narrowing on Killian, then Warwick, and last me. A snarl hitched his lip as he pointed his gun at us.

Pop! Pop! Pop!

"*Kovacs!*" Warwick's shadow bumped me, a bullet grazing my ear, only centimeters from hitting me. My body zigzagged, shooting back. Iain hustled his mother into the backseat of the SUV, firing back. We moved closer, using their trucks and tanks to hide behind.

"I've been looking forward to this for a long time." Boyd's nasally voice shredded at my ear from his position beside the SUV, bubbling hate and disgust through me. "To watch all of you die."

"You first," Warwick snarled, glancing around the truck we were hiding behind.

505

"When I slit Brexley's throat, the joy will be making you watch her die. Choking and gasping for air."

"The joy *I* will feel when I watch you watch her cut off your dick and shove it down your throat," Warwick shot back.

"Too small to choke on," I added. "He's also used to sucking down dicks."

Boyd's rage hit before I heard his bellow, the bullets from his gun bouncing off the car as he barreled toward us, a dozen of Sonya's army with him. Sergui stayed hidden behind the car like the true coward he was.

My eyes met Boyd's, the seething rage we both felt for each other palpable. He fired until his gun ran out of bullets, but he kept coming at me.

Warwick darted out, going for him.

"No!" I grabbed him, my head shaking. *"He's mine,"* I growled through our link. Warwick instantly backed off, turning his energy on the rest of the soldiers, keeping me protected from them while I darted for Boyd.

This was personal.

Boyd's cruel smile grew over his face, both of us understanding this wasn't for revenge.

This was to the death.

"Farkas is going to watch me fuck your corpse." Boyd withdrew a blade, baring his teeth.

"Should have known necrophilia was your thing. Can't get laid unless they're dead, huh?"

"Thought that would make you feel right at home." He gripped the sword, his body curving in offense. "Seems you only like fucking things that were dead too." He flicked his head at Warwick.

Holding my own blade, I countered his move, my head tilting at his words.

Another vile grin tugged at his lips. "I was the one who organized Warwick's attack. His death was because I rallied those men to act. Not Killian or his second. I was the whisper in their ear. The worm that wiggled into their small brains. I let them take the fall when he hunted each one down. Laughed when I threw him into Halálház for his crimes. I saw his dead body on that field that night. He shouldn't be here. Nor should you."

I hated Boyd before, but now deep-seated fury wrapped around my esophagus, the magic flaming in my gut. Wind whipped through the plaza, accompanied by a crack of lightning, and the ghosts of so many dead drifted to my call, brushing by Boyd, jerking his head around at the contact.

It gave me the opportunity.

Lunging forward, I pointed my blade toward his stomach. He twisted, darting out of the way, my knife slicing through his clothes instead, spiking my ire.

I could hear the fighting going on around me, the bullets in the distance, the screams of death from all around, but I was locked on Boyd, my rage simmering to the point I could feel the ghosts slipping from my control, the nectar calling to me... tempting me. All I had to do was reach into my pocket.

More ghosts darted in, skimming Boyd and me, feeling my anger. My desire.

Boyd screamed as a ghost went through him, ripping at his soul. I didn't hesitate; my knife drove through his torso. A guttural grunt escaped him, fury filling his eyes as he yanked himself back, the blade drenched with his blood. He snarled and spit, charging me. Twirling, I shot my arm out as I moved around him, punching him in the temple and stumbling him to the side.

"I'm going to fucking kill you," he snarled, rushing for me. He ducked away from my punch, his elbow slamming into my side, shooting pain along my ribs. His blade stabbed into my thigh, ripping a bellow from my throat. Biting back the agony, I used my other knee, slamming it up into his face. *Crack!* I felt his nose break, the warmth of his blood gushing over my leg.

"You fuckin' bitch!" He jerked back, his eyes glowing with hate. Wild and unfocused. All sense being shoved aside with the urgency to kill me. We lunged, crashing into each other, hitting the ground with force, the blade slipping from his grip.

His teeth snapped at me, his hands going for my throat, his nails digging into my skin as he straddled me, blood and saliva dripping from his mouth.

"Die, you fucking cunt," he sneered, closing down on my throat. Dots ebbed at my vision, air leaking from my lungs. A chuckle spit from my lips, forcing him to blink down at me in confusion.

"Don't you remember?" I coughed out. "I fuck death, and it comes back for more."

Ghosts tore through him, forcing his grip on my throat to loosen, and he cried out. My hand knocked at his elbow, fully breaking his grip from my neck as my other hand drove up. The blade pierced through his throat like an ice pick, gushing air and blood from his neck. His mouth opened and closed, searching for air, his body falling off me as he tried to pull the object from his throat. Climbing up to my feet, I snarled down at him, our gazes meeting.

I could see the panic, taste his fear, and feel death hovering over him. My spirits waited for his to rise, to drag it away like a piece of trash.

"Look who's the smelly dead fish now." I leaned over him, my hand wrapping around the handle, slamming it deeper in his throat, yanking it to the side until I felt bone. "Die, asshole."

His mouth opened in one last gasp, nothing coming in or out, life bleeding from him faster than the blood. His gaze met mine one last time.

Dead.

"Princess..."

I whirled at the feel of his shade. The real man stood yards away, covered in blood, his eyes locked on me. Dead bodies littered the ground at his feet. He moved without another word, our bodies crashing together, his mouth colliding with mine with a brutal kiss. His hands gripped my face, digging into my hair almost painfully. It wasn't passion; it was need. Need to know I was alive. I was here. I was okay.

Tires screeched over the pavement, jerking Warwick and me to the sound.

"No!" Lukas screamed as the black SUV tried to drive away, running for it. Sergui was behind the wheel, Iain in the passenger seat, his mother in the back.

We couldn't let them escape.

Kek's eyes flashed black, her skin turned pale, and her cheekbones stuck out. Her hands went up, and she forced a nearby truck to move, skidding it in front of the SUV, blocking the path. The SUV slammed into it, Sergui's head cracking into the wheel. Blinking, his head bleeding, I could see Iain screaming at him, leaning over, trying to back up the car. Kek held on to it, her body shaking with the effort. She was a demon, but nowhere near as powerful as other demons. This had to be draining her.

"Get Iain," Ash yelled at Lukas. Both ran to stop the SUV from escaping while battling more of Sonya's guards, an endless amount coming from all sides.

Warwick and I moved next to Ember, Eli, Killian, and Wesley, helping cut down some of the numbers, while Lukas ran for the passenger door, shooting at the glass, only cracking the bulletproof window. Sergui punched the gas right when Kek let go, the car slamming back into a tank, trapping them in.

Endless soldiers kept coming for us, giving us no chance to move from a single spot. It would only be a matter of time before one of us messed up and got killed.

"Warwick?" I called him through our link. He knew what I needed. Both he and Scorpion circled around me, protecting me, while I put all my focus on my magic. Before, it had only been a few ghosts that I controlled. Now I needed my own army, and that took all my focus. A guttural cry came from me as I summoned the thousands that hovered near the river and cemetery. My brain shut out everything else. Digging deep, I felt myself leave my body, stepping into the spiritual plane.

"Give them the order, my girl." Tad stood next to me, confirming the claim he would always be near me. "I believe in you. You are strong enough on your own."

I inhaled, staring out at the thousands of spirits around me. "Attack," I ordered. They turned instantly, doing my bidding. Screams and cries burst in the air as each one killed an enemy.

It was sad because, at one time, they were innocent people with lives and families, just trying to make it. Now they were mindless killers, and no matter what, my family came first.

My soldiers and my mother's worked in harmony— armies of death claiming more victims and reaping their souls.

The energy it took to keep them all in my control drained my body quickly. The commotion outside of my body made it hard to concentrate, my hold on the spirits slipping.

A cannon detonated overhead, yanking me out of my

trance, severing my connection to the ghosts with a brutal snap, bending me over. The ball crashed through the bone army like a bowling ball, fragmenting and scattering the skeletons in its path, taking out several hundred.

My stomach sank.

Fuck.

Bullets may not kill them, but cannon fire could obliterate them, making them as good as dead.

"Lukas, watch out!" Ash bellowed, running for him.

My head yanked up to see Lukas, distracted by the cannon fire, his head turning away from his brother. Iain leaped out of the passenger seat, his weapon raised, his mouth moving, though I couldn't hear what he said.

Bang!

A scream stabbed my throat, my body halting in shock as Lukas's frame jerked back at the impact. His head lowered to where the bullet sank. Shock and sadness etched his forehead, his hand going to his heart. He glanced at his brother before his body fell.

No. No. No... please, no.

"Noooo!" Ash's howl cut through me, gripping my lungs like clawed hands, his legs tearing across the plaza to his lover.

"Ash!" Warwick belted a warning. Iain pointed his gun at Ash, ready to fire.

"No!" Instinct moved me forward to get to him, but Kek's thunderous scream froze me in place.

Her skin became translucent, her eyes so black you could see no reflection, only pits of wrath. Objects slid out of her way as she stormed for Iain.

Pop! Pop! Pop!

He twisted, shooting at her, but even if she was hit, her demon was too angry to notice. Terror streaked over Iain's

511

face, his legs stumbling back, about to run like a coward, but Kek caught him first. Snapping the gun out of his grip, he let out a squeak as she drew him in, her arm wrapping around his neck, ready to snap it. She whispered something in his ear, his eyes growing big in response. I could tell her demon wanted to kill him slowly. She wanted this painful and cruel. Her hand started to crack his neck.

The backdoor to the SUV swung open, my mouth opening to scream, to warn Kek of the danger behind her. In a blink, Sonya moved faster than I had ever seen, her violet eyes glowing brightly. Her lip tugged up in a sneer as she swung the sword she had in her hands, the blade cutting at Kek's neck from behind.

A noise wedged in my throat, my body jolting as if I had been the one struck, devastation and agony empaling my soul on a blade.

I know I screamed. I could feel the rawness of my throat, feel the vibration in my chest.

My eyes took in what was happening, but my mind couldn't. Not even as Kek hit the ground next to Lukas, her head almost no longer attached.

Sonya screamed at Iain, both scrambling back into the car. Segui hitting the gas, the car pushing past its blockade, tires squealing as they got away.

I no longer cared. My legs bowed, a sob wailing up as I crawled for my friends. To Ash. Time felt fuzzy, and my perception of the world was hazy. All I felt was more pain. More death.

My hand touched Lukas and Kek, digging into my gut to revive them. I shrieked, trying to bring them back to life, searching for their souls, pulling at nothing. Magic fizzled as I used everything, burning through my energy.

"Kovacs." Arms wrapped around me, trying to pull me back.

"No!" I batted at his hands, trying to push back in their souls, though I knew they were gone, but I didn't care. *"Princess. Stop."* Warwick's link grew weaker the more I pushed my energy into Lukas and Kek. With a growl, he yanked me back in his arms, wrapping me up so I couldn't move, his mouth at my ear. "I can't lose you too," he muttered.

My body went limp, my head bowing, feeling the pounding of his heart, the warmth of his body, the solidness of his love.

"Whatever it takes." His shadow cupped my face.

Ash's grief drew me from my own. Wiggling from Warwick, I scooted to Ash, wrapping my arms around him. His heartache was so heavy, so painful, I could barely hold on to him, sharing in our grief for just a moment. I felt the trees and earth bow to his pain. Mourn with him.

His soul was so kind. He was lightness and life. I felt I was made for the darkness, for the ugly side of death. He wasn't.

Not like this.

Another blast plowed through more of the skeletons near us, flinging bones up in the air like dust, taking out another huge chunk of our fighters.

My agony wanted to wallow in the loss of my friends, but the battle around us wouldn't allow it. Unless we laid down next to them and gave up.

Warwick yanked me to my feet. I didn't want to get up, I didn't want to go on, but in war, you had no choice. You had to sever any part of you that could feel, leaving your fallen comrades where they died, only to grow heavier which each soul you carried on your back as you continued on.

The ones who caused this pain, who took our friends from us, escaped. Anger gripped every muscle, making my shoulders rise in vengeance. It was like I could feel Kek and Lukas near me, telling me to get my ass up and fight.

"Get that bitch for me, little lamb. Take them all down."

Blinking, I glanced down at Kek and Lukas, Ash still bent over them, his heart shattering, as another explosion hit a tank close by.

"Brex!" Warwick tugged me.

"Go! Go!" Wesley motioned for us, moving to Ash. "I'll get him."

"Keep him safe." Warwick's words were a threat, not a plea.

Wesley waved us on, shooting at the enemy as the rest of our group jogged away. The only thing keeping me going was knowing if I didn't, more of my friends would die.

In the end, this war came down to *me*.

Chapter 39
Killian

War.

I had been in many, on the right side and some on the wrong. It was disturbing, horrific, soul-wrenching, hopeless, bleak, depressing, bloody, violent, never-ending, scary, monstrous, overwhelming, inhuman, disheartening, and chilling.

None of those words truly captured the feeling when you were in it. Living it. Breathing it. Your senses couldn't take it all in, holding onto a singular thought.

Survival.

My survival to stay among the living was based solely on the gut feeling that Rosie was alive. Nothing, including death, would stop me from getting to her.

A boom rang out, smashing the last portion of the wall, taking out more of the skeletons fighting for us. I had seen a lot in battle, but beholding thousands of corpses rising from the river to be used to battle for the freedom of our country, went far beyond anything I could ever imagine.

Keeping low, using the remains of the wall and building for cover, we made our way closer to Istvan's convoy. The bastard was probably hiding in the bunkers below, waiting it out.

Our group bulldozed through the units of soldiers, slicing, shooting, and stabbing our way throughout, making me grateful I had these people fighting by my side. I wasn't someone who trusted. Not fully. I always understood as a lord, no one would truly have my back. The closest I came to feeling that way was Sloane.

This group I trusted with more than just my life. I trusted them with Rosie's, which was a hell of a lot more important to me. There was not one who'd second guess going after her, not one who wouldn't fight to the death for her.

That meant they had all of my trust.

There were more faux-fae soldiers, but we had the will. Numbers did not always mean victory. Triumph came from determination, love, and sacrifice. We had a reason to fight. Our lives, our families, friends, and country were on the line.

My expression locked with fury and determination, I moved like a samurai warrior, cutting and gutting Istvan's men. The armored truck Istvan was in was only feet away. The one Rosie should be in as well.

My sword hummed happily in my hands, greedy for action. Slicing through the air, my old friend came back to life, reliving all our tales as a pirate. Old swords were just as alive as fae books. The blood of its victims sank into the metal and became part of its story. They had power and status and could sense weaker or more powerful blades.

I had hidden it in my own safe place for decades. As if I could lock my past up with it too. Keep the truth hidden because it clashed with the noble air I put on.

I turned away from the pirate life. From my truth. Feeling the blade's power, I realized it was as much part of me as the fae lord.

I was a pirate. A lord. A poor starving child. A king.

I was a man who would cut everything down in his wake to reach my mate. I could feel her; I knew she was still alive, but I had no idea what shape she was in. What cruelty Istvan could inflict upon her to punish me.

We slaughtered the last few guards around the truck. Kicking them out of my way, I ripped open the door to the car.

Empty.

"Fuck!" I howled, wrath tightening my muscles. If he had done anything to her, I would gut him like a pig.

"Is this what you are looking for, *Lord* Killian?" A sneer whirled us around, stopping us dead in our tracks. Istvan stood on the steps of HDF, looming over us, a smirk on his face. He was surrounded by guards and two large metal cages, which shook as if live animals were in them. All that disappeared as I spotted the only thing that would bow me to Istvan's will.

Rosie was on the ground like a pet, handcuffed to a chain he was holding. A large soldier stood behind with a gun to her head, ready to blow her brains out if we made one wrong move. Her eyes were black and blue, and her cheek was red as if she had been struck. She kept her chin high, not reacting to the gun threatening to take her life.

"Tsk. Tsk. How the great fae lord has tumbled. Falling for a human *whore*. She spread her legs, and now look at you…" Istvan wrinkled his nose at Killian. "Though she isn't human anymore, is she?" It was not a question. He knew she wasn't.

"Let her go." A gurgling growl rose from my throat.

Istvan laughed. "What wasted words. Is that all you've got, great *noble* leader? Do you really think because you say so, I will? Stupid fool." His lids narrowed. He was right in a

517

way. Though my position gave me more power than other fairies, the iron around my neck in Věrhǎza had wrecked me. I struggled to do the bare minimum. Helplessness rang in my ears like failure. Failure to protect her. "Hand me the nectar."

Brexley stiffened next to me, her mouth parting slightly.

"If you lie and tell me you don't have it, she dies," Istvan snapped, his glower turning to his old pseudo daughter. "Haven't you been the cause of so many deaths, Brexley? Those you claim to call family. Do you even recall shooting Andris dead? Murdering the man you considered an uncle? How about Aron's throat you slashed? Yes, I know you murdered him too."

Her fists rolled into balls, not responding.

It took everything in me not to rip it out of Brexley's pocket and hand it over. Though Istvan might kill Rosie anyway.

My gaze went to my girl. Her crystal blue eyes were already on me, full of words she could not speak, but I felt them in my soul anyway.

"Don't you dare hand it over."

"I will not let you die." I could feel mine were speaking back to her.

"Then all will die." Her head wiggled just slightly. *"Including me. You can't save me, Killian. But you can save everyone else."*

"Fuck everyone else."

She blinked, her eyes glossing over, her lips mouthing, "I love you."

The declaration inscribed itself onto my soul. Those words sank deep into me. All the time I wasted over Kat. I had finally met my mate and most likely would lose her before we could be anything. Her vow of love wasn't in response to my words. It was a goodbye.

Brexley's magic prickled over my skin, a howl of wind, lightning crackling in the air.

"Don't." Istvan glared at Brexley. "You do anything, and her brains will be on the ground before you can even blink."

"You do anything to her, I assure you, Istvan, your guts will be tied around your throat and used to hang you." I took a step closer. His guards twisted to me, prepared to drop me where I stood.

"More empty threats. I'm tired of waiting." Istvan replied, turning his head slightly to his guards. "Kill her."

"NO!" My voice dropped like a bomb, the power of a lord resounding with fury from the back of my throat, but it still didn't come out as strong as I used to be. "Take me instead." I stepped forward. My expression was set with utter sureness. "The fight for this country, people… is between us. She has nothing to do with it."

"Killian." Fear hissed through Rosie, her head shaking.

"You are nothing," Istvan spat. "Nothing more than a figurehead. Utterly useless and inconsequential. You always have been, Killian. All that so-called fae power, and what became of you… a man groveling at my feet." He turned his attention back to Brexley, like I was not worth speaking to any longer.

It was no secret my ego was sizable. I never took kindly, even as a child on the streets, to those who dismissed or belittled me. My temper as a teenager was legendary, and to save him from killing me himself, Croygen directed my anger into something productive. Sword fighting, stealing, and slaying. Having me trained in the styles of the samurai warrior.

I could feel that ingrained anger rise. Markos had always dismissed fae, thinking somehow he was superior in his inferiority. Forgetting we had magic he could never possess.

My magic hadn't been the same since Věrhăza. Having absorbed the iron around my neck for so long had crippled it. Leaving me fangless, but with the dread of my mate being murdered in front of me, I felt it finally hum from deep inside, sparking in my veins. "Let. Her. Go. Now." The glamour I could conjure was an order, a command.

Istvan's head jerked, not ready for the assault. His muscles locked up like his body was telling him one thing while his mind was saying something different. Teeth gritted, he turned to Rosie, his hand reaching for the chain.

"Nooooo." A noise came growling from his throat, his hands stopping, fury shading his cheeks a deep red. Ire ignited his eyes.

"Do. It!" I vibrated with the sheer emphasis on the two words, dripping sweat down my back. Glamour used to be so easy for me, especially with the weak-minded. Istvan's mind was far from weak. He was firm in his belief. A solid mass of ego and righteousness. The strain to control him had my arms and legs shaking, trying to keep my focus on him.

A strangled noise came from him, his hands unlocking Rosie's cuffs.

"Shoot them!" he spat at the guards the moment his fingers unlatched her, giving the order they waited for.

A stream of gunfire came at us, dipping us back behind trucks and tanks to hide, shooting back.

"Rosie?" I bellowed her name, peeking back around. She had scrambled away from Istvan, hiding behind a stone column attached to the arched entry. I needed her in my arms. Safe. Turning to Hanna and Scorpion, I barked at them. "Cover me."

Darting out, firing at the soldiers, my feet took me toward Rosie. I saw Istvan run to the metal cages, opening them. Two forms leaped out.

Terror lodged in my chest, burning like food was stuck in my windpipe.

"Killian!" Rosie's voice filled my ear, hearing the utter panic and horror of what was coming for me.

Just as much animal as they were man, the beast-men we fought in the Games raced for me, their jaws open in a roar.

My gods…

Joska and Samu. The two HDF soldiers who tormented us in Věrhăza and attacked us in the pit. They should have been dead by now, their brains bleeding out of their noses like all the ones I had overseen. But they weren't. They not only were alive but seemed healthy and even stronger. Intelligence fired behind their eyes, telling me they weren't completely wild. Their frames were still man, but both had teeth and claws of monsters.

They weren't human, but they weren't totally fae either.

With the speed of a fae, they came for me. My gun fired, blood spraying from where I hit them, but it did not slow them down. It only angered them more.

"KILLIAN!" The severity of Rosie's voice curved my head, my gaze latching onto her beautiful face, knowing I would never reach her.

"I love you." I mouthed back before I felt Samu's clawed fingers slash across my chest, my body reacting to the pain, though I felt nothing. I kept my eyes on Rosie's, memorizing every nuance until the darkness swallowed me.

I couldn't live in a world where she didn't exist. Now I never had to.

Chapter 40
Brexley

Rosie's scream impaled the sky like it cut a hole in the atmosphere and through my chest. Killian's body dropped, the beasts turning their attention to her.

Joska and Samu were still alive. It had been way past the time the pills should have killed them.

Yet here they were. Both appeared even stronger than before. Joska only wore pants, his body strained with muscles and vigor. He had to have doubled in size, mainly in his chest, his body moving like a gorilla set to kill. Samu was thin but almost completely muscle. His fingers were claws, his teeth sharp and pointed.

Both were heading for Rosie.

A shout bellowed out of my throat, and I leaped from my hiding spot. I fired my gun into my two old HDF comrades, trying to distract them from her. As if the bullets were nothing but mosquito bites, they batted at the hits before their irritation curved their heads to me, stopping their pursuit of Rosie.

Fuck.

Joska's eyes lit up with hunger and desire—to kill and

destroy, to hear my bones snap and feast on my carcass. A grunting noise roared from him, his hands beating his chest. Circling around, he barreled for me.

"Kovacs!" Warwick's warning cry echoed in me, his shadow ready to slam me out of the way.

Taking a deep breath, I pushed him out, holding my ground, pulling on everything Tad ingrained in me. I centered on Joska, feeling everything bubble up inside me. My magic cracked through the sky, wind whipping my hair as lightning zigzagged down to the earth, directed at Joska.

Crack!

Joska leaped out of the way right as it hit, but the power of the fire bolt hitting the ground flung his massive body up in the air.

"Brexley!" Warwick grabbed me, the both of us thumping to the ground, rolling as Joska hit the concrete right where I had been standing.

Another cannon shrieked in the night sky, bursting through a huge section of the bone army, shattering them into pieces before it smashed into the old parliament building, only feet away from us.

BOOM!

The force of the impact ripped me from Warwick, chucking me across the pavement. I felt the object in my pocket dislodge, hitting the ground as I tumbled in a brutal roll, unable to stop. I covered my head as stone and debris showered down, bruising and slicing into my skin.

Coughing and wheezing, my head popped up, searching the demolished plaza.

Fear gripped my throat.

The nectar lay near the steps of HDF. Right where Istvan was rising to his feet. His eyes went to the substance lying innocently before him. His eyes lifted to mine, our gazes meeting. I could see the smugness shifting his features, his lips twisted with arrogance.

"Noooooo!" I screamed, scrambling up to my feet, watching him lean down, his fingers wrapping around the nectar. I froze as he picked it up, his face brimming with voracity.

His lip lifted in a smirk, glancing back at Rosie, who was huddled over Killian, then to me.

"My spies tell me it's like fae food." He brought it to his mouth and bit down on a quarter-size piece. Four times bigger than what I gave Rosie.

Time stopped.

Oh. Holy. Gods.

"There were rumors about the nectar, of its powers, but Kalaraja confirmed it when he watched you bring her back to life. Turn her into fae." He nodded back at Rosie.

Dread wrapped around my lungs, crushing them as terror pumped through my heart. Istvan not only had the nectar, but he had just become fae.

Once again, I failed.

Istvan smiled, his fingers curling around the nectar, his lids shutting briefly, allowing the substance to take over. The abundance of magic he just swallowed down only took a moment.

The sky ignited with bolts of electricity, making the hair on my arms stand on end. Gusts of wind howled off the river, whipping so hard it felt like a hurricane, blowing anything not bolted down to the ground, strewing pieces of bone from the skeletons in the air like daggers. Magic sizzled my skin like fire, pounding down my airways and rattling me to my core.

It was *my* magic, the same that ran in my veins, but it no longer was mine, as though Istvan stole my blanket out of my prison cell, taking it as his. A right which had been taken. A violation.

Lightning sliced down. Death screams from Sonya's army or maybe even Istvan's, shrieked, filled with horror and pain. He didn't care about the army he created. He would gladly watch them all burn as long as he got what he wanted.

The man had no soul. He killed my father and moved me in with them like he pitied my situation, only to use me as his pawn to gain more control and power. Manipulating his own son.

People couldn't seem to understand how someone could be so cruel. Malignant narcissists couldn't understand love. They got off on cruelty, felt power in someone's pain, and felt alive in hurting others. They had no empathy or compassion.

Istvan only lived when others suffered.

His face contorted into something I didn't recognize. His eyes were bright like fire burned behind them. His jaw gritted while the wind whipped through the lightning, sprinkling fire down in a furry. I knew what it felt like to hold the nectar, the overpowering force it sizzled through every nerve and vein. I could barely handle it.

He not only had the magic burning through his gut, but shredding energy through his arms.

There was no way I could stop him. Everything about this felt wrong, as if nature itself was screaming out at the injustice.

"Brexley Kovacs." Scratchy and ancient, I felt the fae book crawl inside my head, jerking me back. *"The girl who challenges nature."* It flickered a memory in my brain. A dream I forgot. Something that was on the fringes of my mind but had gotten lost in the chaos. *"Terrible things happen when nature's laws are broken. Though within terrible, greatness can be found. Power to drain and consume the*

wrong. You are not the only one in this story who defies nature, who should not exist. It is only together you can right nature's balance."

Drain and consume the wrong.

Holy fuck.

Just like I could drain Warwick, I had been able to drain the nectar too. I could take it all from Istvan.

"Kovacs…" Warwick's voice called to me through the deafening gale, already sensing my movement. My head craned over my shoulder, his bright aqua eyes on me. I didn't speak, not even through our link. He knew already. I had no choice.

"No!" his shade bellowed. *"Don't you fucking dare, princess. Whatever it takes, right?"*

Yes, whatever it took to keep *him* alive.

My heart poured through my eyes, my shadow kissing his lips softly before I cut off our connection and turned away.

"NOOOOOOOOOOOOOO!" His voice boomed in the air. I heard Caden, Scorpion, Birdie, and Hanna also screaming for me. My friends tried to stop me, but this was for me to fight on my own. I was the only one who could right the wrong.

Pushing through the winds, I headed for Istvan. Lightning hit the ground near my feet, breaking through the concrete to the earth. I didn't stop. My magic wouldn't hurt me outright. I could feel it, and that was why it had to be me. The one who could get close to Markos.

Istvan's eyes narrowed, squeezing the nectar tighter. The world seemed to denote around me, flames raining down from the sky, setting fire to buildings, cars, living and dead bodies. The wind slammed into me, making me stumble. Getting back up, I grunted, pushing forward, using up a lot of my strength.

My magic was there, but there was no doubt who would win. The nectar had taken the majority of the magic funneling into me the night I was born. It protected me, kept me alive, because no living being could have lived being hit with that much force.

My feelings for it were toxic, like I owed it my life, as if it were alive. It wasn't, and I kept getting people killed because I couldn't see the difference. I couldn't see that it should not exist—see that only one of us could survive this night.

Istvan's face darkened with hate and vengeance, becoming almost unrecognizable.

"You want to die just like your father?" he snapped, lifting his shoulders like he towered over me. "You are just like him," he sneered in an insult.

"Thank you."

Istvan's lip curled. "Both you and my son are worthless. The world will not miss you. Your death will mean nothing."

"No, but they will cheer yours." I slammed my eyes shut, pulling on the power whirling around us. The familiar electricity scorched up my throat and down my veins, wrapping around my spine, burning with agony.

It was like swimming upstream, my legs quaking with the effort to take the power back and let it burn out inside me. It wanted to be free, to be used, and I was trying to dampen and put out the flames inside me. I could feel the magic taking me. Overpowering me.

I was nothing and everything.

Somewhere between life and death.

The Grey.

Like ashes. Burning myself into embers and dust.

I could feel it, but I only pulled harder, squeezing my lids tighter, hearing Istvan yowl.

The icy winds tangled my ponytail and ripped at my skin, but nothing cooled the inferno in me. I was taking on too much. My legs gave out, and I fell to my knees, my physical body starting to lose its battle against it.

The magic from a Seelie queen, her family line, dark magic, druids, and the wall dividing Earth from the Otherworld spun inside me as I consumed more of it.

I wasn't supposed to survive that night. I should have perished next to my mother. I escaped what nature planned for me, but now it had caught up with me. The least I could do in gratitude for the time it gave me was take the nectar with me.

Neither of us should exist.

I tugged harder, a scream tearing from my soul as I held on as hard as I could.

"You are not fucking leaving me, Kovacs!" Warwick's shade burst through, my energy no longer able to keep him out, though he was becoming distant and hazy. *"We came into this world together, and we'll go out of it together."* The feel of his actual hand twined through my fingers, his frame on his knees next to me. "Take it all!"

He was demanding I use his energy—use him as an anchor. Prying my lids apart, I gazed up at him with sorrow. It wouldn't be enough, and he knew that, but he wasn't going anywhere, dying by my side.

"Warwick…" I choked.

"Szeretlek." *I love you.* His sentiment was husky and full of many layers, going far beyond the general meaning. Burrowing deep and claiming me. *"Sötét démonom."* His shadow muttered against my neck. There was no need to say more; I felt his response grazing against my soul, forcing my lids to squeeze briefly together at the intensity.

"Az én farkasom." *My wolf.* My own claim wrapped

around him, branding into his bones, marking him mine forever. In life and death.

My entire body filled with the adrenaline he gave over to me. I carried the past and the present, the dark and the light, life and death... and it still wasn't enough. Istvan's newly acquired magic was at a high level, stronger than many here, putting up a fight against me.

I tore through Warwick's energy, nowhere close to what I needed, pain jolting his body.

Tears slid down my face as I dug deeper, singeing every nerve in my body. A howl filled the air, and I didn't know if it was from Warwick or me.

As lightning hit the ground near us, I felt my shoulders hunch over.

This was it. I just hoped we pulled enough that someone could take Istvan down.

Darkness pulled on me when I felt another hand grip my right one, a body dropping down on my other side.

I looked over, seeing Ember next to me, Eli holding her hand.

Something about it triggered a more vivid memory of that dream.

"I had this dream. I didn't remember it until now," Ember yelled over at me through the wind. "It's my magic in there too." She swallowed nervously and looked at me. "We have to do this together."

It was as if her words wiped away the fog and webs, letting me see the vision with clarity. It hadn't been another version of me, or when he spoke of another, it wasn't Istvan. The book had meant Ember. She was the one in my dream, and Eli was next to her, not a strange version of Warwick.

We were the power source, and they were our anchors.

Like the book showed us, they died and were brought

back to life that night. We had been connected from the very beginning. We shared power; the same magic in the nectar was in both of us. We were family.

"I've helped take that bitch down before." Ember gripped my hand tighter. "I can do it again."

Slamming my eyes shut, I felt the power of the four of us come together. Linked in life and death, bound together in magic. Past and present. From continents far away, all our lives became interconnected on a singular night, like our destinies were always supposed to come to this point.

Ember and I yanked and pulled, taking on the magic that was being used to slaughter and control. Istvan let out a scream like his insides were being fried, but he didn't let go of his grip, his need and greed overpowering anything logical.

"Nooooooo!" Istvan belted, a bolt of lightning slicing down near us. The wind howled, almost pushing us to the ground, before I felt something snap.

POP!

The balance of magic cracked down the middle, bursting in my brain and burning down my vertebra.

A cry from Ember and I tore over the plaza, our hands letting go as we crumbled to the ground. It took me a moment, my insides feeling hollowed out and scorched, but then I heard nothing but the crackle of fire burning.

Like the world had stopped for a moment, holding its breath.

There was no wind, no magic.

No death.

"Brexley?" Warwick struggled to crawl to me, his hands gripping my face, kneeling over me. This time it was my burned and broken body on the battlefield he leaned over. The man willing to die for me.

"*Sötét démonom,*" I whispered to him.

530

"No, princess… I am your *wolf.*" His mouth crashed on mine, raw and brutal, not hiding his emotions as he kissed me with vicious desperation. A cry of relief and love bubbled from my lips as my hands gripped his head. We were alive.

We walked through the shadows of death and made it out—forever scarred and haunted.

Someone's coughing jerked us apart. My bones retaliated as I climbed to my feet. Istvan lay on the ground, blood pooling from his nose, his eyes fluttering open.

I moved, snatching the dead nectar up and shoving it in my pocket. It was empty now, but that didn't mean it would be forever.

Istvan hacked and gulped, appearing decades older than he did before. His clothes were charred, and his skin looked like old, dried, crispy fruit. The fact he was still alive was shocking… that amount of nectar would kill a human.

But he wasn't human anymore.

Caden came up beside me, his disgust and hate pointed at his father.

"So what now?" Istvan hacked, stumbling with pain as he rose to his feet. He brushed off his military suit, his condescending glance going to the gun in Caden's hand, snorting. "You going to kill me, son?"

"Yes."

"Please." Istvan let out a laugh. "You don't have it in you, boy. You never did. Brexley was more of a soldier than you ever were."

Bang!

The gun in Caden's hand went off, striking Istvan's shoulder. Istvan stepped back, his hand going to the wound, touching the blood leaking out.

"Don't underestimate me," Caden snarled. "You created this monster. I tried to fight it, to keep it controlled, but now

531

I crave it. Want it. The human Caden is no longer." He tugged on the trigger.

Caden might have thought he was a monster, but he was anything but. He might be fae, but he was the same guy deep down. Good. Honorable. He thought he wanted to kill his father, but if he did, he already would have killed him. The act would sit with Caden and rot him to his core until he was the very monster he described himself as.

With Birdie, I saw his happiness coming back. I would not let Istvan take that from him again.

"No." I pushed the barrel down, Caden's glare darting to me. "You don't want to do this, Caden."

"Yes, I fucking do."

"Then he will never let you go." I touched his arm, meeting my dear friend's gaze. "He will haunt you forever. He doesn't deserve to be on your conscience." I repeated what Warwick had once said to me, understanding why he killed Dr. Karl for me. "He isn't worth your soul."

Istvan let out a sharp laugh.

"Oh, this is priceless. You're so fucking soft. What a useless piece of shit."

Bang!

Another shot rang out from Caden's gun, hitting his side, bending Markos over. He spat on the ground, his chuckle growing louder.

"Not so easy to kill now."

My fingers wrapped around the blade on my side, whipping it out. The knife hit the target, sinking deep into Istvan's chest, the impact crashing him back on his ass. I was on him in a second, grabbing his jacket and pulling him to my face.

"Maybe harder to kill," I snarled, years of abuse and lies crawling up my spine. "But *not* impossible. This is for me and for all the innocent lives you took." I grabbed the handle and dug it in with a twist. "For Caden and Rebeka." I twisted the blade deeper. His fingers clawed at mine, his mouth gaping, blood pouring down my hands, dripping onto his medals. "And this is for my father." I yanked out the dagger and drove it through his spine, making sure this man could NOT survive. "You lost, Istvan."

Istvan went limp, his head falling back onto the stone steps of his fallen domain, blood staining the concrete.

I stood there, the distant noise of war coming to an end. Blood and bone scarring the earth. The dead bodies of innocent people forced into this all because of ego. What was that saying? When the rich went to war, it was the poor who died.

Fuck that. We had enough.

Though we might have won, it didn't feel like a victory. We lost too many.

"Kovacs," Warwick spoke out loud, our link burned up for now.

He took my hand, pulling me away from Markos. We started to walk away, exactly like my vision, dead bodies lying all around us, fire burning, our boots soaked with blood. Hand in hand through the valley of death.

The Grey and The Wolf.

Epilogue
Brexley

Three months later

"I was not hugging it."

A tiny voice dragged me from sleep, aches twining through my muscles the moment my brain registered consciousness, reminding me why I was so sore.

Chirp!

"Was not! *Buuutttt...* if I was... it's not my fault. It's warm and big, like a monster-size body pillow."

Chirp! Chirp!

"Don't play innocent. You were snuggling it too. I saw you!"

Chirpchirpchirp!

My lashes fluttered open with a groan. Looking around the room, my mind took a moment to register where I was. Light glowed brightly through the window, highlighting the furniture in the large bedroom. The rococo furnishings and luxury fabrics screamed wealth, excess, and extravagance. A symbol of the past, of the huge divide between Leopold and Savage Lands. I hated everything about it, reminding me too much of the life I used to live, but I had been too busy to worry about changing it. It was just a room we laid our heads in, taking advantage of the king-size bed. Through the window, my gaze caught the top of the dome sparkling in the early spring light. Why did I pick this flat? I couldn't live in the building I had spent my youth in, too many memories, but I needed to be close.

"Master Fishy! You're awake!" Opie threw up his arms, drawing my attention to him standing on my leg. "We were getting so bored."

Chirp! Bitzy frowned, flipping me off.

"Good morning to you too." I rubbed my eyes, burning from lack of sleep and the colors attacking my eyeballs.

I had given Opie free rein to use whatever fabric or items he wanted in the abandoned flat, which now, as I looked back, might have been a mistake.

"You like?" His smile engulfed his face, and he twirled around.

Tacky gold tassels from the pillows in the living room were wrapped around his bun, sprouting up like the top of a pineapple. Busy Baroque damask wallpaper was layered in thick strips into a full skirt. He wrapped gold leaf paper like a tube top and wore a bright yellow velvet cape, crystals from a chandelier hanging off it, making him glint and sparkle. His lips and eyes were coated in red lipstick he probably found in the bathroom drawer, left by the previous owners.

Bitzy wore a gold tassel dress and wallpaper folded like wings on her back, her cheeks painted red.

"It's... *so much*... beauty." I sat up, pulling the sheet up to cover me.

"Right?" He tried to twirl again, but the stiff wallpaper and heavy velvet made his moves awkward. "It's a little hard to move in, but you must suffer to achieve true art, right?"

535

"Right." I grinned down at Opie, my heart filling with love. I thought back to the day they walked into my cell. Against all odds, against my own racism toward fae and sub-fae, they wiggled into my life and became part of my family. I couldn't imagine one moment without them.

"If I find *one* paper cut on my dick from wallpaper…" Warwick muttered, curving my head to the man next to me, my heart tripping on itself.

The Man.

The Wolf.

The Legend.

I was still in awe this man was mine. When our paths crossed in Halálház, I had no idea he would be my anchor. Literally and figuratively. The love I felt for him grew with each passing day, tightening our already close bond. We had been through so much—the loss, the heartbreak, the devastation. We slipped into the darkness and crawled out, bloody, wounded, and broken. We refused to give up. We held on to each other and survived.

"Wh-why would you have a paper cut *there*?" Opie straightened the sheet, his nervous cleaning tic kicking in.

Warwick lifted his arm high enough to glare down at Opie, who was fussing with the bedding more.

"I mean, unless you were wrapping the big bad wolfy up for posterity reasons, I have no clue what you are referring to."

Chirp! Chirp!

"Stop saying that! I was not snuggling it!" Opie put his hands on his hips. "That is a total misunderstanding!"

Warwick snorted, shifting on the bed, the blanket barely covering his ripped, tattooed body, the nail and bite marks from last night peppering his skin. We got really rough last night, destroying the desk and coffee table before moving in here.

Over three months after the war, I still held so much excess grief, guilt, and pain. Every death I could never mourn or recognize because we had no time came rushing to the surface every time I closed my eyes. Haunting me. The only way I could sleep was if Warwick made me pass out, which the man took on like it was his only job. He wanted to numb my sorrow, but I knew that would only prolong it. Instead, we shared it through our link and through our bodies.

My magic was returning stronger every day, our link deeper. It had taken weeks after that night for my magic to start coming back. I had used so much, tipped the balance so far off, my body had suffered for it. To feel it again made me feel whole but also scared. That meant the nectar was coming back too.

"Princess…" The feel of his real hands running up and down my ribs as his shadow drew his tongue up my spine forced a gasp up my throat. "Pets need to get off the bed now." His invisible mouth covered my breast, flicking and sucking.

"Pets? Did you call us pets?" Opie screeched out. "How dare you call us that, you chubby meat stick!"

Chirp, chirp, chirp, chirp! Bitzy's finger flew up, circling the air like a helicopter.

"I can fuck your pussy with my tongue right here… them here or not." I reveled in the feel of him doing just that, my thighs parting, my back arching as the real man smirked at me from only a foot away.

"Warwick," I gritted through my teeth.

He cocked an eyebrow, his shade licking me deeper.

"Fuck," I hissed, sweat sliding down my back. "Okay, I'm sure you guys want to go visit Kitty's or…" A groan slipped through, my breath speeding up as Warwick nipped my clit, taking me deeper.

"Or go visit Ash. He'll have lots of mushrooms," I croaked, my hips starting to buck.

Chirp! Chirp! Chirp! Bitzy fingers whipped around in excitement.

"Mushroom man isn't such a *fun guy* anymore." Opie tried to laugh, but it came out flat. A sadness came over him, like he saw what the rest of us did. "Get it? Fun-guy?" He waited for a response, and when none came, he batted at me. "Fine. We're going. Have a good day, Fishy."

Chirp!

"Yes, the big bad wolfy is about to gobble up fish for breakfast."

In a blink, they disappeared.

"About time." Warwick tossed me back on the pillows, climbing over me, widening my legs for him to settle between, his erection parting my folds. There was no hesitation. He thrust in with a grunt, opening my mouth in a silent scream. He slammed in again, his shade cupping my breast as he held onto the headboard, his mood suddenly dark, his hips slamming against mine as he roughly fucked me. All I could do was hold on, overwhelmed by the pleasure and pain.

I knew what triggered him. Not that it took much.

Ash was a sore subject for him. For all of us. None of us expected him to take Kek's and Lukas's deaths well. Hell, I didn't either, but the even-tempered, good-natured tree fairy no longer existed. My best friend, my rock, had become volatile, mean, and short-tempered. I knew he was suffering, as many of us were, and I tried to be there for him, but Ash wasn't even willing to hear one word about them. To even discuss what happened, acting like they never existed, as he grew darker and darker.

It bothered Warwick seeing Ash a drunk, high, angry

mess right now. Getting in fights at brothels and bars. Getting kicked out of places, his mood almost cruel to those who loved him. Warwick and Kitty both tried, and Ash basically told them to fuck off, which was not like him. We all felt helpless.

With Warwick, helplessness turned to anger. Frustration. Violence.

"This pussy is mine, princess." He grabbed my chin, the other hand still on the headboard as he went in harder, cracking the wood, his intensity ripping all logic from my mind, moans heaving from my lungs as my orgasm came barreling for me.

He grunted, feeling me tighten around him.

"No." He pulled out, flipping me around, smashing me up against the broken headboard, rubbing my pussy and breasts against it before he plunged in. My fingers scratched at the wood as he took out all his own heartache and grief on me, and I only asked for more.

There was no line for us, no safe word. We were probably the only people who could handle each other. We took, we punished, we gave, we marked. Our bodies and our souls.

"Warwick!" I bellowed as my body shuddered and convulsed with my orgasm, my mind flashing to moments of us, fucking, fighting, life, death. We were all of it—everything.

"Brex-ley." He growled in my ear as his cum filled me, pushing even deeper into me. The way he said my name, using it as a punishment and worship, shattered another climax through me.

Slowly coming back, our lungs heaved together.

"Bazdmeg." A bubbled laugh hiccupped from my throat.

"That was just the start, Kovacs." His hand brushed away my hair, kissing the curve of my neck.

Right then, a timid knock sounded at the door.

"Brexley?" A woman's voice called me with more taps on the door, clearly waiting until we were finished. *"Kedvesem?"* My dear.

"Yes, Maja?" The woman who was practically a grandmother to me had pretty much followed Warwick and me to this huge penthouse apartment, doing everything she did for me over at HDF.

I had told her she could go anywhere, be with her children and grandchildren, but she batted me away, telling me, "I don't know anything else. I am proud of my job, of what I do. I like it. And you will need me." She wagged her finger at me. "I know because I saw what a mess you made growing up."

I couldn't deny her *or* the truth. I *was* going to need her. With everything I was taking on, Maja's presence was comforting and warm in a time of uncertainty and doubt. I moved Lena and her daughter and Emil's family into the floors below, so they could be together. Emil had never been found, and sadly, we all knew he probably never would. His wife and their kids were on the ground floor, while Lena took the first floor. They all seemed very happy here. This was Maja's domain. We just lived here.

"Edesem?" The door started to open. Warwick groaned against my ear, nipping at my skin before he pulled away, dropping to the bed, not bothering to really cover himself up as the woman moved into our bedroom, heading straight for the closet. "You are late." She tossed clothes for me to wear out on the side chair.

"She's early compared to when I planned on letting her out of here." Warwick peered over at me, stretching out, looking relaxed and satisfied. Though I knew him too well. If I didn't leave now, I wouldn't be for another few hours.

"Thanks, Maja." I nodded at her as she exited the bedroom, tapping on her watch. Warwick's hands tried to grab for me as I leaped out of bed. Smirking over my shoulder, I ignored the clothes she laid out and grabbed my cargo pants and sweater. This meeting was anything but formal.

"Should I ask what you are doing today?" I tugged on my clothes.

"Scorpion and I are checking on business stuff." He tucked his arms under his head.

"Ah. The brothel." I frowned, yanking on my boots. "Spending the day with some of your old fuck buddies?"

"Jealous, Kovacs?" He growled into my ear. *"Thought you loved watching me with all of them? You sure stayed and watched."*

"Fuck off." I cut off the link, making him chuckle from the bed. He shoved the comforter off, rising and prowling toward me, his naked body lining up with mine.

"You know a hundred of them couldn't compete with you." His voice was gravelly, his palms holding my face, turning me to look at him. "I've got my hands full enough with you." His mouth covered mine, and his tongue slipped past my lips, showing me everything he felt, kissing me so deeply that I got dizzy. *"Szeretlek, házisárkány."* *I love you, my domestic dragon (better half).* He said through our link, kissing me again before slapping my ass and strolling off into the bathroom, slamming the door.

I stood there in a daze, his sentiment cascading over me like warm water, a smitten smile growing across my face. Shaking myself out of my stupor, I grabbed my jacket and headed out. Maja handed me a cup of coffee and some files at the door, her grandkids playing on the living room rug, giggling and chattering, lightening the place with sounds of joy. Hearing them, seeing the buds of spring coming out, the sun shining, gave me a thread of hope that a new day had risen and hope was on the horizon.

I sipped my coffee, snuggling against the nippy breeze coming off the Danube, watching the builders reconstruct the longstanding parliament building. My old home. The full wall erected around Leopold had been officially torn down last month, and now we were in the middle of rebuilding all the damage the war caused.

Some damage could never be rebuilt. Blood still marred the cement, left by those who had given their lives for this land. Gazing down at a dark stain under my boots, trying to keep the tears back. I knew who had laid here, who had bled out. The devastation of Rosie's screams as Killian fell still woke me up in a cold sweat. We had lost so many. The absence would never go away, their spirits forever walking this terrain, haunting it with memories, staining it with their souls.

"Almost back to new." A voice came up beside me, a shoulder bumping mine softly, his attention on the work being done as he sipped his own coffee. "We got a lot of work ahead of us, but I think we can open it up to the public by summer."

I gazed up at the man, unable to stop a smile from curling my lips.

"Think you will be okay with a more democratic country?" My shoulder hit his back playfully, noting the bodyguards not far behind him, keeping watch. "No one calling you *lord*?"

Killian glanced down at me with a wicked gleam in his eyes. "I get plenty of that at home." He tipped a brow with innuendo. "Though I'm still not opposed to *King* Killian."

I snorted, my head shaking. "Yeah, because that's less egotistical than lord."

"And because you said that, I was thinking, your role might be more a secretary position, or maybe my coffee girl?"

"Asshole."

Killian laughed, the sound like the clank of bells. Deep, rhythmic, stopping you in your tracks to listen. I took in his profile, my heart still squeezing with the images of him getting attacked by Samu. Half of his guts were left on the pavement. I had been sure another of my family had been taken.

Killian was far too stubborn to die so easily, especially since he had so much to live for. It took him almost a full month to heal, his body in a coma-like state, putting himself together again. Rosie never left his side until one of us came and forced her to go eat, sleep, and bathe, watching over him ourselves. I sat next to Killian's bed many nights, holding his hand and telling him all the things he would be doing once he woke up.

Our city was in ruins, our country a mess. People were scarred, confused, and hurting. No one knew what to do or who was in charge. One night, a week after the battle, sitting next to Killian, I swore I could sense the connection between us, trying to tell me something. It was the part that had always been there. The magic that recognized each other as equals.

He made himself to be a king.

And I was born a queen. Or at least I had the magic of one.

"You are a natural-born leader, Brexley." Andris's voice still rang as sharp in my head as it did the night he died.

543

"All I can hope is I did enough with my time here, made enough difference. Now it's for you to finish it."

So, I had stepped in as temporary leader, recognizing it was my role until Killian was ready to take his seat. I fulfilled my responsibility to Killian, Andris, and even to my father, taking the best parts of each and trying to give this country the same compassion, drive, and hope.

It was Killian who offered a dual leadership position to me. I rejected the idea. I wasn't totally sure it was something I wanted to do forever. There were so many things I felt needed to be done in this world, and the people needed stability and direction. I became more of his second in command, although Killian still treated me like it was a partnership. He joked about royal titles, but it didn't match with the type of ruling he wanted to do. In a place that had endless dictators and autocrats, he didn't want it to feel like just another one was taking over. That nothing would change or be different.

Everything had changed. Sarkis's army rose against the authoritarians… and won. The fae lord himself was a proud member of the rebel alliance, and under him, this country would flourish. The stories my father told me about people walking freely on both sides, having picnics, shopping, going to movies, and meeting friends for lunch, Killian wanted to bring it back.

Neither of us wanted to be above our people. We wanted to be among them. So Killian and I were charting our own way.

Rosie had changed him so much that he no longer was the man high on the throne. He walked the streets, talking to people, getting their thoughts and opinions.

He became a true leader.

"President Killian…" I motioned for him to step toward our new-old parliament building. HDF's former headquarters. Killian changed the name to *A Nép Háza. House of the People*, representing the new rule in this country.

"Okay, not as sexy as king, but still hot. Though I really like commander-in-chief." He winked, motioning for me to go first, heading to our newly renovated offices. It was hard enough to step into the building for work and not see all the shadows of my past like a movie. That's why I could never move back into the rooms here, choosing the penthouse across the plaza instead. We were having it all redone and revamped, taking Istvan's mark off it, though leaving a few things, so we would never forget. While the decor and style stayed the same in the main part of the building, the offices became much more modern and refined to reflect our new government system.

We had a long way to go, but thankfully we had some astronomical donations come in from some private corporation in the Pacific Northwest. Killian and I knew it was from Lars, probably encouraged by his daughter, and we were not above taking it. Gratefully. We were thankful for this secret help from Lars and Kennedy and the debt we would forever owe to Ember and Eli and the Dark Dwellers. We were beholden to them so much for coming to our aid. They showed up without question because that's what they did for family, and now I was strangely a part of it.

Ember and Eli only stayed a few days after the war, needing to get back home, but I enjoyed my time with them. Ember felt like the older sister I never had, and in a way, she was. We were family, sharing something no one else did. Another link in the chain, which tied all of our lives together across time, space, and the world.

Except, I had lied to them. My deceit, if ever found out, might end that relationship, but in my gut, I knew I had to.

No one should have the nectar.

Especially a demon king.

If they thought it still held power, they wouldn't leave without it. I told them the nectar had been destroyed when we sucked all the magic from it. And technically, that was true—at that time.

However, the power I could feel tapping into my hip, waking up a little more every day, spoke a different story. I always kept it on me, needing to protect it. When it was empty, I felt it was my obligation to do so, but now that the power was growing back, I felt more like it was my addiction.

"Halálház is being fully demolished and cemented in today. Construction for the park and monument there will start next week." Killian took another sip, not looking at me. One of the first things we did after the war was destroy everything inside Halálház, killing every experimentation of Sonya's there. I had to remember it was Sonya who took their lives, not us, though the ghosts I felt that day had me in bed, shaking violently with a migraine for the rest of the day.

"I know." My voice came out quiet.

"You didn't want to watch it?"

I pressed my lips together in contemplation. "No." I finally shook my head. I made my peace with that place, knowing I was forever scarred, but I couldn't live my life in the past.

"Brexley—" His Adam's apple bobbed, and I could sense his remorse and shame.

"I forgive you, Killian." I blinked back emotion, cutting him off because I already knew what he wanted to say.

Guilt weighed heavily on him for letting all of us experience that torment—for being okay with how that place was run.

"You shouldn't," he croaked, clearing his voice. "What

I did to Warwick... Eliza." Killian and Warwick might never be extremely close, but I knew they would fight and protect each other without thought. They had been through too much together. It might not be forgotten, but I think forgiveness had come way before either would admit it. Eliza and Killian came to an understanding when they were in the cabin together. Simon called him Uncle Killian. Every Wednesday and Sunday, Simon came to the office to play chess with Killian while Eliza set up schools for children. The way he was with him, I could see Killian would be an amazing father someday.

"We were different people then." I turned to him. "But now you can right those wrongs. Set balance to those crimes."

He stared down at his shoes, nodding before he sucked in, lifting his chin back up. "Yes. Let's get started."

"Let's." I bobbed my head in agreement, walking us to the side doors leading to the offices.

Walking inside, Killian frowned down at his new phone, another anonymous donation to the new President and Vice President of Hungary. High-tech gadgets from the west, enough for everyone in our circle. Killian and I were making trade deals with the west to bring in more products. Injecting much-needed money and life into our country. It would take a while to get on our feet, but at least I saw the light at the end.

"What?" I followed him into our new offices, trying not to recall that once it was used as a conference room.

"My mate." He rubbed his head.

"Let me guess." I dropped the files I was carrying. "She's at the same place as mine."

Madam Kitty's.

Killian huffed, but there was nothing behind it. He acted like Rosie working for Kitty bothered him, and it might a little, but I also knew he was proud of her. She had come a long way. She stood on her own two feet and was making her own way in the world. Not as a prostitute, staying in the back office, working the books, getting orders, and running the backhouse of the business, which also included helping abused women and men or those who had been illegally sex trafficked. Kitty might still run a house of sex, but all who were there wanted to be. And if you didn't, she helped free you of that life and get you back on your feet.

It was a tough decision, but Killian and I decided to make prostitution legal. It was never going to stop, never going to go away. It had been part of the world since the beginning of time, but at least with this, we gave them rights and benefits. Putting an end to the mistreatment Rosie and so many others had suffered.

Kitty had her place rebuilt even bigger, adding a bar and dance stage, which my mate had the ties to supply alcohol for. Another one of his many "businesses."

Carnal Row had come back in full force, which didn't surprise me. The need for an escape from life's cruelties would never go away either. It was already causing a headache. I could see trouble down the road with it, people taking advantage of the fragile ground it was on, but that was not for today.

A bell rang through the room, signaling our meeting was about to commence. Killian hit the talk button on his cell, dropping it on the desk on speaker. "Mykel?" He stayed standing, tugging off his jacket and rolling up the sleeves of his white button-down shirt to his elbows. "How are you doing?"

"As can be expected for a country with a feckless fae leader and the human side in disarray." My uncle's voice came through the phone, automatically warming my heart, his voice reminding me so much of my father's. Czech was suffering from the death of Leon and Sonya's turning on them. And none of us had faith the fae leader would step up. My uncle did. They were still working with the divide between fae and human rule, but Mykel was trying hard to turn his country around to the democracy it once had, following in our footsteps. It was an uphill battle, but he was not the type who gave up.

"Do you have an update?" Killian asked before taking a sip of his coffee. We stayed in close communication with Mykel.

"Yes, the Hounds have reported that hundreds of the faux-fae have been seen crossing into Serbia, Poland, Romania, Bosnia, and Belarus."

Killian's jaw clenched at the name, anger blistering through his eyes.

The Hounds could no longer run free in the Savage Lands, and Vincent, as much as Killian and I hated the asshole, was smart enough to realize it. With Killian as leader, he knew he would have a price on his head and a death wish if he ever stepped back in this city. Vincent made a deal with Mykel, his various groups working as spies and hunters for a hefty price. "Some reported deaths at those times, but no definite link to the faux-fae. We really need a better name for them."

While most of Istvan's experiments died in either the blast at his lab in Kyiv or in the war, there were still many who lived and escaped. Joska and Samu were two of those. The realization that the pills were no longer killing off people was a positive for Hanna, but their living and being out in the world came with problems. No one knew what they would do. Would they kill like wild animals? Adapt? What if they reproduced? What would those kids be like? There were so many unknowns, and sadly, they would never really be accepted into society by fae or humans. They weren't natural. They'd be looked upon as freaks or outcasts.

It was another concern on a growing list Killian and I had to think about.

"You know there is no way to track them once they do. You and I are being treated like hostile countries." Mykel continued on. "The tension between all of us has only risen. Olena stepping up as queen, taking on Istvan's autocrat tendencies, is spurring on her own revolt." We were getting reports from Olek. He and Esmeralda had returned to Ukraine. A strange friendship, or just companionship, developed between them. Esmeralda spoke about finding her grandchildren and getting back into performing, but she was still living with Olek in a new safe house, both spying and reporting back to us. Tad no longer used her, but I felt him around. I saw him every time I trained in my powers, reaching that plane where he was as real to me as anything else. I felt a peace and calmness knowing he was there, that my friend was happy, and just as a part of my life as he was before.

"Things are gonna get ugly in the future there." Mykel's voice shook me from my thoughts. "Rulers of the other countries don't change. They like the power and wealth they live on while their people suffer and starve."

Killian and I foresaw trouble down the line with neighboring countries when citizens would see freedom and a better life here and demand that of their country. Of their rulers.

We would be seen as something to squash. To destroy before we encouraged more to rise up.

"Yeah, I see that coming too." Killian pinched his nose with a heavy sigh. "Any good news?"

"Not really." Mykel huffed. "Though I have the

Mongrels guarding the train line after the last raid in Slovakia. I think things will go a bit smoother now."

My hand rubbed my forehead, feeling the strain already setting in. So many battles, so many fires, but all we could do was put a few out at a time.

On that list was Sonya, Iain, and Kalaraja.

Three of our most wanted. They were smart enough to vanish off the grid for now.

Though I had a feeling I knew where two of them might be—in the protection of Lazar and his son Sergui.

Killian suggested asking Eli and Ember to track them down. As much as I loved getting this country back on its feet, I wanted to be out there… the ones hunting them down. Making them pay for what they took from us.

"Okay, I have a call with the fae leader in Slovakia later. I will speak to him about the raids happening so brazenly in his country." Killian pulled out his chair and sat down. "Anything else we should know?"

"No, I think that's it for today. Who knows about tomorrow?" Mykel replied dryly, hearing the exhaustion in his tone. Some days, this all felt too much, far too many battles to fight while trying to rebuild a country and keep everyone from freaking out. We never gave up on this country before, so we wouldn't now.

"Okay, check in again later this week." Killian picked up a pen, scribbling something down, about to hang up with his other hand, but I grabbed the cell away from him.

"Hey, Uncle Mykel." My voice went soft, showing this was no longer about business.

"Brexley…" I heard a slight crack in my name, like he let down some wall he was keeping up. "How are you doing?"

"I was going to ask you that. You sound tired."

551

"I am, but the world doesn't stop because I need to sleep."

"Take care of yourself, though. Czech needs you at your best, and that means taking care of yourself. When was the last time you even ate?"

"Coffee count?"

"No." Though that had been my main diet too.

Mykel sighed. "Don't worry, I have someone forcing me to eat, even if she has to spoon feed me."

A grin pulled at my cheeks.

"How is *Rebeka*?" I lifted my brow, grinning conspiratorially at Killian.

"Don't say it like that. We're just friends," he huffed, sounding more defensive than he should. "She's a good woman. Helping me."

"Uh-huh…" I teased. "Is that what you kids are calling it nowadays?"

Rebeka decided to go with Mykel back to Prague, stating this city was full of bad memories and she needed to start over. To begin a life as *this* Rebeka, a fresh start she knew she couldn't get here. Too many people knew her face; too many would always associate her with the elite and never let her live in peace. She would be ostracized here, attacked and punished.

We also sensed something was happening between Mykel and Rebeka, but so far, they kept it platonic, leaning on each other in a time of need. She studied to be a healer/nurse, working more with children, while helping Mykel get his country back on its feet. Rebeka probably knew how to lead a country better than all of us. This time she wasn't an armpiece. She was a trusted adviser to Mykel.

My instinct was to message Caden, tease that we could be related down the road, but I wouldn't. After four months, he still was mad at me, avoiding me at all costs, which was hard since he was in this building a lot. He felt I robbed him of something. That he needed to be the one to kill his father.

Caden could hate me forever, but I wouldn't change it. I knew my friend too well. He'd pretend it wouldn't have affected him, but it would only have sunk him into darkness.

"Bye, Brexley," Mykel uttered with exasperation, making me smile more.

"Bye, Uncle."

The day proceeded into the night, interviewing people for positions in our cabinet, taking calls, writing new laws, and banging our heads on the desk. Okay, that was just me.

"Think that's enough for today." Killian rubbed his face, circling his neck back and forth, working out the kinks. "You can get out of here."

"What about you?" I hopped up, grabbing my jacket.

"Gonna work for a bit more, then go get Rosie, have dirty, mind-blowing sex in the back of the car, get some dinner, then more sex until we can't move."

"Really?" I opened my arms. "Didn't need to know that."

"Coming from the girl who this entire city can feel having sex? *Relentlessly*, may I add? And I live across the river," he shot back. "Just giving it back to you."

Right.

"Fair point." I nodded, swinging my bag over my shoulder and heading out. "Night, Killian."

"That's commander-in-chief to you," I heard him yell as I slammed the door, chuckling under my breath. I spotted the head of Killian's protection service working at his desk.

"You're still here too?"

"He's here, I'm here." Zander glanced up with a warm smile. "Plus, I have a lot of work to do."

Zander worked more at a desk than guarding anymore,

but being a double spy for so long, he was the best to know how plans to kill our president might be plotted out. He was in charge of Killian's protection wherever and whenever the president left this building. He might be beloved by some, but not all. A portion of the population still believed in the old racially pure ideals and puritan ways.

"Tell Eliza and Simon hi, and I'll see you guys this weekend." Eliza had set in place a "family" dinner every Sunday. Whoever could show up was welcome, and it gave us time to be with each other outside of work or business.

"I will. Night, Brex."

"Night," I replied, heading out the main doors.

Stepping outside, the early spring temperatures blew across my shoulders, though I could feel a hint of warmer weather coming. The clear night gave no buffer to the cool breeze, the moon and stars shining down with clarity. Most of the streetlamps were still destroyed from the war, leaving the plaza in shadowy darkness, the warm light shining from my apartment across the square.

A wisp of wind curled up my back, blowing through my loose locks.

"Bre-x-ley…" A whisper licked at the back of my head, chills shuddering down my spine.

My feet stopped, my heart speeding up. Fear clutched my lungs. It wasn't a fear that demanded you run. No, this was a fear of knowing time was up. Something you knew was coming was here, and you weren't ready for it.

My muscles locked down, the familiar sensation of death coating my skin. I could feel them before I even turned around, knowing what was coming for me.

"Daugh-ter."

Taking a breath, condensation billowing out of my mouth from their proximity, I spun around.

Eabha, Morgan, Liam, Sam, Roan, Breena, and Rory. My mother's clan. Hooded and almost indistinguishable from the shadows, the necromancers stood with weapons in hand, waiting for me.

Swallowing, my throat stuck, my mind whirling with excuses and promises. Claims I knew I couldn't keep…

"Bre-x-ley." My mother's voice came into my head again, broken and stiff, but telling me far more than her single word said. My shoulders dropped, a sob hiccupping in my chest. Somehow, I knew this was coming, from the night of the war, or even possibly before. Their eyes always watching, their presence never far. They gave me time to say goodbye. That time was up. Like I had, they sensed its growing power. It was something that could no longer be ignored or brushed away.

My hand moved over the pouch I carried on my hip. Unless I was naked, it was with me. A sob choked my throat, my lids squeezing shut. It took me a full minute before I forced my hand to touch the nectar but still couldn't get myself to pull it out.

My mouth was ready to tell her no, that I would promise to protect and keep it safe, declaring we might need it down the road, but the words got stuck in my throat, the lie clotting my airway.

My mother stepped forward, the moon glowing off the metal of her scythe, her bony fingers wrapped around it. She stopped several feet from me, her power and dominance echoing in my bones. She lifted her free hand, her palm up, asking for my sacrifice.

"Mom…" I choked.

"Dau-gh-ter." Eabha stepped closer. *"You can-not pro-te-ct it."* She struggled to get her sentence out, even through our link. *"It is part of you… you are not a part of it. It cannot stay."*

555

I knew that. It was never meant to be mine or anyone's. Power that great was the worst sin of all. It deteriorated the strongest wills. Even if good was intended, darkness would corrupt it, bleeding out any moral virtue. The history of the world showed us this.

The nectar was no different.

Feeling like I was ripping myself in half, I pulled the wrapped object out of my pouch, my chest heaving as I held it out to my mother. Only darkness and a hint of bone under her hood looked back. Even if there was a drop of a mother's love in her, I had no doubt she would fight me for it. It was their mission. Their creed. And they could disappear and hide it from everyone and everything, including fae books.

Without even speaking into my head, I felt her communicate with me, a link only shared between necromancers.

You cannot come look for it again.

"I know," I said out loud to her. A tear rolled down my cheek, knowing it wasn't just the nectar I was letting go. I would never see my mother again after this night.

A noise strangled my throat before I dropped it in her hands. Her skeleton-like fingers curled over it, tucking it back in her robe.

Eabha dipped her head in gratitude before she slipped back into the darkness. My eyes met with my aunt Morgan's, then they all disappeared.

A sob curled in my throat as I stared into the darkness.

"Da-ugh-ter. I-I lo-ve you." They felt like words in the wind, a touch of something I could not see, but sensed all over. A final goodbye.

Bending over, I let my tears fall free, my sobs heaving in my chest. I had been orphaned all over again.

"Kovacs." Warwick was suddenly behind me, his arms

wrapping around me, pulling me, letting me cry my heart out. As a child, I never mourned my mother because I never knew life with her. She was a fantasy, a story my father told. Finding her gave me hope, a mom, a connection.

Now along with my father, Andris, Kek, Lukas, and so many others, I would mourn the loss of my mother too.

"The nectar is gone," I muttered against his chest. It was a hole in me I'd have to become accustomed to. "My mom…" *is gone forever too.*

"I know." Warwick pulled me in tighter.

"I'm…" *Empty, hollow, weak, wrong.*

"You know what you are?" He grabbed my face, tipping it back, his aqua eyes fierce. "*You* are the legend, *sötét démonom.* You are the one who brought me back to life, who saved Scorpion, who survived Halálház and Věrhăza. The girl who saved this country. Not me and not the nectar. *Just you.* And you are fucking mine, Kovacs."

His mouth came down on mine.

"*You* are *The Grey.*" He nipped at my bottom lip, pulling back to look into my eyes. "And I'm just the wolf lucky enough to run by your side."

"Or hump my leg."

He chuckled, drawing me back to him, his hungry eyes moving over me.

"That too."

The nectar might be gone, but I was still me.

The bridge between life and death.

The villain and the hero.

The dark and the light.

I was The Grey.

Caden

Four months after the war

A bottle of pálinka hung from my fingers. The sharp breeze off the Danube ruffled through my hair, stinging my face. My legs dangled from the catwalk, my arms folded over the railing, keeping me from tumbling to my death far below. I squinted down at the completely reconstructed HDF building, which was opening in June to the public as *The House of the People*.

Slapping on fresh paint and changing the carpet would never bury the ghosts of this place. Not to me. Sometimes I swear I could hear my father calling me from his office or see officers and dead friends walking around. It was all in my head, but it still messed with me. Haunted me.

Killian gave a speech tonight in the plaza, and thousands of people turned out for it. He was a born leader. He filled the role as president to a T. Looks, charm, compassion, and drive. The role my father was conditioning me for, though Killian made me see how much I was no longer that person, if I ever was.

Taking another swig, my mind went back to all the times

Brexley and I sat up here, staring across the river at the fae palace, hiding from my father or some mandatory event we escaped. How clueless we were about life, about real sacrifice and pain. How that one night up here, deciding to rob that train, changed the course of our lives forever. It altered everything. If we never left this spot, going to bed instead, she and I would be married to people we hated, playing roles my father forced upon us, living lives that weren't ours. We would be puppets to my father's whims, letting him do everything he wanted without us ever knowing the truth of his real madness.

It frightened me how that single choice could have set our entire lives on a different path. How empty and tragic our lives would have been.

Even knowing all I did, what was ahead...

"Hey." A voice called out to me. It hooked in my chest and tugged at my gut. "Is this a pity party for one, or can another join?"

Curving my head, I took in the petite woman strolling up to me dressed in all black, her white-blonde hair whipping and knotting in the wind, her red lips curved just slightly, causing my dick to twitch.

My fingers rolled into fists at the image of them tugging those very strands last night, making her cry out. We broke the fucking bed.

I shifted, hiding my erection, taking another gulp, my brows furrowing. "How did you find me?"

Birdie lifted a shoulder, settling down next to me.

I knew how. It was how I found her every fuckin' night, no matter if I knew where she was or not.

Like a fucking GPS.

We never talked about it. I didn't even want to think about it, even if my gut knew. It scared the shit out of me.

559

Things were said during the war we both pretended were never spoken. When you think you might die, you get a lot more emotional. Now that we survived and were not in any life and death situations, we went back to pretending we didn't care about each other.

In front of people, anyway.

Though day or night, we fucked like we couldn't ever get enough. In closets, showers, on and under desks, against lockers, in the stairway, *wherever* we could.

I blamed it on the extra adrenaline we both built up throughout the day. Killian had put me, Birdie, and Bakos in charge of training the new military recruits under him. Killian did not forget what Bakos did for us when they were sneaking into HDF. He honored the cryptic message only a few of us knew and helped Killian and Rosie. For his safety, he played a part, but later we found he had defected, turning against HDF.

Killian wanted to acknowledge that.

Bakos held a slightly higher position, staying closer to a desk while Birdie and I were the new trainers, getting worked up and sweaty all day—wrestling on mats, target practice, obstacle courses… nothing seemed to turn my girl on more than fighting.

I went still, realizing what I had just said in my head.

My girl.

Shit.

Lifting the bottle to my lips, I tried to drown all my thoughts. Birdie grabbed it from me, taking some.

"Help yourself."

"*I. Will.*" She stared right at me, letting me know there was a lot more she wanted. It took everything in me not to take the bait, keeping my expression blank.

She sighed, turning her attention out to the palace across

the river. Killian was living in it again but decided to open half of it up for tours and events. He and Rosie stayed in a private wing in the newly built section.

"You're in a mood," she muttered. "You can't still be angry?"

My shoulders went up to my ears. Fuck yes, I could.

"Caden…"

"You don't know how it feels," I snapped. "It should have been me. I should have killed him. Brexley took that from me."

"No, she didn't." Birdie shook her head. "You really think you'd be okay killing your own father?"

I opened my mouth.

"Don't say yes, like it's so easy. No matter what he did, he was *still* your dad." Birdie scooted closer, her hand touching my jaw. "She saved you."

"Saved me?"

"If you had killed him… I'm not sure you would have come back from that. Istvan would have darkened your soul."

"My soul is already dark." I kept my eyes down, feeling the truth somewhere inside.

"Look at me, pretty boy." She forced my chin up. "You can be upset, but don't cut her out of your life. She's too much a part of you. And she doesn't deserve it. It wasn't easy for Brex to make that choice. Now she will live with his death for the rest of her life. Know she did it *because* she loves you, not to take it away from you."

My teeth crunched together, my head turning back out to the water. I knew it; I could feel Warwick berating me daily about forgiving Brexley, but I wasn't quite ready to let it go just yet. Not completely. I would, though. Brexley was far too important to me to not have her in my life. I missed her. It even felt strange to have Birdie up here at our hiding spot

561

instead of Brexley, but as I peered back at the blonde next to me, nothing like what I thought I'd be attracted to, I realized it was no longer Brexley I wanted sitting next to me.

It was time to let go of the past... and christen my future.

A ravenous grin curled my mouth, my hands sliding into Birdie's hair, tugging it firmly. Her eyes flashed, and her nose flared, making my dick so hard it ached. "You know, I've always wanted to have sex up here."

"You never have before?"

"Nope." At the time, this place was sacred to me. It was Brexley's and my safe spot. I would never have brought another girl up here. I always imagined Brex and me finally crossing that line up here, and we almost did before everything went to hell.

Now I was glad, because there was only one I wanted to slide my dick into under the stars, to claim on top of the old HDF building, tearing down all the old ideas and dreams.

Ripping off her clothes, I laid her back on the cool metal, her hands shoving my pants down while I tore off my shirt. The wind whipped against our skin, heightening the sensations. Her legs spread wide for me.

"Caden." Her plea went straight to my cock.

We weren't good at foreplay. We liked fucking each other too much.

I pushed inside her, a groan coming from my chest, my brain not understanding how it seemed to get better. With so many others, I got bored quickly, but with Birdie, I never did.

And that scared me because I had a feeling I never would.

"Fuck! Caden!" She howled, giving back just as hard, her nails digging into me.

Pounding into her, her back arched, my name ringing in the air. Far below, I could hear the sounds of the lapping river and people moving around in the square. In the distance, a train whistle howled into the night, reminding me of so many nights up here with Brexley, hatching her plans to steal from them and give back to the poor. It felt like a symbolic gesture, closing that first part of my life.

My father was dead, and my mother was off in Prague starting a new life. I had a future half-brother, the prince of Ukraine, born to not only replace me but kill me, a bond to a pain in the ass legend that would never go away, and a vengeance seething in the back of my mind for those who escaped us that night. Kalaraja, Sonya, Iain, Joska, and Samu... it wouldn't be long before I desired their blood too much. Even as only half a legend, I understood the craving for death, for revenge. It filled me now and pumped in my veins.

I no longer hated what I was.

I felt alive, like I had lived in a bubble before. Dull. Lifeless.

The story of human Caden had come to an end.

This next story might be tragic, most likely bloody, but it would be fucking *real*.

Scorpion

Five months after the war

"Az istenit!" Dammit. I grabbed my friend's shirt, trying to get him off the ground. *"Mi a fasz van veled?" What the fuck is wrong with you?*

"Get him the hell out of here!" the bartender yelled at me, his face red, his stature telling me he might be half giant or something. "He's not welcome back!"

"Good job, asshole." I went to grab his arm again. "Barred yourself from another place."

"Nyasgem!" Fuck off!

I glowered at the tree fairy—the man who used to be the voice of reason and the solid ground under all our feet.

"Ash." I gritted my teeth, my patience very thin lately. "You are making it really hard for me not to kick your ass myself." I leaned over him; he reeked of alcohol and opium. "Now get up." I pulled on his arm. This time he didn't fight me, his body barely able to stand on his own feet. It seemed Warwick and I were constantly on babysitting duty with him. Picking him off a bar, brothel, or drug den floor. Most of the time bloody and black and blue from whatever fight he got into.

564

"Ash, I'm not carrying you." I put his arm around my shoulders, his feet barely helping me get him out of the pub. The cool night air filled my lungs the moment we stepped outside. The final throes of spring were shaking off, heading into summer.

"I'm finnnneee," he slurred, pushing me away.

"Fine?" I snorted, his eyes half-lidded from being drunk, high, and beat up. "You are fuckin' mess, man."

"Fuck off." He shoved me, stumbling back, anger lining his forehead. "I don't need you."

"Looks like it." I watched him weave, his fingers pulling out a joint, struggling to light it.

"No." I plucked it from his mouth, crunching it under my boot.

"Fuck you!" Ash bellowed. "You can't tell me what to do."

"Someone needs to!" My temper flared. I knew Ash was hurting. Fuck, we all were, but this was getting out of control. At first, we all thought he just needed time, but it had been over five months, and Ash was only getting worse, turning on those who loved him and burning bridges he could never repair. "I know you are going through shit," I growled, feeling all the burdens I was carrying lately. "But *we all* are. Stop thinking of only yourself."

His lids narrowed, his mouth opening to respond.

"No," I barked. "I've had enough. We *all* have. Now it's time to get your shit together. You're pushing away all the people who fucking care about you. You think you're the only one who hurts? Who misses them? Who is suffering?" I stomped closer to him, my disgust moving over him. "I have my girl at home, tearing herself apart because of what was forced upon her. Unsure of what she will become, what will happen to her. Stop being so fucking selfish and look around and see you aren't the only one in pain."

Ash's lips turned down, his feet unstable, but his demeanor didn't change. No indication I was even speaking to him.

I scoffed, my head shaking. "Look at yourself. Drunk, high, and belligerent. Who are you, man? You think they'd be proud of you?" I motioned down to him.

"Screw you." Ash shoved at my chest, but he only tripped himself backward.

"No, Ash, you are only screwing yourself." Damn, when I was the voice of reason over Ash, something was terribly wrong. "I'm done. You can pick yourself up or not. But when you find you've destroyed every relationship and cut off everyone you love, you only have yourself to blame." I turned, stomping away, my own temper about to get the better of me. I'd hit my limit of retrieving him, cleaning up his puke, and tossing his unconscious ass on my sofa, with only anger and resentment being given back. Yeah, I was done. I had enough shit to worry about.

Warwick and I had taken on the distribution of alcohol to Kitty's, which was flourishing, and getting us more clients in Carnal Row. It was all legit and above board, but I wouldn't lie and say there weren't some deals being made. Nothing considered illegal per se. We were getting busier each day. The demand for alcohol was never a waning commodity. Though hope was trickling back into this city, fear of the unknown had people turn to comforts. Turn to something to ease the worry. To let them escape.

Places like Carnal Row would never go away. This world was always changing, going through wars, death, diseases, and heartache since the beginning of time. People would always need an outlet.

Weaving through the streets, you noticed all the construction and places being rebuilt. Grocery stores, pharmacies, bakeries, and even a few restaurants and clothing shops were popping up throughout Savage Lands. Killian had declared it District VII again, putting this whole area back into districts as it once was, but I think it will always be Savage Lands to us. Too much blood, sorrow, and death marred these streets.

Our population had taken a hit after so many died under Istvan and Sonya, so many dying in the war fighting for this land, but I had heard rumors we were getting floods of immigrants from other countries, wanting a better life for their families, seeing Hungary as the land of hope and prosperity.

And President Killian welcomed them all.

I crossed into the old Leopold area, the scar from the old wall engrained in the pavement. I took the stairs up to my flat. Brexley wanted us close, and with Hanna, I felt she needed all the reminders of love and family she could get. Though the memories of her parents probably plagued her more than she claimed being back here.

I could feel Brexley, the sensation always shimmering around me. It would always be there. It was something we would live with, becoming such a part of me, and if anything happened to her or it, I would lose my shit. She saved my life. She led me right to my mate, but because we had this connection, Brex and I were trying to put up some boundaries. I didn't want her coming in on me and Hanna, and I was done being pulled into her and Warwick's endless sex marathons. Though I won't deny a few times with Hanna, the connection, their energy, and "influence" were times I wouldn't mind repeating.

I barreled through the door to an apartment that made me itch. The decor was champagne and caviar, and I was tattoos, motorcycles, and kinky sex.

The lights were off, and the enormous windows facing the old HDF building were the only thing lighting up the space.

Silence filled the four-bedroom flat.

"Hanna?" I slammed the door. A flutter hit my chest, something feeling off. "Hanna?" I moved through the living room to our bedroom, my throat closing in. She had good days and bad days, and then she had *really bad* days.

The good days, my gods, there was nothing better than to see her smile and laugh. She turned me into a fool… in a good way. I couldn't even hide or deny the fact I was so fucking in love with this woman. She had me utterly and completely. She was strong, funny, smart, and fucking wicked in bed. Responsive and willing to push limits with me. She let the wildcat side of her free, like she accepted it. Liked it. And damn… we could get extremely feral. I had never spent an entire day and night with someone and then miss them the moment we parted. I even had her come on some of my business jobs because I didn't want to be away from her. She was an excellent partner and usually talked them into buying more from me.

Then there were the bad days, the melancholy, heartbreaking, sad moments. She'd stare blankly out the window toward where her parents used to live. She drifted around aimlessly as if she couldn't find her place. Those broke my heart, but it was the really bad times that destroyed me.

She was frantic and almost unhinged. Her emotions over what she suffered and her fears of what she was turning into scared her so much that she lost herself. One time I found her using her new clawed fingers she now could shift into as blades against her wrists.

That did it for me. She scared me so much that I knew

she needed help. I forced her to see a therapist-healer after that. It was slow, but I noticed the good days were starting to outweigh the bad ones, but I always had that fear she would slide backward.

"Hanna!" I bellowed, jogging into the bedroom we shared, my gaze scanning the dark room, spotting her standing at the floor to ceiling window, staring out the window, lost in her world.

My hand went to my chest, relief heaving from my lungs, taking a moment to recognize she was okay.

"Hanna?" I said her name, walking to her. Her head jerked to me as if she finally realized I was there, her face streaked with tears. "You didn't respond." My heart still pounded in my chest with terror. The idea of losing her… that wasn't something *I* could live with.

"Sorry." She folded her arms, sniffing, her feet knocking at the things on the rug surrounding her. It was a box full of pictures and trinkets. Bending over, I picked one up, my chest locking up.

It was an image of Hanna when she was in her early teens with her parents. All smiles and happiness, a Christmas tree behind them, and I noticed all the family pictures and small items spread around her feet.

"I went over there today." Her voice was raw from crying.

"Little viper." I drew her into my arms, feeling her chest heave against mine. "Why didn't you call me? I would have been there."

"I needed to do it by myself." She pulled back, wiping her eyes. "I needed to say goodbye."

My hands glided up her jaw, my thumbs wiping away her tears, my chest aching for her.

"You know it's never goodbye; they will always be with

569

you." The sentiment flowed out, sounding very unlike me, but Hanna had turned me into a man with hope.

"I know." She cleared her throat. "But it was time to say goodbye to that life. To not stay trapped in the past because it was safe." She peered up at me, her hand sliding over mine. "I don't know what my future will entail, if I'll become completely feral, or if I will even be alive in a few years."

My muscles clenched at her words.

"I'm not okay right now." Her blue eyes filled with liquid. "But I think I will be. You fought so hard for me, and I want to fight for you. I want to move forward. Try to accept what I am." Though she never could fully embrace it outside our group. There was too much hate, prejudice, and fear of what she was. The faux-fae were not accepted. Maybe Hanna could change that, but I wasn't willing to have her be the test subject. "I want to start healing."

Emotion expanded from my lungs up my throat. I leaned over, claiming her mouth with mine, kissing her with everything I had. It wasn't wild or rough. It was handing my heart to her on a platter.

I inched her back to the bed, kicking off my boots. I laid her down, crawling in next to her, holding her to me.

"I'm not going anywhere, little viper. Whatever it takes, and whatever happens, we will figure it out together."

"I'm still gonna have good and bad days."

"So will I." I kissed her nose. "Just don't ever do anything which takes you away from me, okay?"

She bowed her head, ashamed of the day she tried to harm herself.

"That I promise you."

"Oh, watch what you say, sweetheart. That shit is binding now."

A smile grew on her face, her fingers trailing up my jaw, pulling herself a breath from me.

"Good." She kissed me, my soul feeling everything she gave. "I love you, Scorpion."

I inhaled sharply, our gazes meeting for a moment before my mouth claimed hers as mine. I rolled her slowly onto her back. "I love you too, little viper."

I had no idea what was ahead of us. My focus was on tracking down Joska and Samu, but not to kill them like the others wanted. I wanted to watch them, study them so I could prepare for what lay in wait for Hanna.

As I entered her, slow and deep, our moans mixing, I knew there was nothing in this world I wouldn't do for her.

Nothing I wouldn't hunt, kill, or track down to protect her.

My woman had claws and fangs, but if anything came at her, they would feel the deadly sting of a scorpion.

Ash

Six Months After the War

"Get him out of here!" I felt hands lift me up, the world blurring and moving around me until my gaze caught on a familiar face. My lids narrowed, anger bristling, seeing the disappointment and frustration on her features. Not that anyone could tell. Her expression always came across as unemotional, but I knew her too well. I had seen that look for centuries, only used on me once before. When I ended our friendship because my ego couldn't take the rejection.

Kitty's finger pointed to the door. "You aren't allowed in here anymore."

"Fuuuckk off." I wiggled out of the grip of the huge bouncer Kitty had at the club now. A whole new section of entertainment and alcohol. One I had frequented a lot until she tossed my ass out, but she could never stay mad at me, and I wormed my way back in.

Though tonight she hit her limit.

Get in line.

Warwick, Brexley, Scorpion... shit, the brownie and imp wouldn't even come near me anymore. I was even sick of myself, but I couldn't climb out of the darkness. It had wrapped around my soul, seeping violence and rage into every pore. The only way I could deal was to not be part of reality. The moment I surfaced, the pain was too much. It killed any light.

"Get out, Ash," Kitty lifted her chin.

"Come on…" I slurred, staggering, the room not staying even. "This is a whorehouse!" I tossed up my hands. "I just cut out the going upstairs part. Saved you a room." By getting a blowjob right at the bar, not aware enough to care that it was in front of everyone.

Fury scraped across my memory, me yelling at the girl to go deeper, though it didn't do anything for me no matter what she did. Her hair was too brown, her eyes not dark enough blue. It wasn't *her*…

Or him.

"I run a respectable establishment." Kitty motioned to the door again.

I snorted, lowering Kitty's lids into slits.

"Get out."

This time, the huge ogre practically picked me up, hauling me to the exit.

"Ash?" Kitty's voice curved my head. "I lost you once. Don't force me to lose you again. I want my *brother* back."

Her words hit some place deep in me, like spikes in my gut before the bouncer threw me out, my face hitting the pavement with a smack.

Fuck.

I lay there, feeling people walk right by me, no one giving a second glance to a drunk lying on the ground in the middle of the path. This place was full of losers like me.

I want my brother back.

The echo of her sentiment was the same as Warwick's.

573

And their disappointment in me, and my own, only dragged me down more. They were all thriving, all doing something to help this city move on from the destruction and years of suffering. Killian had officially opened the Parliament building today. Hordes of people were there, awed by the new House of the People, while I stood outside in the exact spot my loves had perished. Their blood could still be seen soaked in the asphalt. Where I should have laid down with them. Their smiles and laughs echoed in my head, never giving me peace.

I found myself at Kitty's, trying to forget the pain.

It was in my nature to help, always being the one everyone leaned on for support. I could hold nothing and no one up, though. It was me, for once, who needed the help. *I* needed to be saved.

I couldn't breathe. I couldn't function. I couldn't stand myself sober. The nightmares pounced on me the moment I started to come down. Reenacting Lukas and Kek's murder over and over.

I dulled every sense with drugs and alcohol, finding my way to seedy opium dens where I'd have moments of clarity, realizing someone was sucking me off or fucking me. Man or woman, it didn't matter because none of them were right. None of them cured what my heart was crying for.

The three of us had never put labels on what we were. At first, we were just enjoying it for what it was, but the more we all got to know each other, the deeper we fell. We just worked. I was happy. Very happy. It felt like something that would last, which was not something I ever had before. The only other person I thought I loved had been Janos. It didn't hit me until I met Kek and Lukas that I had fallen in love with someone who didn't even exist—an idea of someone.

Lukas and Kek opened me up again, made me feel again.

I couldn't let that go. I couldn't let *them* go. The best times were when I forgot they were dead, that my skin hadn't soaked in their blood. That my two lovers hadn't died right in front of me. We would see each other later at home.

I wished it had been me instead.

"Get the hell up." A woman's voice tangled in my ears, wrapping around my heart, lifting my head with hope.

"Kek?" I blinked, my vision blurry, but I saw blue hair and a male figure standing beside her. "Lukas?"

"What are you doing?" Lukas squatted down, his face hazy, but those blue eyes looked sadly into mine.

"I don't want to be here without you guys."

"Tough." Kek put her hands on her hips. "It's time to stand up and sober up. Take a shower. You smell like shit."

A snort coughed up the back of my throat. Kek was always to the point. No time for bullshit.

"I miss you guys so much it hurts." I rolled onto my back, my lids squeezing together at the movement.

"Hey?" A hand nudged me. The voice was all wrong. "Get up."

When I opened them this time, two strangers peered back at me. A girl wearing a blue wig, and a young fae man, trying to push their cart past me.

I blinked, feeling the dagger stab into my heart. The loss all over again. Slowly, rolling up, I moved out of the way, letting their cart pass me.

Sorrow filled my bones, and I staggered forward, stopping where a crowd was building up. My attention went to the girl twirling fire sticks while doing acrobatics on a hoop swing. Her features caught my eye, sobering me up slightly. They were split down the middle. Two different color eyes and hair, reminding me of Ember.

A Dae. They were very rare. To the point I wondered if

575

more than a handful existed in the world. They had been brutally hunted down by Aneira and killed.

Now it was Ember hunting down the monsters.

Like you should be doing. My mind went to Sonya, who gladly let her son be killed by her other son. She murdered Kek.

Sonya and Iain. They took from me. They ripped my world apart. They were still out there. Alive. In hiding. But they were still free.

As the girl flipped and performed, something filled my chest, dissolving all the pain and sorrow and growing my anger into something else.

Something stronger. Something that drove hate into my muscles and poured acid into my veins, but for once I didn't shun or try to escape the feeling. I wanted it. It made me feel alive.

It tasted like…

Revenge.

I would do it for Kek and Lukas.

They deserved everything. They deserved someone who would bring their killers to justice, not get drugged up and pass out on the street.

Pulling back my shoulders, I took in a huge inhale, my hands yanking out the drugs in my pocket. Staring down at them, I paused.

Do it, Ash.

Quickly, I chucked them into the trash, strolling out of Carnal Row.

Whatever I had to do, wherever I had to go, I would track Sonya and Iain down.

I would avenge Lukas, Kek, and all the loved ones she took, the lives she destroyed.

I knew this was what I had to do. Bring justice back into balance.

Tree fairies were known to be calm and even-tempered, in harmony with nature and magic.

And when you fucked with nature, we fucked back.

We rained down in fury and blood.

Until you were Ash…

The End Of One Story Is Merely The Beginning Of Another…

Thank you to all my readers. Your opinion really matters to me and helps others decide if they want to purchase my book. If you enjoyed this book, please consider leaving a review on the site where you purchased it. It would mean a lot. Thank you.

.

About the Author

USA Today Best-Selling Author Stacey Marie Brown is a lover of hot fictional bad boys and sarcastic heroines who kick butt. She also enjoys books, travel, TV shows, hiking, writing, design, and archery.

She grew up in Northern California, where she ran around on her family's farm, raising animals, riding horses, playing flashlight tag, and turning hay bales into cool forts.

When she's not writing, she's out hiking, spending time with friends, and traveling. She also volunteers helping animals and is eco-friendly. She feels all animals, people, and the environment should be treated kindly.

To learn more about Stacey or her books, visit her at:

Author website & Newsletter:
www.staceymariebrown.com

Facebook Author page:
www.facebook.com/SMBauthorpage

Pinterest: www.pinterest.com/s.mariebrown

TikTok: @staceymariebrown

Instagram: www.instagram.com/staceymariebrown/

Twitter: https://twitter.com/S_MarieBrown

Goodreads:
www.goodreads.com/author/show/6938728.StaceyMarie_B
rown

Stacey's Facebook group:
www.facebook.com/groups/1648368945376239/

Bookbub:
www.bookbub.com/authors/stacey-marie-brown

Acknowledgements

Coming to the end of this series is bittersweet. I have fallen so deeply in love with all the characters and it's hard to say goodbye, each becoming so important to me. But I don't think they will stay away forever. So many stories left to tell.

Thank you all so much for living the Savage Lands Series as much as I loved writing it!

Kiki & Colleen at Next Step P.R.–Thank you for all your hard work! I love you ladies so much.
Mo & Emily–You both make it readable! Thank you!
Jay Aheer–So much beauty. I am in love with your work!
Judi Fennell at www.formatting4U.com–Always fast and always spot on!

To all the readers who have supported me: My gratitude is for all you do and how much you help indie authors out of the pure love of reading.

To all the indie/hybrid authors out there who inspire, challenge, support, and push me to be better: I love you!

And to anyone who has picked up an indie book and given an unknown author a chance.

THANK YOU!